THE FIRE AND THE WOOD

A Love Story

THE FIRE AND THE WOOD

A Love Story

BY

R. C. HUTCHINSON

THE LITERARY GUILD OF AMERICA, INC.

New York   *1940*

To M. H. Churchill

My Dear Jeremy,

   You will remember that I told you Josef's story one evening, the summer before last, in the Half Moon at Clare. You thought then that it was worth putting on paper, and I still think it was. But the time, between now and then, has not been a good one for the job: the means by which we know what is happening round the world have become so efficient that it's increasingly hard to concentrate, for several hours a day, on the fortunes of one or two people. The excuse, of course, is not valid: no excuse is valid. The masters of the trade have done it as well, and sometimes better, when the hubbub is loudest. But I myself find difficulty, with these cold winds blowing incessantly against the mind, in raising it to that temperature which seems to me necessary for work which has the smallest pretension to seriousness; and I fancy that some others among the feebler-hearted brethren may be in the same case.

   I mention the handicap as an apology for dedicating such a book as this to you, an amateur suckled by Turgenev and weaned on Henry James. Will you take the gesture as one of gratitude for many kindnesses, and for twenty years of friendship?

Yours ever,

R. C. H.

Infantry Train Centre
R——
March, 1940

THE FIRE AND THE WOOD

IN THE Moltke Hospital at Hartzinnfeld the Director's office is now on the ground floor; directly to your right as you go in by the main entrance. This is obviously the sensible arrangement. It is one of the innumerable minor achievements of the present régime.

Before 1933 the Director had his quarters on the second floor of the west building. There was no lift. You had to go up about fifty steps, then the whole length of the northward corridor; or rather, you were taken first along the southward corridor and round the corner to the waiting-room. This was a long, very narrow room which looked like a piece of the passage chopped-off: it had, in fact, been constructed in that fashion. It was equipped with a little table and two shiny chairs, a portrait of the Reichspräsident, half a dozen recent issues of *Neue Medizinische Monatsschrift*.

This was where Josef Zeppichmann waited for his first interview.

"The Director will be ready for you in a few minutes, Herr Doktor," the porter said.

A little too casual, the man's voice: he would have used the same tone for the patients' visitors. But the 'Herr Doktor' gave Josef Zeppichman a prick of pleasure. Of course, they had called him that all up and down the wards at Zornenwalde, but it made a difference, now, to feel that the title really belonged to him. 'Doctor Zeppichmann.' It was like wearing his first long trousers: knees patched—Max had already worn them two years—but long trousers all the same. Leaning against the table, he took out his father's letter, received that morning, and read a part of it again.

3

'Franz and Moses and old Frau Wagner were in last night just after I had closed the shop. I told them that my son Dr. Zeppichmann had been given a post. My son Dr. Zeppichmann, I said, Doctor of Medicine with full diploma, my son the Doctor has an important post in the Moltke Hospital at Hartzinnfeld. Many candidates, I said, dozens of candidates, but Josef of course beats the lot of them. Ahi, Josef, my lad, that was a fine thing to say. Franz—you should have seen Franz's face! He put his arm round my neck. Ah, Jakob, he said, think of all you have done! In the war you give your right leg for your country. Now you give your son to the glory of science and healing! And Frau Wagner says to send you a kiss on both cheeks, like she gave you when you were a tiny boy.'

Ugh, those fat, moist kisses of Frau Wagner's! But it was nice to think of them gathered in the room behind the shop, Papa garrulous and beaming, Frau Wagner's damply shining eyes, the small, appreciative grunts of Moses Echlinger: all of them talking about him, Josef, the little boy who'd got to be Dr. Zeppichmann: him, about him.

'But you haven't told us yet how long this career is to be. You know, Josef, my darling, how Mamma and I hope that very soon you will come back to work among your own people, here at Richterhausen. Ahi, what a proud day that will be! You won't forget, laddie, that so many of our own people here, in the factory quarter and round about the old market, are always wanting a good doctor. Typhoid there was, last summer. And bad limbs they get at the factory and often there are sore places and much jaundice now that food is so bad. Poor people, yes, but so many between them can give a doctor what is right for a man of such good education who gives up his life to them. Dr. Sponholz has a little motor-car, 10 horsepower, not so bad! But he is getting old, I have heard people say that he would like a young assistant . . .'

Back to Richterhausen! Staring at the bare wall of the waiting-room, Josef saw the street where the shop was, the pump at the corner. You turned left there—to the right the road only led into Bieber's yards—and for three or four straight kilometres you were held between the railway siding and a drawn monotony of workers' houses. You crossed the tramlines and the road gradually shed its workshops, its little garden plots; then the telephone poles ran on dead straight, aimed at the slag hills of Auermund. Richterhausen: old Maria Kuschnitzki, bulbous and dishevelled, sprawling over her barrow; a switch of tabid children playing in the sand by the railway track; torn posters flapping in the damp wind. Everything infected by the stench of the tanneries, which flavoured even your food. Some time he would go there for a few days; later on, when he had saved for a good overcoat and smart shoes, when the last skin of Richterhausen accent had been stripped from his speech. But stay there? devote the rest of life to that copse of crouching houses?

He would have to write very carefully to Papa, very affectionately. Papa, after all, had set him going—done without tobacco for fourteen years. The letter must carry a hint, so gently phrased, that a doctor's career should not be too much fenced, that the people it was useful to know lived in the larger places. Before long he would send a present for Mamma; Mamma liked a dash of colour, and there were fine shawls in a shop he had noticed near the station.

"The Director is ready to see you now."

Along the corridors again, with the old porter puffing officiously ahead. Across the landing, blinking under the candid curiosity of a girl who stood at an open door. Another corridor, where the smell of lysol was intensified. A door covered in scarlet baize, and a sudden guilty feeling, as when he had stood outside the anatomy school waiting for the *viva voce*.

"Doctor Zeppichmann, Herr Direktor!"

"Just sit down a minute, Doctor. I want to get this letter off . . . All right, Gustav!"

Dr. Wildelau shifted his pince-nez, moved a paper-weight to uncover a letter from the dean of the Zornenwalde medical school. *'I have found Zeppichmann a most industrious student, of high intelligence, thoroughly conscientious in all his duties. I have no hesitation in recommending him . . .'* Just so, just so! Old Plünnecke fastened the same encomium to every graduate he despatched. Character, that was one of the things Plünnecke did not fully understand; the others were biology, anatomy, diagnosis . . . And yet, oddly, one of the finest teachers in Hanover. This time he had sent a raw one, by the look of it. A lad from the coal-pits, you'd have said, done up to imitate a suburban gentleman: his square, corneous face pumiced to a horrid brightness; the big loose jacket fitting only on the shoulders, far too broad for the fellow's skimpy height; long, red wrists leading down from the frayed cuffs into hugely awkward paws.

"Well, Doctor Zeppichmann, I've had a most glowing account of you from Doctor Plünnecke."

"Yes, Herr Direktor."

Certainly the eyes were alive. Not intellectual, no, nothing of subtlety; but intense, devoted, like a setter's eyes. Yes, there was something altogether canine about this youth, the air of an ugly watch-dog—a puppy rather, a puppy with its first good beating just behind, desperately keen to show its usefulness, desperately gauche.

"You left Doctor Plünnecke in good health?"

"In fairly good health. He feels his age a good deal, I think."

"Indeed? Doctor Plünnecke is eight years my junior."

"Oh . . ."

Wildelau pulled another letter from the typewritten

pile, altered a word and signed it. If this man had to be invited to dinner, who would Hildegarde get to meet him? He said slowly:

"You are very fortunate to have studied under Plünnecke. A splendid teacher. If I had a son of my own, that is where I should send him. Without a doubt. Without any hesitation at all. But perhaps I ought just to say this. A man who gives up so much of his time to tutorial work cannot—in the nature of things he cannot—keep so well abreast with current medical practice as we are obliged to in our work here, for instance. You will realise that you are now passing on to another stage in your education. You will learn here many new things, you may find that our practice—indeed, our theory—differs in many particulars from what Doctor Plünnecke has taught you. That is inevitable—just as life is inevitably different from the picture of it drawn by a schoolteacher. What I mean is—I don't want your sense of loyalty to Doctor Plünnecke to make you unduly critical of methods you find in use at this hospital. I would say, Observe, Compare, Appreciate—Criticise, if you like, mentally. But to begin with, reserve your judgements."

"Indeed, yes, Herr Direktor, I understand that."

Wildelau re-crossed his legs. There was a faint-hued satisfaction in this familiar duty, like the quiet enjoyment of his own perfected routine: shaving in the morning, opening his private letters with the paper knife which was always laid beside his plate. Pleasure, too, in the sense of his own spirit flowing down into this empty vessel; his own honesty, homeliness, his certainty of purpose.

"Are you interested in politics at all?"

"No, Herr Direktor, I have never concerned myself with politics."

"Ah, so! That is very wise, I think. Of course, we must always remember first of all that we are citizens of a great nation. We must be ready at any moment to devote ourselves, everything we have, to our national duty. But men who want to get on in their profession have no time for political ebullience. There is too much of that among our young men nowadays. Too much speech-making and scrapping, even in a quiet place like this Hartzinnfeld . . . I want you to feel that you are not merely working in this hospital, but that you are a part of it. We are all bound together in one common purpose, we are, as it were, a single weapon forged against the great enemy, disease . . ."

He glanced at the clock. Twenty past four already, and he had to see a visiting surgeon at half-past. A pity. He must have another talk with this boy later on. Something might be made of a creature with such earnest, hungry eyes; if not a doctor, at any rate a wholly reliable ward-man.

". . . To begin with you will be working under Doctor Röstel. His surgery is over there in the north building— the porter will show you. Eight o'clock, will you be there please. And if any questions arise about your work they should go to Doctor Röstel in the first place; he will consult me if there's anything he can't settle himself. Well, Zeppichmann, I hope you'll be happy here. I'll give you just one hint. I have found that one's happiness in life depends on a single condition: on knowing that one has done one's duty."

He held out his hand. Josef rose as if to take it. Stopped short. Fumbled.

"May I just ask something?"

"Certainly, certainly."

"It's just—it's this way. Doctor Plünnecke was kind enough to give me facilities for some private research. I—he encouraged that. I—I was wondering if perhaps you would have no objection to my continuing that research—in my own time, of course. I thought that possibly you might grant me the use of a small laboratory—I mean, a bench, just a bench in the bacteriological laboratory."

Wildelau stretched his lower lip.

"As to your carrying on private research—well, I suppose there's no harm in that, so long as it doesn't intefere with your work. And possibly Doctor Dittmer will not object to your being in his laboratory sometimes, if he knows exactly what you're doing. In what branch are these—researches of yours?"

For a moment Josef's mouth wouldn't open. This was one of the cues for which he had rehearsed, but the sentences which came so fluently in a hotel bedroom would not take shape before Wildelau's fixed, inquiring eyes.

"I am on the track of something important," he said abruptly.

"Yes?"

"A new polyvalent tuberculin."

Wildelau turned his eyes away.

"Doctor Zeppichmann," he said, staring at his blotting-paper, "I don't want to be in any way unsympathetic, but I think—I think you ought to know this: of some twenty thousand revolutionary discoveries in medicine which young men announce every year, something like thirty-five per cent are new and perfect antitoxins for tuberculosis. I suppose that at this very moment hundreds, literally hundreds of scientists who have spent their whole lives in research are at work on just that problem. In America there are huge laboratories with fully-trained staffs engaged on nothing else. Do you—do you really think that your chances of success are very rosy?"

This time there was no hesitation.

"I think I am on the way to success, Herr Direktor."

From the loose jacket came a long, dirty envelope crammed with manuscript.

"I have a record of all my workings up to date. I have used Schulze-Manz's formula as my basis, but I've introduced two new elements which I call Psi Plus and Psi

Minus. I've been experimenting to determine the exact co-efficients, and I think now—"

Wildelau cleared his throat. "Yes yes—"

"—I thought perhaps you might care to glance through my tabulations. It wouldn't take you more than an hour—some time when you're not particularly busy. This top sheet gives a brief explanation of my system—I've divided the data into five groups corresponding with the five hypotheses which I've detailed—"

"—Yes yes, some time, some time I should be very much interested." Wildelau folded the sheets and slid them back into the envelope. He said, "Yes, Zeppichmann, I'm very glad you've occupied your spare time in this way. It is—it is good practice, it develops orderly habits in thinking. Yes, some time I should like to look through your essay. At present I am particularly busy, I'm finding it very hard to get through all my work." He rose. "I'm sure Doctor Röstel will be most interested to see these—these papers. Well now, I have an appointment at half-past four—it's past that already."

But the youth did not move. Grave, awkward, determined: like a dog asking to be taken for a walk, Wildelau thought.

"There is just one more thing I wanted to ask you, Herr Direktor. I thought that you might have some cases here, some cases in the Tuberculosis Department, which are not responding to any standard treatment. I thought—it seems possible that one of those cases would prove to be exactly what I'm looking for. I thought—I mean, when you've had time to go through my analysis of results—I thought you might be willing to hand such a case over to me—for a limited period, of course—"

"Do I understand you to mean," Wildelau asked slowly, "that you want to try out your theories on one of my patients?"

"Well, yes. I don't mean, of course, one of the paying patients—"

"Doctor Zeppichmann:" Wildelau said, "when you have worked under me for twelve months or so you will probably have learnt something about my ethical position, about the creed on which all our work here is based. You will learn that we here regard each single life for which we are responsible as something of inestimable value . . . When that is learnt, we may perhaps discuss your proposals again. In the meantime, Doctor Dittmer may be willing for you to make some experiments on his animals. I can't promise that, of course . . ."

Josef said, politely: "I have already made experiments with two hundred groups of tubercle-infected rats—"

"—And how many of those are still extant?"

"In my last, what I call the M.44 group, the negative results only came to 17.6%."

"Which means, on a broad hypothesis, that you want me to give you a 17% chance of killing one of my patients?"

"I think I could put it at only 15%, given a suitable subject. And of course I'm not asking for a good case—not to begin with—only a case which has passed the line already."

Wildelau went to the door and opened it.

"In a year's time," he said, "I hope you will have shown me that you are not only a conscientious, reliable house-surgeon, but also that you have grown a little more mature, that your sense of proportion has developed. It can, I think—develop a good deal."

2

FROM the station, where he had left his bag, a narrow road curved up to the Bülow fountain. Standing there he had half the town in the sweep of his eyes, right over to where the new summer villas crept up into the pine woods, points of cream and scarlet in a crumpled curtain. One day he would live in a villa like that. The late sun, still strong enough to warm his face, flattered that notion. The street was quiet, the tramway didn't come up here. An old woman in grey clothes, twelve years behind the fashion, moved slowly along the footpath, stopping at all the windows of the smart, bijou shops, appraising, passing on, drinking the sunlight. That was the way to use a quiet town like this, a town of leaning sixteenth-century houses: to share its calmness, sip the small beauties which it held out as you passed, sunlight on an old wall, the smell of coffee; to live as probably she did in one of those sun-drowned villas, or in a little house down the Kirchenstrasse there with dormer windows; with one old servant, and a military pension. But that was a far country.

The working quarter was on the other side of the river. He went down that way, shifting his heavy bag from hand to hand: the same canvas bag that Jakob Zeppichmann had brought to Richterhausen from Lublin. And here the evening wind, coming freshly from the water, chilled his thoughts a little. The sun was in his eyes now, making the roofs black and forlorn. He had an address to go to, he had seen it in an advertisement panel at the station: Handelstrasse 149. *Accommodation for Professional Men and Families. Close to Rumprecht's Works.* It sounded the sort of place. To start with.

It was a Number 4 tram that Josef wanted, the policeman said.

A Number 4 came along the old quay and lurched across the bridge; changed its conductor pole in the square on the other side and barged round into Siemenstrasse. There Josef caught it; gratefully planted his bag on the platform and went inside. How much to Handelstrasse? Five pfennigs and two for the suitcase. Yes, luggage left on the platform was charged extra. Wearily he went to fetch it, and returned to his place heaving it above the passengers' knees. The crowded tram lurched to the right again and began to climb laboriously between the factory walls.

This Dr. Dittmer, Josef thought, he was evidently the man to be cajoled first of all. Dittmer, presumably, was head of the Research Department, and would have to be placated before one could use his tools. To begin with, Josef might pretend to be much interested in whatever Dittmer himself was doing; he might make himself useful, preparing compounds, taking readings. That would be the first stage . . . Dr. Wildelau? Pfui! A garrulous old woman, a little Caesar from the market stalls!

The street narrowed. Here, standing between two houses in the row, you could place your hands on both frontdoors. The tram slowed to a walking pace, squeezing through a crowd which spread across the roadway: a crowd staring at the wreckage of a little shop, chairs with the legs torn off, broken china all over the footpath. With furious clanging the tram ground on, a message chalked on a wall slipped past the window and was lost. 'This happens to traitors.' An elderly man, a clerk from one of the factories, followed Josef's gaze and smiled.

"Communists, you see! The young men hereabouts are mostly that way. Sunday nights, they have to smash something to keep themselves amused." Looking hard at Josef's face he leant a little closer. "Let me just tell you. You're a

stranger to Hartzinnfeld? Well, people of your—people of
your kind, they want to keep quiet as much as possible. I'm
only being friendly, you understand?"

Josef smiled.

"Yes yes, I thank you. But I never meddle with politics. I've too much else to think about."

Handelstrasse was built in the eighties, but it incorpo-
rates, at the end farthest from where the tram stops, a lane
that once ran between two farms. One of the farms still
stands, much chopped about; a Department Manager belonging to Rumprecht's bullied it into a house of 1910 re-
spectability; and Number 149 was once Ruckschade's Inn.
It has been, from time to time, a storehouse and a box factory. Windows have been altered, and on the street side
there is an ugly wing, built with bricks left over from one
of the factories. But at the back its charm remains: the tiny
dormer windows, the little gallery on two sides of the courtyard. The Spühlers, when they occupied the place a few
years after the war, restored so much of its homeliness as
their means and taste allowed. That courtyard holds you
very pleasantly, when you have walked all the way along
the dingy street. And though the rooms have got depress-
ingly shabby, the upper windows give you a sight of the
Graftel woods.

A student's cap was hanging just inside one of the front
windows. The door-bell was out of action. Both these details
were satisfactory to Josef as he stood by the door, sweating,
sizing up the place: it had the air of genteel patronage, and
a smack of comfortable inefficiency. One got on best by em-
ploying slightly inefficient people. Then the window above
his head was jerked open, and Frau Spühler's round face,
porched with a crimson dustcap, was staring down at him.

"If you please?"

Josef took off his hat.

"I understand, madam, that you have a room to let? I mean, for pension-accommodation."

Frau Spühler screwed her eyes, thinking hard.

"I'll come down," she said at last.

That gave her a little time, time to grasp the situation. Life always moved too fast for her, tradesmen were always arriving, lodgers asking for something; they popped things at you, they never gave you time to think. Mainly, she thought now about bolsters: one of the bolsters from the vacant room had gone to Herr Barthol; there was another in the attic, but it scattered feathers all over the place, whatever you did. Josef listened to the creak of the stair-boards as she came slowly down.

When she opened the door she stared at him as if his appearance there were a fresh phenomenon. Stared in silence, until her voice, in its irresponsible way, said suddenly: "Twenty-four Marks a week. That doesn't include a midday meal."

Josef regarded her earnestly.

"I didn't mean to pay more than twenty," he said.

Not more than twenty! And he looked like a vigorous feeder. Why did he stare at her so reproachfully, as if she were trying to cheat him? She said:

"I can show you the room."

Following her along the cracked linoleum, smelling faintly the afterglow of the last meal, his eyes went up and down from the fine grey hair leaking out of her cap to the awkward movement of her huge hips. Something reminded him faintly of his mother, though she was small. But this was a gentlewoman, comparatively; one who had fallen a step or two. Incipient rheumatoid arthritis, possibly. Twenty-four Marks! And he had hardly hoped to pay less than twenty-five at a place of this kind.

"There," she said, "this one."

But he had stopped a few paces back, where an open

door showed him an L-shaped room, half as big again as the one to which Frau Spühler was inviting him.

"May I look in here?"

It was empty, and he went across to the window. This was the sort of room a student of the better class had, a smart pair of shoes stood by the bed, there were pictures which he vaguely recognised as being in respectable taste. Like Herr Niewind's room at Zornenwalde. But what really mattered was that here one had room to work: a bench over there by the long window, with shelves—he could put them up himself—against the adjacent wall. Bring the light over to this corner with a two-way connection and a long flex, and the room would be a laboratory in embryo. The picture that his mind suddenly made went on through time: long evenings at his bench there, hundreds of hours of contented patience. To work as Koch did, alone and utterly confident: that was happiness.

"This is not a bad room," he said. "Of course, it's in rather bad repair . . ."

"But this is Herr Meisel's room."

"He is here for long?"

"Oh yes, there's no talk of his leaving us."

Josef went to the window again. Here, to the left, he could fix up a level table that would take his balance. He said:

"But perhaps Herr Meisel would be willing to change his room?"

Frau Spühler stared at his face, puzzled. You didn't ask lodgers to change their rooms.

"No," she said at last, "no, I don't think he would."

"How much does he pay for it?"

"Herr Meisel? For this room? How much does he pay?"

"Yes yes, what does he pay?"

"Well, I don't know. Let me see. Herr Meisel came

to us in 1929. Yes, we were charging twenty-two Marks then. Meat was a bit cheaper then, you see. The price of meat in Hartzinnfeld, it's become something terrible. We just had to put up our charges."

"But Herr Meisel still pays twenty-two Marks?"

"Well, you see, we couldn't put up the charge to the lodgers we had already, could we?"

She smiled, asking doubtfully for his understanding. Ah God, he thought, was it wise, was it fair to put such people in the world? These women, you could steal the rings off their fingers and they would think you were only doing it to save them from phalangeal cramp.

He said seriously: "Yes, I quite see that, I quite understand. But if I were to offer you twenty-five—no, twenty-four Marks, it would only be fair for me to have the best room. Herr Meisel would surely understand that."

"I don't think he'd like to change," she repeated. "You see, all his things are here."

"But they could be moved. It wouldn't take five minutes." He was calculating swiftly. One could get a good laboratory balance for a deposit of about seventy Marks. Instalments, say eight Marks a week. He ought to send home nine Marks a week—that was more or less agreed. It would be cutting things close, but . . .

"Twenty-five Marks," he said. "For this room. That's a definite offer."

Frau Spühler turned her head away. She was very unhappy. Twenty-five Marks, it wasn't to be sniffed at. The room at the end of the passage had been empty for three months. It was now six weeks since Herr Meisel had last paid his bill. Oh really she did not like this young man, she couldn't like him at all, coming here and wanting Herr Meisel's room and popping figures at her, not giving her time to think.

"I must ask my husband," she said, and went vaguely

away, leaving him in the passage. She knew that August would be no help at all, but it gave her a little more time.

Josef stood still, calculating. The house was very quiet, he heard only the crackle of a board recovering from Frau Spühler's steps, very faintly the murmur of her voice somewhere downstairs. Suddenly a new sound came from below, the sound of some one coughing. A harsh, uncontrolled cough. That was interesting.

He went down and got his bag.

When Frau Spühler returned, Josef's bag was in the middle of Herr Meisel's room, his coat and hat on one of the chairs.

"Well?" he asked.

He was like a hungry man with bread just out of reach.

"I was thinking," she said slowly, "—I mean, my husband says you ought to ask Herr Meisel yourself. You could explain to him."

"Just so. I can quite easily explain to Herr Meisel. Perhaps if we put one or two of Herr Meisel's things into the other room he would see how comfortable he'll be in there. These pictures, they'd show better in the smaller room."

"But not before Herr Meisel comes in," Frau Spühler said anxiously. "He'll be in any moment now. You can wait just a few minutes, surely you can wait! . . ."

"These cushions," Josef asked, "are they Herr Meisel's, or do they belong to the house?"

3

IT TOOK less than fifteen minutes to get most of Herr Meisel's belongings shifted. Josef did the greater part of the work himself. Frau Spühler, faintly hoping that Herr Meisel would hardly notice the change, was trying to put everything in the same order: the two small pictures where you could see them on entering the room, the large ones opposite the window. When it came to moving the wardrobe, that mahogany wardrobe which Herr Meisel had had sent from Berlin, Herr Spühler had to be called up to help.

Shorter than his wife, massive in neck and shoulders, Herr Spühler looked a very bullock for strength. Yes, like one of the young prize bullocks Josef had often seen in the Richterhausen market. "Ah yes," Herr Spühler said, rolling up his sleeves, "when I was in the Navy—a Warrant Officer, you understand—I could carry three men on my back. Three stokers, do you see, a hundred kilograms apiece, three hundred kilograms altogether. Carry them all along the fighting deck."

He walked all round the wardrobe, as if it were a city to conquer.

"Now this," he said, "I shall take upon my back. With my arms going round behind, like this." He took up his stance, back to back with the wardrobe, leaning forward, his big behind pressed against it. Large he might be, Josef thought, but standing like that he looked as flabby as a tortoise. "Now I just want you, Hilde, to tilt it forward till it rests on my back. And you, Doctor, would perhaps support the bottom a little."

"It is quite impossible," Frau Spühler said. "You can't

do that kind of thing, you know perfectly well you can't."

"We could carry it together," Josef suggested.

"Nonsense, little plum. It's quite all right, Doctor."

"But your heart, August! You know what the doctor said about your heart. You, Doctor, I ask you to forbid him. His heart, you can see what it's like."

Josef could only see Herr Spühler's behind. But he thought endocarditis was not unlikely.

"Perhaps if I took out some of the things . . ." he began.

But Herr Spühler, getting impatient, had succeeded in pulling it on to his back. And now, entirely in the semblance of a tortoise, he was moving towards the door, his short legs jerking along an inch at a time, his stomach issuing alarming little grunts. "August, you will kill yourself!" Frau Spühler repeated, hovering miserably on his flank. "Your heart will never get over it, to-morrow you'll be a dead man."

"I doubt if it'll go through the door that way," Josef said gloomily.

"Go through?" Herr Spühler panted. "Of course it— damn and blast it! Hilde, for God's sake! Doctor, get hold of it, can't you! Hold on to her stern!"

"That is the end!" Frau Spühler said.

Yes, it was going, it was through! The moulded top came hard against the passage wall, but somehow Herr Spühler had got it clear, the stern only scraping the lintel. On again, straight on along the passage, Herr Spühler creaking and grunting, his wife damp-eyed, while Josef in sullen exasperation fidgeted uselessly behind. Up the two steps Herr Spühler climbed, a pygmy Atlas in gigantic motion. But the next doorway beat him. Josef cried a warning but it was long too late, the wardrobe came against the lintel mouldings with such a crash that Herr Spühler himself was almost taken off his feet.

"Now he is destroying the house," Frau Spühler said.

Herr Spühler stood shaking like a snapped spring, the wardrobe still aloft.

"Sideways," he jerked out, "just go—sideways. Have goodness—fetch Professor Rupf!"

The trouble, as Professor Rupf and his wife saw it when they arrived, was to turn the wardrobe sideways from its present position. The top of it was jammed now between the ceiling and the architrave, the bottom wedged into the skirting where the passage narrowed. Tall and kindly, Professor Rupf surveyed the situation, measured the distances with his grave eyes.

"If you were to come out, Herr Spühler, then we could make a plan of campaign."

But Herr Spühler, still crouching underneath, could not see it like that.

"If I move it will crash to the ground," he answered.

"He should never have attempted such a thing," Frau Rupf said robustly. "At his age it's fatal to the heart."

"That is what I said," Frau Spühler agreed. "It was the Doctor here who wanted it moved."

"I am only fifty-nine!" Herr Spühler retorted.

The Professor turned to Josef, who stood with his hand in his pocket staring glumly at the wardrobe.

"If you would help me to pull it a little this way, Herr Doktor. The ceiling, you see, it's a bit higher on this side. That will give us a little turning space, then we can swing the bottom round and that will enable us to get it on its side. You, my dear, will you just hold on to the bottom—see that it doesn't scrape the wainscotting. Perhaps you could stoop down, Frau Spühler, just enough to get under and help your husband. Herr Spühler, could you ease yourself back a little?"

"No," said Herr Spühler definitely. "I can't move half an inch. I've got cramp."

"What did I tell you!" Frau Rupf said.

The Professor clicked his tongue. "Never mind, never mind, we shall lift it clear of him!"

"And is my husband to stay there for the rest of his life?" Frau Spühler asked.

Frau Rupf shrugged her shoulders.

"At this rate his life will not be long!"

From downstairs came the sound of glass jangling in a loose frame. That was the front door.

It was characteristic of this house, Erich Meisel thought as he stood gloomily in the entrance hall, that the front door should rattle like that. Characteristic, perhaps, of the whole of Hartzinnfeld: a ramshackle outpost of the provinces, where nothing ever happened quite to time, nothing ever fitted. He called, "Minna! My house-shoes!" but there was no answer. The silly girl in the kitchen was alternately coughing and singing at the top of her voice. He opened the door of the Spühlers' sitting-room, hoping for a morsel of Frau Spühler's constant, unreasoning sympathy. But no one was there.

He sat down, suddenly feeling his tiredness. The whole day, from breakfast, on one plate of soup. And he must have walked twenty kilometres. That did not seem so much; for on his holidays, three years ago, he had done as much as forty kilometres in the day, with nothing but bread and cheese for lunch. He was an athlete, Erich Meisel, trained to endurance. But the hard pavements, the eternal stairs to top-floor offices, worked more severely on that spare, narrow-chested body. It was unlucky to have been born in 1912, to have lost one's father three years later. The thin tightness of his face showed that. They were marks of aristocracy, Erich himself thought, emblems of Junker blood: the high cheek-bones he saw in a mirror, the deeply recessed eyes. But his forbears had mostly been stout-faced.

He would not have said that he was lonely. But there is a congenital disposition to loneliness, and spirits suffer from that affection as constantly as certain bodies from asthma. The attacks come less from solitude than from the sense of being a stranger. And in Hartzinnfeld Erich was a stranger still. Oh yes, he had his friends, he would meet them in the Club this evening: lads of decent intention, honourable, if not of his own rank. But his thoughts were going back over the day's wanderings, and he realised that since leaving the house this morning he had spoken to no one as to a fellow man. "Goodmorning! I understand that you have a vacancy here for an assistant in the advertising department." "Goodmorning! You promised to tell me if you had notice of any openings for a shorthand writer . . . Oh. Oh, I see! Then you will let me know through the post?" That is not conversation.

For more than a month, now, this had been the daily routine. Life sloped downwards from the Tuesday, three years ago, when an army medical board had refused its certificate. That was the day when his spirit's growth had stopped. But the time in which hope and dignity had flickered out together was the moment when he last stood in Birnegarten's office: the fat Birnegarten leaning back in his chair, heavily suave, a little nervous. ". . . This new combination involves the fusion of the two publicity departments. I'm sure, Herr Meisel, you will appreciate the fact that the more experienced men have first claim. I needn't tell you how much I regret that the increasing severity of competition makes these measures necessary . . ." Dust swimming in a column of sunlight, the smell of new distemper, and a door swinging. Then a stocky youth with a big nose and a Hamburg accent asking if Herr Meisel would be so very kind as to show him his record books.

He had told no one, written to none of his friends. In a letter to his mother he had said that the quiet provincial life suited him, that he was too busy to spend a weekend in

Berlin as she suggested. It was pride's last refuge, to keep his wounds in hiding, not to cry out.

Where was Frau Spühler, what was every one doing in this damned house? In the sharp attack of loneliness he would have welcomed old Spühler himself, old Spühler with the eternal question floating on his eternal grin. "Well well, any luck to-day, Herr Meisel?" He took off his shoes—one of them had a nail sticking up—pushed them into a corner and limped across the hall in his socks. The girl Minna, meeting him there, thought, 'How angry Herr Meisel looks to-day!' Like a leopard, she thought, a wounded leopard. Yes, he was just like a leopard, thin and self-contained, with a rather surreptitious pride, the small eyes scowling.

He stopped abruptly when he saw her.

"Didn't you hear me call? I want my house-shoes."

"I put them in your room, Herr Meisel. Yes, I did clean them—this morning."

"Where is everybody?" he asked. "Where's Frau Spühler got to?"

She started to answer but a fit of coughing took her and made her speechless. Oh, damn the girl! Was there no one in this place who could even answer a plain question. "You ought to see a doctor!" he said, but she didn't hear him. He went on upstairs.

They had the wardrobe athwart the passage now, and Frau Rupf, jammed in a corner behind it, was uttering explosive little sarcasms as quickly as her hard, small mind could form them. Herr Spühler was still in the same position, fixed like a figure of stone in the attitude of one about to dive through the floor.

"If only you could move just a few inches to one side," Professor Rupf said reasonably, "then we could cant the thing over and slide it forward obliquely."

"I am not standing like this just to admire the view," was all Herr Spühler answered.

"If you can release me by supper-time," Frau Rupf said stonily, "I shall be perfectly content. Otherwise, perhaps you would bring me my night-things."

Frau Spühler stopped weeping to stare at Frau Rupf disdainfully. She said:

"You can't undress there, with my husband only a few inches away."

"Then you must either remove your husband or put up a small screen."

"Patience, ladies, patience!" the Professor said sadly. "We must try to tackle the problem reasonably. When once we have the wardrobe out of the way we can attend to the disposal of the population."

"Long before that my husband will be dead," Frau Spühler retorted.

Frau Rupf smiled coldly.

"Well, we have a doctor here to do the post mortem. All we shall want is an undertaker."

A quiet, stiff voice asked:

"Just what is happening to my wardrobe?"

The silence that came was the silence of schoolboys at the special jerk of a door-handle. Josef, twisting round, saw a young man with the figure of a delicate boy, a face of almost middle-aged maturity; eyes whose stare was like a flat, wide beam of light.

It was the Professor who first got his tongue loose:

"You might say, Herr Meisel, that everything has happened to your wardrobe except what we want to happen. It persistently objects to going through this door."

"And why should it?"

"Ah, that is Herr Spühler's affair."

From the stiff, doubled trunk of Herr Spühler a voice said uneasily:

"You must ask my wife, it's something she fixed up."

Meisel's eyes, moving round upon Frau Spühler, set

her into speech some five seconds before she intended; and the words came wrong:

"I thought—I thought perhaps you would like the other room. It gets the sun—it gets the sun in the early morning. Just a change, I thought—I knew you wouldn't mind. At least, I thought perhaps it was more suitable."

"More suitable?"

She opened her mouth again, but nothing came at all now. Erich Meisel said coolly, carefully:

"So you've decided to move me into another room? Wouldn't it have been more courteous to consult me before shifting my things?"

The question was pushed at Frau Spühler alone. But every one felt guilty.

"Perhaps we could adjourn to the dining-room and discuss the matter there, in an amiable spirit," Rupf began.

"I personally am unable to adjourn anywhere," his wife said. "And Herr Spühler does not seem very adjournable."

But Frau Spühler had been given time to arrange her mind now.

"It's nothing to do with me," she said boldly. "It was the Doctor's idea."

"The Doctor's?"

"That gentleman."

Josef saluted. "Doctor Zeppichmann!"

Erich had barely noticed him. Dr. Zeppichmann, good God! A flourishing Senior Boy from the agricultural labourers' orphanage.

"So you think my health requires the early morning sun, Herr Doktor?"

Josef smiled. He liked a joke, even when he couldn't quite get his mind round it. Amiably, a little nervously, he said:

"This room here, you see, it's specially suitable for some

research work I'm doing. I have agreed to pay Frau Spühler a special rate to secure my choice of room, and I felt certain you would see that the new arrangement is—quite reasonable. Actually that room is in some ways a better one. As Frau Spühler says, it catches the early sun."

He stopped there, because you cannot go on talking to a man whose back is turned to you. And Erich was already addressing Herr Spühler.

"You know, this is by no means a perfect boarding-house, but as places of this kind go I've always thought it was run on fairly sensible lines. Perhaps I'm over-scrupulous, but isn't it rather surprising, after lodging here for three years, to find that a total stranger has jumped in from no-where and helped himself to my room? Or is it just your ordinary practice to get hold of your guests' private property and bundle it about? Possibly you're under the impression that I only hire a room to sleep in! As for my wardrobe, which happens to have been built by one of the finest cabinet-makers in Germany, I suppose if it gets in your way at all you're at liberty to pitch it into the street! Or have you any reasonable explanation to offer?"

Frau Rupf sighed. "How that young man does talk!"

"Quiet, Trude!"

"Have you any explanation?" Erich repeated. "Why can't you answer me? What are you standing there for in that idiotic way?"

Herr Spühler spoke then. It was Erich's remark about pitching the wardrobe into the street which had mainly provoked him. (Pitch that wardrobe?—let young Meisel try it!) But the personal insult ripped off the coat of decorous restraint which he had worn for his guests these fourteen years.

"Herr Meisel," he suddenly barked, "when you have paid the six weeks' rent you owe me for your room it will be time enough for you to insult my wife and myself. Meanwhile, this is a house, let me tell you, for respectable guests. It is not a charity-home for ruffianly paupers."

A moment of stillness, a moment when the noises from the street seemed to be still. White and shaking, Erich made a step towards Herr Spühler. But a hand stopped him: Josef's.

"One moment, Herr Meisel," Josef said. "Listen please! If I was to advance something towards your arrears, that would make everything all right, wouldn't it? That would be a reasonable settlement, don't you think?"

Erich stared at Josef for an instant; their faces only a few inches apart. Said nothing. Pushed through to the small room at the end and slammed the door.

Along the passage, shuffling in her loose slippers, came the girl Minna.

"Herr Meisel was saying he wanted his house-shoes. Shall I get them and take them to his new room?"

No one answered her.

4

DR. WILDELAU sent down a note to Dr. Röstel:

'The young man I mentioned will report to you to-morrow morning. His name is Zeppichmann. I have already interviewed him.

'Zeppichmann is, I think, a keen youngster, and more intelligent than his rather homely outlines suggest. He should work hard, under careful supervision. On the other hand, I ought to warn you that his success in examinations seems to have given him a slightly exaggerated view of his attainments in Medicine. I suggest that this error in self-appreciation may be rectifiable, without any discouragement of proper keenness, by the concentration of Zeppichmann's energies on that part of the Ward routine which is proper to a junior man.'

Dr. Röstel showed the note to Dr. Dittmer.

"At any rate I hope he will be tidy," Röstel said.

"Yes yes," Dittmer agreed, "I think tidiness is the one really important thing in all scientific work"; and went away to his own regions, where he could laugh out loud.

The Moltke Hospital catered for all the ailments recognised by medical science, and even for some which, refusing classification, are not recognised. But the Staff suffered from one disease, virulent and infectious, an encompassing mania for tidiness. It is needful to be tidy, in a place which gathers all the damaged bodies from a thousand square miles. A new in-patient arrives, on the average, once in every three hours; but they don't come at three-hourly intervals—a dozen or twenty may turn up at once. A new case has to be examined, cleaned, put to bed. That means records, towels,

bedclothes—fifty different material things, as well as the exact application of labour; and one has to find these things in a hurry. The demands of the machine do not cease while emergencies are covered. Cases get hungry, run up temperatures, require the slipper, require medicine, die; irrespective of the Staff's convenience. So if some one fails to put a bottle of iodine back in the proper place the noise of complaint sounds far. *It must go back in the proper place!* The injunction becomes a motto, a war-cry, a permanent knot in the brain. The foot of a bed just out of alignment, some one's thermometer left on a dressing-trolley: these things, in the Moltke mind, were like pictures hung crooked. You could not rest, you could not get on with what you were doing, till the emblem of chaos had been reduced to order and somebody soundly lectured.

Dr. Röstel had come to the hospital on a six months' appointment in 1922, and still meant to find a less exhausting post as soon as he had cleared up an interesting pyelitis case in Ward 14, a hobnail liver in Ward 6. He suffered from the disease in its most acute form. Dr. Röstel had a motto of his own, 'Only the patient matters,' and its application kept him in a smouldering frenzy. With his intense shyness, he never looked at a patient's face, seldom addressed one except conventionally; but as he passed through a ward a little moan, a catching of the breath, would make him pull up in a kind of panic distress. "Sister! Nurse! That man's head is too high. You must take one pillow away. No, that's too low now, you must find a shallower pillow." And then, "This spittoon, when was it last emptied? A spittoon shouldn't be left for more than an hour. This record card, it's not been entered up this morning. Nine o'clock. Where's the senior nurse? That window's too far open, there's a draught along these beds. What's that over there? Look, my girl, look! That clout. Who left it there? What's it doing there? A cleaning rag on a patient's bed, I've never heard of such a thing—don't you realise these things are alive with bacilli!"

So this what's-his-name, this new young man, Zeppichmann, about whom Röstel saw nothing at all remarkable one way or the other, this Zeppichmann had got to be tidy. And ah, God, the number of qualified hobbledehoys that had turned up in these twenty years to borrow Röstel's stethoscope without permission and amble about the wards in dirty overalls and leave their notebooks on the bedtables!

"I am sure," he said, "I am sure, Doctor— Doctor Zepp—Zepp—I am sure, Doctor, we shall work very happily together." Washing his hands once again, his knees bent with rheumatism, his round, cosy little stomach pressed against the basin, he smiled in his friendliest way at the cold tap. "All I ask is that you should be methodical. Methodical, clean in your work, wash hands between the wards, not leave things about, you know. That other man I had, young what's-his-name, Werner—Werner-something, about four years ago, nice fellow, clever, he used to take out his dentures, always said they weren't comfortable, used to put them down and leave them all over the place. I found them on a patient's bed once. A pneumonia case. Just imagine that! A man with lobar pneumonia, about forty-eight hours to live, thinking over his past life no doubt. Suddenly he looks up and sees the doctor's teeth on his bed. I told Werner, Werner-whatever-it-was, I think his name was something like that, I said, 'Only the patient matters.' That's a thing I'd like you to remember: *Only the patient matters.* I said to Werner-whatever-it-was, 'If your dentures aren't comfortable you'd better leave them with the porter when you arrive and get a receipt for them.' Well now, come along to the post-mortem room and I'll show you a liver which I think will interest you. A rather fascinating cirrhosis. It belonged to such a sweet old lady, died on Monday, came from

Dresden. Would you mind going back and just shutting that door! With the handle. It doesn't have to be slammed."

So that was this man's kink, Josef thought. Tidiness. Ah well!

And four days later Dr. Röstel found that all the drawers in his instrument cabinet had been elegantly labelled, and a separate hook had been screwed on to the door for Zeppichmann's overall, and on Zeppichmann's table stood a wooden box, neatly home-made, with the rudiments of a patients' index.

It was observed in the Wards also that the new doctor was a tidy person, in the Moltke tradition. For a day or two this awkward, over-scrubbed young man in the very new overall was seen to trail after Röstel as dumb and sombrely as an aged sheepdog. It got about that he was an undertaker's apprentice, making mental notes for the size of coffins. But presently the tame creature began to move a little way from his master, to straighten somebody's bed clothes, push a chair into its proper place, dust some crumbs off a bedside table. That was significant: Dr. Röstel would have found crumbs on the blades of an electric fan. And presently the new doctor was calling, nervously but not unobtrusively, 'Nurse, this medicine glass, it's empty I think. I thought— perhaps you didn't realize it had been left here.'

That was a treat for the patients. Old Kleinsucker, one-eyed and toothless, dying of pulmonary cancer in Ward 10, called hoarsely to his neighbour, "Hey! Heinrich! What about the new doctor! It's bitten him, ay, it's got him all right, the same bouncing bug! Must have the bolsters straight, must have the pots in a straight line. See him squinting at your heat-map up there? Didn't like the line so twisty, that's what it was. You'll have to get it straight, son, or they'll have you in the hack-up shop. Won't let you go on with a wobbly line like that, not the new boy won't." But Nurse Laupert regarded the manifestations with less amusement. "If Doctor Röstel wants to fuss about medicine-glasses, let him!" she said to her friend Elsa. "We must think of his mental health, poor thing, and if he didn't find something to madden him in every ward he'd go completely crazy. But if this flat-headed cub out of the potato-patch thinks it's my job to go round keeping medicine glasses out of his Holy eyesight . . . We've got as many fusspots here as we can get on with . . . And who the devil, I'd like to know, has pinched my midwifery manual!"

No, they were not agreeably impressed by this young Dr. Zeppichmann, that company of people who hurried all day across the parquet floors of the Moltke Hospital, whose common element was the fierce hygienic draught that swept through every ward, the eternal stench of carbolic. Yet no one could deny that he was a worker. Solemn, officious, he had a way of slipping into one of the wards without being noticed. A nurse tidying a patient at one end would suddenly hear his flat, chesty voice: "I'd better leave the leg as it is. If it goes on hurting I'll come back and do it this evening." And there was the new doctor, bent over a bed with the examination-lamp fixed on the headrail, swiftly undoing a bandage. And then, standing awkwardly with his eyes toward his boots, he would pay out a string of instructions.

"I'd like you to dress that arm again before you go off duty, Nurse, just as I've done it. Fresh vaseline. Don't touch the leg, I want to do that myself. About 6 T, in the corner there: I'm sending a chit to the dispensary as soon as I've checked it with Doctor Röstel. The stuff will be down at four and you're to give the first dose immediately. She may vomit some time afterwards; if that happens I want you to note the exact time and quantity of the vomit, and send a tabbed specimen to Doctor Herbst. He will report to me. I shall be here at 6.30, to give the second dose myself. Now about the next bed, 6 U . . ."

In the Staff Mess it was the same. At luncheon the re-

cruit sat earnest and silent, methodically enveloping fork-
loads as if he were fattening himself for market, always with
Schraube's *Cases in Phthisis* on the table beside him. If
young Ahlwarth asked, "What's on your mind, Zeppichmann? Your sins or your kidneys?" he answered gravely,
"It's a case in the throat ward, I'm very worried about it."
And afterwards, when Röstel was having his one treat of the
day, twenty minutes' chess with Dittmer, he would feel a
tap on his shoulder.

"You must excuse me, Doctor, I wanted just to consult
you about that membranous croup in 14. I want to inject
again, but I don't care to do it without your permission. Perhaps if you could just run up and look at it now, then you
could give me your advice before you go over to the surgical
wing . . ."

"Well," Dittmer said, when he met Röstel again, "that
new tool-sharpener of yours, is he tidy?"

Röstel nodded gloomily.

"Tidy? Yes. Yes, there's no doubt about it. The neatest
man I ever had. Never forgets anything. Always returns my
instruments when he borrows them. Never leaves his dentures on the beds."

"Aha," Dittmer said, nursing his thin hands, "then
you're in luck's way! Gracious Providence has looked fa-
vourably upon the good Doctor Röstel, his prayer for a tidy
man is answered at last."

"Yes," said Röstel, with unusual energy. "Yes, damn
and blast it!"

"Indeed? Indeed? Can there be some unheard of failing in this divinely tidy boy."

"There can. He treats the patients as if they were
cows."

"Is that—technically undesirable?"

"All research people talk like you do," Röstel said
grumpily. "You think that real doctoring's just a joke, you

think the only important thing is to marry bacilli and watch them copulating in your dirty little tubes."

Dittmer stretched his cheek-bones.

"My dear Röstel, why such acerbity? I am but a serving-maid in the outer courts of philosophy, and you talk as if I were the Director of the Berlin Underground Railway. I was only asking what could possibly be wrong with this most exceptional Doctor-Röstel-assistant. Is he rough with the corpses?"

Gathering his words laboriously, as one whose tongue is his least responsive member, Röstel said:

"That Zeppichmann, that great bull-calf that His Majesty Doctor Wildelau has plumped down on my stomach, he thinks of nothing but his work."

"My dear Röstel," Dittmer protested, "you really must be more selective in your use of metaphors. Just now you said that he treated the patients as if they were cows."

Röstel grunted. This Dittmer, this well-meaning trainer of bacilli, had a single fault: he was forever knitting up the most incomprehensible jokes.

"Thinks of nothing but his work!" he repeated.

"That is terrible!" Dittmer said. "A new assistant house-surgeon in the Moltke Hospital, a young man with all his professional life before him, he ought to be thinking about wine, about the colour of his tie, about horses and girls. To think about his work all day long, it's unforgivable! You, for example, my dear colleague, I know you spend all your time thinking whether you can afford an electric horn for your motorcycle."

"You don't understand me, Karl. Of course, yes, it's quite right for a young man to think about his work. But he should—I don't know, I can't put it into words—he ought to have some other interest, some philosophy. A man ought to be a human being, when all's said and done."

Dittmer frowned.

"That is rather a daring hypothesis. The House-Matron on the medical side, if she proved to be a human being I should lose all faith in divine taxonomy."

"No, but don't you see, he ought to think about his work as part of his life. The most important part, of course. As it is, he only thinks of life as part of his work. He eats his dinner just to give him strength enough to pull out somebody's tonsils."

"Dear me! And I suppose if he ate a very big dinner his strength would be such that the patient's bowels would be dragged up too?"

"I shouldn't mind if he took some sort of interest in the source of the tonsils. He just doesn't notice the patients at all, they are merely specimens of dilapidation for him to practise on. Why you, you whose whole business in life is to juggle with bottles, I believe you would be less detached than he is. Yesterday he came to tell me about a gangrened finger in Ward 10. I asked, whose finger, and he said Herr Güttler's. I said, 'Do you mean *Frau* Güttler's?' and he said, 'Oh yes, now I come to think of it, it is a woman.' Just fancy that!"

"It shows a wonderful purity of mind," Dittmer said. He stubbed his cigarette on Röstel's enamel table and steered vaguely towards the door, moving his stiff legs like a pair of compasses.

"At any rate," he said, "the boy is tidy. That is a great virtue."

It was a virtue not much exemplified in Dittmer's own regions. He himself had started the research department at a time when the Moltke Hospital, aloof in its great tradition of good nursing and sound application of proved methods, had still regarded bacteriological research as the eccentric trade of long-haired chemists at the universities. He had been given an old laundry at the very end of the north building and 3000 Marks to spend on 'such tables, chemicals, etc., as may be proved necessary for such investigations.' The department cost thirty thousand a year now, but Wildelau still thought of it as an extravagance, perhaps justifiable because it gave the hospital publicity of a fashionable kind. It was still in the laundry, the benches converted from ironing tables were still used, the drying racks and one of the old boilers had never been moved. What Dittmer did with his thirty thousand Wildelau could never quite understand.

Appropriately, a corridor some forty yards long divided this hunting ground of Dr. Dittmer's from the respectable part of the establishment. Wildelau traversed this corridor seldom, disliking any part of his kingdom where he could not successfully catechise; Röstel hardly went there at all. It was a shabby passage, which the painters always overlooked, and as you went along it the tang of overriding hygiene altered remarkably to the mustiness of houses long deserted, rotting wood, mice, damp distemper. The door you came to was hung with motheaten baize; it had been fixed ostensibly to protect the penetrating labours of Dr. Dittmer's mind from the vulgar racket of convalescence. You went through this door and through a second, the old laundry door with a loose thumb-latch, and then the Moltke Hospital had disappeared altogether.

Here Dr. Dittmer felt at home.

It was a little after eight o'clock when Josef, paying his first visit, carefully closed the laundry-door behind him to make it whine as little as possible. The big room was full of brown steam, through which a naked bulb, hung jauntily from a loose flex at the farther end, showed like a November sunrise. To the left, through a jungle of glass and iron, he saw a second light, a yellow pool depending from a poke of cardboard; beneath, a patch of shiny serge stretched over a giant pair of buttocks. He went that way.

"Can you tell me," he asked politely, "if Doctor Dittmer is by any chance still at work?"

The man he spoke to turned round slowly and took off his pince-nez. It was a stout, lugubrious schoolboy of forty with his chin a week unshaved.

"Be careful where you're standing," he said. "Those flasks are full of nitric, and that box by your left foot has got Dittmer's favourite rats. They hate excitement. You don't mind my telling you? We haven't got the elbow room those people in the hack-and-dope departments have. Just wait a minute while I write down something. What's seven nines? Ah, I knew it was either that or fifty-four. You haven't by any chance got a pencil on you? . . . Dittmer? Well, he was messing about not long ago. I saw him—when was it? Look here, if there's anybody charting readings over there, by the boiler, that would be him."

Josef went over there, and found Dittmer in his shirt-sleeves: a man stretched out to five-foot-ten, with hair like a puff of smoke, whose grey eyes looked at the world with a tourist's tolerance.

"I don't know what time it is," Dittmer said without looking round, "but if you've come to wash the floor I can tell you straight away that the floor doesn't want washing and as long as I'm in charge of this department it will not be washed. Now look here," he continued, "this is rather inter-esting. This curve, look—you see the way the bumps come? Now the odd thing is this: every bump corresponds with an injection; but only alternate injections give the fluctuation. Why? There's no sense in it that I can see. Can you tell me? Who are you, by the way? Oh yes, you're Röstel's new assistant."

Josef's eyes were fixed on the chart. "Of course," he said, "I don't know what you're injecting. But I had a simi-lar curve once, and it simply proved that each second in-jection—or third in my case—was negatived by the one preceding."

"Yes yes, of course it shows that. But why? And if

Number 2 in the series gives no reaction, why does Number 3 give a hell of a reaction? Look at that—it's like an Alpine crag! Wait, I'll show you the formula, then you'll see what I mean. Formula—what have I done with the damned thing!" He shouted, "Korbenhaus! Have you seen a bit of yellow paper, about the shape of a wishbone?"

Korbenhaus shouted back: "With figures on it?"

"Of course, you blockhead!"

"I saw it on the floor, near the fume-cupboard. I expect the cleaners swept it up."

"Hellhounds!" said Dittmer. "Ah well, it may turn up. Listen to me, Zeppichmann! The world is divided into people who work and people whose only business is to stop others working." He swept his hand over the huge disorder which filled the room, wooden boxes stacked on the benches, bottles all over the floor, cages everywhere. "Every single day some busybody comes nosing round my poor little department, upsetting everything. To-morrow morning when I come in I shall find those filthy cleaners have got all this stuff into a hopeless muddle. Tell me, what do you think of my old friend Röstel?"

"He's a splendid man to work under," Josef said. "A most inspiring doctor."

Dittmer started.

"Inspiring? Good God! Yes yes, you're perfectly right, I'm sure. Poor old Röstel—most inspiring, I don't doubt it. But just listen a moment. When you come in here I don't want you making little cupboards and putting up hooks all over the place and labelling all the cages. That only wastes time and puts people out of temper. Half the sorrow in the world springs from people going to a drawer labelled 'Fancy Shirts' and finding it full of neckties. If people didn't label drawers you wouldn't expect to find anything special in them and you wouldn't be disappointed. Where was I? Yes, this one, temperature at the fourteenth injection, Thursday

6.30 p.m. D'you mind standing back a bit, you're giving me a shadow. I can't see why some one doesn't rig these lights so as you can see something. Now you're stepping on my phial-rack. Never mind!"

"Perhaps I could visit you some time when you're less busy," Josef suggested.

Dittmer frowned.

"Forty-eight-point-seven, fifty-one-point-three. Oh yes, what was it you wanted?"

"I—I have Doctor Wildelau's permission to ask if you would be so kind as to allow me to come here occasionally. I mean, to work here. I mean, I thought I might possibly be of some use to you in odd ways, scrubbing the benches, that sort of thing." He saw Dittmer shudder, and skidded on: "No, I don't mean that, I never interfere with things. But I thought I might learn how to prepare nutrient media for you, that might be helpful, I thought, and then perhaps later on I could have part of a bench to do a few experiments of my own. I am—I am just a bit interested in the tubercle bacillus."

"You'd better go over to Doctor Vollmuth and ask to have a look at his patients," Dittmer said. "You can see T.B. in action there. And my God how it acts! A pleasant afternoon-off for you."

Josef nodded.

"Doctor Vollmuth, yes! I haven't had the pleasure of meeting him yet—perhaps you could introduce me one day in the Staff Mess? I suppose—I suppose Doctor Vollmuth sometimes makes tests with preparations you send him?"

"Doctor Vollmuth," said Dittmer, "has not yet been known to admit that tuberculosis is caused by bacilli. As far as I know, he believes it's caused by certain conjunctions of the planets. They're all like that in the hospital out there. They believe that disease can be charmed away by good-humour and tidiness and tact. When I talk to them about genuine scientific methods they think that I'm plotting to take away their living. Now you really must go away, I can't stay chattering all night, it disturbs my rats. Yes yes, come again by all means, yes yes, I suppose I can find somewhere for you to play the fool, heaven knows where, I've so many youngsters in here I've hardly a square yard to call my own. But you're not to meddle with things, mind! I don't want any one making a mess of this place . . ."

Next day the telephone rang in the Research Department, and Dittmer, having moved a stack of cases to get to it, unravelled the receiving wire.

"Hullo hullo hullo!" he said. "Whatever you want isn't ready yet, and if you don't want anything why waste my time!"

The precise, courteous voice of Dr. Vollmuth answered him.

"There is a young man here, his name seems to be Zeppichmann. He tells me he is doing some work for you, and that you have sent him to examine some of my cases in order to prepare some kind of thesis for your inspection. Is that—correct?"

Dittmer let off three great barks of delight.

"I beg your pardon?" Vollmuth said. "I fancy there is something wrong with my instrument."

"It's not me that sent him," Dittmer roared. "It's the devil himself who sends Herr Zeppichmann to try the virtue of honest doctors. Put him to bed, I should, give him some of your open-air treatment! He'll probably make a first-class case for you if you work at him patiently. God bless your efforts, worthy Doctor Vollmuth!"

Vollmuth pulled down his waistcoat and smiled politely. So Dittmer was in one of his boisterous moods: those bugs of his, real or imaginary, they got into a man's brain. He went back to his waiting-room.

"I find that Doctor Dittmer has changed his plans," he

said to Josef. "I regret very much that we cannot show you round this department at the present time, as we happen to be working under unusual pressure. Perhaps in the summer we shall not be quite so busy, and Doctor Wildelau may be disposed to arrange a visit by some of the junior members of the staff. I hope I may have the pleasure of meeting you again."

Outside it was cold but sunny. The beds, fifty of them, each with a scarlet over-blanket, stretched all the way along the terrace, eight feet apart, in perfect line. The patients watched the stolid young man in overalls as he marched slowly past them, bound for the main block; his heavy face important and preoccupied. In the tedium that stretched ahead like a new motor road any such event was welcome: a bird that swooped to pick up a crumb, a young doctor passing. A woman smiled at him, but he did not appear to see her.

He went in at the east door and his own world re-formed about him: new, but already familiar, the pervading carbolic, the grey distemper. He picked his way without thinking through the labyrinth of staircase and corridor. They were quickly at-home, the Zeppichmanns. A bed trolley went by, a floor-boy hurried past with a chit for the dispensary, a door opened and some one called loudly for Nurse Henschel. From the door of 11 Sister Dietert appeared. "I should like you to see Herr Stache, Doctor, there's a change in the breathing I don't like." But before he had got there a nurse came with a message. "Doctor Röstel has just telephoned, he would be glad if you would go to help him in 15. As quickly as you can."

So: he fitted in. But his thoughts were on the line of beds along the terrace. A grey-haired man, six from the end of the line: with a glance from his eye's tail he had noticed that one specially. He wanted that man. Just for twelve months.

5

AH WELL, the trouble was practically over, Frau Spühler
thought. They had bought a reading chair to go in Herr
Meisel's room. It came from the Metropol Stores, where
you really got very nice things for about half what they
charged you at Berghauer's. Really it was a pretty chair, as
well as sensible; the back in tapestry, with a motif of flowers; wallflowers, Frau Spühler thought, though Professor
Rupf maintained they were geraniums. Herr Meisel had
said 'thank-you,' though not very graciously. And Frau
Spühler had wept a little, reminding Herr Meisel that she
had lost her only child in infancy, and that it wasn't easy
for honest people to get along nowadays, with meat so costly,
and something would have to be done about the damp patch
over the door in the dining-room.

Since then, Herr Meisel had gradually come out of his
sulks. He talked a little at meals now, in his oldish, knowing
way: there were things going on in the country that they
knew nothing about, he told them. Ah yes, he heard things
when he went to his club, that club of his where he spent so
much of his time. And once more Frau Spühler was warmed
by a little pride in having this young Berlin gentleman as
her guest, this young man of excellent family who seemed
to know all about what was really going on.

But when Dr. Zeppichmann was about, Herr Meisel
did not talk. His eyes, gripping the cracked vegetable dish,
were the eyes of a man unjustly in the pillory.

Happily, it was Dr. Zeppichmann's custom to hurry
through his meals, excuse himself, and bound away to his
own room; where, having locked the door, he did unimagi-

nable things with the tubes and bottles which seemed to
multiply every day.

"It is not my idea of a doctor," Herr Spühler said,
pouring out more water for Herr Barthol. "A doctor is supposed to go round and see people, or else the people come to
him. He takes the pulsations of the heart, he sees if the
tongue is correctly adjusted, he prescribes the appropriate
drugs and lotions. This mixing up of medicines, that's a
pharmacist's business. Old Julius Gehrmann round the corner, he can do that sort of thing. And he's a man of practically no education at all—gave me wrong change for a
five-Mark note only yesterday."

"Still, he seems to be a hard-working young man,"
Professor Rupf said.

His wife raised her shoulders.

"It's one way to get a reputation for industry," she
said. "To shut yourself up and lock the door. Probably he's
reading the feuilletons."

"There's hardly anything in his room except doctors'
journals," Frau Spühler said cautiously. The tide of her
maternity, flowing so readily to any man under thirty who
had not his own mother about him, was already lapping Dr.
Zeppichmann's rocky shores. "Sometimes he looks to me as
if he's lonely."

"If Doctor Zeppichmann cared to keep his door unlocked," Frau Rupf answered, "then we could all go in and
comfort him. As it is, we might sing choruses in the corridor
outside. That's about the best we can do."

"I see there has been street-fighting in Halberstadt,"
Herr Barthol said boldly.

Frau Spühler glanced at him gratefully. Herr Barthol
was always ready to rescue her from the needle-blows of
Frau Rupf. Not that Frau Rupf was an unkind person: Frau
Spühler did not believe that any one was really unkind. But
being the wife of a professor Frau Rupf was naturally an

intellectual; some people said she knew even more than the Professor himself; and an intellectual had a way of hurting an ordinary person, without meaning to, just as men with big boots had to tread on your toes in the tramcar.

"It is a sign of restlessness," Herr Barthol added. "Whenever I hear of street-fighting I say to myself, 'Ah, that means some kind of discontentment among the common people!'"

He drank the rest of his water, dried the underside of his moustache with two pouncing blows of his handkerchief and looked round defiantly for questions. 'Herr Barthol, he is the very image of the Emperor,' they had said in Ülzwalk, where he had been one of the leading figures in the bakery business; and now, at sixty-seven, he looked as much a cavalryman as ever, the smallish body held so stiff that it seemed gigantic, the eyebrows abundant and ferocious, the cleft chin as tight and stony as a boxer's knuckles.

"Discontentment!" he repeated. "I don't mind saying, in this circle of friends, it would be a good thing for the country if certain people I could name had a rope put round their necks. Yes, that's what I'd do. I'd tie the rope myself. Frau Spühler," he added, "I should like to say, with your permission, that this has been an admirable dinner."

Herr Spühler nodded.

"You'd have to be sure and use the right sort of knot," he said. "It isn't as easy as you think. I saved a man's life once by knowing the right kind of knot. That was at Helsingfors, in March 1907."

"But Herr Barthol doesn't want to save any one's life," Frau Rupf objected. "Just the contrary."

"In the navy you learn a great many things," Frau Spühler explained. "My husband obtained all kinds of useful information, and many different abilities." She faltered, eager to push her man's prestige a little higher still, but feeling on her face the damp stare of Frau Rupf's pale eyes.

"The cold tap in the kitchen is leaking again," she concluded.

Herr Spühler understood her.

"Last time, I had a crick in my back for weeks," he said. "Why did the man put the main cock in such a ridiculous place! Right against the wall, only six inches between the wall and the tank. A naval tradesman would have put it the other side of the floorboards."

"You mean, in the sea?" Frau Rupf asked.

Herr Barthol said slowly: "Cramp in the back has a rheumatic origin. It is a rheumatic condition of the kidneys. One of the evils brought about by our civilization, which is the highest in the history of the world, is that we have forgotten the art of mastication. Goats, for example. Can you remember seeing a goat with a crick in its back?"

Frau Rupf shut her eyes, scouring her memory. She would have liked to say she had, but a certain honesty always forbade her to invent an experience she could not imagine completely and in detail.

Professor Rupf could not picture it either.

"On the other hand," he said, "it may be argued that our eating is more aesthetic, visually, than that of the goat. When I watch a goat nibbling I always find myself moved towards laughter. But to watch my wife's lips as she discusses an apple gives me nothing but pleasure."

"I agree, yes, of course I agree!" Herr Barthol said quickly. "But surely you must admit that this tearing over the roads in motor cars is a sign that we have lost something of our ancient simplicity."

With this Frau Spühler agreed.

"Ah yes, the war," she said stoutly, "the country has never been the same since then."

The door behind her was not quite shut, and in the mirror above the sofa she caught sight of an untidy head, the head of the girl Minna, peeping round to see if she could come and clear away. Well, Minna would have to wait. The philosophical conversation between Herr Barthol and Herr Professor Rupf should not be interrupted.

A cosy hour such as this made up to Frau Spühler for many hardships. Her husband, with all his versatility, had never achieved a fortune. He could fit a new tap-washer, shine up an old saucepan to make it like new; he had made a little shed in the yard for his bicycle, with a shelf for the oil-can, he had once re-distempered a part of the attic. But since his retirement no one had ever come forward to offer him employment. It is a trial of virtue, when you dream of a delicious place of your own, to have a house full of strangers; people who come in at curious times expecting a meal, who shift the furniture in their rooms, leaving ugly patches on the wall where it stood before; to watch the milk-bill mounting, to face every Saturday the business of explaining to Frau Rupf the little entries on her account for extras. But it made a difference if you called these strangers your friends.

And they were gentlefolk, these guests of hers: all of them, until Dr. Zeppichmann's arrival; and he, after all, was a Doctor, which counted for much the same thing. Gentlefolk, and people of intellectual distinction. All her life Frau Spühler had yearned for culture, for the larger philosophy of worlds outside her own. And here, at her table, was Professor Rupf, who had been to Venice, who in his simplest observations used words she did not understand. And here was Herr Barthol, with his Potsdamer dignity, once a leading personality in commerce, a man whose knowledge of practical affairs gave him status to argue with the Professor on equal terms. Sometimes dear August yawned a little, as the two thinkers plodded side by side along the heavy course of cosmic learning; yawned, and undid his waistcoat, and made small stomach noises, altogether permissible in a sailing man. But across Frau Spühler's gentle mind this flow of long, rich words passed with the cleansing grace of her own dusting mop, sweeping away the little webs of trouble, the grocer's bill, the awkwardness about Minna burning Frau Rupf's undergarment. In this hour she was lady of her house, she was mistress of a salon; and if her active part in the conversazione was small, she felt that some genius of her own, a special sympathy with adventurous minds, shone out like morning sun to warm her company's powers.

"My old friend Otto Richtenberger," Herr Barthol was saying, "he used to have a large trade in Brussels. Ornamental iron lampstands, tremendous strength, you could sit on the top of them and they wouldn't bend. He had a turnover of two thousand Marks a month—the Belgian trade alone, that was. Tremendous strength! You could sit on top of them. And very handsome. And this year, if you'll believe me, not one! Trade gone to nothing. Now tell me this: why?"

Frau Rupf, who never entirely understood the art of conversation, said:

"I suppose the Belgians don't like that sort of thing any more."

Happily Herr Barthol did not seem to hear her.

"Government!" he said shrewdly. "I don't mind saying that some of the things I've heard would surprise you." He leant towards Herr Rupf, glancing quickly to see if the others would overhear him. "They fix it up," he said, "they fix it all up with the Communists. It suits their book, you see, to keep us a beaten country. Suits the social-democrats too—a strong country wouldn't put up with them, not for five minutes. Well, you see how it goes! My friend Otto Richtenberger, he goes to see his old customer in Brussels. 'No good!' this man says. 'The public doesn't want that kind of thing nowadays. All electric stuff is what they're using.'

Now listen! Do you think he'd say that to a French manu-facturer?"

Frau Spühler caught sight of danger. When it came to politics Herr Barthol was a hard fighter; there was always a chance of his grazing the sensibilities of those less ardently convinced.

"I am sure Herr Richtenberger's lamp-stands must be very attractive," she said, "as well as useful."

"That's just what I mean!" Herr Barthol said. The graceful adam's-apple in Professor Rupf's throat began to bob, showing that he had a sentence ready.

"Yes, they may call us a beaten people," he said, "but the world still comes to us for our learning. In art, in science, in philosophy, we have always been the world's great teacher. Our learning is the greatest wealth we produce, and no one can prevent us from exporting it. Learning—and beauty" —he smiled at his wife, he bowed modestly towards Frau Spühler—"they are the staples of our national economy."

"But you can't live without selling something," Herr Barthol insisted.

Frau Spühler smiled at the Professor. Not because of his compliment, in which there might be a note of flattery, but as one who shared with him the subtle appreciation of cosmic values.

"Learning and beauty!" she repeated, feeling that by a special utterance of simple words she could invest them with new power. She pushed her chair back a few inches and leaned forward on the table; as once, a small, round, spectacled girl, she had leaned across the schoolroom desk, gulping the words of Herr Loeb, the geography teacher. In a few short sentences Professor Rupf had lifted their thoughts to a higher, more spiritual plane. And now, watch-ing the mist of thoughtfulness in his gentle eyes, the scholar's smile which came to his lips almost without moving them, she felt the glow of spirituality as if it were physical warmth, passing through breast and forehead.

It is like staying in a grand hotel, she obscurely thought.

But the grinding of a hinge, a little breeze stirring her thin back-hair, cut through the magic of her contentment. She knew, she felt him, that Herr Meisel was standing behind her.

"I am sorry to disturb you!"

His voice was that of a departed spirit, a weary spirit whom an unpractised medium has summoned by mistake.

"I am sorry to disturb you, Frau Spühler. I'm not asking for any favour, any special treatment, but on an evening when I happen to have a fairly severe headache it is really quite impossible to stand this noise."

"Noise?"

"You may not be aware that for the last twenty minutes the man who took my room from me has been hammering nails into the wall."

6

THEY waited till Herr Meisel had gone before settling who was to approach Dr. Zeppichmann. On the face of it, it seemed to be Herr Spühler's business. But Dr. Zeppichmann had been invited to the house by his wife, Herr Spühler said, and it was therefore her duty to conduct all subsequent negotiations.

"It's a thing for a man to deal with," Frau Spühler repeated.

Frau Rupf made a good suggestion.

"You, Herr Barthol," she said, "you are used to dealing with men. As a large employer you have learnt how to exert authority . . ."

"I have also learnt the principle of good manners," Herr Barthol said. "To assume the authority which belongs to our hosts would be a grave discourtesy to them."

"But really, Herr Barthol, we should take it as a favour," Frau Spühler pleaded. "It would be so much easier for you to put it to the doctor, as a fellow-guest . . ."

"I can think of nothing more likely to impress the young man than a visit from a gentleman of your presence," Herr Rupf added.

Herr Barthol made up his mind at last. If Frau Spühler would be good enough to show him which was Dr. Zeppichmann's room?

They went upstairs all together, Frau Spühler nervously leading, Herr Barthol grave and resolute behind her. "I feel," the Professor said, "that at times like these we are fortunate in having a man of Herr Barthol's experience to represent us." Frau Spühler knocked gently on Dr. Zeppichmann's door.

"Is it anything important?" Josef called. "I'm very busy."

"Herr Barthol would be glad if you could spare him a few moments."

With their anxious ears close to the door they could not help hearing the Doctor mutter ferociously, "The devil take Herr Barthol!" Then:

"Perhaps Herr Barthol could manage some other time. I'm busy this evening."

This was said politely, but something in the voice told Herr Barthol that the politeness was superficial.

"Yes yes," he said quickly, "some other time will do very well." And to Frau Spühler, "I have just remembered that I must get a letter on the night mail—it is my sister's birthday to-morrow. I will—I will have a talk with Herr Doktor Zeppichmann later on, I shall explain to him the duties of a guest in a high-class boarding establishment."

Before he had reached his own room the hammering began again.

Herr Meisel's door had opened a little way. The diminished party could see Herr Meisel's pale face, his eyes coldly surveying them.

"This is intolerable," Frau Rupf whispered. "Arnold, you are to go in at once and give the young man a sound lecture."

In the Professor's gentle eyes, turned slowly round upon his wife's face, there came the shadow of a child's obstinacy.

"You mean, my precious, that I am to break down the door with an axe?"

"I mean that you're to try and see if the door's locked."

The Gods were against Professor Rupf. Josef had forgotten, this evening, to lock his door. Herr Rupf tried the handle and it swung right open.

"Go on!" his wife insisted.

"Good luck!" Herr Spühler whispered.

The Professor shook himself, as if to get some loose pieces of his body into the folds of his suit; went in and shut the door behind him.

To the party waiting outside he seemed to be gone a long time. They could just hear the two voices, chiefly Dr. Zeppichmann's, which was the louder and more determined. But presently the sounds grew fainter, almost to silence.

"It is really most kind of your husband," Frau Spühler whispered gratefully. "It is a very awkward thing to deal with, really I admire his courage."

"Probably the young doctor has poisoned him," Frau Rupf said curtly.

But it was the Professor whose voice they faintly heard now, and with his ear spread over the keyhole Herr Spühler could just make out what he was saying.

". . . whether we can separate the notion of human personality from all the physical and mental attributes that seem to make it up. You, for example, spend your life with people whose bodies are in some way out of order; and probably you recognise all those people's moods as the effect of their illnesses. A man who would otherwise be good tempered is made sulky by kidney trouble, a vain woman is really one who feels inferior to others because her hearing is bad—that sort of thing. Now I myself am interested in race —I expect a Russian to behave in one way, an Italian in another, a Negro quite differently. And a man who studies heredity in individual families can forecast behaviour much more accurately still. You see what I'm driving at? I want to know whether I, Arnold Rupf, have anything that is peculiar to me, whether I am a personality uniquely created, or whether I am merely a common denominator, the meeting

place of various lines of natural causation. Do you ever
wonder about that? I mean, with your patients for instance,
do you ever try to detach the sick man from his sickness, to
consider how far the complaint is part of his *persona* or how
far it is something completely external, not an attribute but
a detached phenomenon from which the patient can be sepa-
rately considered?"

Then Josef's voice:

"Of course, yes, the mental attitude of the patient
makes a great difference. We regard that as almost ele-
mentary—"

And that of Rupf again:

"No no, I don't think you quite understand me . . ."

Herr Spühler turned round to whisper his report:

"I can't make it out at all. The Professor seems to be
going a long way round."

"Here, let me listen!" Frau Rupf pushed him firmly
aside and put her own ear to the door. She heard Josef say:

"But women are altogether different. They don't live
by thought at all, they live by their instincts. Or so I've
always been told. As a matter of fact they don't interest me
in the least."

"I can't quite agree with that," Herr Rupf said slowly.
"I should agree that a woman is not capable of logical or
continuous thought. She cannot consider any subject for two
minutes without swerving off in another direction as a new
idea chances to come into her head. Her mental processes are
like a motor car without a driver in a field without any
boundaries. In spite of that, I think that if you compare the
human female with the lower animals you must agree that
she is—by that standard—a cogitative being."

Obstructed by Frau Rupf, Frau Spühler could hear
nothing.

"What is he saying?" she asked anxiously.

"He is saying," Frau Rupf replied a little testily, "that you and I are slightly better than hippopotamuses."

Another half hour had passed when Professor Rupf came out, and the corridor was empty. Seeing no light beneath his own door, he went slowly downstairs, smiling. Nearly forty years of schoolteaching, and still he believed in boys, in every fresh one that came into his field. The best of his pupils had often gone on to failure, or what he called failure: they had become acquisitive business men, or politicians of the more tawdry kind, or wooden-headed soldiers. One or two were in prison now. But that was somehow his own fault, he sadly thought. Give him a stocky child with the commonplace bullet head, arms shooting out of frayed cuffs, knees all muddy, and there was the raw material for scholarship as he understood it. You had but patiently to open his eyes, to let him look for a moment steadily on the mind's fair kingdom: its enormous liberty, the variety of its adventures: and surely he could never turn back to the Sodom of dullness. This young Zeppichmann, he had been too much in the laboratories; but his brain was alive, meticulous in the field he understood. There was rich soil between the stones, and in time Arnold Rupf would plant something there.

They were all in the kitchen, and with unusual condescension his wife was helping the Spühlers to do their weekly stock-taking. They talked, almost contentedly, of the price of food.

Frau Rupf did not look round when she heard the cluck of the latch. With an artist's concentration she went on ruling lines across the stock-book.

"How nice it is, Arnold," she said softly, "that at last you have an intellectual equal to talk to in the evenings. I expect you will learn a great deal from Herr Doktor Zeppichmann."

"Trude, you are a great silly!" he said. He came and

leant over her shoulder; not in the least guilty. "I think he is a young man who can be influenced. Quite uneducated, of course, like all scientists; but by no means a fool, and not, I fancy, unteachable."

His hands were on Frau Rupf's shoulders. She moved them away. She said:

"I suppose every one is teachable, except of course a born fool like your wife."

"Trude! My dear, what do you mean?"

"Have you put down two small tins of mustard?" Frau Spühler asked.

Getting no answer, she turned and saw her husband staring with canine interest at Frau Rupf; then Frau Rupf's face, scarlet; the Professor's, sorrowful and puzzled. She suddenly realized that a quarrel had started; unthinkably, a quarrel between a man and his wife, her guests.

"I am only sorry," Frau Rupf pursued, "that I take up so much of your time. If you didn't have to sit in our room reading your books all evening you could devote yourself to influencing intelligent young men—"

"But, Trude, my precious—"

"Listen!" she said sharply. "I can see how much you've influenced him already."

They listened. And heard, once more, the sound of steady hammering.

"I am afraid," Herr Rupf whispered, "I am afraid—I can't have made myself quite plain."

His wife snorted.

"You made yourself plain enough—"

For the second time in a single month—the second time in fourteen years—Herr Spühler's temper gave way.

"Enough!" he shouted. "I won't have women snapping and scratching in this kitchen." And then to Rupf, "You—you and this Zeppichmann, the devil take you both." A little cry came from behind him, and he turned upon his wife. "Well, what are you whimpering for!"

The whimper stopped. For a moment she stared at the three faces with the ghastly curiosity of a bear when the trapper comes, then her head dropped and she wept without control.

It was arranged some minutes later that the girl Minna should be sent to Dr. Zeppichmann with a message. She was to say politely that Herr and Frau Spühler presented their compliments, and would be much obliged if Dr. Zeppichmann could refrain from his carpentering in the evenings, since it troubled some of the other guests.

So once again Josef was disturbed.

He was using the time between two readings to finish putting up a tube-rack, when he felt a draught at his back and found the girl standing behind him, her weight on one leg, hands crossed on her dirty wet apron, foolish eyes pointed stubbornly at the wall.

"Well, what in hell is it now?"

She started coughing. This creature always coughed explosively when you asked her a question, stopped to grin at you in a silly, confiding way and then went on until you could have thrashed her.

"Please," she got out at last, "Frau Spühler sends her kind regards and you're to stop making that filthy row, it's driving Herr Meisel cracked."

Apparently he did not hear her. He was regarding her face as if she had spoken in a foreign language. He said:

"Here, come over here a minute! I want to look at you. How long have you had that cough?"

7

DR. DITTMER'S regard for his animals was akin to that of the prize cattle-breeder. The use of animals is to get him money, he is quite callous about that; and yet, as he tends them each day to increase their cash-value, his possessive feeling becomes a kind of affection. A complex sadism, some would say. Inaccurately, but let it pass.

He kept a big cage of rats, beauties, in reserve for future use. And as long as they were not required for experiments they had every luxury he could contrive for them. On Sundays he made a special journey to feed them, not trusting the lab-boy. Sentimentalist or brute as you please, he was naturally upset when, one morning, he found three of them dead.

His analysis of the contents of the stomachs showed no trace of any toxin. Two of the carcases had what looked like minute punctures in the neck, where a very little tuft of fur might have been cut away; but both these specimens had been notorious fighters, and in any case the indication was too small to build on.

He did make some inquiries; and learnt from Proske, the lab-boy, that Dr. Zeppichmann had been arriving very early several mornings lately. At what time? Oh, about half-past five, when the cleaners came. Proske himself checked in at six o'clock, and three times in the last week he had found Dr. Zeppichmann already at work. At work, whereabouts? Over there preparing nutrient media—or so Proske thought. "Nowhere near the rats?" "Not that I remember, Doctor."

Later on he tackled Josef himself.

"Well, Zeppichmann, you seem to find my poor little department beneficial to your health. I hear you are bounding in here when the cock crows."

Josef smiled.

"Yes, Doctor, yes, I like to get a little laboratory work done before my daily duties begin. You'll see, I've done three more tubes of your delta-four, I thought they might be useful."

"Ah yes, yes, that's possible. Thank you. I was going to ask you—have you noticed any of my rats looking at all out-of-sorts lately? Bismarck IV—you know, the big dark fellow—you haven't noticed anything peculiar about him?"

Josef hesitated.

"Well, I did wonder whether he was moulting a bit when I saw him the other day—I was over there using Herr Korbenhaus's balance. But of course I didn't think anything of it—I know the animals there are under your own supervision."

"You've never given them anything to eat? A bit of sugar or something?"

"To eat? No, Doctor Dittmer, no—I shouldn't think of doing such a thing."

No one could have doubted the honesty of Josef's eyes. No one, except Dittmer. Not that he disliked the boy: it was impossible wholly to dislike a youth of such keenness, one who was never out of temper, always ready to do an odd job of the humblest kind, always sharp in comprehension. But he did not trust him. The boy's curiosity was more than academic—he could not see a paper on the floor without turning it over, in a roundabout way he was always finding out exactly what Dittmer was doing. Dittmer, moreover, was not used to being treated with so much deference. He liked to think of his department as a small republic, he liked his young men to argue with him, didn't mind a little unqualified rudeness; for that assured him that he was a human-being, not yet a mere muscle of the hospital like poor dear Röstel. This Zeppichmann, he was too punctilious, he had altogether too much virtue. Dittmer suspected, moreover, that he had secret designs to bring a Röstellian tidiness into the department; once or twice he had found a book he wanted most conveniently near his elbow, and Zeppichmann had been in the room not long before.

That, of course, was not quite the same thing as poisoning rats. But a tidy man could not be watched too closely.

Sitting opposite Röstel, as usual, at the midday meal, he said:

"I suppose you give that Zeppichmann of yours a dog's life. He's always taking refuge in my humble department."

Röstel sniffed.

"A dog's life? I suppose you think because you are allowed to take six months, if you feel like it, to prepare an overdose of toxins and administer it to one guinea-pig, we, we others, in the working part of the hospital, can also arrange the lives of our patients to suit our own convenience. I suppose you suppose that we have infinite leisure in which—"

"Stop, my dear friend, stop!" Dittmer pleaded. "Another sentence as long as that, with your mouth full of mashed potato, and you'll turn into a patient yourself. What I really wondered was whether you are finding Zeppichmann enough work to do. He seems to have a lot of time and energy left over. Perhaps you're rather slack in the wards at present?"

"Slack?" A shrapnel burst of potato shot over the table. "I tell you, Karl, if one of you people from the slop-shop over there had to tackle the work I do in a single morning, day after day—"

"Yes yes! I was only suggesting that you might hand over a bit more of it to your assistant. Seeing that he's a tidy man, not likely to put back a set of kidneys in the wrong patient—"

"Do you mean," Röstel asked bluntly, "that you're finding him a nuisance? Because if so you must complain to Doctor Wildelau. It's nothing to do with me, I didn't engage him, I can't arrange what he does in his spare time."

Dittmer dug at a caved tooth, pondering. No, it wouldn't be fair to call Zeppichmann a nuisance.

"I lost three of my rats this morning," he said inconsequently.

"God in Heaven! If I find them in one of my wards—"

"No, I mean they've died."

"Well, that's what they're meant for, isn't it?"

"Yes, like your patients, my dear Röstel, that's what they're meant for. But it's better, in both cases, that death should take place at the proper time."

"Are you trying to make out that my assistant has poisoned your rats? If so, you must refer the matter to Doctor Wildelau, it's nothing to do with me, I'm not responsible. God bless my soul, I've got enough to do, six wards to look after, not including the casualty room, these young nurses they get nowadays never knowing where anything is, man died of haemorrhage the night before last, silly girl on night duty got the form filled up all wrong, without chasing my young man all over the place to see he doesn't interfere with your menagerie. You'd better keep them locked up, it seems to me . . ."

Nevertheless, he had his eye on Josef that afternoon.

The boy was kept busy enough, in all conscience. Röstel never saw him idle, and wherever he went there were signs of his activity. In Ward 9 he found one of the beds in a new position. "Here, nurse, sister, Fräulein Laupert, what's this bed doing over here?" "It's Doctor Zeppichmann's orders, Herr Doktor. He thought there was too much sun over there, it might be bad for Frau Meyer's skin-trouble." Here there was an extra bolster, brought at Dr. Zeppichmann's instructions, here a man was wearing tinted glasses, as Dr. Zeppichmann had required, here a probationer called in from another ward was preparing half-hourly compresses for an incipient ulcer. Röstel himself had thought the ulcer too trivial to be worth attention—the man's real trouble was a groin-wound—but Zeppichmann had decided otherwise. Well, it did no harm, that attention to detail. Everything that Zeppichmann ordered was sensible. He bothered the patients, he sometimes brought the nursing staff to the verge of mutiny, but in theory it was all sound doctoring . . . In the next ward he found Zeppichmann himself, washing an impetigo case. A middle-grade nurse stood by, one of those tall girls who achieved a Charlottenburg distinction even in uniform, holding the basin and cutting Josef into shreds with her angry eyes.

"Couldn't you leave that to Fräulein Henschel?" Röstel asked mildly.

Josef shook his head.

"I was not quite satisfied. I mean, I wanted to be sure that the skin was properly sterilised all round the points of eruption."

"Herr Bercovitz told me he was perfectly comfortable after I did it," the nurse said, her voice like Juno through a drain-pipe.

"Yes, but—I was not thinking of the patient's comfort," Josef said bleakly.

"Well," said Röstel, "I think perhaps you might leave that now, Fräulein Henschel will finish it off, and come to the theatre. I've got an examination to make."

"Certainly, Doctor Röstel. I'll be there in four minutes. I can quite well leave the other jobs and do them this evening."

That was just it, Röstel thought: young Zeppichmann never did think of the patients' comfort, except where comfort had a physiological importance. And Healing, after all, was not an industry . . . And yet, the boy had good hands, he could do a dressing more expertly than most of the nurses . . .

'Ah, if I could only catch him doing something really stupid!' Röstel thought; and afterwards blamed himself severely for such lack of charity.

Up on the fourth floor Sister Dahms was having five minutes' rest and coffee with her friend Sister Taübler.

"Of course the young man is quite inhuman," Sister Taübler said. "He's interested in nothing but himself."

"I don't think you're quite right, dear! If he was interested in himself, surely he'd get a decent pair of shoes instead of those ploughboy things, and surely he'd try to do something about his hair—did you ever see a head more like an old clothes-brush? No, he seems to me to think of nothing but medicine-glasses. Always hunting for empty medicine-glasses, so that he can call the duty-nurse and try to make her feel like a murderess. I really believe it's the only thing that makes him happy—finding an unwashed medicine-glass. I think there must be some dark story behind it—I think Doctor Röstel must have made a misalliance with a machine hand in a bottle-factory."

"Or perhaps Doctor Zeppichmann's mother trod on a medicine-glass during the period of gestation."

"Or more likely she trod on little Zeppichmann's head *after* the period of gestation."

"You mean you think he's really not quite compos?"

"My dear, he couldn't be!"

"At any rate the patients hate him."

"Oh *don't* they!"

In truth, Josef Zeppichmann was thinking not of medicine-glasses but of Dittmer's rats. Standing beside Röstel, taking over specimens of blood and urine, sealing and labelling them, asking questions, he was concentrating all the time on the problem of Dittmer's rats.

Those three rats ought not to have died.

His object had been to see how far the percentage of his Theta agent, which he had proved to be favourable to tissue instauration, could be increased. In his final experiments at Zornenwalde he had got the figure up to 2.65, and he had hoped to advance it as far as 3.50, which would allow the Kappa to be reduced proportionately. The actual proportions he had used with Dittmer's rats were 3.00, 3.25, 3.75; half-fearing that the last might be lethal. But that 3.00 had proved lethal was a bitter disappointment. It meant, on a rough mental calculation, that his safety index would be reduced to 22 degrees. And old Sinsteden at Zornenwalde, lecturing on Elements of Bacteriology, had laid it down that to proceed from animals to the human subject was not ethically justifiable with an index lower than 30.

In short, he was not yet ready to experiment on the human subject.

He would have to find a new Theta agent, or else in some way modify the Kappa. Probably he would have to try both. With luck, he might stumble on a satisfactory Theta in two or three hundred experiments—say three months' work. Much more likely it would be six months. Six months —and somewhere else a man working on a similar hypothesis, with all the proper equipment, might announce a formula to-morrow.

("Yes, Doctor Röstel, I sterilised it myself this morning. And that one too.")

And after all, what real grounds had old Sinsteden for his calculus of safety? On what principle could he maintain that it was right to experiment on the human subject with an index of 30, wrong with 29? Surely every scientist must make his own judgement on the basis of life values.

There was an anecdote his father was fond of telling in

his war reminiscences, about an old ruin of a place called Les Deux Ecureuils, which they had disputed with a French battalion right through the autumn of '16. Possession of this place had become a point of honour. And one night when the French had kept it for a month or so, the divisional commandant had sent out a party to get it back. "A birthday present for the General," he had said. A hundred and fifty men were involved in that spree. Twenty-eight had got back. Just twenty-eight. One hundred and twenty-two lives—gone —to settle a little matter of prestige. Well, he, Josef, was not asking for a hundred and twenty-two lives. He was asking for just one. One fairly hopeless life that he might restore or might possibly destroy.

Not even a whole life: half a life, one might say.

He had visited frequently the sanatorium near Zornenwalde and studied the patients there. They existed, they breathed: many of them asleep for long periods in the day, awake and in pain through much of the night: people who could not read right through a magazine article because they no longer had the mental stamina to concentrate on print for half an hour. Pointless lives, because all the hope had gone out of them.

Those tuberculous guinea-pigs, the last batch he had used at Zornenwalde, had looked so much like that; lying all day in the little cages, staring at him with apathetic eyes. The test group had got much worse after the sixth injection, they had refused even to drink water, become unconscious. That had been a wretched night, when he was expecting them to die. But only one had died. That moment, twelve hours later, when one had started to push its nose against the wire, asking for food, had brought a curious, intense excitement. And six weeks later, watching the surviving nine as they tumbled and gobbled, climbed up the wire to snatch at the greenery he held for them, he had felt his first great happiness. The triumph had seemed to be complete. That day he was certain that he, a young medical student whom nobody had ever heard of, had defeated one of the oldest enemies.

But triumph cannot be enjoyed in privacy. Between the moment of great discovery and the day of recognition you are whipped by a scarcely tolerable impatience. Nine guinea-pigs, running and gobbling in full enjoyment of their animal life: that was nothing to tell the world about. To take a man—or a woman—whose case looked hopeless and restore him to full health . . . publish a meticulously detailed account of the case in *Neue Medizinische Monatsschrift*, with an outline of the working basis, synopsis of previous experiments . . . Send marked copies to one or two specialists in Vienna, to the Berlin newspapers . . . That would start the headlines. There, still ahead but almost within grasp, there was Josef's day!

But it was rather worrying about Dittmer's rats. No reason, on the face of it, why in this respect the rat and guinea-pig reactions should differ.

"Yes, Doctor Röstel, if you care to leave it to me I'll clear up everything here and enter the report. Yes, I'll bring the book to the surgery for you to check over. Yes, Doctor Röstel . . ."

There was a mastoid in Ward 9 to look at, a lost case that one had to be careful about, with the quadruplicate report in mind: one or two other things. He was free at half-past seven and decided to work for an hour in Dittmer's laboratory, giving supper a miss. At times like these, when his mind was driving hard, he could go a long time without food.

Dittmer was not there. Only Korbenhaus, the chief assistant, sprawled over his bench, grunting and belching like a cowherd. It might be worth while, Josef thought, to try bringing Kappa to a higher temperature before passing it into solution with the saline compound; this might offset the violence of the subsequent reaction, leaving Theta in a purer form, without reducing the compensating value. Or possibly, by using Fischer's compound instead of the Löchert stuff, he could afford to introduce a stronger alkaline agent. The formula would be in one of Dittmer's manuals, the materials were at hand. Two hours' work, then he could leave the solution to settle and get Dittmer's microscope on it to-morrow morning before he came. In the meantime he could be preparing in his own room (his own laboratory, as he mentally called it) a sufficient quantity of Psi Plus emulsion to provide for the further experiments. And he would still get nearly three hours' sleep.

"Do you mind lending me that set of retorts?"

"Certainly, certainly, my dear Zeppichmann! They are the ones I was just about to use, but it makes no difference. No doubt you are starting some epoch-making experiments?"

"No no, Herr Korbenhaus, I am only fiddling a little to amuse myself."

At nine o'clock Dittmer came back, pitched off his coat and went to examine his new cultures, singing *Kennst Du das Land?* in his chesty bass. "I've been to see our good Director," he suddenly announced, negligently twiddling the micro-adjustment. "Satan's sins, how that man does fuss! Heidkamp's bill, that's the trouble this time. That busybody Zinkler must needs go and show it him, and he wanted to know what the hospital had got for the money. Two hundred miserable Marks!"

"What was it?" Korbenhaus shouted across the room, "rat food?"

"Don't talk to me about rats—rats are off the menu to-day! What was the bill for? How should I know—I'm not an accounting clerk! D'you know what I did? I showed Wildelau a tube of water coloured with a pinch of potassium permanganate, and I told him it was a specimen of the rarest fluid in Europe."

"But there's nothing rare about potassium permanganate solution," Korbenhaus objected. "I could make gallons of it myself."

"That," said Dittmer, "is because of the specialised training you have had under my care."

He climbed up to kneel on the bench—he liked to be well over his work—and started singing again. He was a very happy man, who easily expelled the small cares that came his way with noisy explosions of temper; and these were his best moments. The smudge he was watching had been a uniform cloudy blue this morning. Now it had a hard rim of dirty orange. That rim meant, to him, a military tribal movement which made the Tartar migrations seem trivial. A minute drop delicately released from his pipette, and the instinct in a billion particles had worked to his will, forming a new empire. Instinct? He doubted that. Those specks of protoplasm which he had never seen were equipped, he thought, with something equivalent to reason: else how, when he attacked them, did they always find the single chance of escape? And now, as he worked the muscles of his eyes, trying to detect some fainter streak of colour within the orange, his thoughts swept down into the kingdom he watched. To be one of those, to be among that billion of individuals? Yes, individuals, he believed that, he had lived with them so long. Would he, down there in that multitude, conceive a purpose different from mere survival? Was there, down there, ambition, leadership? He could believe that as well . . .

"Excuse me, Doctor Dittmer. I wonder if you will be so kind as to lend me your Pelzer? It's just a little point I want to clear up."

"Who the devil are you?" he shouted. "Oh, it's you! Yes yes damn it, help yourself to Pelzer, only don't believe a word he says. A typical chemist, a fundamental bungler. What are you up to?"

Josef hesitated.

"Well, really, I was only making up something to keep the moths out of my clothes. It's a great nuisance, they eat up everything I possess."

"Well they've got to eat something, haven't they! Moths, my dear Zeppichmann, are sent by a wise providence to curtail the vanity of young doctors. Good God, what a caboodle you're rigging over there!"

He slid to the floor and drifted across to the corner bench, cursing the lengths of tube and glass stoppers as he trod on them.

"All this infernal machinery," he said sadly, "for the single purpose of destroying the humble moth! Explain it to me, good Zeppichmann, I am a child in these matters. Your moth, I suppose, slides up the tube here, he takes a sip from this flask, he passes on through this rubber connection towards the pleasant warmth of the bunsen burner. Is that it?"

Josef constructed his smile.

"It always interests me," he said, "trying to work out new arrangements of apparatus."

Very young! Dittmer thought. Really, when rats arrived at maturity in a few weeks, it seemed absurd that human beings grew up so slowly, and in the end had rather less intelligence. And yet, this youngster whose big hands worked so deftly, who grasped so quickly any point in the mathematics of research . . .

"By the way," he said, "I'd prefer you not to use this place before I come in the mornings. Or any time when I'm not here. It's just that Doctor Wildelau might think materials were being wasted, he expects me to keep my eye on everything . . ."

8

HE THOUGHT it advisable to see Frau Spühler about it
first of all.

Once a week she made a formal call in his room, bringing the bill: she liked to do this in person, feeling that by a
tactful charm she could make the commercial transaction
into one of social pleasantness.

"Good-evening, Herr Doktor! Well, the time has come
again for us to exchange our little weekly tokens of honesty
and friendship!" Then her dainty laugh. Then, "The little
bits of paper that make the wheels go round!"

As a rule he had the money ready. He would give her
his distant smile, with "It is a pleasure, gnädige Frau!" and
the business was over. But this time, with a touch of cere-
mony, he asked her to be seated.

"If you are not too busy, Frau Spühler, and can spare me
a few minutes, there is a little matter I should like to discuss
with you."

Frau Spühler had no wish to sit down. Tired as she always was, she much preferred to stand when in the guests'
rooms, feeling vaguely that she must keep an easy escape.
But now her mind had set off on such a wild career that her
body, uncontrolled, dropped into the chair he set for her.
'A little matter.' That terrible phrase could only mean one
thing: Dr. Zeppichmann was angry that she had stopped his
evening carpentry, the Professor had said something that
evening which impugned the Doctor's honour, Minna had
given the message insultingly, the Doctor was going to de-
mand an apology, he was going to insist on Herr Meisel being asked to leave the house, he was going to leave himself,

he would refuse to pay this week's bill, there would be a lawyer's letter and dear August would say it was all her fault.

"It's just a suggestion I wanted to make," Josef began. "Of course I don't want to interfere with what's no business of mine——"

"But you don't understand," she said. "It's just that Herr Meisel had a headache that evening, otherwise I'm sure he would not have made any objection to your construction-work."

"Herr Meisel?—a headache—?"

"You see, really Herr Meisel has a very nice nature, he comes of a distinguished family, one of the oldest families in Berlin. Herr Meisel is going through a very difficult time, even the finest brains are left idle nowadays, the government does nothing. And he is so young. I wish you could have heard the charming things he has said to me sometimes— when he is quite well, I mean—such a sweet thing he said once when he was in bed and I took him up some soup. When you think of his living all this long way from his mother, and naturally he had grown fond of this room, the outlook is so nice."

"Indeed, yes!" Josef agreed. "I am only sorry that there aren't two rooms with the same outlook. It was about your servant-girl that I wanted to speak to you."

Ah! With that direction Frau Spühler could run before the wind. How often had Frau Rupf said 'That girl of yours!—' and how many times had she swamped the wrath of Frau Rupf with her own!

"Minna?" she said. "I tell you, Herr Doktor, I can do nothing with the girl. You can't imagine how it vexes me, her slovenly behaviour, her carelessness over the visitors' rooms. But you see how it is, the child has no mother, when I first took her she couldn't even sew properly, and in these days there's no one to teach a motherless child the proper way of addressing educated people. Herr Spühler, you see, suffers from his heart a great deal, so when I am doing the cooking I can't keep the same eye on Minna as if she was working with somebody who could show her what she does wrong. I'm sure she does try, in her own way. You see, with the price of greenfood going up twice in one week—"

"I've noticed that she has a little cough," Josef said.

"Her cough, yes! Of course it's not easy to teach these things to a child who's had no proper schooling, but in time I shall get her to put her hand up. I constantly tell her—"

"I was wondering," Josef persisted, "if I could do something for it."

Frau Spühler nodded.

"Why yes, Herr Doktor, if you were to tell her about putting her hand up I'm sure—"

"No, I mean, I was wondering if I could do something to make the cough better."

"Better?"

It was confusing to talk to a young man like this, who seemed to be always running away from you. For an instant, with her thoughts tripped in headlong flight, she had a vision of Minna, under Herr Zeppichmann's tuition, diligently practising a more tuneful cough. But almost at once her mind regained its balance and she saw the danger. That last girl she had had, the voluminous Elsa, Elsa had complained so much about her legs aching that she had sent her to a doctor; and the doctor, naturally, since he had to earn his living like every one else, had announced that Elsa had varicose veins. That had meant a fortnight in bed, and afterwards two trips every week to the Moltke Hospital.

"It's habit," she said, "just a bad habit. She had a little cold and that started her coughing and now she can't make up her mind to leave off. It's very kind of you, Herr Doktor, all the same."

"I'd like just to examine her," Josef said woodenly.

"Oh, but if it goes on I can get Doctor Wohlfahrt to see her. Doctor Wohlfahrt attends to all the working people, he has special rates."

"But it would be a pleasure to me to give my professional service without charge. It would—it would allow me to show some appreciation of what has been done for me in this house. You have been most kind—in arranging about this room, and sometimes giving me supper at special hours."

Frau Spühler found that tears were coming up into her throat. Such a long and difficult conversation always weakened her, the moment came when her tired brain seemed to slip out of gear and powerful emotion swept up into the space her thoughts had left. That this difficult young man, with all the doctors' books he had read, and operations and things too—that he should be so kind! Even when Herr Meisel, who had really a sweet nature—and naturally a young man of aristocratic birth was highly-strung—had said unkind things to him in her house! To have all these young men in her care, with their mothers so far away, and then to have them saying such kind things to her! But she did not cry. August hated to see her crying—it was naturally upsetting to a naval man—and she had discovered that if she spoke very fast indeed, holding her throat very stiff, the sobs could not overtake her words.

"You don't know how hard it is!" she said. "Dear Herr Doktor, I try so hard to make everything right, I put a new chair in Herr Meisel's room, I thought that would make up to him for the view out of the window. I only want us all to be happy. If Minna would only take the syrup I made for her, it's an old recipe of my mother's, but I knew from the mess in the sink she had just poured it away. I do try to get round to all the rooms myself, I want all my guests to feel that they are just one family."

He was looking at her with a patient kindness, but he

did not seem to understand. Something else was needed to make him understand her.

"Herr Barthol will be sixty-eight on Sunday," she said desperately, "in spite of all the trouble he has with his kidneys."

"Well, perhaps I ought to be getting on with some work," Josef said. "It is most kind of you to have given me so much of your time."

When she had gone he smoked a cigarette; a treat he generally kept for Saturdays. He would have to try again later on, and if the good fool could not be brought to the point he would act without her. Actually another week's delay was, in strict theory, essential. Sinsteden's dictum about safety was still lodged in his mind. Another week might give him the clue for an improvement in Theta. Possibly Frau Spühler would let him keep a cage of rats in the bicycle shed, if he explained that they were very tame and really quite lovable . . .

It was worrying about those rats of Dittmer's. All three of them, dead within twenty-four hours of the injection. If a human subject went off like that . . . But it was a case of one life against thousands. Somewhere, in a newspaper, he had come across a phrase used by a political speaker. 'It is the many we have to think of. The individual does not matter.' Yes, that was it.

The individual does not matter.

9

EVENTS danced to the tune of his impatience.

At supper on Tuesday Frau Spühler brought in the dishes herself. When it came to changing the courses everybody helped, Herr Spühler carrying the tray, Herr Barthol getting out of his chair to put a plate on the sideboard, even Herr Meisel taking a dish or two along to the kitchen. From a certain delicacy, no one asked why Minna was away from duty until Josef himself put the question.

"The girl is lying down," Frau Spühler answered. "She says she has a headache."

It was generally felt that Dr. Zeppichmann had been wanting in decent manners; like one who, with a dead body in the house, carelessly asks why a chair is empty.

But later in the evening he had a visit from the Spühlers together. They stood in the middle of his room, side by side.

Herr Spühler said: "You must understand that we don't want to impose on you. It must be arranged on a proper financial basis. I shall meet the charge myself, and the girl will repay as much as she can out of her wages."

Frau Spühler said: "Of course you will realize that it's nothing serious. She has often had these headaches before, it's only that I feel it my duty to do everything possible, supposing there might be something wrong with Minna."

"Doctor Wohlfahrt was out when I went for him," Herr Spühler added. "His usual charge for working people is three-Marks-fifty. Of course he is a man of very great experience, with six letters after his name."

"Possibly something in the way of a tonic," Frau Spühler suggested. "The cause is low spirits, it comes from the blood. You see how difficult it is for me, with the house-work on top of the cooking. It made me so ashamed, seeing poor Herr Barthol having to take his own plate away as if he was in a common lodging-house."

"And naturally we want to do what is right," Herr Spühler continued. "She is not really a bad girl, and in any case we feel a duty towards her. We take an interest in her health, just as the captain of a warship is concerned with the health of his most junior gunner."

Like an expert bidder at an auction, Josef waited for them to run dry; without impatience, for he wanted time to prepare his answer. The mention of Dr. Wohlfahrt found a spring in his nature. So, there was competition! This fuddle-witted Spühler would play off another doctor against him! Well, if they wanted to haggle he would lay down his own terms.

When a pause came he was all ready.

"I don't want to alarm you," he said, "but you must realise that the girl's trouble may be more serious than you think. I don't care for that cough."

"Oh, but she's had that for a long time——"

"Exactly! Perhaps too long! You may not know, but certain kinds of cough are infectious——"

Frau Spühler was appalled.

"But, Doctor Zeppichmann, if it's infectious she must go to the hospital at once! With all these people in the house, Herr Barthol sixty-eight last Sunday——"

"——The only thing is, if we take her to the hospital, and they find the trouble to be serious, we may be blamed for not giving the case more attention in its earlier stages. Of course I myself have had nothing to go on——"

"But Minna never asked to see a doctor!" Frau Spühler protested. "If she'd told me——"

Her husband cut across her. He had done some private manoeuvring in his navy days, he grasped Josef's point.

"You mean, you would like to treat her yourself?" he asked bluntly.

"It must be just as you like, Herr Spühler. Doctor Wohlfahrt's experience must be far greater than mine—though possibly my medical knowledge is rather more up-to-date."

"Doctor Wohlfahrt," Spühler said slowly, "makes special terms to poor people. Minna's treatment will be partly at our own expense, but——"

Josef smiled. The table was ready for his card.

"I have already told Frau Spühler that I should be glad to take the case without a fee. Minna has done many small services for me, she has—she has always cleaned my boots very nicely. And of course"—a special smile for Frau Spühler—"I have come to feel myself a member of your household. I make only one condition, which I'm sure you will find quite reasonable. The case must be left entirely in my hands—that is, unless I myself think it desirable to invite another opinion."

Spühler hesitated. Suppose the girl was to die or something? A young chap like this . . . But his wife's mind was driving on again, working her tongue as a steamboat's wash draws little waves along the river bank.

"But you know, Herr Doktor, you ought not to take in all she says. Minna is rather a lazy girl, sometimes when she says she's not up to her work——"

"You can leave that to the doctor!" Spühler said.

"I promise you," Josef added, "that I shan't keep her in bed any more than is absolutely essential."

Frau Spühler opened her mouth, but nothing more came. It hurt her deepest feelings to settle a question all in a moment like this. A dozen new aspects rose to the surface —her position in relation to a paying guest, her responsibility towards a hired girl, the question whether this young man would know about certain things that young women had to go through (which of course could not be discussed with dear August present), the problem of who was to take up the coffee to Frau Rupf in the mornings . . . The crowd of uncertainties, storming to escape in speech, jammed all together at the exit.

"I—I don't know," she said. "I don't—I really don't know . . . Very well, I'll go and get her room tidy."

"There's no need to do that," Josef said with decision. He reached back for an exercise book which lay on his table and slipped it into his pocket. "I know where her room is," he said.

He was calmly slipping past her, out of the room. He was going upstairs.

"Herr Doktor!" she called.

She heard his heavy boots going on up the attic staircase; his voice, quite like a real doctor's voice, saying "May I come in!"; the squeak and then the bang of the attic door.

10

IT WAS rather as if Minna had only just arrived in this room, for a short visit. Her small travelling-box stood open in the middle of the floor, her belongings tumbling over the sides, everything else was on the bed or the floor, clothes, cigarette ends, cracked ink-bottle, a crumpled copy of *Der Westöstliche Divan*. Her cap lay in the pool of grey water which a dip in the boards had collected from a little roof-hole; and amusingly, a giant spider who had found this island refuge stood fast at Josef's entrance, seeming to glare at him resentfully. Only the tight, damp-woollen odour of the room suggested her four years' occupation.

It reminded Josef of his own room at Richterhausen. That, of course, had always been beautifully clean; even in a woodshed his mother would not have allowed this jungle of webs, the green mould on this flaking plaster, the basin rimmed with brown soapstains; but the shape was similar— a minute window where the wall was shallowest, the way the rickety door, half-opened, came against the side of the bed. This kind of disorder he also knew, from the recent days at Zornenwalde, where students were sent out to the factory district to try their hands at a confinement. A smell like this no longer disturbed him, the woodlice crawling along the bedrail were what he expected in quarters of this kind. But he found it all distasteful. The shape of poverty, to one a fraction past its margin, was in a peculiar way offensive.

He shoved his way along the wall to the head of the bed, where the roof's slope let him stand upright.

Minna, sleeping, took her place in the room's careless-ness: the cotton slip flung down at one end of the bed, the girl at the other; with one arm hanging down to the floor. The thick dark hair sprawled across her face like a wild horse's mane, the small face was white and damp. She breathed quite steadily, not coughing at all. Only a small movement of the muscles in her eyes and cheeks showed that some pain had followed her into sleep.

He had not been able to study her so closely before; and now he felt the same sharp excitement that buying his own stethoscope had given him. All those hours of work, the lost sleep, the tedium of meticulous checking: and this was the climax, perhaps the gateway into triumph. For an instant as he watched the face the lips, dividing in a curious smile, sent his thoughts in a new direction: the chance of danger . . . But his resolution shut that door at once. She had, after all, so little to lose. *The individual does not matter.*

"Minna!" he whispered.

As soon as her eyes opened, the cough, like an engine started with the throttle wide, began to shake her with continuous violence. The attack went on for half a minute. Josef had been ready for this. He slipped his arm round her shoulders, pulled her up and a little forward, seized a tooth-mug standing on the floor and held it for the sputum. When it was over he straightened the bolster and put her back against it, carefully, as one lowering a crate of china. He said: "There, that's over now, that's better, just keep quiet a minute!"

The voice was an echo of Dr. Plünnecke's, far more smoothly rounded than the one Josef used in the hospital; he was surprised to find how easily it came, the Plünnecke patient-voice. And like a magic cloak, cut down to fit, the whole of Plünnecke's clinical technique seemed to fall about him: the careful movement of the hands, eyes confident and thoughtful, even the changeless sympathy of Plünnecke's smile.

"You told me, didn't you, that the cough started about a year ago, as far as you remember?"

The girl looked at him stupidly.

"Did *she* tell you to come up here?"

"Yes," he said, "yes, Frau Spühler thought I might be able to make you a bit more comfortable. It makes you feel tired, that cough, doesn't it?"

"I'll come down when I'm better," she answered hoarsely. "I've got to feel bad sometimes, haven't I! I'm not trying to get her money for nothing. I felt bad all last week but didn't say anything. I can't make Herr Meisel's boots shine when they're wet, whatever I feel like."

Josef said: "You're not going to do any more work, Minna, until I give my permission."

"I'm going to do as I like," she said, and turned to face the other way.

Blessings on old Plünnecke, shabby, short-sighted, terrified of boys: old Plünnecke with his loose-knitted tie flopping out of his waistcoat, lecture-notes drifting all over the classroom in the boisterous draught—he had told them chapter-and-verse how you dealt with a patient like this!

Josef moved a pair of shoes, sat on the end of the bed, and pulled out the exercise book: brand new, a week ago, for only forty pfennigs. They had offered him one with a stiffer cover for fifty, but he had decided that he could strengthen the cover of the cheaper one with cardboard. The first page was already headed, 'First Test with Human Subject: Minna Wersen,' with a list of spaces marked for primary data.

"Do you know," he said, "I used to have a room just like this. At home, I mean. I lived in a place called Zornenwalde, my father had a little hardware shop there. Yes, I never slept anywhere except that little room till I was seventeen—I'm twenty-four now. How old are you?"

"I don't know," she said.

He wrote against 'Age': 'Estimated nineteen.'

"What part of the country do *you* come from?"

"I don't know."

But he was neither disturbed nor vexed. 'All patients are evasive,' Plünnecke had said, 'except the kind that are garrulous and misleading. Many behave like guilty prisoners under cross-examination.' Yes, Josef was prepared for this; and in time he would get what he wanted out of the little wretch. He went on talking, slowly, silkily: about his home life, the hard conditions when his father was away at the war, a bad illness he had had in the cold winter of '22, when food was so scarce. His eyes were searching the room, imagining an enlargement of the window, a little home-made table slipped in beside the bed for tools and medicine. They fell on another exercise book which protruded from under the bolster, grubby and dogeared but the twin of his own. So Minna also kept a notebook! What in the world would she write in it?

"I suppose you don't remember the war? You're too young for that."

"I remember the French soldiers," she said. "One of them came into our place. I went and bit his leg."

"So you lived in the Rhine country?"

"That was ever so long ago. I don't remember anything about it, except biting the French soldier."

"Oh, your parents moved later on?"

"Not unless some one dug them up."

"I see." He was looking round for a towel, anything he could use to cool her face. "Well, I hope you gave up biting people later on."

"I bit a girl at school."

"Good heavens! Why?"

"She said that Fräulein Rother was a pious humbug. That wasn't true. Fräulein Rother was kind to me, she was the only decent one among all the bitches."

"You didn't like school?"

"No, I only liked Fräulein Rother. When she died I bunked."

"It was a boarding-school, was it? I never went to one."

"You're lucky. They're hell."

"As bad as being here? I mean, working for Frau Spühler?"

"One bitch is better than half a dozen. I don't mean Fräulein Rother. She was a Bride of God."

Surprised, Josef asked:

"What sort of school was it? A religious school?"

"I don't know. Yes, they had religion, they had a Pastor to do that. It was a thingummy school—a dump. They had all of the bad lots, stealers, dirty-minds, balmies, kids with no parents."

"Which bunch did you come in?"

"No parents, of course. 'Unfortunates,' that's what they called our lot. That meant orphans and bastards."

She had turned to face him again, speaking with a small animation that changed her curiously. With a little blood in her cheeks, hair pushed back and eyes coming to life, she might have been a normal subject under a bout of common fever. So much that for a moment he was scared, thinking that his longing had forced his imagination. It might be some ordinary bronchial affection, severe, but of no interest whatever.

"That cough's a nuisance, isn't it!" he said. "I know— I had one just like it, went on for months. I could give you something for it if you like."

Even as he spoke the animation faded out. He waited for another salvo of coughing, but it didn't come. There was just a silent struggle, all the motions of a man tied to a stake. She whispered:

"It gets—it gets my breath—sometimes!"

"Let's look at your chest, can I?" he said.

He could not hear her answer. Her head had fallen right back, her eyes were shut as if she slept again. But from the tension of her body he knew she was conscious, and he saw her lips moving. Well, he had been very patient, he couldn't wait any longer. Carefully, as when he worked in the theatre, he moved the draggled blanket. And knew immediately, with a giant relief, that he had not been wrong.

When he saw the body itself he wanted to shout. The condition, for his purpose, was almost as good as it could be; perhaps dangerously good: the flesh so thin that it showed the pectoral structure like a window, the left mamma shrunken to an empty pocket, the left chest-wall collapsed upon the upper lobe. He had seen a similar formation twenty times in middle-life cases; never so perfect an example in adolescence. Move this girl up to the hospital, put her under Vollmuth's standard treatment, and her chances of getting back to normal life were perhaps one in ten. Say, to be fair, one in five. And under his, the Zeppichmann treatment? Well, six months would settle it. Yes, from carefully weighted calculation he was confident that in only six months she would be safe; or, of course, dead. The excitement was so urgent that he could not resist it. He felt for his pencil, which had dropped into a fold of the bedclothes, and began to write.

'When case first examined, disease already well advanced . . . deepening of supraclavicular fossae . . . flattening of the mammae . . . râles everywhere . . . whispered pectoriloquy . . . cavitation at the left apex . . . superficial examination indicated left lung too far affected to respond to any treatment . . .'

A hoarse whisper:

"Can't you—do anything—better than that!"

The smile he had let drop came back again.

"I'm such a stupid fellow," he said, "I always have to write things down, otherwise I forget everything."

"What d'you want to remember?"

"The way your chest goes when you cough. Wait a minute, I'll get you something."

He covered her and slipped away. To his relief the stairs and passage were empty—he had expected that Frau Spühler would be listening at the door and he would have to cut his way through a jungle of questions. Confidence, he thought, must get the girl's confidence—stupid to have made that note, childish—first injection to-morrow?—no, too soon.

Back in his own room, he used all the quickness which hospital work had given him. Medicine—ignorant people always liked to have medicine—something harmless, with an emollient: there was some stuff he used himself—yes, here in the drawer—this with a fourth part of Frerk's solution would quieten the cough a little; and ten minims of laudanum wouldn't hurt. Ten? Make it fifteen. He sped about the room, putting a saucepan on the stove, collecting instruments, lysol, basin, cottonwool, clean towels, his own bedclothes. Within ten minutes he was at the attic door again, arms weighed with paraphernalia.

He found her sitting up, staring with a child's ignorant expectancy. (Like Dittmer's rats, he thought.) She said:

"Oh, you've come back!"

"Yes. And I've got you some medicine. Quick, wasn't I? I made it myself. Quite nice, you try!"

"I'd rather have something from the chemist's. They know how to make it right."

"I used to be a chemist," he told her.

(Near enough.)

"Oh well!" She drank it off, with the air of closing a poor business deal. "Just the same as Frau Spühler's!" she said. "Is that all you want?"

"All I want you to drink. I'll bring you up some better stuff to-morrow."

"I'll be down to-morrow," she said carelessly.

"Not if I know it!"

"Whether you know it or not! I'm going to get my money, and I don't take money for nothing. Or medicine," she added. "What does this cost?"

He ignored the question.

"It's silly, you know, to talk about going downstairs to-morrow. You couldn't do it, however much you wanted to. Don't you realise that you're ill? You couldn't stand up for two minutes."

"Stand up? Of course I could!"

"Not for more than ten seconds."

"All right, look!" she said.

With all the appearance of vigour—it would not have deceived a first-year student—she jerked herself out of bed and stood, with her arms folded, barefoot on the bare floor; solemnly defiant. But Josef didn't even trouble to look. He pounced at the bed and ripped everything off it, twisted the six-weeks-dirty linen into one bundle and pitched it into the corner. For the time being the mattress—if you called it that—would have to stay. The rug he had brought went on top of it, then his own decke with sheets clean the day before. By that time she was limp and gasping. "You'd better sit down," he said quietly, and she sat on the side of the bed. He had brought up an old shirt of his own, it was coarse and much darned but better than what she was wearing and newly-washed. "I'd like you to put this on, it'll be comfier than that thing." He gathered the old bedclothes again and took them outside. He heard another burst of coughing, and when he re-entered she was lying back, her small ration of recovered strength all consumed; but she had changed into his shirt. That gave him confidence.

He said quietly, in the Plünnecke voice: "I'm going to tidy you up a bit." And slipped one of the towels under her shoulders.

It wasn't easy, working from the other side of the bed where a capricious joist prevented his kneeling upright; with nothing to stand the basin on but the bed itself, the soap collecting plaster and cobwebs the moment he put it down. But that was in the way of the trade. And he felt the pleasure of good workmanship as, without one motion of roughness, he cleaned the crust of grime away from the forehead, leaving the pale skin quite soft and fresh; as with delicate strokes of twisted cotton wool he purged the cavities of the eyes. Now a smear of vaseline where the skin was rough, now a clean handkerchief to dry the creases under the chin. Gentle, gentle, but quick, while the passive state lasted.

She did not interrupt him, however, she didn't wriggle or say anything. He became ambitious, and hating that a patient of his should have her hair in such a dirty tangle he set to work to comb it out and then shampoo it. "I've got to pull a bit," he said. "You've let it get in such a state . . . Did that hurt?" "Not much." And a little later, kneading the soapy mass and glancing at the face upside-down, he noticed the lips faintly smiling.

"Do you like this?" he asked.

"Fräulein Rother used to do it," was all she said.

He was eager to start a more thorough examination. It might be some days before he could get hold of a portable X-ray apparatus from the hospital, and in the meantime his verbal account of the pulmonary condition must be so meticulous as by itself to parry all scepticism. But the girl must have a rest first, he had to go carefully, he was not sure how far he had overcome her ignorant hostility.

"There now! Don't you feel more comfy?"

He looked round for something else to do, and realised that it had been a waste of time cleaning up the girl if the room was to stay in this condition. No, he wouldn't allow it. He went downstairs to the passage cupboard where the household things were kept and came back with another load: a brush and pan, a pail of hot water, scrubbing brushes. With the same care that he had used on Minna, but without the gentleness, he set upon the filth in the room.

He did not dislike the work. This was his own patient, not an odd case in a long ward, not just a piece of Röstel's leavings. She was more than that, this decrepit parcel of humanity, she was the instrument for proving his case. (He thought of Wildelau, the pompous Dr. Wildelau who had snubbed him for daring to undertake research.) And with such an instrument he was ready to take unlimited trouble. Moving on hands and knees, with his head so close to the floor, he found the stench almost unbearable; but to see all the grease in flight before his brush, the woodbugs turning over in the brown, soapy wave, this was a new and quickening pleasure. To-morrow he would consult Herr Spühler on the subject of enlarging the window, later on he might do something about the plaster. Meanwhile his excitement must find release in vast exertion, and he'd have his patient's room clean if he had to scrub all night.

He thought the girl was asleep, but when he looked up she was watching him, with the isolated curiosity that he was beginning to find a nuisance. He could not help thinking of Dittmer's rats, the way they had watched him one day as he was cleaning out their cage; their eyes following each movement of his hands with a certain small shrewdness, with just a little apprehension. He said:

"Don't you want to sleep a bit?"

"No," she said, "not when there's something to watch. I can sleep when you've gone."

Curious, he thought, how self-assured she was, with nothing of an invalid's demeanour. Seeing her sitting up like this one could hardly believe that she was living with practically no lung at all.

"The room's looking better, isn't it!" he said.

"Yes. But it's not worth bothering. I only sleep here, no one ever sees it."

"Well, you'll be seeing it a good deal at present."

"D'you mean I'm going to be ill?"

"Yes, you're pretty ill. That chest, it's in a bad state."

"Yes," she said, "it hurts a lot. When I'm coughing, mostly." Then, "Am I going to die, do you think? I mean, fairly soon?"

That took him off his guard.

"You—you'll have to go carefully," he said. "You'll have to do what I tell you, take things easy." He got up and sat on the bed again, for the first time rather nervous; it was delicate and important, this, getting the mental attitude right. "Listen, Minna: I've taken on the job of getting you well again—quite well again—and I'm going to do it if you'll only help me—"

"I don't mind about it," she said. "You might just as well die as go on washing all those plates and things three times every day. She won't even give me new drying-cloths, it's awful drying all that stuff with the cloths always wet."

"But I'll get you some new cloths myself as soon as you're well again—"

"I don't see why I can't die if I want to," she said obstinately. "What's it got to do with anybody except me?"

He had to begin again.

"Now, listen, Minna! . . ."

A little afterwards it occurred to him that she had, at least, taken away the last of his scruples. What harm in gambling with your neighbour's money if your neighbour had no use for it?

FROM Bruddestrasse, shabby and foul-odoured, a flight of worn steps cuts between the workshops to go down in zig-zags to the ferry. In summer workpeople go that way at the dinner-hour to sit on the narrow terrace half-way down and eat their sandwiches, with the steam barges plodding below to amuse them. The movement of the scene is agreeable, drays and yellow trams jostling past the half-timbered wharfhouses; and the river always brings enough wind to clear away the brewery odour in which they spend most of their lives. On fine nights these steps are a place for lovers.

That river breeze which makes the terrace so pleasant in summer turns, by October, into a damp and bullying wind: a wind such as you can enjoy, in a hardy way, when you face it on wide moorlands. In a town its vigour is only spiteful, rattling windows, scattering rubbish as it cries through narrow streets; and to have it whipping about the face, as Erich Meisel had that night, is a trial of the steadiest temper. He was going home this way partly because it was dark and unfrequented; he had formed the habit, these last weeks, of avoiding casual encounters with his friends which might mean the price of drinks; and now, wretched with the chill and solitude, he wished he had gone through to the Drenkerstrasse and taken the tram.

Ten minutes before, he had been sitting in the Club, and that was the place to be on a winter night. Nothing but an old storeroom, with two glaring lights which were always flickering from some fault in the connection, a rusty stove belching smoke through its cracked lid; but it was warmed with the breath of thirty men, made cheerful by their loud voices and brave songs. Nobody there as a rule but clerks and shopkeepers; yet they had the right spirit, those trades-men, the old nation-spirit, believing that a man's worth lies in his own right arm. In that place he caught something which had belonged to his fathers, a comradeship of soldiers. There he could lose himself, forget the dinginess of Hartz-innfeld, the kitchen odours and the smell of polish which the draught took all along the corridors at Handelstrasse 149. To-night there had been two men of his own stamp, delegates from divisional headquarters at Frankfurt, one of them a general's son whom he had known in Berlin. They had gossiped a bit, he and Karl von Schüttenwalde, about the old Academy days. And Fuldenkraus's speech, promising victory over their persecutors far sooner than they imagined, had whipped the fighting blood in him till he had seemed on fire with courage. They had broken spontaneously into the party song, Karl gripping his hand, with one great shout they had reaffirmed their oath of loyalty. In that high mo-ment he believed that he could never be lonely again.

That was barely fifteen minutes ago. And now he was in his deepest loneliness.

He had left the meeting before it closed, whispering some excuse. Karl would have wanted to take him some-where afterwards, one of the hotels, and he couldn't face that: this suit, he had worn it every day for more than two years; and there was the eternal question of paying for drinks, tipping waiters. Yes, it would have been a glorious end to the evening: Karl and he together, affectionate and rather rowdy, with the bourgeoisie of Hartzinnfeld staring at them in envious disapproval. But the price was too high.

A swift 'goodnight.' The door closing, darkness and reality.

On the steps a man and woman passed, bound together with their arms. They stared at him in the scanty light, the man said something inaudible and the girl tittered. He hadn't heard what the man said, but he recognized the local accent. They were blessed by their meanness, he thought, people like that: a place so small and mean as Hartzinnfeld was the only scene they knew, and fitted comfortably to their own small spirit. Well, he was not like that, thank God, he belonged to a larger world.

Belonged?

He had to clutch his hat, the wind was so capricious here. And with his other hand he held to the rail, frightened of stumbling; in the evening's excitement he had forgotten his hunger, but he felt the weakness now.

So silent here. The steps of the couple passing him had dwindled and ceased, there was no sound from the river; with the wind flooding his ears he heard only faintly the jangle of the trams which he saw crawling along the other bank. Those trams, they would be taking late-shift men along to the ironworks, men chatting and laughing, men who had a job. Others were lounging along the quay down there, workless like himself; he could just see them as they passed the lamps, just catch the twinkle of a lighted match. Yes, like himself, but he did not belong to them. They were born, that sort, to narrow lives, to shoddy clothes, scant rations. They had lost nothing, having no heritage. What he himself had lost he knew from a hundred glimpses: photographs in family albums, the chatter of other soldiers' sons at the Academy: enough to make a general picture of the life he should have had, the Mess's comradeship, the welcome rigour of military service. Yet it was not those things he grudged, the flavour of that life and its dignity. All he wanted was to serve his fatherland; and the fatherland had become too mean to want or merit his service.

The sound of laughter came to him feebly, carried across the water. A nation's poverty, he thought, is borne by every one. But her spiritual anguish has all to be suffered by the few who keep her soul.

The ferryman had gone off duty, he had to go and thump at the ferry house door. A woman with a candle, opening the door an inch or two, said that her husband had gone to bed, he was in pain with rheumatism: no doubt his honour would be willing to go round by the bridge. It was always like that in Hartzinnfeld, no one ever lacked an excuse for laziness.

"The ferry service is supposed to operate till 11.30," he told her. "I can wait while he dresses."

Standing here at the water's edge he could see the life of the other bank more clearly; but still as something separate from his own, unreal, as when you watch a street from a sick-room window: a waiter hurrying about a lighted café, always the rocking trams. For a moment he felt a huge impatience, longing to merge himself in that activity; and then a dread of it, knowing the loneliness of streets where no one spoke to him, laughter he did not share. Only the river, high in this season, the brown swirls travelling swiftly away from the town's infection, gave him a remote comfort: that was like his country as he dreamed it, like himself; it would flow as full and steady when those things had gone.

He shivered. The surface wind, wrapping about his neck and forehead, brought gusts of river fog, foul-odoured. From the coldness of his forehead he knew he would have neuralgia to-morrow, a pain sharper than fire. That fellow, why couldn't he hurry!

He was trying to recall the exaltation of the evening, but all he could think of now was the circumstance which had spoiled it. They had passed round a slip for subscriptions: divisional headquarters were opening a new propaganda fund, and every member was supposed to contribute according to his means. He had put himself down for ten Marks, the very highest sum he could hope to raise in the time. Some of the rank-and-file—lads who served behind counters—had promised fifteen or even twenty Marks. Karl von Schüttenwalde had seen the list as it went round, he must have noticed Erich's entry. A fellow like that, naturally, would make no comment; neither would he ascribe the small subscription to any lack of zeal—Karl knew him too well. No, Karl would have drawn the obvious, the correct conclusion that he, Erich, had become a pauper. And it wasn't only Karl. The list would be posted for later subscriptions, every one of those boys would know that while Albert Terber, son of a petty house-agent, was giving twenty-five Marks Erich Meisel was only giving ten. That meant in practice that he would have to avoid the Club for a fortnight. Even then his position could not be the same. They would treat him as their equal, they might even call him by his first name . . .

The door behind him opened, the ferryman limped across to the boat and untied it. Erich said, getting in, "You've been a hell of a time."

He stood facing the bank he had left. That way, for a few moments, he could faintly enjoy the sense of isolation, freedom from the streets which had hedged and wearied him all day. Out here the air was fresh, like mountain air, and the smoothness of the boat's travel passed into his senses, as if some power of his own moved him so easily. The brown water lay astern like a silken fan. The ferryman was jabbering as he rowed, something about his four children and their lack of clothes, about what the ferry had earned before the war. "Nowadays they all go round by the bridge, no money, you see . . . comes of the politicians, what do they do? What's the good of working if the politicians throw it all away? . . . and now, you see, they all go round by the bridge . . ." But Erich wasn't listening. A thought had come as if a dark room were suddenly lighted: here was depth and stillness, here was purpose; from poverty and the Club's contempt, the country's rottenness, one leap would take him out of reach.

His friends would understand. They would recognise it as an act of supreme nobility.

But the chance of escape came without resolution. Huddled and pensive, he had not moved his feet when the stern swung in and the town surrounded him, voices close above his head, a motor bleating, the café's light sculpturing the boatman's face. That, too, had been a dream. Walking slowly up the steps he felt for a coin, found only a two-Mark piece, impulsively pitched it over his shoulder.

"Something for your children!"

He had meant to take a tram from the Lindenmeister crossing, risking an encounter with some one from the Club; but his stupid charity had made that impossible. And now, added to the constant soreness of his feet, he felt a small wriggling pain across the chest. Where the road was darkest he stopped to lean against a warehouse wall, watching the uncollared loads that joggled past in the frowsty comfort of the trams. A girl with crumpled skirts above her knees, breasts stuck out like mitres, came across the road to give him a pert good-evening; but a whistle from a man in a sleek overcoat made her turn and go off with him. Shivering, he turned the corner and began the climb towards the Mühlstrasse.

It was nearly twelve when he got home. As usual, a light was showing in his old room, the one which the Zeppichmann creature had stolen; the door was open, and as he went along the passage he noticed that the room was empty. A sudden curiosity made him turn and go inside.

So this was Zeppichmann's idea of elegance and comfort: shelves and basins, shabby text-books, bottles all over the place. Well, Erich had expected nothing else. Bottles with neat little labels, they were the boundary-posts of such a fellow's mind. It was not even a doctor's room, it was a cheap apothecary's.

The neuralgia was beginning, the warmth of indoors

seemed to spur its attack. He crossed the room to look more closely at the line of bottles on the wall-shelf: among all these, surely there might be something to give him relief.

Most of the labels had only formulae which were meaningless. But one small bottle, standing out of its place, was marked *Tinctura Opii*. He knew what that was.

Laudanum: how did you take it? The usual dose was very small, he fancied, not more than a drop or two. Dangerous to take too much. And yet, what was the danger? Down there on the river he had seen the chance of peace, a deep and lasting peace which no one could steal from him. Close as it was, that peace had been fenced off by a fearful boundary, the gripping coldness of the water, horror of suffocation, the struggle . . . With this stuff, as he supposed, you slept, slept deeply, passed unknowing into the deepest of all sleeps. He could leave a message to say that his death was an act of protest, the only witness that an honourable man could make against a country fallen into the hands of charlatans. That message would be read in court, published in the newspapers . . . A current of warm emotion ran through his cheeks and temples: like his father, his grandfather, he would be remembered as one who had sacrificed himself for his nation's honour.

He took the top off the bottle and sniffed.

A board rattled outside, that loose board which Frau Spühler complained of once a week and her husband never remembered to nail down. He tried, in one movement, to put back the stopper and shove the bottle into his pocket, forgetting that he wore an overcoat with the pocket entrance vertical. When Josef appeared at the door the bottle was still in his hand.

He did not try to conceal it now: he wouldn't play schoolboy to this fellow. Hardly glancing at Josef, he held up the bottle and turned it round to read the label again. He said, carelessly:

"This is laudanum, isn't it?"

Josef nodded and smiled.

"Yes, that's quite right. I was making up a draught for the maid—poor Minna, she's in a bad way with that cough. Can I—won't you sit down? I've got cigarettes some-where—"

Still looking at the bottle, Erich said:

"No. No, I only came in here to see how you've arranged my room. I thought as you were so keen on the room you'd probably have some special furniture for it—good pictures and so on. Of course my pictures are only relatively good—"

"Oh, but they're excellent, Herr Meisel! I admired them very much when I was moving them. No, I'm afraid I've nothing like that, I look on this as just a workroom—"

Erich said, hardly moving his lips, "Yes, I see that . . . I looked at it differently." Then, "I'm going to borrow this, if you don't mind. Or for that matter, even if you do."

He was strolling towards the door, but Josef came round and stood in his way, still smiling.

"Excuse me, Herr Meisel, but I'm afraid—I can't—that, you see, is a very dangerous drug, it mustn't be in the hands of any one who doesn't understand these things—"

"I understand it all right. I'm not an ignoramus—"

"No, but please, Herr Meisel, that drug must only be used by qualified doctors—"

Erich, standing with his feet apart, caressing the bottle, surveyed Josef with a leopard's eyes, taking his time. He said softly:

"Just listen a minute! A young hobnail from the slums who comes into a house like this at no one's invitation but his own has got to learn a few things—"

"Herr Meisel," Josef said earnestly, "I can see you're not well, you look feverish. Won't you sit down a minute, let me make you up something? Please, I should like to do that! No charge—just as a friend—"

"If I ever want your damned professional attention," Erich said, "I shall tell you. Meanwhile, will you please get out of my way!"

Smiling again, Josef stood aside. But as Erich passed he grabbed at the bottle.

Erich said between his teeth:

"Let that go, will you, you young bast—"

"No, please, Herr Meis—"

The blow of Erich's fist, delivered at such close range, would have broken the jaw of a nicely-nurtured man; but not the jaw of Josef, who had fought the pick of his contemporaries in all the alleys of Richterhausen. Josef simply dropped back, surprised and smarting. But the bottle crashed on the floor.

It was Erich who smiled now.

"Well, that's smashed the bloody thing," he said.

"Do you know," said Josef, taut with fury, "that bottle cost nine Marks! I'll ask you to pay for that!—"

Erich laughed. The sting in his knuckles had, for the moment, driven the neuralgia right away. He went on to his own room, laughing copiously.

12

BEFORE making the first injection, Josef smoked a cigarette in his room: not to steady his nerves—they never gave the smallest trouble—but to satisfy a certain instinct for drama. He would go without his cigarette on Saturday.

The shiny instrument-case he had bought lay on the table: 28 Marks, with neat compartments for ampoules and a section to hold the working diary. Also a little book for Minna, *The Adventures of Hedwig Sachse*—she had said she enjoyed reading. It was all very extravagant, but extravagance is curiously easy to one who has spent the greater part of his savings in a few weeks. (The bill for Bovine Tuberculin alone had reached 180 Marks.) Yes, he had used up a big slice of his money and the whole of his spare time. How many hours since he had come to Hartzinnfeld?—it must have run into hundreds. In a peculiar way that expenditure of time seemed the heavier price: he could feel that in the tiredness of his tough body, the headaches he was beginning to notice. In all that time a man with his wits about him could have done many things, could have made money in odd ways, tried to get on with people, improved himself. And about this gamble he was under no delusions. His polyvalent tuberculin might not work. You might get 100% positive results with animal subjects and a lethal result with humans—he knew that. If he only succeeded in accelerating the disease in this girl it meant that five years' work was wasted. Then he would have to decide whether to risk another five years, another ten, twenty years—poverty, overwork, loneliness—or to become just a good doctor. It was frightening, the thought of becoming a plain, good doctor.

One might as well be a schoolmaster, like the idiotic Rupf.

The cigarette was starting to burn his fingers. He crushed it and put the stump away in a little tin he kept for cigarette ends. On to battle!

The girl grinned when he came in. She always grinned nowadays. So: he was not such a bad doctor!

The psychological side of this case had been tricky. From his first visit to her room he had understood the girl through and through: she was an empty adolescent without any kind of mental ability; she had acquired, for self-protection, a special insolence made out of certain poses picked up in the schoolroom; she had a cheap armoury of gauche polysyllables, borrowed apparently from this Fräulein Rother for whom she had once conceived a Schwärmerei. It was the *gamin* type, the would-be adventuress serving in a beer-garden: you found it in all the textbooks of psychotherapy. But it had proved a harder type to break down than the textbooks said. This Minna had answered his cheerfulness with sulks, his gravity with something like mockery. She had never shown him the smallest respect, and yet his efforts at intimate conversation had been treated with incomprehension. She would not talk about herself, she revealed none of the trifling vanities which can be exploited. Hardest of all, she did not seem to want his or any one else's company. She lived in some foolish daydream and was quite content with that.

But he had brought her as far as acquiescence. He had been so patient, always treating her as if her own wishes were paramount. 'You will let me come and attend to you again to-morrow? Just to make you comfortable!' At first her answer had been 'If you want to!' And now it was 'Yes, Herr Doktor, that's all right.' The grin she gave him now, that was another advance. It meant that she recognised him as a human being of some kind. He had, in professional terms, made psychological contact.

"This new window," he said, sitting down on his home-made stool, "it makes a difference, doesn't it! Makes the room fresher."

"Yes, I suppose so."

"Look, I've got you a book, an adventure story. You told me you'd like something to read."

"Oh yes, yes. Thank you."

She took his gift with a trace of pleasure, but when she read the title her face was puzzled, disappointed.

"Do you think it's too hard for you to read?" he asked. "I don't think there are any difficult words."

"No, I suppose not. I haven't read a book like this be-fore."

"Oh? What sort of books have you read?"

"Only what Fräulein Rother gave me."

That Rother woman again!

"What were those?"

"Poetry, most of them. There was a book called *Hermann und Dorothea*. Have you read that?"

"No. I've heard of it."

"And one called *Das Lied von der Glocke*."

"We did bits of that at my school," he said. "Now listen, I'm going to try something new to-day. The way you're breathing—that pain in the chest—it won't ever get right if we don't go for it. I've got some stuff here I've made specially, it's a kind of medicine only I put it into your arm. A bit of a prick—it hardly hurts at all . . ."

As he got out his tools, chatting like a conjuror, he was eyeing her obliquely for general condition: often one saw more in these sidelong appraisals than in the formal exami-nation which followed. He was lucky, he thought. The col-our in the face was good, the texture of the pupils normal. He might have waited a month without getting a better day for her to resist the primary reaction.

"I'm going to listen to your heart," he said.

She said rather fretfully: "You did that yesterday. It can't sound all that different."

"Oh, can't it!"

The day's excitement slightly affected his muscles, making his movements a little clumsy; but his brain was going as neatly as a jenny, noting and holding every detail for the record: pulse, respirations, resonance. Pulse was interesting, down to 98.

"You're feeling better than you did a fortnight ago?" he asked her.

"Yes, I'm quite all right now."

'All right!' But undoubtedly the general condition was improved, improved rather remarkably. The change might be partly due to normal fluctuation, but only partly. His own rough-and-ready nursing had something to do with it, the scouring he had given the room, the new nightgown and clean sheets, above all the new window which he and Herr Spühler had constructed together. The thought came, as he bent over her listening to the rhonchi:

'Suppose I'd given the case to old Vollmuth up at the hospital? A scientifically constructed chalet, first-class nursing, the sweet air from the pines. Would the pulse be down to 90 by now? Would Vollmuth, in the end, have made a job of it?'

An odd sentence from Schankhäuschen's Manual floated into his mind's eye (at the top of the grubby page, underlined by the book's last owner). 'In such cases sanatorium treatment is indicated: and where there is doubt a period of such treatment should always precede experiment with tuberculins . . .' And Schankhäuschen, after all, was not a nature fanatic . . . Appearances did suggest that this particular case was one which might benefit from Vollmuth's pedestrian methods. If the patient were offered her choice, and had wit enough to understand the alternatives as well as he did, she would most likely opt for sanatorium.

It wasn't too late to hand the case over. He could make up some sort of story for Vollmuth, be a little imprecise about dates.

He found that his hands and tongue had stopped moving, he saw that the girl was watching him with curiosity.

"What are you thinking about?" he asked.

She said: "Guinea-pigs. Frau Spühler says you've got guinea-pigs in your room. What do you do to them?"

"Do to them?" The ratchet of his brain slipped, it was a physical sensation. "I give them medicine," he said; and then the rest of the lie came easily. "Yes, they're sick, poor things—they belong to a friend of mine, he asked me to look after them and try and get them better."

"But one of them died, Frau Spühler told me."

"Yes. Yes, I was terribly upset about that. But it was in a very bad way when it came to me, I couldn't do anything for it."

She nodded. She seemed quite satisfied.

"Does he pay you—your friend?" she asked.

"Pay me? Oh well, no—no, nothing to speak of. A trifle—just what their food costs me."

"But you can't go on doctoring everybody for nothing. How can you live? I wouldn't do Frau Spühler's filthy work for nothing."

He said quickly: "Oh, but I get paid at the hospital. That's where my real work is. I only do these odd jobs because I like it. It helps me, you know, it's good practice."

"I see," she said; and then, with perfect simplicity, "Am I good practice?"

Oh, damn and blast the woman!

No, he would not consider any sentimental point of view. If you took the standpoint of every patient who came your way you would never get anywhere in research, you would always be wondering and doubting. He said gently, smiling:

"No, Minna, I only give you my treatment because I like you. It's nice to work for people you like occasionally. Well now, let's have that arm of yours."

He held her arm very tenderly. With an artist's care, with something of an artist's satisfaction, he painted a neat circle of formaldehyde.

"Now," he said, "this is where you're going to feel a little tiny prick."

"Is that what's going to make my chest better?"

"Yes yes, I hope so. Now still, please, just keep as still as you can!"

13

HE WAS glad to have got the first step over.

The attack of sentimentality had been quite unexpected. He supposed that every scientist was subject to such dangers in the early stages, a moment when the patient's private interest blocked out the view of one's objective. Well, he had stood his ground, and the onslaught would not come again. If the girl suffered pain under his treatment, if in the end he lost her, he would certainly feel a personal regret; for she was not ill-looking now that he had cleaned her up, and there was something attractive in her simplicity. But nothing would make him waver now. The supreme experiment had started.

He began to calculate dates. Nine weeks, he reckoned, was the minimum in which he could expect any reaction. Dosage would then be up to 0.12 C.C. D5. In fourteen weeks . . .

To-morrow he would scrub the floor again, using some of the hospital soap; and he would substitute his own mattress for the lousy thing she had at present. Possibly get her a new pillow. He was feeling already a possessive pride in her, the pride a man takes in some piece of machinery he has put together. She was something far more important than his first private patient: the instrument of his inventive genius, the screen on which new knowledge, so laboriously designed, might be projected. Oh yes, at the sanatorium she would have lived under better therapeutic conditions, received more constant attention; but for Vollmuth she would only have been one patient in the endless succession, one more article on the travelling band. If Vollmuth cured her she would simply go back into circulation, back to Frau Spühler's draughty, underlighted kitchen. If Josef killed her she would still have been some use.

Stop, enough, mustn't think like that! The sickly gas of sentimentality was leaking in again. Figures, they were Josef's business, figures, records, charts. To-day's entry in the record would have to be minutely accurate.

He cleared a space at the end of the bench, moved the electric bulb which he had fixed on a running flex. The record-book, where was it? Not in its proper compartment in the instrument-case. Oh yes, he remembered, the book had fallen off the bed just as he was measuring out the dose; he had picked it up and crammed it in his pocket. He was annoyed, now, to see that it was badly crumpled and had a brown stain across the cover.

When he opened it he did not see his carefully ruled margins, his own neat handwriting. It was covered, page after page, with the swaying, stumbling hand of a child.

Unpardonable carelessness! He had come away with Minna's scribbling book by mistake. He must run up again quickly and get his own book before she started reading it: to let her understand the grim details of her condition might be disastrous.

But his alarm lasted only a moment. Ridiculous to suppose that she could make head or tail of his record, with its tabulated data, figures and symbols. She would learn as much from an Egyptian papyrus. He smiled, turning over Minna's pages: what a contrast with his own precision, this caricature of handwriting, this battlefield of blots and smudges. What was it all about—the story of Minna's life? With a sudden, pale curiosity he began to read.

14

'ANOTHER plate last night. Smithereens. The Witch went on for 20 mins, all about sense of duty etc: I said you can't expect a plate not to smash the floor being brick like that. She said why do you drop it on the floor then. I said there's such a hell of a pile of plates after supper one of thems got to fall off, it was cracked anyway. I said I can't go on wash-ing all those plates three times a day not with this feeling giddy the way I do, why can't you send the Frog to help, what does he do all day long except read the newspapers. So then she slapped me and I laughed and she cried. Then afterwards I cried because the Witch hasn't got hardly any money on account of the Leopard not paying and the Social Democrats ruling the country wrong, and she gets pains in the back which are worse than pains in the chest. I shall tell Fräulein Rother and God.

'Fräulein Rother came last night when I was waiting to clear away supper. She came and sat in the Witch's chair. Her robe was made of peacock's wings and her hair was like a waterfall of golden sparks. I told her I was rude to the Witch and she said I must get up at 4 next morning and do the front passage the Witch generally does. So I did that this morning.

'Sick again, no breakfast. I got the pain, doing Herr Barthol's room, the bit behind Herr Barthol's writing table where you can't get at the dust with the nails sticking up and catching my clout. The pain was like a hot dark sea. It is all right if you don't try to get to the shore again, you must go where the sea takes you, you must be like a fish in the sea. Minna went deep down into the sea, Minna was not frightened, it was hot down there and she swam easily like the fishes do. The grey fish came to swim beside me, his body is like the evening clouds, he is the sign of God's humility. Minna spoke to the fish, she asked why God had sent her into the sea of pain, the fish said that Minna was proud and God must punish her. Minna had been too proud, she thought she was better than all the people in the Witch's house, even better than Herr Rupf. But when you go far down in the sea it is not too hot any more, God does not punish you so much, you can breathe quite easily there.

'Down there I was quiet and not lonely or frightened. I swam with great strokes thrusting back a hill of water thrusting a mountain of hot water at each great stroke. My feet stamped against the water I sprang from the mound of water on which my feet had been, my head pierced through the range of waters like a scythe's stroke cutting the young soft grass. Here the darkness of the sea was broken, the wave of darkness broke into a chain of quiet hills. Here I saw the sun's rosy light showing behind the hills of darkness, like the darkness of the Tastehausen forest pitched on morning sky, like the dark shadows on the curtain of Fräulein Rother's room. Here the sun's light breaking the dark sea cut ribbons of rose and gold, the mist that fell across the sea was gold and green. The fish that swam with me caught a new coat from the sun, his new coat was of green and gold, shining like new snow on the Tastehausen hills, like the evening robes in Berghauer's window. I laughed as I swam and the fish laughed beside me, we were so strong against the water, I and the fish that Fräulein Rother sent to make me un-lonely. Fräulein Rother's fish laughed like a trumpet, our laughing was like the wind in the pine trees at Tastehausen and the music of Tastehausen orchestra in the municipal gardens, it was like all God's angels laughing together in the morning.

'Minna passed by the cave, the dark cave in the bed of the sea. I thought the sea's current wrapped about Minna the garment of water folding Minna's body would draw her to the dark sea-cave where Fräulein Rother lies. I thought I felt the current drawing Minna's body, I saw in the shadows of the caves the satin pillows where they stretch in sleep, in long unbroken sleep, those ones, where they hear no sound but the water's music, the quiet music of the water warmly flowing, the water flowing through their deep cool chambers. Minna would care for the sleepers in that cave, Minna would get up early to get their food, she would dry their plates with a silken cloth, a new silk cloth for every plate she dried. She would not be tired there. But the Witch's voice came down to call her back, Minna was frightened and her arms beat hard against the water, her body rose again, leaving the quietness of the coloured shadows, she struggled up to the high hot sea. The hands of pain caught her by throat and forehead, she could not sink again to the quiet water, she saw the cold light far above and fought to free herself from the angry pain.

'The Witch said that only lazy sluts went to sleep at their work, she said I must come back after dinner and do Herr Barthol's room all over again. She said she would take fifty pfennige off my wages. I told the Witch she was a crumple-bellied sow with a wasp in its mouth, I said you can't clean a floor properly with nails sticking up, I told her the dust all got into my nose and throat and made me sleepy. She said I would find myself in the gutter if I talked to her like that, I said the gutter wouldn't be so hot and sticky as her filthy kitchen. Frog Spühler came to the kitchen after dinner, he said the Witch had gone to bed cum headache.

'I will write more diary to-morrow night. Too tired now.

'I woke up early and the pain was bad. I cried a long time. I wasn't crying for the pain hurting me, I was crying because I can't beat it, the pain takes hold of my head to make me angry and proud. That is why I am cruel to the Witch.

'But it is only the wicked who are proud and cruel when they have pain. Fräulein Rother had cancer of the breast, the man who came to do her up for the funeral told me that. Sometimes in the classroom she went quite white, her face was like the statue of the old queen in the municipal museum, she held the sides of the desk as if she was trying to break it, she could not speak for a long time and all of us were frightened. But afterwards she said she was sorry to have made us frightened, it was only a chill she said, and then she smiled and was specially kind to us. Fräulein Rother told me the pain did her good, it put her in the same family as the blind and cripples and hunchbacks and all the poor bastards with hare lips and squidgy eyes and spotty faces. I said it was how you were made, to feel like that when the pain got you. She told me she was not made like that, she was made proud and wicked, she had only got like that. But the headaches don't make me get like that.

'To-day when I was doing out the flues I thought it was because the pain wasn't bad enough. Fräulein Rother used to go as if she was being frozen from the inside, she bit her lips so as once there was blood there afterwards, she made a singing noise like the old dog Fritzel when he was asleep. We could all of us feel it then inside ourselves how it was hurting her. I thought while I was doing the flues, it must have been because it was so bad that she got so beautiful and loving. But oh God I don't want that oh dear God I can't put up with pain like that, it only makes me worse oh God, the pains I have, I don't want to go all white and sweating and have my face twitching and my finger nails dug into my hands like that. Oh God isn't there some other way to kill the wicked part of me, it's only the outside part that's proud and selfish, couldn't you take that away without so much freezing pain like Fräulein Rother's?

'To-morrow I'll do the beds in the Witch's room and Frau Rupf's room, that the Witch generally does.

'Herr Rupf spoke to me this morning, he stopped in the

passage and asked what I did on my holidays. It is moving to feel that Herr Rupf is my friend, in this place I haven't many friends. I didn't say anything because my mouth wouldn't work and I heard the Witch calling.

'A lot of coughing to-day. I was frightened in case the Witch saw my handkerchief that had got all bloody. Must go down and clean it in the sink when the Witch has gone to bed.

'The coughing would not make me angry and cruel if it wasn't for pride. It is because I think all the people in this house except Herr Rupf and the young doctor are all stupider than me and I am the only important person. I suppose when you get old you get better about that, you get to see it isn't other people's fault that they're so stupid and unimportant. I want to get old so that I can be humble enough to love other people.

'But it takes so long to get old. The days go by like the tired horses dragging sandcarts up the Hügelstrasse, the days are so heavy and there are still so many to come.

'Oh God let me get back in the end to Fräulein Rother, don't let her get too far away, don't let her forget me. Fräulein Rother's hands were as gentle as a dove's breast, her voice was warm like morning sunshine, she was never too tired or ill to talk to me. Even if my heart is proud I will do unselfish things, I will do more work to make up what I owe Frau Spühler. And if the pride has to be burnt away with pain I will go into that fire with my heart singing as your own saints used to sing, I will keep my eyes wide open looking for Fräulein Rother beyond the flames, I will march with head held bravely and gather the flames to me like gathering sheaves of wheat. But oh God don't take my brain away, let my brain stay clear to read some books and listen to the talk when I go into the dining-room. Only hurt me enough to make me humble like Fräulein Rother was, enough to make me love all lovely things, and all the ugly things, as Fräulein Rother did . . .'

15

HE WAS sleeping badly, a new experience. Having got to bed shortly before two o'clock he regularly woke at about half-past three, with head aching and a dead tired body, his brain fully conscious. The darkness became intolerable then, he would turn on the light and go through some notes, try to do some calculations he had jotted down for odd moments. But at that hour his mind worked like a leaky pump, the room's familiar shape oppressed him, he could always hear faintly, like the faulty undertones of an engine, the noise of Minna coughing.

To a patient in that condition he would glibly have advised a change of scene. He had never thought of taking a holiday himself: with the Zeppichmanns the word holiday meant a day when you were obliged to close your shop and lose money: but now, two days after the third injection, he decided to give himself an evening's amusement.

A copy of *Hartzinnfelde Zeitung* which he found in the staff mess gave him a choice of entertainments: there were five political meetings in different parts of the town, Rosa Wittke was singing in the Feurich-Saal, Dr. Hermann Linderstädt was to lecture on Paranoia. No, those would not do, he wanted gaiety, he wanted to talk and laugh with his friends . . . Friends? He hadn't any.

He had almost decided to spend the evening reading the medical papers when he thought of an invitation that Ahlwarth had given him. Dr. Ahlwarth, the young assistant in the out-patients' department who was always enjoying some obscure joke of his own, had treated him most amiably. He had said, shortly after Josef's arrival, "If you're ever at a loose end, come round to my digs. 24C Zeugerstrasse. My girl and I are nearly always there, we keep open house . . ." Yes, one ought to have some friends, to get some practice in social behaviour. An evening call was not irregular, he supposed: it was seven o'clock now, and by the time he got to the other side of the town the Ahlwarths would certainly have finished their evening meal. After hunting in the chest of drawers he found that he had one clean collar.

As the crowded tram pitched and squealed down the Langebergstrasse he remembered that he had said nothing to his patient about going out. As a rule he made a last visit shortly before nine o'clock to note her temperature and make her comfortable for the night. Well, that last visit was scarcely more than a formality; she would surely have the sense to turn the light out and settle down by herself. But he should have said something: the ridiculous diary had shown him that the girl suffered from an advanced neurosis, and he had to keep her mind's field as smoothly rolled as he could. For a moment he thought of getting off the tram and going back.

That was ridiculous, too fussy. From the shop lights passing he saw they were near the river now, and he had taken a through ticket to the Burchardt terminus. He kept his seat, and got off at the Statsfurter Square.

Remotely, as he stood and shivered on the pavement, he realised that he was glad to go for fourteen hours without seeing her. The hospital wards were tedious enough, but there you saw a succession of invalids, most of them only once a day; you did or said what was required and passed on, it was the nurses' business to see to them after that, the nurses had brain enough for nothing else. To see a feeble-minded girl three times a day, to spend from ten to thirty minutes every time in her mousetrap of a room, always feeling the intentness of her strange eyes: that was a heavy trial to a young man's patience. He deserved an evening off.

After ten minutes the wriggling lights of the Burchardt tram came loose from the thicket of lamps beyond the river, it tilted up and swung across the bridge. This was to take him into a part of the town he did not know, and the tram's population gave him the key of it: faces like perished rubber, boots that were hardly more than sandals, a boy's cheek and forehead raked with impetigo. For the first time he wondered whether he had been right to put on his better suit. The smell of these people was familiar, a smell of wool baked in sweat, the drifting aromas of vegetables and fish. In his boyhood every house except his own had its smell on that foundation, and even in boyhood he had found it distasteful. Now it had become as strange to him as doublet-and-hose, and he was faintly surprised that Ahlwarth, unpretentious as he was, lived on such a tram-route. Yes, the blue serge was probably wrong.

Already he felt that this evening was a mistake, he was spending time and getting nothing for it. This tram moved like a wounded ox, it seemed to be always waiting in the loopways. His fellow passengers, accustomed all their lives to awaiting other people's convenience, sat in a dull complacency, the air grew thicker with their breathing. In a bout of nausea Josef shut his eyes and at once he was back in Minna's room.

The state of the arm, that was his real worry. The general condition was worse, but he had expected such a setback at this stage. He had also expected a local morbid reaction at the place of injection. But the swelling should have abated by now. There was a rash he could not precisely identify spreading right down to the wrist, and a still larger area of cutaneous sensitivity, which interfered with the girl's sleep. He remembered a case that Plünnecke had mentioned where an ordinary calf-lymph inoculation had produced toxic reactions so severe that the arm had to be amputated. Supposing, now, that it came to calling in a surgeon! That would

not only mean the end of this experiment: one way or another news would reach the Moltke Hospital almost as soon
as the surgeon arrived and then there would be Wildelau to
settle . . . Perhaps he should have applied a Zeliche poultice before leaving her this evening . . . He was beginning
to feel it like an ulcer in his temples, this anxiety which he
had to carry all by himself.

It was starting to rain when they got to the terminus.
The conductor, pointing eastwards, told him that Zeugerstrasse was under a kilometre that way.

This was another town, it was like a city punished by
war. Sparse lamps showed a house in every three boarded for
sale, a window in every ten gave the street a wisp of light.
The people were abroad; but they weren't hurrying to reach
the shops before closing hour, there was no group of boys
shouting their way along the road as they did in Handelstrasse. They stood in a line against the wall, the people
here, with no protection against the gusty rain; they did not
seem to notice it. They stared at Josef as he passed, discussed him in a phlegmy undertone; and where there was
light enough to see their faces they were like the faces of a
theatre chorus, the eyes feverishly brilliant.

He had come to a web of streets, a camp of little houses
thrown where it took the builder's fancy.

"Can you direct me please," he asked a boy sitting on
a doorstep, "I'm trying to find my way to Zeugerstrasse."

The child giggled.

"Zeugerstrasse? He's gone away, gone away, gone away
a-wenching. Knock on the bed and pull the sheets and surely
you will find him."

But a woman leaning from an upper window called
hoarsely that he should go straight on, and in another hundred yards he reached a street of greater maturity, an an-
tenna of Hartzinnfeld trimmed with bourgeois houses. This
was Zeugerstrasse, and the house he wanted stood right op-

posite, a villa of some pretension, huge in the darkness. He saw no light in any window, the bell-pull only brought a rattle of rusty wire and the patter of plaster falling; but the door stood open and he went inside.

The air was musty, and his footsteps on the tiled floor cracked hollowly against the high bare walls. It was like a theatre when the audience has gone. There were voices somewhere, he thought they came from above; and a door continually banging. He struck a match and went up the bare staircase to the first landing, another match and on again. But at the second landing he stopped, a little scared by the weight of emptiness. He thought he could hear, now, the sound of a bed creaking; and suddenly a woman's voice quite close to him said, "Oh God, my arm, my arm!"

He ran then, back to the stairs, clung to the handrail and let his feet find what steps they could, was down both flights before he could collect himself. The pan of light from the door, with the moist air blowing in, brought him to his senses. What feebleness, to let his nerves play such a trick! But he could still have sworn the voice he had heard was Minna's.

As he stood in the darkness, letting the vibration of his body work itself out, the rectangle of light was broken; a man who smelt of onions came in and began to feel his way down the passage towards the back of the house. He would have walked right into him if Josef had not spoken.

"Excuse me, I wonder—"

The man jumped.

"Who's that?"

A pair of hands, skinnily strong, seized Josef's wrists as neatly as if the two men stood in broad daylight.

"Keep still," the man said hoarsely, and called out, "Franz! Come here, quick!"

From a lower floor footsteps came up to the end of the passage, there a door was kicked open, letting out a sprinkle of light. Mercifully, it was Ahlwarth's voice that Josef heard.

"Well, Neuling, what the devil's wrong with you?"

"Bloody spy!" Neuling shouted.

Josef brought his heels together.

"Doctor Zeppichmann!" he said.

As the candle which Ahlwarth carried came nearer he could see that the man who held him so fiercely had a boy's figure; only his dark head, dripping with rain, showed the size and hardness of a man's: a miner's head, the face spare and white, eyes far recessed and brilliant.

"There is some misunderstanding!" Josef said.

Ahlwarth, coming up to them, broke into laughter.

"Spy indeed—you slug-wit! Let him go, fool, this is my friend Zeppichmann, the most respectable member of the Moltke staff—we're all of us proud of our Doctor Zeppichmann!"

He took an arm of each and led them along the passage.

"Well, how was I to know!" Neuling said gloomily. "The bastards are everywhere, they follow me about."

But at the end of the passage he stopped and took Josef's hand. "Apologies, brother!" he said warmly. "I get scared, you see, in dark places. They shot at me once, down on the canal bank. It's like that, you get scared. People that smell flush, always scared of them! No harm intended."

"I myself sometimes find darkness rather alarming," Josef said.

They followed Ahlwarth down to the basement.

The long room, floored with cheap linoleum, had the smell of a beershop, and all its hardworn furniture might have come from beerhouse auctions.

"I'm sorry the light's not better," Ahlwarth said. "They've cut off the current for some reason so we have to make do with these lamps. This is Friede Tscherloh who lives with me."

Unused to the light, Josef saw indistinctly a plump girl who lay across a bed at the end of the room. Nervously, he went that way and clicked.

"Doctor Zeppichmann."

Fräulein Tscherloh took out her cigarette but did not move.

"You should have come earlier," she said in the friendliest way, "that awful Dreigerschmidt has been here, he's finished all the beer."

"Dreigerschmidt, he's always in front of me!" Neuling said, with a child's temper in his voice.

Friede laughed.

"Come here then and give me a kiss! . . . There, is that better?" She swept her eyes round to Josef. "You too?"

"Well, thank-you, gnädiges Fräulein, no!" Josef said unhappily. "Er—not this evening!"

"She means well," Ahlwarth remarked. "I'm sorry about the beer. One minute, I've got cigarettes somewhere. Yes, you must have one. Wait a mo', just let me shift this gramophone . . . Now, you can sit here—I'm sorry the place is so untidy, the one trouble with Friede is she's lazy. Yes, my precious, you're a lazy slut and you know it, you make my life a misery."

But he did not look unhappy. At the hospital he was always pertly cheerful, here his cheerfulness had become a glowing warmth. With a young host's eager restlessness he shoved his clumsy length about the room, smiling, raking his lanky hair, hunting for cigarettes; stopped to wipe some beer-slop off the arm of Josef's chair, to pat Neuling's shoulder, to plant a resounding kiss on Friede's cheek.

"You," he said to Neuling, "you ought to be at home looking after your family instead of trying to murder respectable doctors in my mansion. Who've you got to put your children to bed?"

Neuling grinned. "I did it myself an hour ago. All four of them."

"I thought it was five now," Friede said.

Neuling shut his eyes.

"No, four it is. The last one died, thank God." He turned, smiling, to Josef. "My wife's got trouble in the breast," he said, "not much, you know, but painful. You'll understand that, being a doctor. That's why I mind the children—I've nothing else to do. Hurts her, you understand, across here. Herr Ahlwarth here'll tell you, cancer he **says** it is. That right?"

Ahlwarth nodded, and Neuling smiled.

"Well, there it is. It's bad at night, you know, comes on then. She cries a lot, and that sets the children off. That's why I go out of an evening, I can't stand that, not all through the night. Cheerful girl she always was—a good girl too, earned ten Marks a week doing the schoolhouse over there, kept the children lovely. I don't know how it is, but I can't stand it when she's blubbing."

Ahlwarth, sitting on the table and playing an imaginary violin, said with sudden ferocity:

"I'll get it fixed this week, I'll have her in the hospital if I have to murder some one!" He turned to Josef. "Five times I've been to Wildelau already, and all he says is that the cancer ward's full-up. Did you ever hear such impertinence!"

Josef said modestly: "I believe they are overcrowded in that department—"

"Then why the devil can't they enlarge the department! Why can't they stick up a new building, get some more doctors and nurses. D'you think there are no doctors out of a job? And no bricklayers?"

"I imagine it would be a question of capital—"

"Exactly, yes, capital! If there were two hundred wealthy Junkers on the waiting-list, d'you suppose Wildelau would simply tell 'em the ward was full? D'you think he'd say he must limit the number of cases received in order to maintain his nursing standards? You'd think from the way he talks that medicine is just a decoration of life, practised by enthusiastic artists!"

Friede, rolling over on to her back, said:

"But, Franz, darling, if the money isn't there I don't see how Wildelau is going to make it."

"The money *is* there!" Ahlwarth said furiously. "Go and look in the windows of Obermüller's and you'll see evening gowns priced at RM 600, you'll see fur coats at three or four thousand. Well, some one's going to buy that stuff, I suppose!"

"Well, Franz!"

The door had opened very quietly, Josef had only noticed a whiff of brandy. The man who stood there, smiling, had a grey suit that matched his hair, perfectly tailored; only the cloth was thin, covered with stains, and the trousers were frayed at the shoes.

"A bloody night, don't you think?"

He came forward with a popular actor's confidence, pushed a hand into Ahlwarth's hair, went over to the bed and patted Friede's quarters.

"Got a job to-day!" he said. "Selling tickets for some screecher. Agreeable. Remuneration dainty. It lasted, unhappily, for just five hours. Result!" He pulled up a bottle from his trousers. "All right, Friede, don't get so excited!"

Ahlwarth gazed at him abstractedly.

"Listen, Major! I was telling these people that if the population of Hartzinnfeld can afford RM 600 for an evening dress it can afford to put more beds in the hospital."

The Major nodded.

"I expect you're right. Has no one in this bloody outfit got a knife?—I can't get this cork out with my finger-nails. Yes, I expect you're right. More beds, I'm all in favour. Complete with lovely occupants. Only question is, where the devil d'you find the wherewithal to pay the lovely occupants?"

"I tell you," said Ahlwarth, "there's money in this town enough——"

"Yes yes, I know there's money in this town. There's everything you want in this bloody town except a job. (Wash this mug for me, Friede, there's a duck.) Take me back to the war, that's what I say. They treated you like dirt and they fed you like swine, but at least they gave you something to do. How's your lady, Neuling?"

"Not good. She blubs almost all the time."

"I say, I'm sorry about that. I'm damned sorry. Mine's dead, thank God, so I don't have that worry. Here, have a drink. Prosit! Here's to all the swine that have got us like we are. You, I don't know your name——"

"Doctor Zeppichmann, if you please."

"——That'll do as well as anything. Drink! Go on, get on with it! Here's to the swine aforesaid, may they burn!"

"The question," Ahlwarth said, "is——which particular swine?"

The Major threw out a generous arm.

"The bankers, the stock-wanglers, the landowners; town councillors, pimps and pawnbrokers. Any one who's had a good square meal since the war. That'll do to get on with. Prosit! May they scorch slowly!"

Josef modestly drank.

He thought that without rudeness he might take his leave now, but did not know quite how to manage it. Perhaps he need only say a word in Ahlwarth's ear, thanking him for his hospitality and begging to be excused, then make a general bow and slip upstairs. He began edging his way along the wall to where Ahlwarth, with his back turned to the Major, was now arguing trenchantly with Friede.

His movement was cut off. The door, violently kicked, swung open again, a girl with grey hair hanging in rat-tails round her yellow face splashed into the room, a trio of men behind her. "God!" the girl said, "how this place stinks! Whose is the Schnapps?"

"Help yourself!" the Major said. "Here, use Neuling's glass, he's not more consumptive than you are."

"A pleasure!" Neuling said.

Ahlwarth looked round and smiled.

"No business for you here, Anna. The Major had five Marks but he's blued it. No one else has got any."

The girl drank the glass half-empty and passed it to the man behind her.

"I don't want business," she said quietly, "I want some one's face smashed in. Heard what they've done to Paul?"

The man behind her, gently stroking the red skin on the side of his face where eye and cheek were missing, said: "Fftt! Every one knows about that."

"You shut up!"

"Let her vomit it!" the Major said. "No good strapping up a wench's tongue. Here, Anna, here's a cigarette for you. It's my last, so give me your blessing."

"I'll give you more than that," she said. Like one deliberately focussing attention on herself she took a long time to light the cigarette, staring at the flame as if it were an animal whose tricks amused her. "Well, they've got Paul where they wanted now." She hardly moved her lips when she spoke, you had said she was a marionette for which a conjuror used a tiny, harsh falsetto. "Spraacke, it was, he fixed the whole thing. He wanted Paul's job. Paul's first job in ten years, and Spraacke wanted it. Spraacke fixed it with the foreman."

The Major shrugged his shoulders. "That's natural. You don't expect to hold a job if you don't fix the foreman."

"Yes, and the foreman, d'you know how *he* fixed it? Told Paul to oil the worm-gears in the Spann husker. Watched him till he had his hand in. Then he kicked on the power."

Ahlwarth whistled. "My God, what's happened to Paul's hand?"

"Happened?" Anna laughed. "You should know! I expect they've sent it up to your hospital for you to play with, forearm and all. You can do things with a disused forearm, can't you? Use it to teach the young doctors." Her face was whiter than a mushroom, but she still seemed perfectly steady; she smoked fast, gobbling at the cigarette, hunting every cloud of smoke with another jerked from her nostrils. "Or do you think I've cooked it up for the kids? I tell you I would if I could get it. It's not a lot of fresh meat they ever taste, with the men all beating me down to RM 4.50 a night."

The Major eyed her with interest. He always admired Anna, there was so much resilience in her wasted, concave body.

"You can bring an action," he said. "Get damages off the company."

"Damages?" She put an arm round the Major's neck, leant forward and laughed as if a pair of prize cocks were fighting in her chest. "Damages! With Drenker-Schersking on the Bench?" The laughter stopped and she pushed his head away brutally. "D'you remember what happened to the last Marxist that went in front of Drenker-Schersking?"

Sitting all by himself, contented in his own sombre way, Neuling nodded gravely.

"That's right," he said, "the Court's no good. No good for a working person. May be all right if you're in a job. No good for a working person if you've not got a job. They come down on you."

Anna did not hear him. She was clutching the Major's arm, leaning on his shoulder and faintly giggling. "Listen, listen, I haven't told you the funniest part. We went to the police-office, Willi here and I, we went to the police-office, we told the officer about it, I said I'd sue the Company. And what d'you think? He'd had the Company's lawyer in, the

Company's going to act against Paul for inattention to
duty."

She was weeping now. The stiffness left her face as
when the wire is drawn from a crinoline, it was the face of a
child weeping.

"That's right," the one-cheeked man said. "It put the
machinery all wrong, Paul's arm being stuck in it like that.
They'll claim on him for spoiling the machinery."

The Major had been listening as a lawyer would, nodding and nodding, while his cigarette burnt down to his lips.
Suddenly he stiffened.

"Who did you say it was? Who was the bastard who
fixed it?"

Neuling answered him:

"Spraacke, she said it was. That would be him, I know
that bastard. Always round with the Nationalists."

The Major nodded.

"Spraacke, yes, I know him! Herr Spraacke is in for a
surprise . . ."

The voice was as soft as a cat's paw, the claws still
retracted. Watching his eyes, Josef knew from Richterhausen
days that the man had reached a further stage in intoxica-
tion: that point where the brain is quick and sure as a surgeon's hands, only the judgement left in cloud. There was
danger here. And he would have stolen away, but the close-
ness held him. There had come into this tawdry room
something more than the warmth of stale bodies drying and
breathing together: it was Kameradschaft, it was a religious
unity.

Ahlwarth had moved round the table, he caught hold
of Anna's wrists.

"Quiet!" he said urgently. "Come, Anna, loosen-up.
What's happening to Paul now? Why didn't you bring him
to me?"

She said jerkily: "He's in the Lützowstrasse clinic.
They said there wasn't a bed in the Moltke."

"Who's the doctor? Who's looking after him?"

"Doctor Grohne."

Ahlwarth spat. "What the devil does Grohne know about a surgical case! Might as well go to a blasted vet." He turned to Josef, letting his voice dive beneath the hub-bub. "Look here, Zeppichmann, I'll want you in on this. We've got to get hold of Wildelau and put the fear of God in him. That hospital was built for the poor and the poor have got first claim on it. My God, we'll see him now, we'll rout him out in his blasted mansion and drive some sense at him. Where's your hat, or haven't you got one?"

For Josef it was like being casually asked to take a jump from a church tower.

"But—one can't call on a gentleman at this time! . . . I understand that Doctor Grohne is a very able clinician, he has been in practice many years—"

"You," Ahlwarth said shortly, "would *you* treat a serious case in a poky half-lit shack of a place about eight metres by ten? D'you think it's a doctor's business to hang on to cases just so as to test some crank theory of his own?—that's what Grohne's doing every day!"

Josef put his hands in his coat-pockets. "In any case I was about to tell you," he said resolutely, "I must be get-ting home now, I have some private work to do. I am most obliged—"

"Private work?" Ahlwarth stared at him, no longer angry, only overcome by curiosity. "But surely—with a doc-tor—there's no such thing as private work. I mean—we're all in it, aren't we? We're all at the same thing, trying to reduce the world's filthy flood of pain—"

"But we go about it in different ways," Josef said.

They were talking in the special privacy which you can find in noisy, crowded rooms. A wave of quietness dis-turbed them. Then Neuling spoke:

"At the Bierstube Moritz, that's where you'd find him now. The Moritz, that's where Spraacke and his lot go."

The one-cheeked man buttoned his coat.

"The Moritz? Good! We'll start by smashing that."

"Stop!" the Major said. "You listen to me, I understand these things. No good smashing up the Moritz, it's as like as not Spraacke gets away without a dent on him. You never get your man that way."

"I don't mind who I get," Anna said quietly. "I just want to smash up the face of one bloody Nationalist. They've had Paul's arm and that's going to pay for it—I'll get a night's sleep after that. Some one give me a fag!"

"Much better make Spraacke pay the bill himself!" the Major said reasonably. "It's easy enough. There's a back way out of the Moritz—into Verbin's yard. Just chuck in one fuldner bomb and Spraacke'll go out that way as sure as sodomy, having Paul's arm on his mind. The yard's a tidy place to deal with him."

"What's the good?" Ahlwarth said quietly. "If you smash up Spraacke they'll only get their own back."

He was answered by Friede. "Don't interfere, Franz! They've got to learn, those people. If Spraacke gets off without a mark on him they'll think they can do what they like."

The Major had crossed over to Neuling.

"The first thing is to secure a fuldner," he said.

"And where do we get that?"

"Off Simon Gehrmann. He's got 'em in a cellar under the shop. Eight Marks, and they're dead reliable. Police stuff."

"Yes, and who's got eight Marks?"

"I've got 1.50," Willi said, and threw the coins on the table.

It had become a business meeting, they were sober and thoughtful. Five more coins landed on the table and Friede counted.

"7.60," she said, and looked all round. "I suppose, Doctor Zeppichmann, you haven't by any chance—?"

Josef hardly hesitated. If a handful of pfennige would

get him out of this he was ready to lose it. He put down a five-Mark note.

"If that will help you——" he said awkwardly.

To his horror, Friede leant over the table, caught him by the shoulders and kissed his lips.

"Franz! Why didn't you tell us? Why didn't you say he was a millionaire?"

They were all staring at the note as if it were ectoplasm, and Neuling was beginning to cry. "Something over," he said hoarsely, "there'll be something over! If I could have something—just fifty pfennige—just to buy a pastry for my babies . . ." Josef felt Ahlwarth's hands pulling him away.

"Here, come with me a moment!" Ahlwarth whispered.

Thankfully, Josef followed him out of the room. They stopped at the top of the stairs.

"Listen!" Ahlwarth said quietly. "It's my fault, I suppose, I shouldn't have had you here, my friends are people you don't understand. But why were you such a fool as to chuck your money about? Don't you see what'll happen? Neuling will get that bomb for them, so as to have the change. Oh yes, they'll make him, nothing'll stop 'em now. If he gets caught with it he'll get twelve months. What happens to his wife then?"

Josef breathed heavily.

"I'm sorry, but it isn't my affair. I don't understand people like that, my parents always kept with respectable people, I don't want to be mixed up with any rowdiness——"

"Yes, but that girl—Anna—don't you want to help her? Don't you see what a state she's in? That husband of hers, the only man on earth who's ever really loved her——"

"Well, I've paid for their bomb, haven't I! I don't see——"

Ahlwarth said with his teeth fastened: "Yes, you've paid for their bomb all right. That was bloody helpful, wasn't it! You think it'll do them all a world of good, going off and raising hell in the Moritz!"

"Well, that was what they wanted. They wanted excitement, I suppose——"

Ahlwarth no longer troubled to keep his voice down. "Yes, of course they want excitement, it's all they've got to live on! And do you think it's a doctor's business to give sick people what they want?"

"But I'm not their doctor."

"Well, whose doctor are you? Do you mean you'll only use your knowledge of healing for people who pay you? Do you think any one needs a doctor more than people like those?"

The man was surely not quite sane, Josef thought: this talk of doctoring as if it were a kind of evangelism! . . . It was interesting, of course; a German proud of his nation was interested in all such philosophical notions; but to raise them at such a moment as this!

"I think you must leave these things to my own judgement," he said. "My medical course involved great sacrifices, and—and really I am not unsympathetic with poor people, I lived among them for many years . . . I must be getting home now, it was kind of you——"

Ahlwarth was holding his arm.

"I want you," he said steadily, "to go and get back that note. Now, quickly, before they've got a chance to use it."

"I'm sorry, Doctor Ahlwarth, I—I haven't time now. It's up to you, you must persuade them to use it sensibly— get some food or something. I should be glad to think I'd done something to help them."

Ahlwarth let go.

"Very well!" he said, and went down the stairs again. From the bottom he called back, coolly, "I must say, Zeppichmann, I thank God I'm not a patient of yours."

16

WHY should he feel faintly guilty? If he had done something wrong it was Ahlwarth's fault. Ahlwarth had asked him to come here, had seemed to welcome him. Ahlwarth should have made it clear to his peculiar friends that he, Josef, was some one of a different kind, a respectable person, a man of education. Really he had been placed in a most difficult position.

As he groped towards the street door he decided it was not a sense of guilt that rubbed him. He was somehow a little envious of Ahlwarth, that was all: envious of the self-assurance which gave him a philosopher's spectacles. Yes, it was simply a question of background. From Ahlwarth's speech, his walk, the way he wore his shabby clothes, one knew he had never had to struggle. Life came to you differently when you started from a backstreet in Richterhausen, you had to fight every inch of it . . . Well, that was over, thank God, and he wouldn't waste an evening on social exercises again.

Reaching the door he breathed the clean air gratefully. The clouds had risen, and a scudding moon broke the wet street into solid shapes. He seemed to have woken from a liverish dream.

He was half-way over the road when he noticed a group of men standing by the wall of a house a little way up the street; a dozen, perhaps—the wall gave them its shadow and he could not see them distinctly. To reach the tram-stop by the way he had come meant passing close to them, and he did not care for that; they stood so very still, so quietly. He turned to go the other way, and instinctively increased his pace; but he heard swift footsteps following, and some one called,

"One moment, please!"

The voice was cultured, but its tone hard-stropped. Josef turned round.

It was quite a youngster, seventeen or so, who stood there pointing a torch at Josef's face.

"Excuse me," he said, with the quick pleasantness of a hotel receptionist, "I think you came out of that house over there, 24 C?"

"Yes yes."

"You have been to see some one there?"

"Yes, I was visiting my friend Doctor Ahlwarth."

"Doctor Ahlwarth, oh yes! And your name is—?"

With the torch splashing his eyes Josef could see nothing distinctly, but he realised that a second member of the silent group had moved a little towards him. Mentally he was not frightened. But in this situation the shape of a forgotten incident was repeated: a cul-de-sac in Richterhausen, a stifling afternoon in August when one of the schoolboy feuds was on: and he found that his pulse had quickened. Whatever they wanted, these men, one thing was clear enough: they could do what they liked with him. The obvious course was simplicity.

"My name?" he said. "Why, I'm no one of any importance, I'm just a junior house-surgeon from the Moltke Hospital. Doctor Zeppichmann, that's my name . . . Good night!"

"One moment!" the boy said again. He cocked the torch under one arm, pulled out a notebook and wrote the name down. "And your address?"

"I happen to be in rather a hurry—"

"And your address?" the boy repeated.

"Handelstrasse 149."

Recording it, the boy asked, "Number 149, you said? That's where Herr Erich Meisel lives, isn't it?"

"Herr Meisel, yes. Yes, quite a friend of mine."

"Indeed! . . . And who else is with Doctor Ahlwarth this evening?"

That question took Josef by surprise; and because the scientist's mind is quickened by the unexpected it made his thoughts move like the links of a slack chain suddenly brought into tension: Ahlwarth's friends—these men's enemies—Ahlwarth's friends coming out any moment—betrayal —Ahlwarth despising him more than ever.

"I beg your pardon?" he was saying. "I didn't quite hear."

The boy said sharply: "I asked you who else is there this evening!"

Who else? In his mind's camera he saw them all together—Anna's racked form and bloodless face, the naïve, hurt face attached to Neuling's froglike body, Friede with her fat legs waving in the air . . . They were friends, those people sharing out their last few cigarettes in Ahlwarth's dingy basement; they were nearer to himself than this presumptuous jackanapes. With sudden resolution, he said:

"If you really want to know, there wasn't anybody— no one but myself. And now if you don't mind I'll be getting on."

That unexpected firmness had its effect. The boy, aiming his torch, held Josef's face for a moment in a clawing scrutiny. "Oh!" he said, with a trace of confusion. "Well then, that's all right, you can go now." He turned and walked back towards his friends.

Josef went on at a stroll, even pausing to light a cigarette. That was the way, he thought—ignore these swashbucklers, show them he wasn't scared. He would keep on like this till he reached the first corner, then turn and put on pace. But he had not got so far when he heard a noise behind him: the Major's whistling laugh, and then, quite clearly through the night's silence, the hysterical voice of Anna: ". . . care who it is as long as I smash up some one."

The sensible course was to run—he knew that. Instead of running he turned round, shouted with all the wind in his lungs:

"Look out! Go back!"

If Ahlwarth's friends had been clearheaded enough to take that warning they might have got back in time. But they had reached the middle of the road, chattering like school-boys, before they seemed to hear anything. They stopped then, and their halt served as signal to the men who were waiting.

Josef was standing still. Out of an instant's silence the first sounds that reached him were a thud and a scream to-gether. Then the rush of feet over the gritty surface of the road, a cry cut off as if a switch were turned, the hiss of clothes tearing. The moon was behind a cloud and he saw the scuffle only as in early cinematograph, a clot of wrig-gling shapes that bunched and spread. But when the shifting clouds spilt a moment's light he had a glimpse of a circle neatly formed, the men on its circumference stooping and rising with the regularity of labourers beating a carpet. The screaming had all stopped by then; nothing was going on except this methodical swing of shoulders, and beyond the thumping noise there was no sound but a chain of throaty cries, as if a stammerer were trying to shout a message to the whole of Hartzinnfeld.

Some one got loose from the shambles and came towards him at the loping hobble of a hen with a weight on its legs: it was Neuling, whimpering like a child; his face, as Josef saw it, a wet dish-cloth squeezed into a ball. He was ten yards off when another man broke from the skirmish and came in pursuit.

As if he were a child watching his first circus Josef

stayed where he was and let Neuling stumble blindly past him; his eyes were on the man who followed. He would have stayed like that, a bemused spectator, if Neuling hadn't fallen. The shaking thump of that fall, the pitiful cry, made him turn his head; in one moment he saw Neuling's body like a black pillow pitched in the roadway, heard the pursuer's excited shout and the speeded clatter of his feet; then a spurt of reckless anger tightened all his limbs and he jumped across to intercept.

The man was coming too fast to dodge, his weight poured over Josef's body like a landslide. Sight and hearing went out together. Josef only knew that his shoulder was in biting pain, that his right hand clutched at something soft, his left struck flesh and struck it again as the roadway and the patchy sky swept up together round his head. Then he was lying on his stomach with his mouth full of blood and grit, and the man who had charged him lay a yard away, as quietly as a shepherd boy on a summer hillside. Afterwards he remembered that Neuling had disappeared, the moon had shown only the two of them on that expanse of road; but at the time it made no difference. His body took complete control, got itself upright, and then against the tether of pain he was running as he'd never run since boyhood.

17

HE FOUND himself back in the main road, and there the brighter lamps pushed open a little way the sliding shutters of consciousness. One of his trouser-legs was ripped from thigh to ankle. There was some one who mended a tear like that, a little Jew in Karlsruherstrasse. What was his name? —Kurt Wolfe. Wolfe might do it—not an easy job—cost six or seven Marks. But the suit had cost sixty-five—worth it . . . He wondered why he felt so faint, and then as he moved his arm he knew: fracture of the left clavicle. The lamp he watched was bouncing, bouncing, like a harbour-light seen through a port-hole. He sat down on the foot-path.

A cab drew up and the driver helped him in. "Take you to a doctor?" Yes, he must see a doctor. "Doctor Frerk, he's the nearest." No, Frerk belonged to the hospital, he didn't want any one who knew him to see him in this state. Who was it that Ahlwarth had talked about? Grohne! Yes, he would do.

"Doctor Grohne in Lützowstrasse, if you please."

He must have slept in the cab. When he came to himself he was sitting on a leather sofa in a narrow, distempered room, he remembered as from a dream that the cabman had helped him up some steps and that he had paid him, bringing his right hand to his left pocket. Now a door opened and some one said, "Come in here, will you!" He obeyed, walking quite steadily. His brain seemed to be clear now.

"Well, you've been scrapping in the streets, I suppose?"

It was a small, untidy surgery: Josef noticed that a pot of ferns stood in the wash-basin. The man who addressed him—Grohne, he supposed—smelt faintly of brandy; he was an elderly Prussian with pigeon's-egg eyes whose hair and skin looked to have been bleached by equatorial sun. He said:

"I don't know how many more times my evening's work is going to be cut up by rowdies coming in here for treatment. I don't know why you always pick on me."

"I happen to have been attacked," Josef said.

"Indeed, yes, how surprising! Well, you'd better get your coat and shirt off, then we'll see what wants cleaning up."

Josef tried, and the pain nearly tumbled him over.

"If you will help me, please!" he said.

Grohne eyed him more attentively.

"Collar-bone?"

"Yes."

"Wait a bit, then, we'd better cut the sleeve. I've got some scissors somewhere."

"No no, it's a fairly new suit, I—I can manage, I think."

Somehow he managed, with Grohne giving a push or a tug where it seemed to be wanted, rather as a foreman takes a hand in dismantling an old toolshed. Stripped, he stood and waited for Grohne to do something. So long as he kept his arm quite still and his eyes fixed on one object he seemed to be all right. He stared at the table, which was loaded with books and crumpled journals, jars full of mossy growths, a bicycle tyre and an ancient sporting-gun.

Grohne walked all round him, surveying his body with an archaeologist's suspicious eyes.

"You want me to set it, I suppose?"

"If you would be so kind!"

"Right! Well, come over here! You know, I suppose, that this little job hurts like hell?"

"Yes, it seems to. I mean, I've done it scores of times myself."

"What—are you a doctor? Wait, I'll get you some brandy, you'll need that. It's not the best thing, but I haven't anything else. Well, you're a doctor, are you? Shouldn't have thought it!"

"Yes, I work at the Moltke Hospital."

"Oh, that carcass factory!"

"I imagine," Josef said quietly, "that the Moltke has a fairly high reputation all over Germany."

Grohne was hunting for a tumbler.

"Yes," he said, with his lips stretched. "Like the Church of Rome and other pompous institutions it has a reputation equal to its own crazy pretensions. (I thought I had another glass—d'you mind drinking out of mine?) Yes, I know all about the Molkte, worked there myself for a time—until I found I could scrape along better by running a clinic of my own. Not that the clinic counts for anything—it just gives me my bread and butter. Tropical diseases, that's what I'm interested in. I've had most of 'em. I know more about that than any one in Germany, only you can't get anywhere in research unless you've got money behind you. They've had two or three cases at the Moltke that I'd have liked to handle—recurring tertian malaria, that kind of thing. But d'you think they'd let me? I tell you, Wildelau was positively abusive when I saw him about it. Oh no, they've treated cases like that the same way these last thirty years, 'Our Hospital, my dear sir, is dedicated to healing, not to experimentation'—he thought I might kill one of his patients and that would look bad. As if medicine could ever make any progress when you take that attitude! . . . Hullo, are you still feeling groggy?"

"Well, the shoulder's—rather painful. I think I'll—feel better when you've got the bone positioned."

"Yes, I suppose so. Here, you'd better sit down. One minute: look here, does this hurt?"

"No, I don't think the acromion process is damaged at all."

"Does this?"

"Yes."

"Much?"

"Yes."

"Fine! That shows us where we are. Just a simple fracture. I thought as much. Want some more brandy?"

"N-no. Only I—wish you—"

"All right, hold on . . . Oh damn the thing! . . . There! Wait now, where's something to prop you? This'll have to do. Now for God's sake keep it still while I get a bandage . . . You're a bad patient, you know—you resist. Know what I mean?"

". . . Yes."

He had got hold of his handkerchief, he bit it as if his teeth were holding him above a precipice. Would this evening never end! There was still the bandaging, and that might give him as much agony over again. This fellow's hands were like the grapnel of a steam-hoist, a stoker would have treated him more gently. God! he had found a bandage already, he was coming back, here were the stubby yellow fingers under Josef's nose again.

His anticipation was right: Grohne bandaged like a peasant lashing a broken shaft. "The great obstacle to my work," he was saying, "is this having to break off and attend chance patients at every hour of the day and night. No, I'm not quarrelling with you, I realise that fellows of your age have to let off a certain amount of pugnacity in the streets, since we're not yet in a position to fight our real enemies. I'm not blaming you at all. Only you see how it is? This damnable business of earning a living makes my real work practically impossible . . . Do you think you could keep a bit steadier—I can't get any tension if you wriggle . . . Yes, and the people who come to me aren't in the least grateful."

There was something Josef had wanted to say, and between two spasms of pain he got it out.

"I believe you've got a man in your clinic—Paul something—a man who had his arm crushed in a machine?"

Grohne tugged again.

"Arm crushed? Yes, I know the man you mean. I got Mintzler to help me amputate. Fellow's not too good—weedy type, very sensitive to shock. I don't much hope to keep him."

"It's a kind of case we—it's a kind of case they rather specialise in at the Moltke."

"The Moltke's full up."

"But I was thinking, I might arrange things with Doctor Röstel—he's my senior. I mean, if you felt the case—"

"Whatever I feel," said Grohne with finality, "I don't pass on cases to our friend the worthy Wildelau. He's quite as conceited as he need be without that . . . There, how does that feel?"

"I was wondering if you haven't got a shade too much pressure?"

"Fault on the right side!" Grohne said. "Let's just glance over the rest of you. These abrasions don't seem to amount to much. Do you want me to disinfect them?"

"Well, I could do it myself when I got home—"

Grohne nodded.

"Well, yes, that would save a little of my time—I've got a job I badly want to get through to-night. We can fix this shirt on again somehow just to get you home—won't do any harm. I expect you find them pretty fussy about that kind of thing at the Moltke?—I did. It's the same with all these hospitals, they've all got sepsis on the brain . . . Now we'll put the coat over like that—wait a mo', I'll pin it. You feel all right, don't you?"

"Yes yes. I am very much obliged."

"Good. You can go out through this door over here."

"Oh yes! Thank you!"

The trams had stopped. He would have liked to take another cab, but the evening's gaiety had been costly enough already. It wasn't at all certain that Wolfe would be able to mend the trousers . . . There was not much strength left in his legs, but he thought his head was strong enough to drive them.

In daylight he knew the way well enough: the distance was less than four kilometres. Now his concentration was fitful, the streets looked all alike, twice he found himself back at the Statsfurter Square. But weariness gave him a curious patience, and his feet seemed ready to shuffle on for ever if he didn't whip them. For the time his shoulder was not hurting as badly as he had expected, the lingering soreness of the scratches only warmed that tired contentment which is given to soldiers after battle: he had moved about this evening, met new people, he had faced a powerful man and seen him fall. That gin-soaked doctor—he had forgotten the name already—that buttock-fisted dilettante had thought him a common rowdy. Well, that was a stimulating change, for generally he was regarded as a reserved and bookish person. Indeed, he was faintly satisfied to be taken as buccaneer, he was a larger man than he had been five hours ago.

Empty, the town had grown much smaller, all the daytime smells were damp and pale. In the long upward stretch of the Langebergstrasse the sightless ghosts of familiar houses passed him slowly, drawing peculiar shadows across the cobbled road, the farther tramline picking the moon's light was a trail of little fires. The last green lighthouse wearily flashing ODOL . . . ODOL was behind him now, but his brain held on to its soothing monotony, and with a hobbling tune caught from a radio-shop that evening his throat was humming *Odolodól-dol, Odolodól*. A sleepless woman saw from the window beside her shop a torn, bedraggled man elbowing himself along the wall like a leg-chained convict. A strip of light between two houses brushed across him as he passed her; she was startled to see that his tired face was matted with dry blood, and that he was faintly smiling.

Mysteriously, he felt the evening had been a good one. That feeling came from the moment when he stepped between the crumpled Neuling and the man pursuing him. Was that a relic of the Richterhausen days, when he had fought the miners' children to relieve his boredom? He did not think so: since then he had grown to be a rational being, who did not want to fight with any one. He remembered now, as you call to mind the colour of a day long past, his loneliness in Ahlwarth's room, the chilly pride in being different from such gipsies, his tickling envy of their communion: those were people who accepted each other from a common poverty, and Ahlwarth by some power he did not understand had shared their spirit. Such friends were valueless, yet he desired such friendship: something, something they had, and Ahlwarth had, which he had never found . . . He let his eyelids fall, trusting his feet to keep their own direction. His mind was freer now and he seemed to understand in part the little, steady flame of his contentment. Hadn't he flung himself against an enemy of Ahlwarth's friends, did that not entitle him to some part of their mysterious possession? . . . The footpath dropped for a side-street, he stumbled and fell on his knees. Lucky, he vaguely thought, lucky that Grohne had made the bandage so tight. Grohne, most interesting, though of course a charlatan. An interesting evening, meeting new people. But must one fight and break a collar-bone to have such satisfaction? Friends, that was what he wanted: the peculiar sense of unity which friends seemed to have. As yet he hadn't grasped the trick of it, but later, when his great experiment was done and he was famous, Josef would learn the trick and get some.

The fall had shaken him, when at last he turned into Handelstrasse he found it difficult not to wander over into the gutter. The humming in his mouth had given place to an intermittent murmur, as if an old man tucked away in his chest was dying, and now the exaltation flickered out, leaving a summer mist of melancholy. High up, and infinitely far ahead, a single light was showing: that would be somewhere near the Spühlers' house. He began to wonder if he would ever reach it; to wonder if, when all his plans had been achieved, the peculiar happiness of which he had caught a glimpse to-night would ever come to him.

18

BUT while he drowsed his legs went on as doggedly as time, the light became the square of a little window, then his elbow caught the upright of the Spühlers' porch. Inside, the ordinary life from which he had made a wild excursion took hold of him again. This house, with all the windows locked, kept faithfully its homely daytime smells. Automatically, as he had been taught in childhood, he took off his boots, and felt his way across the hall. His hand found unerringly the edge of the coatstand, the newel post, the latch of his own room. There was a certain comfort in these things. Now he would sleep.

He had not switched on the light when a cry came from above, the cry of a child frightened by dreams. It cleared his mind as the single prod of a fork sets a choked conduit flowing: that light, of course, had come from Minna's room.

His faculties fell into service like a tired battalion paraded at dawn. He put the usual things together, sponges, thermometer, lotion; washed his hands as well as the bandages allowed and went upstairs.

She lay across the bed with her head hanging down towards the floor, the bedclothes in a ragged typhoon about her legs. His quiet "Minna! What are you up to?" did not reach her, and for a few moments he stood still, gazing at her luxurious hair (it struck him as pretty in that disorder), listening to the little, inhuman noise she made. "You know," he said, still quietly, "it's silly to lie like that with all the clothes off you. It makes your cough worse, doing things like that. Why didn't you put the light out and go to sleep?"

Impossible, he found, to work with one arm pinioned: to get her back with her shoulders on the pillow, straighten out the blankets. Well, with this one supremely important case he'd spare himself nothing. The girl had taken advantage of his absence to work up a fever—knowing what he did about her mental state he should have expected that—and now he was in for an hour's labour to prevent any further damage. It was tiresome, but as much his fault as hers . . . He sat on the foot of the bed with his back to her and gradually worked his hand and arm free of the bandages. He wanted a rest after that.

When his faintness passed, and the pain had quieted enough to be overridden, he set to work preparing a capital compress. Her moaning had stopped now.

"Why didn't you put the light out?" he repeated. "You're a silly girl, you know, you'll never get to sleep with the light on."

She didn't answer at once; but presently: "My arm. The stuff you stuck in it's burning all the veins."

Yes, he should have looked at that to begin with, he seemed incredibly dull to-night; but the inflammation could hardly have increased to the point of danger during these few hours.

"Here, let me look!"

He had miscalculated. The inflamed area was considerably larger, it frightened him. He thought quickly: 'Impurity in the bovine element? impossible, stuff came from Isenheim. In the nutrient media? no, he had taken every known precaution. Needle? sterilized in Dittmer's plant, resterilized immediately before use . . . Get some one, get some one quickly! Ahlwarth? No, unfriendly now. Some one else from the Staff—Röstel? No, not give himself away. Grohne?—the patron saint of anti-hygienic surgery! Must get some one, some one immediately. Swelling in the arm-pit. A few hours, anything might happen. Amputation . . .'

"I'd like—more water." Her voice was quieter, she had pulled herself together since he came. "It's warm, this in the glass, it tastes like washing-up water."

"Of course, yes!" It meant going down to the draw tap in the passage, and he felt that every moment was of value, and he was so desperately tired. Still . . . "I'll get you some straightaway—here, I'll take the glass, I'll have to clean it."

The journey downstairs gave him time to think more steadily. He had lost his head, it was all nonsense to con-template getting some one in now. If it came to amputation —no, that wasn't to be thought of. There were lots of things to try, starting with Vehne's antiphlogistin—that stuff, they said, would draw the toxins from the base of a cesspit.

He washed the tumbler with Hippler solution and care-fully dried it.

Yes, but what effect would the antiphlogistin have on the P.T.? He had never examined such a question, and could only suppose that the cardinal as well as local P.T. reaction would be mitigated. That would throw out his whole scheme of dosage, and if he took the same measures with every febrile reaction he would never get anywhere . . . It was, after all, a win-or-lose experiment, and the logical course was to trust to luck. Fall by lysis seemed to have started already, and the local toxic reaction might be-gin to work itself out in a few hours . . . He was in his room, putting a kettle on the gas-ring, collecting the Vehne paste, spiritus coloniensis, tincturae aurantii, quininae sul-phatis . . . When he reached the attic again he had still not made up his mind.

"Here you are, it's beautifully cold—I ran the water two or three minutes. I've put something in, it hardly tastes. Make you cooler!"

She had been égarée like a sleepwalker. Now, sitting forward to take the glass, she seemed to come awake, and her eyes gradually brought Josef into focus. She said sharply:

"What is it? What've you done to yourself?"

"What?" He had forgotten that his face was still in such a mess—he hadn't stopped to clean it. "Oh, I had a bit of an accident, I fell down in the road. Come on, there's a good girl, I want you to drink all of that."

"But that bandage, what's the bandage for?"

"Bandage? That's to put my arm in, when I'm not using it."

"But what's wrong with your arm?"

"It's the shoulder. The bone went and snapped. It's a part that often goes—very weak."

"Doesn't it hurt?"

At this moment, when he came to think of it, it was giving him hell.

"Comes and goes," he said. "Now do drink up that stuff and I'll get you comfortable again."

She finished the draught but she wouldn't settle down. It was maddening, just when he wanted her in a comatose condition so that he could handle the sensitive area without much interference. Her large, ophelian eyes followed his movements like a searchlight, he endured once more the sensation of being examined in surgery.

"I could do the bandage again for you," she said suddenly. "I expect I could do it all right."

He laughed. "It takes five years to learn how to bandage a fracture, even as badly as this."

She nodded seriously. It was always a surprise to him that with so frail and fluid a brain she could often appear so intelligent.

"Then you'd better go to bed," she said. "You can't stand about here when you're all bust up like that. There's nothing more I want, my arm won't come off. Go on, go to bed! Yes, please!"

Ah! so the baggage was starting to order him about! If he had lacked any impulse to be thorough to-night he had it now. "I'm going to see to that arm before I think about bed," he said tersely; and realised a moment afterwards that he had committed himself.

No, he wouldn't use the Vehne, but he would apply linseed fomentations hourly. It was ten times the work, but far safer, a thoroughly practical solution: that was, if she could stand up to it—the cutaneous sensitivity of the arm was acute and she might be difficult after the first application. He said:

"Just wait a few moments, I'm going to make up a warm poultice."

"Will that hurt a lot?"

"A bit."

In his room he found the kettle boiling already, but preparing the poultice was a long job. She was asleep when he returned. He took the opportunity to examine her face, looking for the indications detailed in Basel-Hirsch, but his eyes were too tired for scientific vision. All that they showed him, more vividly than he had ever observed it before, was the startling change that a human face can undergo in the few seconds of passing from consciousness to sleep. It was as if he had seen in quick succession two different beings, the one a resolute young woman, the second a girl worn out with the evening's hardship, passive, tenderly young. Still holding the kettle, he stood motionless; and his mind, left on an easy rein, went off to another night: something the queer man Rupf had said about an invalid's *persona*. Rupf should be here now, to philosophise upon the personality of Minna . . . For himself, he thought he preferred her in the present aspect: a patient should be altogether under your control, and in this gentleness she seemed so. His case, his private case! At the moment when he touched her, pulling down the blanket to loose her swollen arm, she would be turned to a thinking, will-exerting creature. The pain which waited for her returning senses would show its ugliness again in the lines of her face; though her face, he reflected now, was never ugly. Once more she might be troublesome, with her callow talk of his own need for rest. He would stifle that, one could not allow a patient such equality. It nettled him that she should try to peep beneath his cloak of doctorhood; and yet he saw that it was kindness.

He tied one end of the wringing-cloth to the bedpost. He was getting sleepy and must ward it off with action. The poultice, what had he done with that? Even as he fidgeted the poultice into position his eyes closed, and he saw immediately the whole of Ahlwarth's room: Minna was sitting close to Neuling, she seemed quite natural and happy there. He called to Neuling across the room: "That's Minna beside you, I'd like you to talk to her. She's a patient of mine, and very kind."

"What are you doing?" Minna asked, and his eyes sprang open.

"I—it's all right, I'm just getting the poultice ready. Wait, I'll have to heat the kettle again, it's gone off the boil."

Yes, he was tired, and the pain was overhauling him. It seemed a regular business getting upstairs after he had boiled the kettle again. But the poulticing went off well, he was surprised at his own one-handed skill. She held her arm quite steadily, he thought it must be less sensitive than he had supposed; until he glanced at her face and remembered his experience of Grohne's setting. It was curious, in one of her type, that fortitude.

Well, that was over, now he must wait an hour and then if she was awake do the whole thing again. Must get the arm right. Patience, it was going to need a lot of patience.

He sat on the edge of the bed, observing her quiet, pain-bleached face. Yes, a kind person. And curiously, he felt a certain pride in her: she was a good girl, this patient of his; the war he conducted in her body was near the stage of crisis, and she bore its fierceness hardily. Watching the small, tormented movements of her lips and chin he wondered for a moment how far away her mind was, whether in sleep she really left the wasted body to struggle by itself. It was interesting, this question of personality: perhaps Professor Rupf would recommend a book from which he could work it up . . . At any rate he would do his best for her, she was the most important of his medical belongings and he'd spare himself nothing.

In his labouring eyes her face spread and vibrated. He got to a better position with his head on his right hand, he might give himself five minutes' rest he thought. Something cool touched his forehead. He opened his eyes to see sunlight on the little window, and Minna, kneeling beside the bed, was bathing his face.

19

"IN MY opinion," Frau Rupf said, "—not that any one ever listens to anything I say—you ought to get a proper doctor for the girl. I met one of the nurses from the hospital and she told me that Doctor Zeppichmann is a person of no importance there, they keep him to wash the patients and that sort of thing. You can't expect a young man like that to cure people, only a few months after taking his diploma."

She expected no answer from Herr Spühler and got none: he went on sweeping the room with the rapid, vicious strokes of a soldier digging trenches under fire.

"If you will allow us," the Professor said, "I'm sure my wife and I can manage the cleaning of the room ourselves. Just for a few weeks, the exercise would do us good. My wife is a splendid cleaner."

It was no good. Frau Spühler had been heard to say, in one of her moments of depression, that August was utterly useless in the house, a mere burden. This was Herr Spühler's answer. He came every day just after lunch, with an armoury of tools. With polite insistence he pushed all the furniture to one side of the room, where Rupf and his wife cowered and boiled with embarrassment, he rolled up the carpet and attacked the floor, filling the room with a fog of dust. "I am never frightened of any kind of work," he would say, sweating with energy and shame. "In the great days of Germany I commanded fifty men. Fifty men would have blown their own brains out at an order from me—a mere nod of my head and the whole lot of them would have blown out their brains. A Warrant Officer, you understand, first-class certificate in gunnery. Well, that August Spühler is dead now. His heart is under the sea with the great ships of the Imperial Navy. This August Spühler you see is just a nobody, he's all ready to do the work of a cabin-boy."

The Professor, huddled up on the sofa, would nod with sympathetic gravity.

"It is my feeling, Herr Spühler, that our greatness as a nation lies in our adaptability. It is only a finely-tempered spirit that can hold high office at one stage of life and at another bend all his powers to the performance of simple but arduous duties. That versatility, it seems to me, is evidence of the finest form of self-discipline. So long as Germany has men of your kind, sir——"

"But if you would be good enough to keep your broom away from that little desk," Frau Rupf would say faintly, "——it is perhaps of no great value, but it has been in my family for one hundred and fifty years, and repeated battering on the legs seems likely to weaken them. Also if you would give us a little more notice to-morrow I will get some of my things shut away in the drawers, they were not really intended by the manufacturers to be impregnated with dust and grit——"

"My wife must have her little joke, Herr Spühler, she is really jealous of your skill in household-work . . ."

It came up again and again, this question of Dr. Zeppichmann, whenever Frau Rupf was finding her landlord's presence particularly aggravating.

"It seems that Minna is not making very rapid progress under Doctor Zeppichmann's ministrations?"

"I don't know, Frau Rupf, I'm really not at all sure. At any rate Doctor Zeppichmann will not hear of another medical man being called in. He is strongly against what he calls 'dual responsibility.' "

"But surely it's for you and Frau Spühler to say whether another doctor should be consulted."

"I'm not so sure. In any case it would probably result in Doctor Zeppichmann leaving us altogether. It's not at all easy nowadays to find guests of the right stamp for an establishment of this kind. The lodging houses in Philipstrasse, they can naturally get as many people as they like—they cater for the riff-raff. It's quite a different matter, with things as they are, to find guests at all suitable to associate with such people as yourselves and Herr Barthol."

"As far as associating with me is concerned, I see no necessity for bringing in callow and fraudulent doctors. If I—"

"Trude, my love, you are really giving us more of your wisdom than we can absorb at one sitting. You are upsetting Herr Spühler's concentration."

So Herr Spühler had ceased to pay any attention to Frau Rupf's observations on that subject. It was a conspiracy between Frau Rupf and his wife, he thought. Dear Hilde, who was suffering from arthritis and from overwork, poor girl, dear Hilde with all her patience was becoming hard to bear, constantly urging him to give the young doctor a straight talk. As if you could give straight talks to people on whom you depended for RM 25 a week! Well, he could put up with that; he had not lived with Hilde all these years without developing a technique for dodging her whims. He could evade the importunities of Frau Rupf also, simply by wearing his wooden-sailor face and refusing to understand a word she said. But on the rare occasions when the two ladies were agreed their alliance was terrible. He could counter-attack only with material weapons; and now, as Frau Rupf lectured him from her place by the wall, clutching her skirts to her legs with one hand, the other fastening a handkerchief over her scanty hair, he played the broom about her feet as if he were trying to bolt a rat from under them.

". . . If Doctor Zeppichmann really knew what he

was doing to the girl, Herr Spühler, surely he'd let your wife be in there as often as she wished! I understand he has her door locked and keeps the key in his pocket. You've got the material for a scandal there, it seems to me!"

"I had always supposed, Frau Rupf, that there were no scandal-mongers in my household. Will you be kind enough, please, to move a little towards the corner."

"Really, Herr Spühler, my feet are not so very enormous, they can't conceal such a vast amount of dust. I don't see why you have to make me into a nomad. After all, my husband pays for this as a living-room."

"And it is understood that we are under an obligation to keep it clean. Frau Spühler and I regard our obligations seriously, we cannot take money for services that aren't properly performed."

"And that includes, I suppose, the provision of a young ruffian with a stethoscope to attend on us in case we are ill? . . . No, Herr Spühler, no, that I will not have, stop it please, stop it at once!"

He had produced the duster, he was flapping at the table where she kept her most precious belongings, the little Buddha from Geneva, the photograph of her brother Artur who had been killed in a railway accident. A little fluff from her needle-work had settled between the Dresden ornaments and Herr Spühler was flogging it as if it were a cobra.

"Arnold! If you have any manhood in you I beg you to stop this maniac! In two minutes he will have cut the whole of our property into shreds."

Herr Rupf undid his legs and came out into the arena, caressing his fine, smooth temples.

"Perhaps my wife and I could put the finishing touches to this opus, Herr Spühler. We are both most grateful for all the pains you have taken. Really the room looks quite different now."

"Just as you wish, Herr Professor!"

He gathered his tools, bowed courteously to Frau Rupf, and went downstairs. He was mildly pleased. Humble as the work might be, it still gave him a certain satisfaction to do a job with that thoroughness which had once earned him rapid promotion. And to-day, betrayed into repartee, he had really out-argued that terrible woman, his logical powers had driven her right off the field. It was the time now when he had an hour with his pipe by the kitchen stove; but to-day he would celebrate a little, he would go to the Kronprinz and see his friends.

Frau Spühler was in the dining-room, setting the table for supper; in her anxiety to keep level with the work she did everything earlier and earlier every day. He tried to slip past the open door, but he trod on the wrong board and she heard him.

"August!"

"My dear, I have a little business in the town, I won't be very long."

"Perhaps you could just help me with the supper things. I've got the baking to do this afternoon."

"As soon as I come back, sweet—"

"August, my legs are hurting a good deal to-day."

"I shan't be very long!"

He made for the door and got outside. Through the window he caught a glimpse of her face, the face of a woman whose last child drowns before her eyes; with Viking resolution he turned and set off towards the tram-stop, a mighty ant-hill of a man with a brown weather-coat stretched on his shoulders, a slab of naval headgear spread across his wide, square skull.

But his happiness had gone already. Hilde's legs, he knew what pain they gave her in this weather; he knew how she worked to maintain her standards with Minna out of action, he remembered that she had been up late the night before sewing a new square into one of his shirts. He realised now that he was hardly better than the blackguards he'd read about, men who got tipsy twice a week and flogged their wives with fire-irons. He would turn and go back, that was the only decent thing to do. No, he would buy Hilde a pastry with plum-preserve in it.

It was raining, he would have to take the tram.

Well, as he was being so cruel to Hilde he must at least get all the pleasure he could out of the excursion. He turned up his collar, pushed his hands far down in the coat pockets and increased his pace. Rain? It was nothing, a mere dampness in the air which the wind chivvied about, an old sailor hardly noticed such weather as this. His fingers, skirmishing in the pocket linings, came on a twist of paper, and he pulled it out. Of course! That was the real worry at the back of his mind, that was what had put him out of temper all day. He had found it in the passage this morning, just as he was starting for the post: a little note addressed to himself, done with a typewriter and unsigned. 'A friend thinks it well to inform you that the person who calls himself Dr. Zeppichmann is a notorious communist. The injury to his shoulder, which he ascribed to a fall in the street, was actually incurred when he with a large gang of communists savagely attacked a small party of townsfolk returning from a political meeting. Be warned!' Such foolishness! Why, Dr. Zeppichmann held a staff appointment at the Moltke Hospital, any one there would vouch for him. He had supposed that some one was playing a joke on him, a particularly childish kind of joke: as if they would have communists in a guest-house such as his! Still, it had worried him a little. Notes without any one's name at the bottom, that kind of thing belonged to the world of police and criminals, it was not the sort of thing he and Hilde were used to. And now he thought of Frau Rupf's remark: she had told him that Dr. Zeppichmann was not really a doctor at all, he was only employed at the hospital to clean out the wards. That showed that the fellow was not really honest—he had always pretended to be a doctor. And that story of his about how he had come to break his shoulder a few weeks ago, it certainly wasn't quite convincing, now that Herr Spühler came to think about it. It was queer, too, his staying up in Minna's room all one night—Hilde seemed to be quite certain that this had happened: such behaviour was just what you expected from communists, who had no more respect for a young girl's virginity than for other people's money.

No, he wouldn't take the tram after all. It cost five pfennige, and the trams were stuffy on a day like this, and now that the weather-coat was getting old, people were inclined to look at him and nudge each other. A good walk would give him an appetite for his glass of coffee when he got to the Kronprinz.

This Zeppichmann trouble, it was the latest of many worries. Two weeks, now, since Herr Barthol had settled his weekly account. A little temporary difficulty, Herr Barthol had said, and Hilde had politely agreed to let the matter stand over: what else could you say to an old gentleman who looked like a cavalry officer, a man acknowledged to be the very image of the Emperor himself? Herr Spühler knew perfectly well what the difficulty was: Herr Barthol had put most of his money into an iron foundry at Düsseldorf—the old chap was an uncommonly shrewd investor—and now the labourers had all gone on strike and the communists had broken up a great deal of the machinery. It was hard on an old gentleman like that to find his dividends ceasing all of a sudden, really you could only admire the courage he was showing. When the letter came (which Hilde had accidentally read as she emptied the rubbish-basket) he had betrayed no emotion at all, not even his appetite had suffered. For himself, Herr Spühler would have allowed his distinguished guest to keep his room as long as he liked, without paying at all; only that the mortgage company expected their interest monthly, and flour was dearer than it had been since '24.

Flour. Yes, of course, it was Wednesday, and Hilde always baked on Wednesday afternoons. It was wonderful how she kept things going without any servant, the baking, all the washing, the weekly turn-out of the visitors' rooms. And with the cold weather getting into her legs! Could you wonder that she was sometimes a little out of temper, that she was inclined to spend the evenings weeping in a way that was very trying to the nerves of a naval man! And yet he had left her all alone this afternoon, he had treated her like a dog . . . Wretchedly unhappy, he stumped across the Statsfurter square and turned into Obstrasse.

The Kronprinz looked rather forlorn, with the outside tables all packed away, the rain streaming from the drenched sunblind. The place could do with a lick of paint, he thought as he went inside. Here, in a stale twilight, a young woman sat fiddling with a thimble of a Kirschwasser and exhibiting her pink knees to a row of empty tables. *"Herr Ober!"* A chair scraped and the boy Julius, shoulders poked as if he waited for a flogging, shuffled out from the Service.

"Good afternoon, Herr Spühler!"

Spühler peered at him.

"Some light, boy, if you please! Then I can see if any of my friends are here."

The waiter giggled, knuckling his bald head. "I'm afraid there's never much business at this time of day . . . I'm sorry, but Herr Ullrich won't allow the light to be put on before five o'clock. The electricity rate's gone up. What can I get you?"

"Nothing," Spühler said, "nothing at all. I shall wait till some of my friends come. Sergeant Beuloh should be here before long, this is about his time."

"But Sergeant Beuloh doesn't come at all now. Didn't you hear? There was some trouble about the rent, he had to give up his rooms. No, I don't know where he's gone."

Spühler nodded. He liked to give the impression that he had expected everything.

"And Herr Schulze," he asked, "does he come in the afternoons now?"

"No, Herr Spühler, he never comes now."

"What about Georg Erhardt?"

"Not since the summer. His business was in a bad way, sold up I think."

Spühler nodded again. "Sold up, yes, I expect he hadn't much head for business. An army man, of course—they're not used to that sort of thing. These are bad times, Julius."

"Yes, but they'll get better I think, now that we have this new Group. They're people who understand the government business, they won't put up with all these rowdies for long. A strong man, I understand, this von Papen. Make them work, that's what these young men want! They were in here last night, a whole mob of them, breaking up the place. That chair, look, it's only good for firewood. Herr Ullrich was in two minds about sending for the police."

"The police are no good with communists."

"But these were Nationalists. I tell you, I only just saved the windows."

"Ah so!"

"And they said, the first policeman that came they'd break his head open."

"Yes, a political faction I've no doubt!" Herr Spühler stared critically at the slop-mat advertising Mielke's Lager. This had gone a little too far, he was not going to be told about things by a chestless youth in a grubby serving-jacket. He knew what was to be known, all about the new Group; his own eyes were not so good nowadays, but Hilde often read him bits from Herr Barthol's paper when it came down in the evening. "Politics is a very difficult subject," he said. "A man can only understand the way things are going when he's had a long experience. You'll learn a lot as time goes on. You can bring my bill now."

"But you haven't had anything."

"Ah, then you can bring me a small coffee. I shall take that while I'm waiting for some of my friends to come."

The boy Julius uttered his nervous giggle and creaked away. It was a good omen, Papa Spühler coming in again, it might mean that things would look up presently. In all his forty years' service he could not remember business being quite so bad as it was at present . . .

"A small coffee for Papa Spühler. He asked to have the light on."

Frau Ullrich heaved her hundred and thirty kilograms down from the high stool. "Well, he'll bring us luck perhaps. He can have the light when he orders the second coffee."

"Your coffee, Herr Spühler."

"What? Oh yes."

Herr Spühler sat with both hands round the coffee glass and waited patiently, while the wet fell in a steady drip from the peak of his cap to the table. He noticed that the girl had gone. That was a good thing perhaps. For himself, he did not mind looking at a pair of pink legs when Hilde was not with him, but some of his old friends, when they came, would not have cared to find petticoats strewn about their kaffee . . . If Beuloh came he would put out a few questions about this von Papen that Julius had mentioned; now he came to think of it, he was not as clear as he might be about the new Group—he had supposed it was just the same old hopeless social-democrats arranged in a slightly different order. Well, it was good to hear of some one who meant to take things in hand. But no, Beuloh wasn't coming. Poor old Beuloh had had to quit, trouble about the rent. That was enough to show how things were going: an honest man couldn't get along these days . . . He stared through the gloom at the flyblown cherubs hanging by their navels from the edge of the huge mirror, he looked up at the cluster of blind electric spheres and down again at the slop-mat. *Trinken Sie immer Mielke.* What pleasant times he had had here! His cap seemed to have soaked up the rain like a sponge, it was still casting regular drops on the table, *putt, putt.* Yes, a man must get away from home sometimes, and when his friends came he would have a really enjoyable half-hour. A pair of students sauntered in, carrying a load of conversation. "You will excuse me, gentlemen, but perhaps you would care to drink a glass of wine with me?" "Thank-you, sir, but we've only come for a packet of cigarettes. Good-day, sir." They left the street-door slightly open, and the cold breath of the rain-soaked street came in, killing the Kronprinz odour of old wood steeped in wine-slop and the smoke of twenty-pfennige cigars. If only they would let him have the light, Herr Spühler thought. The draught was catching his face as neatly as a well-aimed arrow; but that was nothing, he determined, to a seafaring man.

"I can get you something else, please?"

The boy Julius again: nature had meant him for a gadfly rather than a waiter.

"Something else? No, nothing else! What time is it?"

"Just after five, Herr Spühler."

"After five!" He got out his own watch. Yes, that was right. "I shall have to be leaving now, I must see people in other parts of the town. You will please tell my friends, any that come, that I hope to meet them on another afternoon."

"You won't take another coffee?"

"No, nothing more. Wait! The gramophone is still in use, I suppose? And you still keep *Ich hatt' 'n Kamerad?* Very well, I should like that played for me, if you please."

In ten years' usage the record had lost its best condition, but Herr Spühler did not mind that. This was music!

He had it played through twice, he sat erect and beat the time with his heels. It had been worth while, after all, his firmness with Hilde, the dreary walk through the rain. Dear God what beauty! It was a fierce wine blazing to his heart, it was electricity which ran in cold and quivering threads from spine to temples, setting a thousand feet in steady tramp, the turbines hammering as the line of cruisers trod in ghostly grandeur through the mist of Jade Bay. Here was the peace of desperate battle, here the glory which would flame for ever deep in a nation's soul!

The last notes faltered and the needle scratched. Julius jerked up the diaphragm.

"Good?" he asked.

No answer. Herr Spühler was standing up, his eyes were overflowing.

"You will have another coffee now?"

"Only the Fatherland can make such music!" Spühler said. He fumbled for his purse, cleared his eyes and picked out ten pfennige. "No, nothing else! . . . Wait! Frau Ullrich still makes those pastries, the ones with plum-preserve in them?"

"They're a little stale to-day."

"That doesn't matter. One, please. Wrapped up in paper."

With the pastry held tightly under his arm, his eyes still hazy with tears, he found himself in the street again. Glorious, he thought, such glory! The daylight was going and the rain was heavier now. Such glory! He marched erect and bravely, across the tramlines and through the Co-operative arcade, back again to the Square.

20

FOR half a mile his senses floated in that ecstasy. He found he was going home the old and longer way, but it didn't matter with his limbs so powerful, he had found himself a fighter once again. What if the Fatherland was cankered with the lice of treachery, the money-lenders, Kommunisten, the sneaking pacifists who sucked her blood!—a dozen men like him, one loyal corps, could sweep away that crew and set her free. In his pride and happiness he swung his arms, his jaw was tight, his heavy eyebrows clutched with resolution. From now he would think of nothing but his country, he would fight with all his heart and strength against the rabble that betrayed her.

The road pitched up towards the Leydentor and he had to slack his pace. *His country's enemies, the money-lenders, communists* . . . At the top of the hill he paused to gather breath, his coat was open and the rain whipped in against his skin. Yes, they were all about him, perhaps within his house!

The entrance to the Wilhelm park was open; he would save his legs by cutting across to the northeast gate. He had gone a little way when a figure came towards him through the dusk, a voice called, "Halt! Don't you know you're not allowed to cross the grass!" "I'm sorry, Herr Parkaufseher, I'd quite forgotten!" Returning to the gravel path, he tried to make up for the extra distance by walking faster, but his legs had gone a little stiff. 'If Doctor Zeppichmann's a communist,' he thought, 'it means that twenty-five Marks a week will have to go.'

He would have liked to have some one with him now, old Beuloh, any one would do.

Already the winter had been so long. Where the line of houses stopped the trees were skeletons on the washed-out sky, their leaves mixed up with tramway-tickets made a greasy carpet to the path. Here, where the main paths joined, there had surely been a plot of shrubs, but he did not see them now; the line of children's swings stood motionless, and beneath the bandstand all the chairs were stacked away. From this morning's waywardness the wind had settled to a steady thrust, and the sleety rain, held to a constant slope, fixed all the desolation in a milky screen. Under that tide the earthy smells were fastened down, the smell of rain was tainted with a smeech from the refuse-yards. With darkness sucking out the last drab shades this seemed the final winter, from the bare and sodden turf no flower would spring, no children's voices come to this place again. Herr Spühler's hands were cold, and the rain was trickling down inside his shirt. As he stumbled on towards the railings he wondered if the cloud that lay on Germany would ever, ever yield to sun.

It was after six when he got home. Having taken off his boots he waited like a stranger in the hall, trying to hear where Hilde was, putting-off the moment when he had to meet her. And emerging suddenly from the dining-room she found him there.

Like Venus from the sea he stood, sock-footed, in the pool he had made, a sodden package in one hand, boots in the other. He didn't look at her, and she, with her tear-swamped eyes, avoided his. The water running down from his cap seemed to have damped his voice, when he tried to speak only a whisper came. "Kept in the town, didn't mean to be so long." Without a glance he pushed his gift into her hand and hobbled off to the kitchen stairs.

"August!"

Her voice was nearly as faint as his, but he couldn't pretend not to hear it—he never admitted any deafness.

"Yes, my dear?"

"Minna is worse, she's been crying all afternoon."

"Minna? Oh dear!"

"Herr Barthol's been complaining, he says it gets on his nerves."

"Herr Barthol, yes!" How tired he was: but with her sad eyes watching him he had to answer something. "Well, I must see what Doctor Zeppichmann says; as soon as he comes in I'll have a word with him."

She said relentlessly: "He came back early to-day, he's in his room."

So, there was no escape! Without speaking, as a wrestler strips for combat, he took off his coat and hat, letting them fall on the floor. His shirt and trousers clung like a bathing dress but he knew that the courage of necessity ebbs quickly and he would not stop to change them. A sudden anger helped him. This Zeppichmann, he obscurely thought, he's at the back of all this trouble: coming here, taking Herr Meisel's room, gaining favours by paying his weekly bill, sending Minna to bed and making every one do her work. This Zeppichmann had been riding for a fall and now the fall was coming.

Frau Spühler watched him, on his way to the stairs, as the crowd watches the funeral cortège of a great general passing. Knowing all his gestures, she had realised by the way he jerked the coat off his shoulders that his mind was made up. He did not speak as he passed her, he did not even look at her. There was grandeur, there was something rather terrible in the white determination of his square, windburnt face. Only when her eyes had followed him half-way up the stairs did her heart suddenly fail. She called, "August! August, you ought to change your trousers first!" He took no notice. He steamed gigantically along the passage and thumped the door of Dr. Zeppichmann's room.

Josef's eyes were on Kleim's *Febrile Conditions*. He was

tired, and his shoulder was rather painful: all that clumsy Grohne's fault, he thought—it should have practically healed by now. Through the clotted screen of reaction curves he saw Minna's face as he had observed it a few minutes before, grey, with her thin arm lying across the forehead. The two tremendous blows on the door came like gunfire into sleep. He turned from the bench and shouted furiously, "What do you want!"

At Herr Spühler's appearance, damp and panting like a frog, his anger changed its shape. He said sharply:

"What's the matter, Herr Spühler—have you had an accident? Your clothes! Do please shut the door—you can't stand in a draught like that!"

Herr Spühler came towards the middle of the room and took up his stance there.

"I have come about Minna," he said, looking just beside Josef's head. "I am going to speak quite straightforwardly. It's about Minna. I don't want to have any shilly-shallying. Herr Barthol has been making complaints. And there's the girl herself to think about. You can't treat a human being like a Negro. I won't have that kind of thing in my house."

Leaning back against the bench, Josef regarded Herr Spühler's face with concern.

"I must warn you," he said, "that you're acting very dangerously. A man of your age who stands about in soaking wet trousers is just asking for trouble."

"I stood about in wet trousers long before you were born," Herr Spühler said tersely. "I have spent fifteen hours in a whaleboat with the water up to my stomach."

"Exactly, and that is why you are now subject to chronic rheumatism."

"I have a perfect right to rheumatism or any other complaint I choose to have. Many notable people suffer from rheumatism."

"Yes, and many notable people die early, as soon as it

reaches the heart. Of course it's nothing to do with me. I only do my duty as a doctor when I tell you that the country is going to lose a retired naval officer whom it holds in high respect, simply because he won't be troubled to change his trousers."

"I shall change my trousers as soon as I've thrashed this matter out."

Josef changed his tone.

"Herr Spühler," he said seriously, "the question is one that concerns some one else besides yourself, some one I esteem very warmly. It concerns Frau Spühler."

"It most certainly concerns her!"

"Naturally a man like yourself, who's been accustomed all his life to facing every kind of risk, thinks nothing of endangering his life with rheumatism. I only ask you to think of all that Frau Spühler does for us, and then to think of her feelings if you were suddenly taken from her in the prime of life."

"I've not come here to talk about rheumatism. I've come to talk about Minna."

Josef nodded.

"Yes, that's what I want to talk about myself. I only ask you—as a friend, if I may call myself that, and out of my regard for Frau Spühler—to take off your trousers and stand here by the stove. Won't you do that, please!"

If the appeal had come from Hilde herself he would have ignored it: a man had to be firm against women's fuss. But in Dr. Zeppichmann's eyes was all the gravity of mysterious learning, and it was no surrender to accept another man's opinion in his own field.

"Very well!" he said. He let the trousers fall and stood by the stove in his underpants. "Now then!"

"You wanted to speak about Minna," Josef prompted.

"Exactly!"

"Well?"

Herr Spühler hesitated. In addressing a medical man

one had to pick one's words: he didn't want this young fellow to think him an ignoramus.

"It's about her condition. I have—my wife and I have been talking about Minna's condition—her physical condition, you understand. We consider that we are justified in asking for new indications. I mean, new medical indications. With medical patients one expects to have—indications."

Josef's eyes, polite and earnest, travelled the short distance from Herr Spühler's tremendous knees to his face.

"I—I am not altogether clear," he said.

"Well, damn and blast it, man, you've had the girl for weeks now, what the devil have you done to her?"

"Done to her?"

"Do you think my wife and I can go on doing the girl's work for the rest of our lives! Cleaning out the Professor's room, that sort of thing! What's a doctor for, that's what I want to know. A doctor's supposed to make people well. If he can't do that—well, you'd better get some one who can. Or I will. I'll get a doctor who knows his business, I tell you. I hear you're a communist too. If you think you're the only doctor in Hartzinnfeld you're much mistaken. If I tell a man he's got to lubricate a gun-mounting, then he's got to do it. And if I put a doctor on to a girl with a headache he's got to make her right. Damn and blast it, that's plain common-sense!"

Well, they had taught him something at the Moltke Hospital, Josef reflected: just one thing, to deal with fools patiently. With his hands behind his back he walked slowly to the door, turned there, looked at Herr Spühler across the room as if he were fifty yards away. (He had learnt that trick from a visiting surgeon.) He paused just long enough to survey Herr Spühler's person in three sections, face, body, knees, before he answered.

"I'm very glad you've spoken so plainly, Herr Spühler. It makes me see how entirely reasonable your position is.

Obviously, when you're paying a girl full wages and getting nothing out of her—"

"Full wages?" Herr Spühler was much startled. "My dear Doctor, you can't imagine I can afford that! What would the girl do with the money?"

"I meant, of course, you still have the expenses of her keep, and then there is the room she occupies."

"Just so!"

"Ah, that's what I wanted to discuss with you. You will realise, of course, that I'm a comparatively poor man. For the sake of the patients, hospital salaries have to be kept as low as possible. But I thought that if I could manage to contribute a little—say seven Marks a week—towards Minna's living-expenses: and then perhaps the little box-room opposite Herr Barthol's room might be fitted up with a bed—possibly Herr Meisel would be willing to occupy that and leave his present room vacant—then the difficulty about getting a new servant—"

"No," Herr Spühler said firmly, "you misunderstand me. I'm not asking you to supervise my domestic arrangements. I'm asking you to cure the girl of whatever-it-is. If you can't do it I'm going to get another doctor."

Josef was carefully arranging Herr Spühler's trousers over the back of a chair. He brought it near the stove.

"In that case," he said, "the man I should recommend is Doctor Dürerhaus of Leipzig—he's the man I've been corresponding with about the case. Of course his fees are rather high, since he's the leading man in his field, but I might be able to arrange some reduction."

Herr Spühler shook his head.

"There's Doctor Wohlfahrt round the corner," he said. "He's always looked after us very well."

So realistic was Josef's start of surprise that the chair fell over.

"Doctor Wohlfahrt! You can't mean Doctor Wohlfahrt in Tetzelstrasse! You don't mean that you're going to

ask him to deal with an advanced case of pulmonary tuberculosis!"

"No," said Herr Spühler, "I'm going to ask him to deal
with Minna."

Josef made another pilgrimage to the door; realising,
now, that the trick was something more than pure histri-
onics. He was suddenly frightened. The hand of cards he
had kept ready for this game with Spühler were all played
now; played, as he thought, correctly. He had underesti-
mated the old fool's obstinacy. This Spühler, this little fat
frog of a creature propped up there in his underclothes, this
bottle-headed mariner was going to rob him of his most
precious possession.

"Very well!" he said, swinging round like a dancer.
"You will get Doctor Wohlfahrt. He can take the case from
this very moment. With his long experience of cut fingers
and whooping-cough I suppose he can treat a consumptive
girl far better than a man who's merely specialised in that
branch of medicine for the last six years! I don't suppose
he'll want to consult an expensive specialist, he'll put her
right with syrup-of-figs and Pach's Ointment! You will tell
Frau Spühler, please, that I am looking for other accommodation. It's a pity, only my professional dignity demands
that, as you'll understand. I shall be glad to send Doctor
Wohlfahrt any particulars of the case that may possibly be
helpful to him. I only reserve the right—which belongs to
me in any case—of publishing a full report. I shall do that
as soon as the girl is dead."

"Dead! What do you mean?" Herr Spühler asked
dully.

Josef shrugged his shoulders.

"Well, in the hands of a doctor like Wohlfahrt I give
her about fourteen days to live . . . I'm sorry, because I
find her an amiable young person. I have already given up
all my spare time and a good deal of money for her benefit
since I came here. I was quite ready to devote myself further

to the girl's welfare. I myself hold the curious view that a
life which can be saved is worth saving, and that one has no
right to hand over helpless people to jobbing doctors who
can't possibly understand their complaint. But it's no use my
arguing. The girl's a nuisance to you, naturally you want to
get her out of your way and get the room clear. As you say,
speaking from a practical point of view the life of a pauper
has no importance. You must forgive me for feeling rather
differently about a patient who's occupied all my spare time
for many weeks."

Herr Spühler's lips were fluttering in a useless dance.
It was like trying to build a pontoon bridge across a stream
which had suddenly become an angry torrent: no sooner
were two of the rafts fixed together than the current swept
them away. A moment came when the flood slackened and
he seized his chance.

"Naturally, Herr Doktor, we are very grateful for all
that you have done—"

"No!" said Josef sharply, and then his voice came down
like a horse reined-in by a perfect rider. "No, in practice I
have done nothing for Minna. I have progressed a certain
way with a course of treatment, that's all. It will amount to
nothing now, the effects will all be washed out. It is—it is
very sad for me, but that can't be helped. If I were a quack
who pretended to do quick cures my own position would
have been much better. Perhaps I should not have been
obliged to leave this house, to say good-bye to people I've
grown so fond of."

"How long would it take you to get the girl right?"
Herr Spühler asked gruffly.

Josef shook his head and smiled.

"She would have turned the corner in a few days from
now," he said sadly. "And now, if you will excuse me, I shall
have to get on with my work—I have important reading to
do. But please make use of my stove as long as you wish."

The trousers were still wet; all the stove had done was

to make the legs look like crumpled railway tunnels. But
Herr Spühler put them on again, enduring the clamminess
about his waist. What did a little more discomfort matter in
the chain of small discomforts through which he lived—the
draught from a crack in the kitchen window, the way dear
Hilde wound herself up in the bedclothes, the chilly morning journey to the ash-heap when he had raked out the
kitchen stove! Now they were going to lose this Zeppichmann, and the money-trouble would get still worse. That
was the intolerable thing about young Zeppichmann: his
having enough money to do what he liked. For the rest, you
couldn't exactly find anything wrong with the fellow. He
was honest enough, surely; pleasant-spoken, as a rule,
friendly, and of a deep seriousness which Herr Spühler was
ready to respect in any young man. Was it really Dr. Zeppichmann's fault if you felt that you couldn't altogether
trust him? In his slow, unshakable honesty, Herr Spühler
thought that perhaps he had spoken to the young chap too
severely.

At all events the interview was over.

But as he reached the door, Josef turned round again.

"If you will give me just five minutes," Josef said
quietly, "I'll run round to get Doctor Wohlfahrt myself.
It's still raining hard, I shouldn't like you to go out again.
It will be no trouble to me."

Herr Spühler did not turn round. He wouldn't look at
those searching eyes again. He said harshly:

"No! I do not wish any action to be taken. Not yet. I
have to give the matter serious consideration. I shall discuss
the matter with my wife."

He slammed the door behind him. He had made it
clear, he thought, that he was not a man to be trifled with.
But already a new dread was upon him. Lowering his damp,
tired body a step at a time down the stairs, he knew that he
had to face Hilde again.

21

HAVING reached the bottom of the page, Josef gave himself time for a smile before he turned it over. Another fence crossed: really he had done it exquisitely well, his heels just scraping. And he had been so near failure.

Rebounding from Herr Spühler's violence, the door had swung open again. As his footsteps ceased to sound, a faint cry of Minna's came down to the room: that peculiar cry which she made at the edge of delirium. It killed Josef's triumph, that single cry.

Lies were a necessity, but a boast was something almost sacred. He had told Spühler now, without the smallest reservation, that he would get the girl all right. He had said that under Wohlfahrt (a thoroughly sound practitioner who would have sent the girl to a sanatorium at once) she had not the smallest chance. The facts of the case were that under sanatorium treatment her condition might be stabilized, if only for the time being; that under his own hands she might easily die within a few days. When that happened there would be a less amusing interview. People smiled at him behind their hands for his stocky figure and big ears, his cheap clothes, the flavour of the Richterhausen back-streets which still hung about him. He knew that, he was used to it, he didn't care. It would be another matter when these worthy turnips could call him a fool.

That was more than a possibility, it was likely now. And yet, in a sense, he had already succeeded.

When he next got hold of the X-ray apparatus he would be quite certain: but he didn't need that. A tyro could see from the superficial indications that the wasting was already arrested: the fuller shape of the mammae, increase of flesh above the ribs, the tone of the skin, those signs proclaimed the formation of fibrous tissue as clearly as birds proclaim the Spring. The quieting of the cough, the measurable decrease of sputum, these alone would have satisfied him that that P.T. was doing its work even more brilliantly than he had hoped. Those special indications which he noted constantly told the same story: the curve of pulse had changed from a cock's comb to something more like a woodman's saw, the sedimentation rate was nearing normal. Recording a hundred details every day he was starting to live in a high excitement, akin to a composer's excitement when his concerto is first played by full orchestra: the smallest effects according minutely with his preaudition. He had started the experiment with that kind of certainty which comes from mathematical reasoning. What he watched was almost a process separate from his own contrivance, a law of true causation steadily working out. There was a fault, however: a question of utility. A cure might be the apotheosis of scientific mastery; yet it was judged a failure if—from some piffling secondary cause—the patient died.

He kept two principal charts, which he called Charts A and N. The first was based on a condition index, which he worked mathematically from a co-ordination of condition-data. This curve, while maintaining an upward trend, showed an invariable fall some ninety-six hours before each injection. Curve N, which recorded the positive incidents of febrile reactions, touched a slightly higher point at a space of about thirty-six hours after each injection. On the upper part of this second chart he had drawn two lines, based on Kleim's observations, a danger line and a fatal line. In its last upward leap the curve had crossed the danger line.

Another curve was pencilled in on this chart, joining the successive high points. This curve was concave towards the base. It showed that, while the upper points of the main curve had so far been progressively higher, that progression would presently be turned. As general condition improved, the body would resist the febrile reactions more positively, and each of the high points should come a little lower than the one preceding it. But the smoothing of these curves was artificial. Like all curves of phenomena they were, in their pure state, jagged. And in the next upward jag the line of fatality might be crossed.

In effect, Chart A showed that he could not reduce either the strength or the frequency of the injections. Chart N showed that the next one might kill her.

A clock struck in the dining-room: seven-thirty. According to his programme he wasn't due to see her again till 8.15, when he had finished supper. But he would just look in now, and if there was anything useful to do he would cut the meal.

Not that he wanted to go. To-day he had spent already a total of three hours in the attic—he always bicycled home at midday to see that she was comfortable. The headache with which he lived was partly due to lack of food and sleep, partly to spending too long each day in the air of beds and illness. That room of Minna's depressed him: his daily scouring, the magazine pictures he had nailed on the flaky walls, could not offset its smallness and familiarity. But he could not keep away.

Atropine: he might have to give her that to-night, much as he disliked it: he put the tablets in his pocket and took the kettle from the gas-ring. Crossing the passage, his eyes heavy with speculation, he collided with Herr Meisel. He murmured 'Verzeihung!' and went on to the attic stairs.

He had a shock at the moment when he went in. She was in a position he had never seen before, arms stretched straight by her sides, head pitched back across the bolster so that the skin of the neck was taut, the mouth open in a fish's gasp. *Dead!* he thought. *Left her twenty minutes, and she's gone and died!* It passed in an instant, that wild conjecture. She was obviously alive, with the respirations over-quick and noisy, she was burning hot and dripping with sweat; but apparently asleep. His hand went for the tablets, but no, he would not disturb her. Foolish, to tumble into panic at so slight a variation of the febrile symptoms. He poured the warm water into a graded basin and measured out a portion of spiritus coloniensis with unnecessary precision; but he noticed that his hand was shaking.

Sponging was all he could do for the present: he folded the bedclothes over, arranged the towels and set to work. Calmness slowly returned with the careful movements of his hands; as when a painter, too stale to work, finds some relief in cleaning out his brushes; yet every precise action—the squeezing of the wool, the careful towelling as each small area was done—was pushed a little faster by anxiety. Instinct, as much as knowledge, told him that he was near the height of danger; and he felt obscurely that so long as he watched and worked upon the body she could not steal herself away.

She went on sleeping, or appeared to sleep; he could move the arms or legs as if they belonged to a corpse. Absorbed, he seemed to have been in this room all day, watching the small movements of the lower ribs, listening to the respirations. The traffic of the Moltke, his four long rides through the rainy streets, were all pushed back in the darkest part of memory. From that separate life only one thing stayed with him now, his own voice as he talked to Spühler.

I myself hold the curious view that a life which can be saved is worth saving.

I was ready to give myself to the girl's welfare.

One has no right to hand over helpless people.

You say that the life of a pauper has no importance. You must forgive me for feeling rather differently.

Those sentences were strangely clear, and held in the

very tones he had used, as the lines hammer in a tired actor's head. Uttering them, he had enjoyed his virtuosity: this doctoring, it taught you how to use your tongue on simple folk! Now, they became a sour after-taste, like jokes repeated from old journals. It seemed a waste to have poured out so much cleverness in deceiving a stupid man.

It was harder than he had thought, to work so utterly alone. The need to hide his purpose with a cloud of subterfuge had once made it more amusing, but the play had gone on too long. He was angry now that a serious man should have to dress in fancy clothes, that a scientist could only do his job by pretending to be a journeyman. The time of uncertainty was over. The experiment had shown already that his formula was essentially sound, whatever its imperfections; it was no longer a dream that he was giving something of large importance to his calling. And still, to get the peace that was all he wanted, he had to invent ingenious lies about his treatment of a working girl.

You say that the life of a pauper has no importance. You must forgive me for feeling rather differently.

In reality, was his vision different from the one he had thrown at Spühler? It was different, yes, because of his sense of values: against a pauper's life he measured the lives of thousands . . . He had gone through that so often, there was nothing left to argue now.

Yet faintly, as when the smell of brine first comes to a boy who has never seen the sea, he felt the need to break away from reason. To Spühler he had made himself out a simple man, who worked for Minna out of common kindness. Mysteriously, he wished that that were true.

22

LEAVE it alone! The fight against his sentimental weakness need not begin till another injection was due: enough, for now, to get her past the immediate crisis. The sleep held fast, as if she were under morphine, her respiration was a trifle slower. "Careful!" he said aloud, and a little wildly, "careful, Minna, hold on, you mustn't die!"

It almost appeared that she heard his appeal and tried to make some answer. The little whine from her throat changed to a guttural noise like the first motions of a vomit, the muscles of her breast and stomach began to labour, in her right leg the muscles tightened and vibrated. He had seen movements not unlike these in the early period of tertian fever, never at a sweating stage; the signs were outside the books and left him helpless. He slipped his arm behind her shoulders, his wrist into the farther armpit, as he had seen Röstel do with convulsive children: raised the body and turned it gradually to Matussék's position, taking the weight of her head on his weaker arm. The syringe was close to hand, but he wouldn't use that yet: if, as he supposed, the toxins were driving the fever towards an early crisis it was dangerous prudence to interfere. He put his free hand on the thorax, encouraging the muscular effort there. But the spasms were already diminishing, the joints a little relaxed. He moved himself a little further on the bed so as to hold her more comfortably, and sat intensely still, watching the twitches of the leg, listening intently to the respirations; watching and listening, listening.

The signs changed from moment to moment, it was like observing a sea battle through drifting fog. A noise like wood scratching on plaster came from the lower trachea; he understood that. There were short periods of apnoea; that was outside his understanding. He had the curious sense that from where she hid, somewhere inside this body, Minna was helping him: that she herself was managing a battle passed beyond his scope. He tried to think what she was like, that creature who had been present at every stage of the experiment, whose chatter often upset his concentration; but he could not remember her now, he saw only the face which had belonged to her, a blind shape of flesh twitching and burning. It was what he had wanted, a passive vehicle for his exploration. But the sounds of struggling within this body were strangely distressing, and he felt very lonely.

He didn't know what time it was. He thought that the bell had gone for supper about half an hour ago. Something must happen soon, she couldn't hold up a temperature like this much longer—and stay alive.

He grew impatient. Sounds coming up from the house, the distant murmur of trams through the frush of rain, reminded him of a world outside. Here he could touch the ceiling as he sat, he could have sketched from memory all the dirty shapes along the walls. If she meant to die, let her hurry and be done with it. Then he would find another case, begin all over again . . . But a change in her breathing instantly alarmed him, he called sharply, "Minna!" and felt his own heart thrusting as he bent to listen. Her breath had a new odour, which he thought he recognised; and the lips and tongue were working in the way he had seen after fatal operations. He put his hand back for wool and etherised water, put the moist wool to her parched lips and then drew it carefully along the gums. Foolishly, he whispered to her as he worked about the mouth, "It's all right, Minna, it's all right, don't talk now, take it easy! . . ." Her breath went in sharply, as if to explode in a fit of coughing, and came out in a long sigh.

Then his gaze travelled upwards over her face, and he saw that her eyes were open.

They were not like the eyes of the dead, fixed and lustreless. But they stared past his arm to the farther corner of the room, trying, as it appeared, to follow some movement there; with such intensity that Josef turned to see what it was, and was surprised for a moment at seeing nothing. And while he looked that way he heard some one speaking: Minna, speaking.

Not with the faint, spasmodic speech of the very ill, but with almost her normal power; huskily, but in the quiet tones she used when answering his serious questions.

"I'll be down in a minute. Tell Frau Spühler I'll be down soon. I overslept a bit, I won't be long."

It took Josef only a second or two to get over his shock. He said quickly:

"Not to-day, you can't go down to-day. To-morrow perhaps."

"No," she said, "I can't stop now, I've got to see Frau Spühler. I want to tell her something."

"What is it?" he asked. "I'll tell her."

"It's about the butter-plate. I said it fell off the shelf. That isn't right, I knocked the damned thing off with my elbow."

"But that doesn't matter in the least!" He was back in his stride now: he knew his trade, Josef did, he was specially good at the psychological part. "Frau Spühler told me it didn't matter about the butter-plate, it was a very old one. And in any case I've bought her a new one instead."

"Oh. Then I must pay you. How much did it cost?"

"It doesn't matter," he said, "it was nothing, it doesn't matter at all. You must have a rest now—Frau Spühler said you were to rest."

"How much?" she repeated.

"Oh it was—it was 1.50."

"Oh yes, 1.50." She hadn't moved at all, her eyes were still raking the corner of the room. "That's one year's interest on fifty Marks at three per cent. Yes yes, I used to do it with Fräulein Zenke, she told me how to work it out. A year's interest on fifty at three per cent, that's a month's interest on six hundred at three per cent, a week's interest on two thousand four hundred at three per cent. But I haven't got that."

"You can settle up when you're quite well again," he said. "You must go to sleep now."

"The English lesson comes next," she told him. " 'My cousins and I are going to London. We go by the boat. In London there are many great buildings, which we shall visit, also the River Thames and the Palace of Waxworks.' If I pay twenty-five pfennige every week, I'll have paid it off in six weeks. Can you wait six weeks?"

"Yes yes, easily."

Let her go on, he thought, no use struggling against it: she'll tire herself soon. The temperature did not seem to be altered, something was delaying the crisis. Atropine now? No.

He thought the chatter was finished, but the eyes were still open, and presently it began again, the voice still firm and even.

"Fräulein! Fräulein, listen! I want to know how much it costs to get to Giessbach. Second-class would do. Do you think it would be more than fifty Marks, there and back?"

Josef said quietly: "No no, less than that."

"Well, say forty Marks. Then there's the cost of the guest house. Three weeks altogether, twenty-five Marks a week, that makes seventy-five. Seventy-five and forty. That's a hundred and thirty-five. Say a hundred and fifty for everything."

"Yes yes, that's right, that would cover it."

"I've got forty-two," she went on, "that leaves a hundred and eight to get. I can save three Marks a week if I don't have to get any more stockings. That's—how many weeks?—thirty-six. Thirty-six—oh, that's much too long! Too long, too long!"

"Now listen, Minna!" he said seriously: it wouldn't do, all this talking, this weaving of figures. "Listen, you don't want to worry about that. Directly you get better I'll see what I can do. I'll help you a bit. I'll see you get a holiday."

That stopped her: but only for a few moments.

"It isn't for me," she said suddenly, "I don't want a holiday. I haven't done any work for weeks."

"Well then, there's nothing for you to worry about. Wait, I want to move your head a bit. There, that's more comfortable, isn't it! Are you thirsty?"

"Perhaps I could save four Marks," she persisted. "Four a week, unless that filthy woman tries to cheat me over the washing, and then I'd get interest on the forty-two. About twenty-five weeks then. Twenty-five weeks, when does that go up to?"

He tried firmness now. "I wish you wouldn't talk so much!" he said sharply. "You're only making yourself worse."

"Worse? Oh God, I couldn't be worse—my head, it's like barbed-wire dragging over a stone wall."

"Who do you want the holiday for, anyhow?"

"But I told you, Fräulein, I told you about it! It's for the doctor. He never gets a holiday, he told me that, he's never had a holiday in his life."

He didn't answer for a minute or more. She was still rambling on, something about the interest you got from a savings bank, about some school row over stolen money: he wasn't listening. Then, involuntarily, he spoke again.

"But the doctor doesn't want a holiday!" he said. "He's much too busy, he's always got masses of work to get through."

"Yes," she said, staring hard at the corner, "yes, that's just the point. He thinks of nothing but his work, he'll kill himself." Then, sharply, "Not so fast, not so fast. I can't keep up!"

He moved her again, lowering her shoulders slowly on to the pillow. "It's all right, Minna!" he said. "Take it easy, take it easy!" He wished to God she'd stop this gibbering, it made it four times harder for him to watch and listen. God knew, it was job enough to watch this case, this fragile body incandescent with its toxic energy, burning out the last of its strength—without the distraction of a chattering stranger. It was not his first experience of delirium: in the fever wards at Zornenwalde such rubbish had filled the air like the trilling of birds, and like the trilling of birds it passed through his ears unnoticed. It was different, in this small room, with these eyes pointing across his shoulder, awake, and seeing something he did not see. He turned his back to her for a moment, shook out two of the tablets and occupied himself in dissolving them. That was something sensible to get on with. It was an ordinary job, after all, a patient with fever, in a dangerous condition; the delirium was incidental, one had to ignore that. Everything was in its usual place on the little shelf he had made, the cotton wool, phenacetin, inspection-lamp, the box with the hypodermic syringe . . . This was his first experimental case, if it failed he must re-examine the P.T. for its toxic element and then find another patient. A pity, if he lost this one, but she had served a greater purpose than thirty years of scrubbing floors. And, after all, the individual did not matter.

But the voice, the voice of this intruder he was trying not to hear, went on persistently; strangely precise in its unreason.

"Fräulein, Fräulein, don't go away, it's dark over there, I can't see you! Listen, Fräulein! Oh, I'm so tired, I must tell you before I go to sleep. You wanted me, you wanted me to do something. You said I'd got to make something out of myself, you said I'd got to give the world something."

"Yes, but not now," Josef said. "Another time, when you're not so tired."

"But I can't do anything in this house. There isn't time and my chest's always hurting. If I painted pictures that would be doing something. Professor Tappert said my pictures were good, didn't he! But there isn't any time, there isn't any time. It's this damned cough, I can't, I can't keep up with it. Closer, Fräulein, closer! Hold my hand. Not tight, not tight, the arm hurts. He put something in my arm. He didn't mean to hurt it, he only put something in. You see, don't you, he didn't mean to hurt me. He wouldn't hurt anybody, he's always so good, so good, he sits with me, he puts cool things on my head. Listen, listen! I want to give him a holiday. That's worth doing, isn't it—that's something to do. Then he'd think about something else besides illness. He doesn't think about anything else now, he's never learnt anything. Wouldn't it be worth doing, sending the doctor to Giessbach so he could see some things. He'd be worth something then. His head's all right, only there's nothing in it, nothing but illness and medicines. He's never heard anything, poor dear thing, he doesn't know anything at all."

Again Josef interrupted. He didn't want to be a party to this crazy conversation, but there was no other way to stop the flow.

"You'd much better have the holiday yourself," he said practically. "I mean, as soon as you're better."

She seemed to be puzzled then. The eyes, still set to find a distant object, turned in his direction, and the hands were moving, feeling for something. She said impatiently:

"But don't you see, I'm no use! I tried—I tried to, but I couldn't, I can't even do the blasted housework decently. I can't, I've got no patience, I quarrel with the old bitch all the time. He's so good, Fräulein, so good, and his head's better than mine. So kind! He'd be useful, Fräulein, he'd do something if he got something in his head." Suddenly she clenched her fists and jerked herself up. "I tell you I'll do it!" she said fiercely. "I'm going to do it, I'm going to send him to Giessbach. He's going to be a great man, Fräulein. Minna's going to make him a great man!"

He caught her by the arms, he almost shouted, "Quiet, Minna, quiet!" That force wasn't needed. Like a marionette thrown to the wings after its last violent antics she fell back on the bolster, crumpled and spent. Done for herself, he thought: over now, all over!

It was relief, of a kind, to see her lying so still: her body relaxed, the flush in her face already dwindling. And her eyes were quiet now, cloudy, no longer strained. He put his hand on her breast, with a certain instinctive gentleness, as the unaccustomed handle the dead; and found that her heart was still beating.

Clumsily, like an old engine dragging a load uphill, but still beating.

His relief broadened, not so much because she was still alive as because he could be active again. In a moment he had the body covered over. The chapter in Suhr's *Practice* came before his mind's eye as when a new slide is slipped into a lantern: Paragraph 12, *Manual Assistance,* with a dirty crease stretching across the corner. Back on familiar ground he forgot the disturbing Minna, he forgot the room itself, the yellow light and awkward shadows poured across the cheapjack furniture. He could work now. The digitalis was always ready in graded doses, but the heating pads had to be prepared, the vessels he had used to be scalded out, fresh water in the drinking-cup . . . With four different jobs on hand he was listening, always listening, to the respirations, a slice of his vision was always on the sheet above her ribs, he no longer noticed her face at all. He heard stealthy footsteps on the stairs outside, some one listening and going away again; a clock striking ten and then eleven. They were like the faces of the crowd in a runner's eyes, those noises, fretwork beside the narrow strip of reality. It was beating, still beating, and the pulse was firmer now. He might bring it off once more, he might still get her through.

Now, as his body tired, his brain like a horse with the bridle loosed came into a longer stride. The work on hand, long reduced to automatism, had not the weight to hold it back. He began to wonder if he would hear her voice again; he dreaded it, the voice of the unknown who hid inside the small, quiet body; and yet, in a new access of loneliness, he wanted her to break the silence.

He wanted more than that. Some curiosity, a private need he had not known before, made him long for a moment's understanding between them. He wanted her thoughts close to his for a moment, close as their faces were. They had made a long journey together, and her face, as it seemed to him now, had always been in shadow. The voyage might be nearly over. Half-consciously, he wanted to see her in the full light before it was done.

The room, a box of broken yellow light, stuffy with their breathing, seemed to sway a little, like the cabin of a yacht at anchor. At some time in the early morning, when she lay like last year's doll in the nursery corner, perfectly still, the colour all washed out, her breathing only perceptible to Josef's hungering ears, he found that he was speaking to her again.

"Minna! Minna, are you still there?" And presently, "Why do you want me to go to Giessbach, Minna, what do you know about that place?"

She did not wake; in such a sleep a shout would not have woken her. But when a little time had passed (an hour perhaps, when time was moving like a stream through boulders) he caught a whisper from her, "hills . . . Fräulein Rother told me . . . beautiful hills."

This was different from the voice of her delirium; how-

ever ragged and small, it belonged to her as the small forehead and the sharply-cut chin belonged, it was the private
voice she used when most at ease. It altered her from a body
with life in it to a creature still alive; and soon, with his face
leant close to hers, he could hear that she was speaking
steadily, as if she counted on a listener's attention.

". . . clear, it's all perfectly clear. The little station's
almost in the middle, an old sergeant with a wooden leg
takes your ticket and you go out into the square. The square,
yes, it's very wide, with trees on both sides where they set
out the little tables. There's always a smell of coffee right
across the square, the priest stands in the sunshine and
watches the boys as they race each other on old bicycles.
You'll stay at Wiezerzick's Gasthaus, Frau Wiezerzick will
talk in the evenings about the French war. In the morning
you take a loaf and sausages. The road goes over a stone
bridge and past the Resurrection Church, then there's only
the little wooden houses squatting under their snow roofs
and the road goes up into the pines. You walk till you're all
sweaty and covered with dust, then you get off the road and
you climb up with your feet on pine needles till you're right
above the pines, and you see the lake from there, it's a shining blue eye with great green eyebrows. You lie on the short
grass between the rocks munching your dinner and you watch
the tiny steamers paddling along the lake like ducklings.
There's always a cool wind up there, and the ground's so
soft you don't feel your body any more. Yes, yes, it will be
just like that! Your body stays behind like an old pair of
pinching shoes you've thrown away, you float away on the
smell of trees and you drink up all the summer."

Just for a second her eyes opened.

"You'll write to me, Herr Josef? You'll write and tell
me if it's all like that?"

As her voice was washed out by a gasp, Josef remembered what he was about. To be listening to such chatter,
when her life was a candle which he carried through a

draughty corridor! Reaching with one hand for the phial of Stritze's valerate he slid the other under the bolster and shifted it so as to relax the carotid arteries. A piece of card fell on the floor, and as he turned to measure out the solution he caught sight of a faded photograph, a girl with hideous teeth and pince-nez, the inscription *Lovingly, your Hedwig Rother.* As he watched the yellow smudge of Minna's face through the medicine-glass the idea pricked him: 'So that is the other of her heroes; the spotty schoolma'am and the doctor!' There was a name for these delusions—he had it, Romanticism. Yes, he thought, that was the kernel of the matter, romance-psychology.

His tiredness was changing to a new form, a mental apathy. The excitement of the battle had ebbed away, he could only see a rusty bedstead with two of the uprights out of their sockets, the colourless remains of a kitchen girl like those which made the eternal scenery of the hospital. He had emptied his resources now, he was too tired to care if he lost or won. A holiday, he needed a holiday. And then, if need be, he would find another case.

His thoughts would not stop there, they squeezed and ran to find a farther playground. His next experiment: the first approach, the empty record-sheet, the first injection: would every stage be so exciting at the second time, would he feel again the private glory in a patient of his own? Something, he knew, would not be there. In some peculiar way his second case could not be so *sympathisch.*

He had his ear to the heart again, straining for its flimsy tread. She turned a little, and as a sleeping child clutches a woolly bear she brought her arm across his face: that very thin left arm.

He let it stay there, cold on the rough skin of his cheek. He said, all of a sudden: "I'll take you to Giessbach, Minna! I promise that, my dear I promise that! As soon as you've got well we'll go there, you and me!"

23

THE window of Röstel's surgery commanded the courtyard and a shed where the Staff kept bicycles. There, waiting for Röstel to come and go down to lunch with him, Dittmer saw young Zeppichmann wheeling out his machine as he did every day. For Dittmer, who found all the corners of life amusing, this was an entertainment. Efficiently clothed in cape and leggings the youth looked like a peripatetic mushroom. His machine was a portentous affair with unheard-of stabilizing bars, he wheeled it as if he were leading out a General's charger, invariably he stopped to test the brakes. Then the handlebars were firmly grasped, the mushroom's stalk made three deliberate punts, and lo! it was become a centaur, a floating mound of dignity and purpose.

"Our poor luncheons are not good enough for your distinguished assistant," Dittmer said over his shoulder.

Röstel closed the door behind him and went over to the basin.

"I hope you've gargled," he said abruptly. "If people who have nothing better to do must spend their time blowing on my window panes I require them first to sterilise their breath with carbolic . . . Zeppichmann? I don't know why he goes home for midday, I don't know what he does, I can't understand him at all. He looks as if he never goes to bed. They tell me he's a Communist, they say he spends his time scrapping in the streets. I don't know, his work's all right, I can't help what he does out of hours, I can't spend all my time chasing my subordinates all over the place. Please, if you don't mind, I'd rather you didn't fiddle with those instruments. They're for the use of properly qualified doctors who wash their hands at regular intervals."

Dittmer put down the umbilical scissors with which he had been cutting his nails.

"A Communist? Well, really, that surprises me very much. One day, I suppose, I shall hear that my old friend Doctor Röstel has become a Flat Earth enthusiast." He picked up a bandage and started twisting it into the shape of a daffodil. "Not a good thing to be, just at present—a Communist! You've seen the news this morning?"

"The news? You mean about the duodenal operation on Herr von Abschwanger? Yes, indeed, a most remarkable accomplishment! . . . If you really need bandages to amuse yourself I can send some old ones along to your workshop . . ."

Overnight, a stiff, dry wind from the northeast had broken up the mist; the drizzle had stopped and the sky, still haggard with rain, was drawn to a greater height. Above the town its colour deepened, and the clouds were puckered there, as if rough hands had dragged it down. But behind that angry curtain the winter light was brilliant, sharpening its folds, and where the clouds were torn it leaked into the rain-washed air, flooding the roofs and chimneys with an icy radiance. Josef, free-wheeling down the drive, let his eyes rest on the town for the first time. A spread of factories and houses, always in the same place, was no more worth attention than the colour of his own skin; but to-day, with the wind cooling his face, a curious wakefulness penetrating his fatigue, he thought it was pretty, this jumble of red and grey lit by a yellow shaft. He even held on his brake, ekeing out the moments till the drive would turn and the view be covered by the new laundry wall. Up here you felt so light and free, with the stale hubbub of the wards behind; and with winter's dirty coat unclasped he suddenly saw the beauty of her nakedness.

Where the drive turned into the public road the wind stood against him like a net, he had to pedal to keep going down the hill. He was surprised to feel so great a reserve of strength, to find himself so far detached from the lumbering pain of his forehead.

It was another victory. He had left her dozing, with a temperature hardly over 98.6°, respirations back to the average of the previous week: she had taken a little food, even asked for something to read: he was satisfied that one more hazard lay behind. That quickening relief, as when a tired swimmer feels the sand, had come at every stage in the treatment. But this emotion burnt more warmly than relief, and with a brighter flame. From such a state of mind he could not pick the separate threads as when he diagnosed an illness: he scarcely knew that his mind had altered, only that a certain happiness had come, like sunshine to the faces of the blind; that something was alight inside himself which resisted all external coldness.

There remained, across this inner light, a streak of darkness: a final problem to be solved. But he would not allow his thoughts to turn that way.

Without reflection, as he pedalled industriously along the Gardelegen avenue, he knew he had suffered a needless poverty: he had driven himself to clear the nettles from a garden without once noticing the flowers which grew there. But that was over, and nothing was really lost. The aim of all his work was still the same, only made luminous by his new discovery. He no longer spent his powers just to confirm a theory but to recreate something with a tender value of its own. The relief, the sense of escape he had! No longer to watch himself playing the assiduous, sympathetic nurse, to fill his eyes with calculated optimism whenever they encountered hers. From now she was companion in his adventure, he worked for her as well as for himself, instead of suspicion he would have her constant understanding . . .

The impetus of the long glide carried him under the railway bridge and on to the main road. Her patience, that was all he could think of now, her patience and humility. Her body was so small, her hands were too fragile to bear the marks of so much labour. She won't go back to that, he thought, I'll fix up something else, I won't let the old dame have her! At the Türkeplatz a coloured ball ran out in front of his wheel, he pulled up sharply and gave the ball back to the child who had let it run. The child's mother smiled at him, and he bowed and smiled, thinking how frail she was. Everywhere, he thought, there are people who are small and frail and who need protection. Where the road started to climb towards the Bülow fountain he got off and pushed the bicycle. And there the sun broke cleanly from the clouds, breathing warmth on his cold cheeks, and he caught a smell of new bread from the door of a bakery, and the loneliness of Hartzinnfeld had melted away. I found her in this town, he thought, I am at home here.

This was a street of busy shops, and as he plodded up its slope, leaning on the handlebars, smiling, he did not realise that the pavements were more crowded than was usual at this hour; until a business man hurrying across the road collided with his front wheel and ran on without even stopping to curse. Josef looked up then, and saw the scoliotic who sold *Hartzinnfelde-Zeitung* hobbling as fast as he could along the other pavement, sowing copies to right and left as he went.

In the sweep of his eyes he caught the face of a girl, a tall girl with tight shoes which kept her to a broken gait as she ran. That pale face, it was blind with eagerness, and in a flick of time he felt he had seen it before: a woman running along his own street in Richterhausen, some summer afternoon when he had been sitting on the hot kerbstone. It had frightened him, that woman's face, and now this face frightened him. The sun stayed brilliant, but as he reached the level and got on the bicycle again he felt obscurely that the glitter of the windows, the warmth on his hands, were both illusory; like the daylight which a motor's headlamps thrust across dark fields.

He pedalled slowly, calling "If you please! . . . Excuse me!": it was difficult to get along with people walking about the roadway as carelessly as in a fairground. He saw what they were making for: the Radio-Haus am Schüster stood at the next corner with a trio of trumpets sprouting from its entrance like a monstrous flower, and there the crowd across the road was damming the traffic altogether. He had to walk again, manoeuvring his front wheel as if he were thrusting a spoon through a bag of apples, "Excuse me please . . . Thank you!" and then for a moment or two he was quite shut in. The radio was in clumsy order, vomiting a chequered stream of broken sentences and music, he caught only a phrase or two, '*He will release us . . . all that is done with now.*' It seemed to be enough for the crowd, they caught at a group of words and pitched it out to neighbours at the fringe, a knot of boys with arms round each others' necks were laughing and cheering. "Please—excuse me—I am in a hurry." The man he spoke to squeezed to let him pass, giving a friendly smile.

It increased, the sense of separation and of insecurity, as if some cloud pursued him with a private shadow. It derived from fragments belonging to a world outside his own, bits of a conversation he had heard in the Staff Mess, newspaper headings. He had thought it was no concern of a scientist with his job to do, this uproar from the mart of argument and rumour. And now he felt as if free wine were being poured in the street, and he alone had come without a pitcher. They were shouting to each other between the houses, "Heard the news?" A child with a little flag held right above her head was singing triumphantly as she stamped along the kerb. It was the sun, perhaps, which drew good humour to these faces as it draws new colour to the earth's dun crust; the sun breaking the drab half-tones of the Friedrich wharf to a pattern of shadow, plucking a sword of light from the mud-sodden water; perhaps it was the sun which made them smile. Even old Margarete smiled, pushing her barrow up the slope, Margarete with the man's overcoat just buttoned across her gigantic breasts and her faint eyes soaked with tears, she too was smiling.

Across the river the floating crowd had a new direction, a whiff of music came from somewhere along the Siemenstrasse and they were hurrying that way. Josef would have turned to avoid the crush by going the long way round, but his time was limited and he thought he could hustle through.

These were a shabbier mob, these shoppers from the little Siemenstrasse stores: women who no longer tried to be young with bundles as shapeless as themselves, tired children dragging their fingers along the boards with the auction bills: they seemed to catch their tone from the grey of the besieging houses, from the dirty chocolate of the trams. The procession emerging from the Haubold passage had the same low colour. These boys belonged to the region north and east of the Burchardt crossing, they were awkwardly built out of narrow purses, their clothes were coarse and tight and heterogeneous. But they marched, in ranks of eight, with the port and stamp of soldiers, their feet fell to the drum's quick beat with a crash of a single bar. They wheeled at the corner, clean as a cartwheel's spokes, and came on rigidly towards the bridge, a grill of shoulders fixed to a common frame. A lanky milkman's boy; the second cashier from a bank in Mählstrasse; a swarthy youth from Rumprecht's works: they had lost their separate selves in the single pulse of their feet, narrow or bold their heads were held as if on a bearing rein, their lips were close, their young stern eyes drove on with a bright devotion. "Our men!" a woman said as she squeezed through the tightening crowd, and whispered again, wiping her eyes, "Our men!"

The sun had gone when the tail of shouting children reached the bridge, but as Josef made his way through the drifting crowd the new strange light was still on their faces. Old Frau Pfeiffer at the door of her shop with the meat-saw in her hand, a man who had come out of the barber's with the lather still on his face, they laughed and shook each other's hands, a woman seized a grocer's boy and kissed him. "We've got it!" Hans Brose called, "it's come at last!" and with great tears falling on his cheeks and his belly bouncing like a trawler he danced a jig on the pavement. The tram which the crowd had stopped jerked on a foot at a time with the driver leaning down to shake hands with his friends, the people inside stood up and banged the windows and waved their handkerchiefs. *It's come, it's come!* Carefully guiding his bicycle, murmuring "Excuse me, please, excuse me!", Josef did not quite understand it all; his own sunshine had disappeared and he got no warmth from theirs. But he smiled, as he had learnt to do at a hundred bedsides, he smiled and gave his good-humoured nod to any one he knew. Only when a girl stepped out with a sudden cry of *Jude!* and rammed her umbrella at his front wheel did he realise fully that the festival was not for him. When he had picked up the umbrella, and gravely returned it, he rode on as fast as he could.

24

THE news had got through to Handelstrasse and Herr Spühler had put on his medals. He did not altogether understand: he couldn't see how a swap-round of politicians in Berlin was going to make old Barthol pay his rent, to clear up the troubles which had thickened about them like cobwebs these fourteen years. But young Herr Meisel seemed to know all about it, Herr Meisel with his important friends in Berlin, and Spühler had more sense than to bother himself with schoolbook questions. That burst of sunshine, it had come right in through the kitchen window; and Herr Spühler's heart, his heart had told him that once again he was free.

Nobody understood how Herr Barthol had got the news, lying in his bed all week, too ill as they thought to read his papers. But here was the old gentleman fully dressed, fully dressed and standing by the kitchen table, with a tiny bottle in his hand.

"Gnädige Frau—Herr Spühler—my two old friends, old friends who have travelled beside me on a long, hard road! I beg of you one thing, one sacred act to crown this day's happiness! This little flask, I've kept it many years for this day. I beg you (if you have no suitable glasses the coffee cups will do just as well), I beg you to join me in this pledge: *Deutschland!*"

The tears which had beleaguered Frau Spühler's eyes could not be restrained now. They came as a summer storm against the window panes, she saw Herr Barthol and her own August like giants enwrapped in cloud, her throat was drowned with tears and she couldn't speak. From the deep,

delicious mist she heard a burst of music. It was August singing, August singing and stamping his short, wide feet as he
had last done nearly thirty years ago.

He saw that she was blind, leaning against the sink and
oblivious of the cup Herr Barthol held. He went to her and
gathered her breast against his shoulder, stroked the sleeve
of her satin dress, whispered endearments he had long forgotten. "My Hildchen, my Hildelein, we are happy now!"
Herr Barthol stood with a cup in either hand, more soldierly
than he had ever been, and gazed at them with a vast affection, and bowed and smiled again. "Dear friends, that we
should have lived to see this day!" "This day!" Frau
Spühler whispered. She did not fully understand, but she
knew that August was happy, happy and proud; and that
made all her happiness. The sunshine and the satin gown,
and now the buttons of his naval coat pressing against her
breast: she was young again, and beautiful, and her lover
was brave and strong.

They were standing at the street door when Josef arrived: a triad of the resurrection. Hilde had found the little
flags which had lain all crumpled in a cupboard with her
wedding shoes and August's stormcoat; their colour still
showed well enough, and there was one for each of them.
She held her own flag high and bravely, waving it at passers-
by as if to drench them with her inward glory. Herr Barthol
handled his a trifle awkwardly, like an old lady practising
revolver shots, and he flinched a little from the friendly
thumps Herr Spühler kept giving him across the reins. But
he felt obscurely that he himself had brought this joy to
them, these good old friends of his, these children holding
each other's hands and smiling through their tears, and in his
aging heart their ecstasy lit up a bright reflection. He knew
that a button of his coat was off, that the knees of his trousers
sagged, his left boot gaped where the lace had broken; but
forgotten dreams were driving a warm live blood into his

veins, with his neck and shoulders braced like a bow he once more thought himself a soldier. "It has come, old friend!" Herr Spühler said again. And Herr Barthol, with his eyes shining over his proud moustache, said, "It has come!"

With this new spring of kindness bursting from her heart Frau Spühler would have run to welcome Josef, poor Dr. Zeppichmann who worked so hard and was always so tired-out. But something stopped her. Perhaps it was the doctor's face, so very pale to-day, his eyes so guarded and so dead. Herr Spühler called as he approached, "Herr Doktor, have you heard——?" but he too fell silent, and Josef did not answer him.

Josef propped his bicycle against the wall; it fell over, but he didn't go back to pick it up. Closed in himself, hardly feeling the eyes which followed him, he went upstairs; past the door of his own room, straight up to the attic. The old excitement of entering that room had gone, he only wanted to find peace there.

She was awake. She looked at him cautiously, as if he might be coming to scold or to praise her. He didn't say anything, he sat on the side of the bed and held her hand, with his eyes not quite meeting hers. He sat there for a long time, almost happy, nervously pressing her hand.

25

RÖSTEL stood outside Dr. Wildelau's room for at least half a minute before he went in. He couldn't understand how it was, but these interviews with Wildelau always chilled his bowels. Leaving his own room two minutes ago he had felt quite sturdy, and now his hands were fluttering like a skylark's wings. This red baize door, it was oddly redoubtable: standing here for the first time, shaking all over, he had almost read the words *Lasciate ogni speranza voi ch' entrate* along the architrave. He had grown less fanciful since then, eleven years of scolding nurses had made a man of him; but the physical sensation was the same, the way the trousers felt loose on his legs, the peculiar shallowness of his breathing . . . He furtively knocked the door and pushed it just wide enough to squeeze himself inside.

"Ah, Röstel, yes! Sit down, sit down!"

Yes, Röstel's intuition had not misled him: something was wrong. Of all Wildelau's manners, the breezy one was the most dangerous; and he was wearing his light grey tie as well.

"Sit down, there's a good fellow, do sit down! I'm sorry I had to send for you at a busy time of day, but it's rather important."

Important, God in Heaven! Had some one bungled a post-mortem form?

". . . about young Zeppichmann. I want to know exactly what you think about his work."

Röstel hesitated. When starting to speak to Dr. Wildelau he invariably found that his first sentence had telescoped, he must always give himself time to pull the words apart before he released them.

"About his work, Herr Direktor, well, I've nothing to say about his work. I mean, as to his work, I can't find anything wrong with it. Nothing wrong, Herr Direktor. Works very well. His work, I mean to say, is excellent, quite excellent."

"You've not had any trouble with him? No trouble of any kind?"

There was a catch in that, something like the horrible traps that lawyers prepared for witnesses: Röstel knew it, he knew it from the easy, purring tone. Well, he was not going to be caught, not at his time of life. A plain, straightforward statement, that was all anybody was going to get from him.

"Trouble, Herr Direktor? No, Herr Direktor! I mean to say, no, nothing, nothing that you could call trouble. Naturally we all have our feelings, it stands to reason, one can't always judge by personal feelings, as long as a young man's work is all right, whatever one may feel."

Dr. Wildelau accepted the deposition with a certain dullness.

"I'm not—absolutely clear, Doctor." ('Oh God, now he's calling me Doctor!' Röstel thought.) "Do I understand you to mean that Zeppichmann is—insubordinate, or rough in his manner toward the patients, or—"

"Exactly!" Röstel said firmly. "That's quite right, Herr Direktor. All wrong! Manner towards the patients. I don't mean that his manner towards the patients is wrong, I shouldn't dream of saying so. Very good hands, doesn't leave things about, every attention to patients' comfort. I'm sure the boy means well, very hard-working young fellow, never had a better man. It's just—oh well, I suppose it's all my imagination."

"You mean—?"

"I mean, he treats them as if they were blocks of wood.

No no, I don't mean that. Excellent at his ward-work, couldn't be better. I mean—well, he never seems to me to think about patients in the same way as I think about them. Of course it may be all my imagination, in fact I've no doubt it's all my imagination, it's just a feeling I have, if you know what I mean. I can't put it plainer than that, can I?"

Wildelau nodded.

"No, you could hardly put it plainer than that."

He got up and walked across the room. This was a difficult matter, he wanted to be quite sure that he was dealing justly with every one concerned, and he found that by pacing slowly up and down the room he acquired a sense of detachment, a feeling of almost divine impartiality.

"I myself," he said thoughtfully, "have formed a similar impression. As you may know, I take some trouble to keep acquainted with the work and—personalities—of all my Staff. I like to feel that I am, as it were, a personal friend —perhaps I might say a father—to every man and woman who works under me."

Röstel nodded devoutly. Really—though he could be most alarming, and wasn't by any means what Röstel called a doctor—there was a certain greatness about their Director, a certain grand humanity, a certain . . .

". . . And, as I say, I have recently become aware of a tendency in Zeppichmann which seems to me exactly as you describe it. I shouldn't like to think ill of the young man, I'm sure he has his good points, but I can't help feeling that his treatment of patients is utterly at variance with the clinical standards and the—philosophy of our society. Naturally—"

Röstel coughed. "Pardon me, Herr Direktor, but I think you—I don't think you quite understand—understood me. I shouldn't think of suggesting that Doctor Zeppichmann's treatment of patients is anything but what it should be. I should be the last person—"

"Exactly yes, I appreciate that! I fully understand your position, I see your meaning very clearly indeed. I'm very glad that you've been so frank with me, and I'm also glad that you're willing to make the most generous allowance for youth and inexperience. I feel that that is the spirit which should animate all our work here. On the other hand, I ask you to believe that I, too, leave nothing out of consideration in judging a case of this kind—nothing, I mean, that could be urged in Zeppichmann's favour. You see, Röstel, a man in my position has to take the longest view. I have to consider what is in the best interests of the hospital, looking some ten or twenty years ahead. That means I can never afford to lose any opportunity of recruiting the finest available material. (The fact that I selected you, some years ago, from a large field of applicants goes to show that my judgement in these matters is—not without wisdom.) Now I have here a letter about a Doctor Maus, from Munich, a young man who's been very highly recommended. His academic qualifications are not quite so good—formally speaking—as Zeppichmann's. But in the art of healing, as you will be the first to agree, it is not always the academic qualifications which are the most important. Doctor Maus has been working in the Kronprinz hospital at Munich, and he seems to have earned the highest esteem, both of his colleagues and of the patients themselves. That is really the kind of man we want here—don't you agree?"

"Why, yes, Herr Direktor, certainly, there's always work for a good man. Very short-handed we've been lately, it's quite a struggle to get through."

"Just so! Well, I thought I would consult you before writing to Doctor Maus—I value your opinion on these matters and I wanted to be quite sure you agree with me. I think I can get Doctor Maus here by the beginning of next week. I expect you'd like to keep Zeppichmann a few days more after that, just to show the new man his work."

"But—but you mean, Herr Direktor, that Doctor Zeppichmann has to go? You mean that this other man is taking his place?"

"My dear Röstel, there is one person who governs us all, and that is the Treasurer. It's all I can do to make him pass the present salary-list. I think if I suggested lengthening it he would become one of our patients! Well now, I don't think I need keep you any longer. I'm very grateful to you for giving me your opinion."

So that was all! As if the chair had been gently tipped up from behind Röstel found himself on his feet. ('You can say your *Mahlzeit* and get down now, Heinrich!' 'You can go now, Röstel!' 'That's all we want to ask you, Herr Röstel!'—that pattern had been repeating all through his fifty years and he took his place in it quite automatically.) He made his little bow to the top of Wildelau's head—the Director was already busy with the next problem—and turned towards the door. From the roll-top desk in the corner the yellowish bust of Galen stared at him a little sardonically. He always welcomed that gaze: it meant that one more period of discomfort was over and he could hide again in his narrow, cosy world.

But at the door he stopped. It came to him, as if in the voice of an indignant angel, that at the age of fifty-three he should no longer be treated like a child. Really and truly, this man Wildelau, this glorified office-clerk who had almost forgotten how to read a thermometer, this Wildelau with his pot-bellied eyes and his tight little trousers, who was known to take quack tablets to relieve his dyspepsia . . . He turned abruptly.

"Herr Direktor!"

"I've rather a lot to get through this morning, Röstel. If you want a talk with me, perhaps you'll be good enough to arrange with my Secretary . . ."

"Herr Direktor, I want to make myself plain. I think

you've misunderstood me, misunderstood me altogether. I mean to say, if Doctor Zeppichmann goes we shall be losing a very good man. A most conscientious doctor. I mean to say, you don't find them every day, young men who are so thoroughly well up in their bookwork and yet willing to do what they're told, a fellow who takes as much trouble with a twopenny-halfpenny ulcer as over something really interesting. A very rare thing, Herr Direktor, to find a man like that. I think we should be making the greatest mistake if we let Doctor Zeppichmann go. The greatest mistake!"

Wildelau did not look up. Still writing steadily on his pad, he said:

"I have been Director of this Hospital, Doctor Röstel, for something like twenty years. In the course of that time I think I may say that I've learnt a little about the business of selecting staff. I've learnt that there are many qualities to be considered, and that they are not all immediately obvious to those who cannot regard the issues with the same detachment as myself. I think that's all I want to say just at present."

"Yes, Herr Direktor!"

There was hardly a sound as the door opened and shut, but when Wildelau looked up again Röstel had gone. Only Galen stared at him; with his customary approval, Wildelau thought.

He was vexed about the position Röstel had taken. But it was always like that, it was one of the factors which made his work so very exacting: you could never rely on the men below you to take the broader view, to examine questions of personnel with absolute impartiality . . . He took a typewritten letter and wrote across the top: '*Arranged. Z to have one month's sal. in lieu of notice. Fräulein Berger to advise Treasurer.*' Then he put the letter in the basket labelled *Disposed*.

He had a free hour now—ninety minutes with any

luck—and he settled down to the work which in his view was really important. He was preparing a treatise on *The Basic Principles of Hospital Management Considered in Relation to the Place of the Hospital in the National Health-Progress-Organisation,* and this week should see the completion of Chapter XXVI (*Some Factors in Hospital Dietary*). He was unlucky, however. Only half an hour had gone when he became aware of a slight draught on the back of his neck, a faint smell of cough lozenge: Fräulein Berger.

He said without raising his head: "Put the letters on that other table, will you. I'll start signing at five o'clock."

"It's not the letters," his secretary said. "It's Doctor Dittmer—he would like to have a word with you."

"Dittmer? I'll see him at ten o'clock to-morrow. Make a note of that, will you: Dittmer, ten o'clock."

The smell of lozenge increased. Pale and pince-nezed, like a bad man's conscience, Fräulein Berger came up to his shoulder.

"I think you ought to see Doctor Dittmer now, Herr Direktor. You remember that last month he sent his estimates direct to the Treasurer. He reported to the Board Meeting that he hadn't been able to see you."

One of the frilly sleeves she wore, a kind of sex-membership badge, was almost touching his ear. Surely, Wildelau thought, it was a cynical stroke of providence to give the same creature so exceptional a capability and such a voice, to say nothing of her tusks.

"Well, can't you find out what he wants? See if it's anything really important?"

"I think you ought to see him yourself, Herr Direktor."

"I didn't ask you what you thought!"

"No, Herr Direktor."

"Well, you'd better send him in."

Much as Wildelau detested Röstel's furtive entrances,

Dittmer's contemplative style annoyed him more. To-day, as usual, the man's slow, sceptical eyes were hovering about the office as he came in—from the carpet to the bookshelves, resting for a moment on the bust of Galen, travelling across to the window, everywhere except on Wildelau's desk—as if to suggest that he had cleaned his boots in better rooms than this; while his lips were stretched into their private, pitying smile.

"You wanted to see me, Doctor Dittmer?"

Dittmer's smile revolved and came to rest on Wildelau's face with a faint surprise.

"Poor Galen!" he said. "They've chipped his ears a bit since I was last in here. Those cleaning women, they'll make Heaven uninhabitable when they die."

"And the matter you wanted to discuss with me?" Wildelau said patiently.

"Discuss with you? Oh yes, it was about young Zeppichmann. Röstel tells me you're sacking him."

Wildelau scraped an imaginary crumb from his lower lip.

"If you wouldn't mind just leaving that paper-knife alone—!" he said. "Zeppichmann? Let me see, yes, I was talking to Doctor Röstel about Zeppichmann. But I'm not sure that I see the—precise connection between Doctor Röstel's assistants and the—bacteriological research department."

Dittmer carefully fitted his right buttock into a little space he had cleared on the desk. He said:

"That's just what I've come to talk about. That boy, for all I know, may be a cabbage-fisted doctor. But he happens by the inscrutable decrees of fate to be a born bacteriologist. For some reason that completely defeats me his very unpleasing head is fitted with the apparatus for advanced mathematics. And what is far more startling, he has grasped the elusive truth that mathematics is not without form and void. When you add to that the fact—"

"Doctor Dittmer," Wildelau said frigidly, "the Hospital spends some thirty thousand Marks a year on providing you with things to fiddle with. Is it absolutely necessary for you to manhandle my inkstand as well?"

"Oh, this is yours?"

Dittmer dutifully put it down and closed the three lids, *click, click, click*. His eyes had dawdled on to the *Disposed* basket and he was trying to read from the wrong end the letter which lay on top. A Reichsministerium letter, by the smell of it: yes, he could see the heading now.

"As I was saying," he continued pleasantly, "if you've no use for Zeppichmann in the outer courts of this place I can take him into the Inner Sanctuary. I mean, in fact, that I've got a job for him."

"And has the Treasurer got a new salary for him?" Wildelau asked gently.

"Yes!" Dittmer said. "You know that Korbenhaus is leaving at the end of this month, Allah be praised! Well, little as Korbenhaus has ever contributed to the work of the department, I shall want some one to replace him. Young Zeppichmann is my sausage."

Wildelau took off his glasses and swung them delicately from the cord, apparently timing the rate of swing. "Hitherto," he said, "I have been under the impression that staff appointments were a matter in which I myself am a good deal concerned . . ."

Dittmer nodded. "Exactly! That's why I came early to make sure you'll give me the man I want."

The glasses fell, smack, on to the blotting pad.

"Doctor Dittmer, as you've chosen to raise this matter with me—instead of waiting till I sent for you—I may as well give you my decision straight away. For reasons which I shan't trouble to discuss with you, I have decided that Zeppichmann is not a desirable person to belong to my staff. That is final."

For the first time, Dittmer looked straight into Wilde-lau's eyes. His own were still mild and clear.

"*You* have decided?" he asked.

"Precisely!"

Again Dittmer's glance went over to the letter in the basket, and returned to Wildelau's face.

"Am I not right in thinking that the decision has been made by some pertinacious busybody in Berlin?"

Wildelau suddenly struck the table.

"Doctor Dittmer, the relationship between this Hospital and the central authority for German health organisation is nothing whatever to do with you! Do you understand?"

He pressed the porter's bell.

Dittmer stood up. "But the advancement of medical science is very much to do with me," he said. His voice suddenly changed: it was as if a second valve had been opened in his throat, releasing a whole reservoir of angry power. "It so happens that Zeppichmann has a more astonishing aptitude for research and greater powers of concentration than any man who's ever stepped inside my laboratory. If he's given the proper facilities there's no limit to what he may accomplish. And because you haven't got the nerve to run this hospital yourself, because you're such an old woman you've got to take orders from a pack of numbskull politicians——"

The door opened and the porter clicked his heels.

Wildelau said: "Gustav, Doctor Dittmer is not feeling very well. Will you please accompany him back to his own department."

Dittmer shrugged his shoulders and turned away. But as he passed the bust of Galen he stopped to run his fingers over the stubborn chin. "You and me," he said softly, "our day is done," and laughed uncannily in his thin nose, and went out softly laughing.

26

"I MAY say, Doctor Zeppichmann, that I very much regret the Director's decision," Röstel repeated. "In fact, to be perfectly candid, I strongly urged him to reconsider it. I—I went as far as it was possible to go with proper regard to the Director's position. Naturally, in such matters of high policy as the appointment of staff one must respect the Director's judgement. I can only say that I regret the decision, I—I regret it very much."

"You are really most kind, Herr Doktor!" Josef said.

They watched him, on his last day, to see how he would carry it off. (Every one knew he was going.) They were not much rewarded. His ordinary reserve was fastened a little tighter, he seemed to be short-sighted when they passed him in the corridors. But he went through his routine as steadily as if this were a normal day, initialling a record-sheet, examining a new case of endocarditis, switching his clinical smile on and off between the beds. An old woman in 14 clutched his wrist and bellowed hoarsely, "They tell me you're packing your traps, Doctor-boy! Well, you'll have to come back and put the poultices on my stomach. You'll have to, I tell you. Those bitches in the fancy pinafores, they don't know how to do it. Nor the old fellow either! I tell you you'll have to come back for that job!" He told her, in his elderly voice, that he would mention the matter to Dr. Röstel; and moved on quickly to the Incipient Cancer at the other end of the ward. But Sister Täubler, patrolling at his side, caught a look in his eyes which she had not seen before.

"Say what you like," she afterwards observed to Sister

Dahms, "I don't mind swearing that he looked quite human. Just for a moment, I mean. Quite human! You know, when all's said and done, we've had more poisonous specimens of ward-trotter on our hands. I mean, he does at least know something about it. I can't help thinking it's a pity in some ways, his having to go."

Sister Dahms put down her cup.

"Not half such a pity as it is about Doctor Hirschstein. *He* knows his job better than the whole lot of them put together, *and* he's got nice eyes."

"Oh well, I suppose they know what they're doing."

"I suppose so. Pass me the other cake, dear, will you!"

At half-past six Josef went to get his things from Röstel's surgery, but when he reached the door he heard voices inside. Maus, the new man, was there. Dr. Maus was living up to his reputation, his manners with everybody were delightful. "I quite agree, Doctor, I quite agree!" Josef heard him say. "You know, really, it's a great thing, it's a wonderful thing for me, to find myself working under some one whose outlook on our profession is so entirely ethical . . ." while Röstel said a little wearily, "Quite so! . . . Indeed, yes! . . . Quite so!" He decided not to go in: his overcoat was in the lobby and Ahlwarth or some one would send on the rest of his stuff. He returned quickly along the passage, pretending not to see a Ward Sister who passed him, and went down by the porter's stairs.

The long row of wash-basins with the chipped mirrors advertising Kain's Haemorrhoidal Suppositories, Gustav sprawling over the evening-paper, the smell of liquid soap: these had become like the wheel's rumble in a miller's ears, it was difficult for Josef to realise they were done with now. Gustav, glancing up, said, "I understand you won't be wanting that peg any more?" "Thank-you, no!" Josef said, and jerked the swing-door open with his knee, twisting into his coat as he went along.

This was something he had learnt to enjoy, as you enjoy the day's first cup of coffee: the moment when the swing-door opened, letting a cool air wash into his face, and closed again to shut away the staring light, the hum and heat of three hundred people at work. But the pleasure had been unreflective, he only realised it now. He stood still for a moment, catching the faint, damp smell of trees, and looked up at the rows of lights across the yard. Ward 11, with the main dispensary just above it, No. 2 theatre over that: it was curious that he would never see those again. He got his bicycle and lit the lamps.

As he stopped to test the brakes a window went up, a voice called out, "Is that you, Zeppichmann? I'd like a word before you go." That was Dittmer, but Josef did not want to see him. He was a little unhappy now about those rats of Dittmer's; and afraid, in a peculiar way, of Dittmer's kindness. Pretending not to hear, he made his three energetic punts, got on and pedalled down the drive.

27

HE WENT through the back streets, partly out of prudence, partly to fence his thoughts with the comparative darkness.

At present, the money problem was uppermost. With a month's salary in hand he was all right for living expenses until he found work of some kind. (Part-time assistance to Dr. Wohlfahrt? A job in one of the co-operative dispensaries?) But without the hospital facilities he would have to improve his own laboratory before he could do further work on the theoretical side. He wanted more chemicals, a further supply of tuberculins. As to the main experiment, it was vital that Minna should be moved before long: he had planned to get her into a bungalow high up on the other side of the town. Meanwhile, there was something like two hundred Marks to be paid on Teppers' account . . . Yes, the important thing was to get a job, any sort of job, immediately . . . But Hirschstein, whispering in a corner of the Staff Room, had told him there would be at least a dozen doctors out of work in Hartzinnfeld alone.

There was one way out, simple and final. A letter from Papa had come this morning, urging him to go back to Richterhausen. Old Dr. Sponholz was looking for a young man who could give him part-time assistance, and at Richterhausen the new regulations were not yet being imposed very rigorously. Josef could live at home, sleep in his old room: then, Papa wrote, they would all be happy. His mind had worked on that as he made his round in the wards. Possibly old Sponholz would let him use a part of his surgery as a laboratory, Minna could be transported to Richterhausen

and live—live where? Richterhausen, with its yellow fog
and its stench of tanneries, with the third highest T.B. mor-
tality in the country . . . And then he thought of the humiliation: Zeppichmann, the boy from the little hardware
shop they had all heard so much about, the one who had
gone to college and was going to be a great doctor—here
he was, living behind the shop again, doing odd jobs for
Dr. Sponholz. Workmen from Bieber's yards, men pushing
barrows along the Büttelstrasse or even cleaning out the
drains, they would all hail him as an old schoolfellow; it
would be, 'Hey, Josef, so you're back again after all!' And
in five years' time, perhaps, he would have a share of Sponholz's practice, and would spend the rest of his life trapesing
up and down the endless, dingy streets . . . No! No! Ah
God, not that!

The coat he had on was a good one; he had bought it
in a moment of extravagance and hardly worn it. He could
do without that—in very cold weather you could sew newspapers inside the lining of your jacket—and he might sell it
back for 75 per cent of the purchase price, with luck. The
bicycle, of course, could go. Then there were things he had
brought from Zornenwalde, a copy of Vielehr's *Lectures on
Anatomy* in quite good condition, the sateen bedspread . . .
He would cut out the cigarettes (which he was smoking at
the rate of twenty a week now) and make do with one good
meal a day, which he could cook for himself on the gas-ring
. . . It was a question of time: he had only to hang on for
two or three months, and then—unless the unthinkable happened—he would be in a position to publish his first report.
It would have to be written under a *nom de guerre,* and with
some ambiguity as to the way the case had been obtained.
Directly it was published, inquiries would come from specialists all over the country. He would simply have to choose
the most influential and make a frank, confidential statement
to him . . .

Yes, that was the objective. He would have to sell nearly all his personal belongings, he might have to starve himself; but somehow, somehow he was going to reach it.

He was riding fast through the Old Market, drawing a physical refreshment from the cold air flowing to his cheeks, the soft hum of his well-oiled wheels. But at the Adrianstrasse crossing he was brought to a stop by a little crowd spreading across the roadway. "The tram," he heard some one say, "it was the tram did it! Caught her back wheel and sent her flying." He propped his bicycle against the kerb and started to push towards the centre of the crowd, calling, "Is some one hurt? I'm a doctor." "Let him through!" a policeman shouted. "Let the doctor through!"

They had got her under a streetlamp, with her head on a policeman's surcoat: a girl of Minna's age and rather like her. All the way from the tramlines there was a trail of blood, flagged out with the contents of her handbag. A young policeman was anxiously dabbing at the girl's cheek with a small handkerchief, while another held the bicycle and was trying to twist it into its former shape. With tiny, frightened ejaculations which sounded like jokes a busy old woman was taking off the girl's shoes.

To Josef the shape of it was plain at the first glance: femoral fracture and probably fracture of the tibia on the same side; the facial wound was superficial, it was the blood from the armpit he didn't like. His coat was off already, he said, "Just get out of the light, will you! Somebody give me a pen-knife—no, don't move her yet!" But a man came up behind and got him by both arms, a thin voice said, "You, we can do without your sort, you clear out!" and Josef found himself face-down in the road.

As he made his way back through the crowd he saw they were staring at him intently, some without malice. But he did not bother about that. His rage, while it lasted, was a coat of armour against such curiosity, and his lips were smiling. He thought, "Well, she can die, if that's how they want it. It's not my business, she belongs to them." And he hoped, just then, that she would die before another doctor came. He wiped off some of the blood and dust from his trousers, turned on to the canal bank and rode away.

It was dark in this narrow lane, between the trees and the lightermen's houses, and the scene which had broken his journey came back like the taste of food: the light across the cobbles, the twisted bicycle, a compact and a lace handkerchief in the dark, widening pool. Strangely, for his eyes had never rested there, the face of the unconscious girl stayed clearest in that image, like the focussed patch in a cloudy photograph: dark hair spilt over the white forehead, the small, two-knuckled chin. It had no meaning for him, the face of a young woman he had never seen before. A dead face, or nearly so: and he had watched so many in the Moltke wards. Yet the image kept close to him as he crossed the bridge and turned into a better-lit street, that patch of white against the dark coat, the slightly parted lips. So near to Minna's face, Minna as she had looked after the last injection, as she would look when dead.

So, it had crept into his privacy again, the voice which he had tried to silence through these days and nights, which had always sounded faintly through the hubbub of worry and calculation, demanding to be answered. The value of Minna, not to his work but to himself: the distorting glass which he had kept to hide his face and which had grown too heavy for him to hold there: these things could not be evaded now.

The next, most critical injection was due to-night. The 'condition curve' had begun to fall as it had done at every corresponding stage, though this time far less steeply. It was a reasonable assumption that if further tuberculin treatment were withheld this curve would continue to slope down gently for several days, perhaps for weeks. Then, if the case

were under ordinary, sound treatment, the drop would be
arrested. Life would continue, perhaps for years, on a lower
level; she would remain as one of those who lie on little
beds, dozing, occasionally coughing, sometimes reading a
page in a book before letting it fall . . . Another injection
might push the curve of crises up again: possibly above his
hypothetical line of fatality. He didn't know, it was all
guesswork, he simply didn't know.

That was the technical problem: he had been all
through it again and again, and his thoughts only traversed
that ground once more as a prisoner in the exercise yard
always turns at a particular stone. The real problem was far
larger now. He had thought there was only one more hedge
to be broken through, and the hedge had become a forest.
The task was no longer merely to justify his action to himself, but to justify himself to her.

He was in Handelstrasse now; unconscious of his actions he had climbed the steep hill from the brewery and
crossed the main road. The white face still lay on the screen
of his mind, but he had forgotten the affair in Adrianstrasse
altogether: it was Minna's face now.

He had come to long for the moments when he should
see her again: as he went through the wards he had found
himself glancing at the clocks, calculating the minutes which
lay between him and her bedside. Yet he made no progress.
When he left her in the mornings he carried for an hour or
more a pleasantness which had come from their meeting:
they had spoken to each other kindly, they had laughed a
little: but that was all, the fragrance of a meal he had smelt
and never eaten. He knew dimly that her spirit had far more
to give him, that only a weakness in himself was keeping
him from her generosity. It was as if the miracle of sight
had been given to one born blind, and the August fields and
the mysterious hills were waiting for his vision, and he yet
lacked nerve to loose his eyes from the familiar bandage.

The sunshine was already on his face but he could not look at it.

He had put the bicycle away, entered the house by the back door, slipped up to his room before any one had seen him: this was his way now, to hide from the quickfire of curiosity. He started mechanically to make his preparations: drawing off a minute quantity of the P.T. and slightly raising its temperature; sterilising the needle. He was oddly nervous, dreading the moment which was running towards him, the moment when he would take her arm and press the needle in. 'This,' he thought beneath his thoughts, 'is climax, this is the last stage in the old happenings between her and me. When this is over, and when its effect is over, I can rule a line across what is past. She will have ceased to be an instrument, she will be a woman and my friend, and I shall be released.' But he knew that this last stage might never be over, never in that way. He longed for her, he wanted his freedom now, he was terrified to drive her through this new battle before he was free.

THE gap which caught his heel on the third step of the attic stairs; the way one pressed the door to get the latch up; the moan of the hinge and the room's peculiar smell: these were a framework as familiar as the rubs and crinkles in his oldest shoes. But the feel of it had altered now, as when you reach a square in your own town by an alley you have not used before.

She was sitting up, just as he had arranged her at midday. Awake, but apathetic, as she always was in what he called the Pre-injection Period. He said:

"Well, how are we feeling now?"

Then, as if in a cheval-glass, he saw himself as part of the picture: his hands clasped together like Papa's behind the counter, the slight stoop of his shoulders, the fake, ingratiating smile. And his voice echoed inside as if it had come from another throat, the shiny, lavender-scented voice, 'Well, how are we feeling now?'

She was looking at the things he had put down on the chair: the little grey box which held the phial, the blue box with the syringe.

"Is it time for that again?" she asked wearily.

"I think we'd better," he said. The same voice, the same smile fastened on his lips like sticky paper. "It doesn't hurt so very much, does it? Just one little prick!"

"It's what happens afterwards."

"Oh, it won't be so bad this time," he said. "Not half so bad!"

The mask he had put on in his early days with her had seemed such a work of art: it fitted so well, looked so convincing, felt so natural. The mask was grafted to his face now. And it was not only his face which went on posturing, separate from his feelings and his will: the carefulness of his feet as he moved about the room, the gentle way his hands had as they raised her shoulders on the pillow, the attitudes of every limb were false. He was trying to express his tenderness with kindly motions, and all his motions were as glib as actors' tears.

He was dumb with awkwardness, his hands were trembling. He would have liked to busy himself with something on the table, but there was nothing to do there, all the tools were ready. When he started the usual examination he could not altogether avoid her face; and her eyes, which always followed him, were expectant. Expecting what? He knew that she wanted some sign from him, a word or two of reassurance. But the only words he could think of were ones he had used a dozen times before, they had no more blood in them than a printed sermon. He could have put his hand on her forehead, stroked her hair, as he had seen men do in moving pictures. That, too, would have been unreal, no real gesture like that would come from his stiff, shy body. And how could he give her any caress, when she was still the subject of his experiment; now, when the drops of fluid he would soon force into her arm might end in killing her? His distress came out in heavy-handedness; his fingers, exploring above her lungs, had lost their sensitivity, he had never been so clumsy. The smile remained, his lips held fast in a curve of sleek compassion. The threat which nursery-maids hold over children had come to pass: the wind had changed; and his absurd grimace, all the small tricks of sham benevolence, were fastened round him for eternity.

Without intention he was hurrying, jotting a note and jabbing the pencil back to his ear like a shopkeeper in a busy morning: the examination was done in half the usual time. Without speaking, he rolled up the sleeve of her nightgown (the green nightgown with ribbon at the sleeves, his gift to encourage her for the second injection), moved a bolster under her arm and slipped a towel in between. This arm, he didn't much like it, its condition had never entirely recovered since the first injection: but that was a small worry among so many, he couldn't think of it now. Just now he must forget about Minna altogether, he must think only of the gap closing up inside her breast, of the crucial offensive he had to make against a remorseless enemy, the report he would write for *Neue Medizinische Monatsschrift* . . . He reached for the formaldehyde, carefully painted the little circle.

Now the syringe. "Steady now, just keep as still as you can!"

The muscles in the arm tightened, he saw obliquely that she shut her eyes, getting ready for the stab. She whispered:

"Be quick, be quick please!"

It didn't come.

She opened her eyes again and saw him standing by the table, empty-handed. His face was that of a man who has lost something, one who watches his house burning.

"Herr Doktor! What's the matter?"

The smile should have come back, but it didn't.

"I'm not doing it," he said to his own hands.

"Not to-day?"

"Never. I shan't do it any more. I can't go on with it."

"You mean—you're not going to go on making me better?"

He was looking into the corner near the foot of the bed. A new cobweb there. He stretched for the duster which he kept on a special cuphook and cleared the mess away; stood and stared at the place as if he were expecting it to reappear.

"No, I'm not going on with it."

He sat on the end of the bed with the duster on his knees, folded it meticulously in half, into quarters, over again. The sounds of the house began leaking into the room, old Barthol fumbling along the passage till he found the switch, the crash of a saucepan lid on the stone floor of the kitchen. When Josef spoke again his voice was quick and breathless, like that of a boy caught in an orchard.

"You'd better have some one else. Much better. I'm no good at this. I'm not a proper doctor at all."

She did not seem to be startled by that. When she answered, it was in her tired way:

"You mean you haven't learnt it? You don't really work in the hospital? Or do you do the cleaning there or something?"

He said: "Well, you can think that if you like. You'll hear about it, anyway—I'm going to send you up there. It's a man called Doctor Vollmuth, he understands about chests, I'll send you to him. Yes, that's what I'll do."

"So that you won't see me any more?"

"Well, not as a doctor . . . You'll like it up there. They look after you properly—nurses and people. You get clean sheets every day."

He started to collect his instruments. His thoughts, having found a positive direction, were running now. Vollmuth had his living quarters in the hospital, he would get him on the telephone straightaway, tell him a likely story, then get the call switched over to the out-patients' office and arrange about the ambulance. Get it done with, wind up the whole thing and start again. (Case No. 2—but he would have to call it Case No. 1—a man this time, some wreck of a man, some one he couldn't possibly grow fond of.) Forget about Minna, forget her . . . Then he remembered: at the Moltke he no longer had any position. '. . . regret that your work is not wholly in accordance with the ethical and professional standards of this Establishment, and that we

therefore no longer require your services . . .' Vollmuth
would know about that, and if any one cared about the nice-
ties of discipline it was Vollmuth. Vollmuth make special
arrangements, squeeze another bed into his crowded wards,
to please a sacked junior?

". . . you listen, please!"

What was that? She was saying something in her sleepy
voice, he hadn't done with her yet.

"Yes," he said impatiently, "what is it?"

"I say I don't want to go anywhere else."

"Not out of this wretched room?"

"I don't want any one else mucking about with me.
You do it all right. I'm used to that."

"But don't you understand, there are doctors who do
nothing else but your sort of illness. They—they know more
about it than I do."

She seemed to be in difficulty then. Her words came
like a file of sheep, tethered hindleg to foreleg:

"I thought you liked doing me. I didn't think you
thought—I was such a filthy nuisance, I figured I was all
right. I thought you liked—I thought you liked it."

"You're all right," he said roughly. "It's me that's
wrong."

That was like the magic sentence in a fairy-tale, changing his form. He was free at last, stripped of his grinning
philanthropy. And when he went on speaking the words
came almost as easily as if he had rehearsed them. He stood
against the door with his hands crossed on his stomach: it
was the way they made you stand for reciting impositions
at the Richterhausen primary school. He spoke at her chin,
without wavering.

"Listen, Minna. I didn't take you on because I wanted
to make you better. I did want to make you better, but only
to please myself. I'm not interested in doctoring, I'm only
interested in new ways of attacking disease. I'd worked out

some new stuff for attacking tuberculosis—which is what you've got—and I wanted to test it. That's all."

She accepted this as if it were a commonplace announcement; as if he were returning a kettle he'd borrowed with the remark that he'd burnt a hole in it. She said,

"What were you going to do after that?"

"After that? Well, if it worked I was going to publish a report. Then all the hospitals would have sent for specimens and every one would have used the stuff. They'd have cured loads of people with it." He hesitated. "But I wasn't thinking about that. I was just thinking what it would do for me. It would've made me famous."

She said suddenly: "Why do you stand up at the door like that? I don't like you standing up. Why don't you sit on the bed like you always do?" Her voice was staccato, almost imperious. "That's better, yes, that's better . . . I'd like to know, why doesn't it work, that stuff? I thought I was getting on all right. Don't you know enough to make it properly?"

He answered slowly, as in an examination: "It's like this. The stuff's a sort of poison. It's meant to poison the bugs inside you. Only sometimes it poisons the patient as well. That's the difficulty, you've got to mix it so it'll kill the bugs and not kill the patient. It means trying all kinds of different things, making hundreds of experiments. I've been at it six years, all my spare time, up all night very often. I thought I'd got it right. Well, it's no good talking."

"But I want to know!" she insisted. "What's gone wrong with it? Doesn't it kill the bugs any more?"

"It kills 'em all right," he said; and he could not hide a trace of eagerness. "I'd got 'em in hand, I can tell you that. You wear them out, you see. The first dose doesn't make an awful lot of difference, it only gets to the shell of the bacilli, the second gets a bit further, it makes the disease weaken a bit, you begin to see the effect then. At least, you do after the third and fourth. You get a better result every time. Only you have to keep on with it. There's a point where you have the disease beaten; but until you've reached it you've got to keep plugging away, otherwise the filthy thing gets stronger again, catches you napping. You can't leave it, else you've got to start the whole thing over again."

"But you are leaving it, aren't you? You said you weren't going to prick me any more."

"It's too much risk," he said flatly. "I told you, the stuff poisons the patient as well. You know how it makes you bad, a bit worse every time. We might've got over that —you develop resistance. But you haven't developed enough yet, I'm not sure you could stand another shot."

"You mean I might die?"

"Yes. You nearly did last time."

"I know," she said. Then, "Couldn't you make it a smaller dose?"

"No good! It wouldn't get through the shell, the shell I told you about. That's the point about my stuff, it's all worked out more closely than any one else's, you've got to give the exact dose to get any effect."

He realised then that he was talking like a fool; talking as if the experiment were still in progress, as if she were a pupil and they worked together on some one else's body. It was no use sitting about here. Later on, when he'd had time to think things over, he would try to talk to her again, to speak from that strange spring of sensation which had newly burst in him. He started to fasten his case. Something was missing—yes, the record-book, he had left it on the bed and it had fallen down on the other side. He was about to retrieve it, when he thought, 'No, useless, it doesn't matter any more!'

"I'll come back later on and get you comfortable for the night," he told her.

"Why?" she asked.

"Why? I always do, don't I?"

"But you said you'd given me up."

"As an experiment," he said. "I'm going to look after you, all the same, till some one else takes on."

Oh, couldn't she understand how wretched he was! Didn't she realise he wanted to get away! But the tired voice went on, like a tap dripping in the darkness.

"You'll get some one else now? Some one to try the stuff on?"

"I suppose so."

"Another girl?"

"I don't know. Women react better in some ways. No, not a girl. Some one fairly old, if I can."

"And start all over again?"

"Yes."

"And all the time you've spent on me will be wasted?"

"More or less."

"I don't see why it's got to be. I don't mind dying."

"But I mind," he said.

He hadn't noticed her hand creeping towards him, he was surprised to feel her clutching his sleeve.

"Listen, please listen!" She was weeping, but her voice came unbroken and curiously strong. "I don't care what happens as long as you finish it off with me. You've got to do that! You've put all that muck into me, you've made me sweat and burn with it, and now you've got to pay me back."

"Pay you back?"

"You've got to let me have my share. You go off and do it on some one else and it works all right on her and you get famous, and then what happens to me? I'm just lying up there in the filthy hospital with those bitches of nurses all round me! I tell you it's my experiment as well as yours. I'm the one who's been through it, all those pricks, feeling like hell. It's mine, I tell you! If you're going to show some one off to all the other doctors and tell them you've cured her it's got to be me."

"Minna!" he said, "Minna, don't you realise, don't you believe me—the next dose may kill you! Kill you!"

"Well, you knew that all along, didn't you!"

"Yes, I did. But I didn't—I didn't care about you to begin with. I care about you now. The experiment doesn't matter, it's—I hate the whole bloody business. It's you I care about now."

She was silent. Just for a few moments. And her voice dropped to quietness when she spoke again.

"Then why won't you do what I want?"

"I'll do anything, except kill you."

"It needn't. You said it wasn't bound to, you said I might have got enough resistance. I've got more than you think. It wanted me to die last time, that stuff you put in, but I wouldn't. I just wouldn't die." As if to show the force she wielded against death her grip on his arm tightened. But her voice stayed low. "Josef! Josef, there's only one thing I want, only one thing for myself. I want to be the one you show off, the one you've cured. I've never had anything to be proud of, I've never had any one being proud of me. You wouldn't have to say anything about me, you could just say it was a kitchen-slut called Minna Wersen. It'll all go to you just the same, I want you to have it all, the write-ups, photo in the papers, all that. You ought to have that, after all the sweating you've done, you must have that! Josef, I want it to be a success, I want you to have it all. Only I want it to be me that you've used, all the way through. That's all I want."

It was a long time before he gave in.

When he surrendered it was from spiritual exhaustion. He had lost all understanding of himself, he couldn't think any more. She was so much the stronger, lying there with her forehead burning and her eyes constantly falling shut, her thin fingers biting his sleeve.

The job, when he came to it, was ridiculously hard: to hold her arm firmly, when his fingers only shaped to gentleness; to insert the needle with a clean thrust, and deeply enough, when all his feeling was to save her the smallest moment of pain. Yet he did it properly, as a master pianist who cannot fumble a chord; making sure that the full dose went in, whispering inside himself *Don't let it kill her, don't let her die!* While she, instead of lying back as she had done at previous times, pushed herself up on the pillows to watch his work, watched quietly as the needle went in.

It was just then, just at the moment when he held the point beneath her skin, that he felt her lips pressed against his neck; and he answered her, as he withdrew the point, with his own lips pressed where it had been. This was the first acknowledged tenderness between them; their first embrace.

29

THE curve of reactions indicated that the post-injection crisis should occur, on this occasion, from the time of injection plus twenty-seven hours. That meant, approximately, at midnight on the night following.

She was still sleeping then; she had spent most of that day in what looked like natural sleep, drowsy and contented. Her temperature was up, but only a little above the normal for the day's last reading. There was no sweating yet. From some cause, of the kind which buckles the mathematics of research, the febrile reaction was being delayed.

A little after twelve, Josef went down to his own room and took off his shoes and collar for an hour's rest. It had always been the worst part of attending Minna, these times when there was nothing for him to do; when he only sat, as if on the heights above a harbour, and watched the ship with all his possessions fighting through violent seas. And now the ship was out again, bearing himself as well as his ambitions; the newfound core of his existence, the fresh warm springs that soothed his tiredness, were all at hazard there. He had hardly left her through the day, dreading to be out of sight at any moment when she might want him. Stale-mouthed, he had sat with the little broken chair grooving his flesh while the shadow of the window-frame passed across the bed from one wall to the other; until, with darkness shutting a lid upon the room, the walls had leaned together like coffin sides against the streak of paleness where her face was; until there was only the broken, mournful noise of her breathing, and the cold fingers that he held. With the light switched on another day had seemed to begin, yellow and hungry. His eyes grew watery, his ears created fearful sounds for themselves. Time loitering, the angles of the room, the familiarity of walls and shadows, had become like creases in his clothes, rubbing a soreness on his sensibility. His loneliness took no relief from the deaf and silent figure there. The edge of anxiety pressed deeper, he had to move away.

There was half a bottle of milk in his cupboard, and he thought of making coffee; but it meant getting out a cup and spoon, finding some matches, and he was too tired for all that. Not really hungry, now: he had had a piece of liver-sausage for breakfast, and had learnt in childhood to keep his stomach stretched on a memory. There should be biscuits somewhere—somewhere on the writing-desk—but he couldn't find them. Some one had been in here, shifting his things. That poor cabbage-pated old Spühler woman, he supposed . . . He put a chair on the bed and arranged the back of it under his legs to give a certain discomfort: he didn't want to sleep soundly. But he was fairly confident that a cry from above would wake him.

He began going back to his earliest acquaintance with Minna and tried to see her as she had appeared then. It was a curious picture, part of memory and part home-made. Standing there, a few feet from where he lay, she had been a wretched object, her face smeared and red with coughing, the sodden rag of an apron lashed to her waist with string, a big toe sprouting naked from her ancient slippers. But he seemed to see, now, the beauty lying behind that soiled façade: the enchanting smallness of her forehead and chin against the weight and darkness of her hair, the depth in her steady, brilliant eyes. And now, as the tongue will haunt an ulcer in the mouth, his mind went back and back to the way he had treated her, to the dryness of his former thoughts, the fashioned geniality. He tried to see himself at every stage, to mark the worst in every attitude of his, to purge himself. That day when she had said the darkness frightened her, and he had smiled and told her not to surrender to childish fears: the evening of the third injection, when she had begged him to leave it till to-morrow . . . And now, when he would have talked to her of all those things, and tried to bury them in the depth of her compassion, a weight was fastening across his mouth to hold it silent. A kind of press, closed up with nut and bolt. They wanted to screw it tighter still, but some one had lost the spanner, and a messenger must go right back to Richterhausen where the spanner hung from a nail in Papa's toolshed. The toolshed door was locked, they had to hammer it, two mighty strokes, two mighty strokes again.

He had not switched off the light. When his eyes opened, painfully, he did not think he had been asleep. But something had disturbed him, and he lay, stiff with overdriven nerves, listening for some sound from the attic. Then the knocking at the front door began again.

There were sounds like the romping of mice in old farm-houses, then the flap of slippers along the corridor, and Frau Spühler's frightened voice, "Keep them talking, August, keep them talking while I go and hide the gravy-spoons!" Presently, the scrape and jar of the front-door bolts, crisp, official voices, heavy boots on the stairs. In some way Josef knew that they were coming to his room, but he didn't stir. To his reluctant body was harnessed a mind that would only pull in one direction: he would not be troubled with these people who promenaded the farther world, who were neither tuberculous nor tired.

"This way, Herr Schutzmann, if you will be so kind. This is the person's room, if you please. Of course we know nothing about him, you understand, he thrust himself into our house, we had no means of turning him away."

Like a kettle boiling, Josef thought dimly, this voice

of Herr Spühler's: steam pouring forth and the lid bobbing up and down.

The man came in as if the room were his own: the face of a bank-manager just out of the barber's, the thin body uniformed. He went straight over to the desk and pulled out the top drawer. Two young men in ordinary clothes were also in the room, standing motionless by the door: the picture seemed to have arrived already formed, as when the curtain rises in a theatre.

"Key of this drawer!" the man said.

Josef's thoughts moved like those of a man pitched suddenly into space. Case-book, record of all his work—they mustn't get hold of that: where? second drawer as a rule: not to-night: no, up in Minna's room.

He got up, took the key from his trouser pocket and gave it over. But the officer had already found something.

"This document—what is it?"

"That? I—I don't know. Some notes, I expect. Some notes on some experiment of mine."

"Yes," the officer said, "it looks like that."

Moving a little nearer, Josef caught sight of the paper. It was amateurishly typewritten, all blobs and genuflections, with a manuscript heading in giant capitals: *Action-Plan for Hand Grenade Attack on Nazional-Sozialist Party Meeting 26th February.*

"You say these are some notes of yours?" the officer asked. "Some notes for an experiment?"

"No, that paper's nothing to do with me. I've never seen it before."

"But you said just now it was your own notes."

"I—I didn't realise—I didn't see what it was you had."

The officer folded the paper carefully and put it in his pocket. "No, evidently you did not realise. I imagine you generally keep these things in the drawers that are locked."

Josef said: "I wish to state positively that—"

"Exactly!" the man said. The voice was in accord with his appearance, the voice of a bank-manager helping a woman-customer through some financial intricacy. "Naturally, yes, you would like to make an explanation. That will be arranged for, you will make an explanation at the central office to-morrow morning."

Josef nodded. "I see . . . What time shall I come?"

"Now!" the officer said. His eyes smiled faintly. "You'll come along with us now, then you're sure not to be late."

One of the boys at the door turned and signalled with his chin: there was no ambiguity.

"I'll just put my shoes on," Josef said.

That would give him a minute, if he fumbled the laces, a whole minute to get his mind moving.

"It is unnecessary," the officer said.

"May I—may I see a patient of mine before I go? She's upstairs, it won't take me two minutes. It's most important . . ." He had to think and speak at the same time, he had to flog his thoughts out of their sluggish pace, make up his story as he went along. The young man at the door yawned, he was barely eighteen, patiently dutiful but half asleep. The senior man shook his head. "It's important, very important," Josef repeated, as if he were keeping pace with a moving train. "This girl, you see, she's in a bad way, she may be dying, yes I think so, I don't want to be responsible—"

The officer said: "Hauser, take him, will you!"

"—you see, she's a relation of Captain Feldhardt, Captain Feldhardt of the Sturmabteilungen, she's Captain Feldhardt's niece. Captain Feldhardt gave me special instructions—I am a specialist in pulmonary tuberculosis, you understand—he said that I was to give all my attention to Fräulein Wersen till he could have her moved to the sanatorium at Freiendorf."

They had got him out in the passage.

"Hauser," the officer said, "you know Feldhardt. Has he got a niece?"

The boy yawned again. "Feldhardt? A niece? I don't know. I suppose so."

The officer looked at his watch.

"You can see her for one minute," he said. "Wait, I'm coming with you. You can stay here, Hauser—and you, Dubiel. This way, is it?"

The officer marched ahead up the attic stairs, swift and competent, buttocks working like cams in the tight trousers, a racehorse going over plough. He rapped once and jerked open the door.

"You are Fräulein Wersen?"

A voice out of sleep: "Yes."

"You have an uncle—Captain Feldhardt?"

He was standing in the middle of the doorway, but by leaning over, Josef could just see past his arm. Minna had not moved. Her eyes were open now, but she was just across the border of her quasi-cataleptic stage, she would see no separate object in the room.

"Is Captain Feldhardt an uncle of yours?" the officer repeated.

"What do you say?"

"Captain Feldhardt, is he your uncle?"

Silence: but her lips were twisting up for speech. They waited, Josef and the officer together.

"Josef!" she called suddenly. "Josef, some one's making an awful row. Josef darling, can't you make him go to hell."

The officer stood aside.

"You can have just one minute," he said.

Josef went to the bed and put his fingers on her forehead; kept them there for a moment, drawing refreshment from the softness of her skin.

The officer said: "Well, aren't you going to do something?"

Do something? There was nothing to be done, at present. Bewildered, he tried to steady his thoughts, to recover the doctoring mind. It was curious: the appearance of her eyes would have shown that the usual reaction was well advanced, and yet he judged that her temperature had hardly risen since he had left her an hour before. He said urgently, "Minna! Minna, how are you feeling now?" but he knew she wouldn't answer. He put the thermometer in her armpit and started to prepare his usual febrifuge. The officer observed him closely. No, Josef thought, he wouldn't leave anything like that about. Some fool would come and pour it into her at exactly the wrong time. What! Couldn't he come back and see to it himself? Would he never be in this room again? He tipped a fingernail of the mixture into another glass and filled it up with water; while the officer, intently watching, supposed it was the usual procedure.

The case-book: it was on the shelf at the other side of the bed, hardly four feet away. He would have stretched and taken it, but the machinery of his intelligence was still at work beneath his panic confusion: stupid to do that, you couldn't hide the thing, they'd have their hands on it at once.

"What are you doing?" the officer said. "Why can't you hurry?"

Josef took out the thermometer. Yes, the temperature had hardly risen at all since the previous reading. It was possible, just possible, that there was going to be no febrile reaction. On the other hand . . . His mind, volatile in the air of crisis, fled back to the hospital at Zornenwalde: a curly-haired boy from Chemnitz in the Nose and Throat Ward— the bed next the door, malignant diphtheria; temperature at the same high point night after night; and then one evening it hadn't gone up at all, the boy had been smiling and cheerful, and two hours afterwards he was dead. What was it that Plünnecke had said about that? . . .

"Well, can't you read it?"

"Yes—yes, perfectly. Only, I'm rather puzzled—"

"I can't spare time for your being puzzled. Is there anything you want to do?"

"No, there's nothing—yes, yes I ought to feel the pulse."

Anything—it didn't matter how absurd—anything for the chance to stay with her a minute longer! The officer came closer, watching the work with critical attention: it was all the same to him that a pulse-rate had never been taken like that before.

"If I may suggest—" Josef said—"not too close! There's a danger of infection."

"What, is she infectious?"

"Very! As a rule no one comes in this room besides myself."

"Then why in hell didn't you say so before?" He was back at the door already. "I'll want you in thirty seconds from now," he said, and went down the stairs.

Josef sat still, holding her wrist. They were alone together, another thirty seconds, and he didn't know what to do with it. Her eyes, half open, were as fixed and meaningless as the eyes of a draper's model; she seemed to be in another country, only her body was close. He put his mouth to her ear and whispered, "Minna! Minna, do you hear me? Minna, my own, my darling, can you hear?" All his strength was in that whisper, as if he were shouting at the top of his voice; and although there was no response he went on desperately, "Minna, Minna darling, you must get Doctor Ahlwarth! Doctor Ahlwarth, do you hear? Don't have any one else, make them get you Doctor Ahlwarth! Do you hear, darling, *Doctor Ahlwarth,* make Frau Spühler get him!"

He snatched a piece of paper and wrote across it: *'Very important: Doctor Ahlwarth of the Moltke hospital must be asked to take over this case.'* And while he was writing she stirred a little, and her free hand started to feel along the decke.

"Josef! Darling Josef! Where have you gone?"

Josef couldn't speak any more. He took the creeping hand into his own, he put his arm behind her shoulders and pulled her up to him and kissed her mouth. And while his lips were pressed on hers the hand he had loosed came weakly round his neck, and the thin fingers pushed into his hair. And when he released her her voice came to him again, from very far away, "Josef, dear darling Josef, Josef darling!"

From the foot of the stairs the officer shouted, "Here, what are you doing?"

Josef could not kiss her again; his strength had given out. He made a little cup in the pillow, as he always did, and put her head there. He slid the smaller pillow under her shoulders, in the expert way he had; and going to the door he said, "I'll be back soon, Minna. I'll be back again—before long—you understand! You understand, my dear?" At the door he turned, and saw her hand feeling out again, searching. He turned away then, not wanting to see that any more. He said once again, "I'm coming back—won't be long—I'm coming back!" and shut the door after him.

30

HE WAS protected, as Hauser led him collarless and sock-footed along the passage, by the sense of unreality. This youth who clutched his arm had the gentle mouth of a drawing-room pianist, his companion was only a sulky child, the officer a most respectable man, of reassuring stupidity: these were not of a kind to keep a doctor long from his patient. There was, in all their movements, a naïve solemnity, as of children holding funeral service for a dormouse: so that Josef, who was not of the frivolous cast, felt a sudden desire to relieve himself with a crash of laughter.

They were all on the landing now: Frau Rupf with her hair tricked out in tiny pokes like a pheasant packed for the railway, Herr Barthol flaunting a foot of nightshirt between an old frock coat and his blue bedsocks, they stood like mourners at the funeral of a very old, unnecessary man; Frau Spühler letting her warm and easy tears slop down to the quilt she held round her shoulders, her husband with his staunch protective arm about her hips, his face set brave and resolute between the naval cap and striped pyjamas, they were clustered all together under the green lampshade in a little, hardy corps, ready to defend themselves if need be. Only the Professor stood a little apart; and he, leaning forward as Josef passed, whispered, "Good luck, old friend, keep courage!" They joined in the rear as the procession passed and followed down to the front door, a susurrus of slippered feet trailed sympathetically behind the tramp of martial boots. At the door they grouped themselves again and watched the little party on its way, the two tired boys tramping bravely with the limping prisoner between them, the alert officer guarding the rear, watched in silence till the darkness drowned them. Only then was Frau Spühler's emotion released in a trickle of anxious words. "His boots— he forgot his boots—I shouldn't have let him go without them!"

That sorrow could not last in the sunshine of their liberation. As when the dead body has been taken away, and the venetian blinds are rattled up at last, and an almost for- gotten daylight surges in, so they were plunged into a glow of freedom. Instinctively, without a word of invitation, they trooped together to the kitchen, where Spühler stirred the cinders in the stove and his wife put on a kettle; where Frau Rupf, leaning against the dresser and softly smiling, found that she had her hand in the crook of Herr Barthol's arm.

So, he had gone, that stranger to their company: and they realised now, as they had never clearly understood be- fore, how heavily his presence had weighed on them. They had known that he was not of their kind, they had found their conversation curbed when he was at meals, had tried to avoid him in the passages, almost resenting his polite 'good- morning.' Now the truth was out, and they saw that their distrust had been built on somethnig deeper than a fancy. That night when he had hammered on his walls; his habit of slipping away as soon as a meal was over; the sound of his footsteps and of his door softly closing in the middle hours of night: all those small, disturbing things were remem- bered now, and they realised that an evil personality must betray itself in just such signs as those.

"I never trusted him!" Herr Barthol said.

In the big Krossen chair which his great-uncle had left him, August Spühler felt himself once more the master of his household. He had lit his old cutty, which Hilde as a rule would not allow in the kitchen; with his forearms on the table he sucked it learnedly, and his lips gripping the stem took back the line of purpose they had shown on the after-deck of the *Schneckenburger,* his eyes gathering the homely circle were quiet and wise, with a small, steady flame of courage.

"I've known it," he said thoughtfully, "since the day he told us that he took no interest in politics. Something in the way he said it! When you've been in command of men—always new men coming along, have to be put through their paces, hundreds I must have trimmed up in my time—when you get to know all sorts of men the way I do you can tell in the flick of a cod's tail when they're not speaking the truth. And that time he broke his arm—an accident, he said—do you think I believed that? I made some inquiries about that broken arm—I've friends of my own in the town, you know, big people—and I got the truth about it . . . Oh yes, I've been watching that young fellow, I've had correspondence about him these many weeks past. But you can't get things cleared up all in a day, you've got to lie low and watch 'em, those young Marxists. You've got to just bide your time till they make a false step and give 'emselves away. He thought he'd got me fooled, that young Herr Doktor Lenin-Trotsky Zeppichmann—but I knew I'd catch him in the end!"

"It's what comes of a navy-training," Frau Spühler told them. The brilliance of rejoicing eyes had dried her tears already, her warm gaze moved luxuriously from her vindicated August to her guests, and back again to August's rugged face, and yet again to the guests admiring him. "You learn such lessons there," she murmured, "patience and watchfulness!" There was something more she would have said, but her happiness forbade it; through the sweet warmth in throat and cheeks her words were too fragile to make their way.

Even Frau Rupf was moved by her friend's emotion. Remembering how this Zeppichmann had caused the only quarrel between herself and Arnold in many years, she felt that fortune had worked for her a special justice; and though she despised Frau Spühler's joyful tears, she felt a kindred spring in her own sandy spirit. This cosiness, the refound friendship of their small society, it had been impossible while that creature's presence was poisoning the house.

"I hope," she said, "that Arnold will give up scoffing at my woman's intuition now. I told him fifty times, I felt it in my bones that young man was up to no good. And it wasn't only my feelings. When a young man wanders about the house at all hours of the night, when you hear him feeling along the walls and trying the door handles—well, you can't help wondering if that's how an honest man behaves. I think I mentioned the matter once or twice, Herr Spühler?"

Herr Barthol laughed like a punctured tyre.

"A lot of good—the young snake—trying *my* door handle! A trunk in front of it—pushed my trunk up against the door every night." He smiled in reminiscence; they had never realised what a merry gentleman he was. "I had a good look at that young fellow, you understand—the first time I saw him, I took a good look at him. 'That's a snake,' I said to myself, 'that young fellow's a snake!' In business, you see, you've got to sum a man up as soon as you see him. It's a kind of gift that a leading business-man always has. I had one look at that young chap and I went up to my room—that delicious room which I owe to your hospitality, Gnädige Frau—and put the trunk up against the door. A trunkful of old documents—important business papers, that kind of thing. 'Just let him try!' I said, 'just let that snaky communist try getting in here!'"

He laughed again. They were frightened that he would hurt himself with so much laughter, going on for seventy as he was now, and having been through so much with his kidneys. It crossed Herr Spühler's mind that this might be a fruitful moment to speak of the nine weeks' rent which

was due on that charming room. But no, that was a merce-
nary thought; he would not allow the foetid smell of money
matters to leak into this garden of sweet odours. He knew
that he had piloted this ship of his, with all these friends
aboard, through dark and treacherous straits; they had not
always trusted him, and yet his quiet skill, his fortitude, had
brought them all to safety. Dear Hilde, she at least knew
something of the hardships of his lonely watch, she shared
his triumph. Her ageing, timid eyes were holding him no less
devoutly than when, on their wedding day, her little hand
crept out to his. Herr Barthol, who had sometimes been so
stern, Herr Barthol whom he had always regarded with a
certain awe, had changed into a mountain of good humour.
Frau Rupf herself, for all the sharpness which had often
spoilt her fragile femininity, was smiling now with all her
little teeth, and he thought her tiny eyes gazed at him
through the pince-nez with a new esteem. It's like with
a rotten tooth, he thought: you screw up your courage and
have it wrenched away, and at once you feel a giant liberty;
slack limbs begin to work, and the blood flows warm, and
the body rejoices once again in its lusty splendour.

Only the smallest clouds were passing over Hilde's sky.
Herr Meisel had gone out late, for one of his political
duties, and had not returned; she was not quite sure if he
had his thicker waistcoat. And dear Professor Rupf was so
overcome with the night's alarms that he had gone back
to bed.

31

THEY were putting up direction signs in the Wilhelm park, ready for the rally this afternoon: here, at the west gate, the people would turn left and go round the trees to their places on the observation mound, leaving the broad avenue free for the procession of the Sturmabteilungen; over there, between the striped posts, the schoolchildren would be marshalled, carrying their little flags. Odin knew that this was a day of glory for Hartzinnfeld, for again the sun had broken free, drawing out the infinite tones of red and brown from old roofs in the Schneiderstrasse, shaping the pattern of bare trees and trampled turf to a dry-point brilliance. The wind, which seemed to stand against this city like a boundary wall, held hard and keen; to children in threadbare clothes, to the shrunk flesh of men standing against the railings, it was a persistent cruelty. But you could endure that violence for a few weeks more, in the strength of knowing that the season of humiliation was already past; and in this pale facsimile of summer you felt an answer to your spirit's stirring. The boys working with icy hands on the rotted roof of the bandstand had got the flag-pole in position now, and presently the new proud flag was tearing at its leash. Old Sergeant Beuloh, with the guide-stakes under his arm, went over to his orderly and grasped his hand; and they stood for a moment, very straight, to smile with hungry eyes at the standard leaping in the sun.

In Gottwaldstrasse, a little after eleven, the sunshine caught the windows on the river side, and falling across the desk of Commissioner Fietz it reminded him of the afternoon's parade. It would take him half an hour to get into his uniform, and as Paula hated to be jostled by crowds he must see her to her place in plenty of time. He said: "I shan't be able to see the prisoners this morning. To-morrow —make a note of it, will you—to-morrow I'll examine prisoners at eighteen minutes after ten."

And through the tall library windows of the Victoria Philosophical Ladies' Club the sun shone invitingly.

"I don't see why I've got to moulder in this hen-coop all day long," Hauser said, treading out his cigarette on the Turkish rug. "You, Sauerborn, you could look after forty prisoners by yourself. They won't try to break away with those claws of yours about. At least it doesn't want a dozen of us."

Sauerborn yawned. "You, child," he said, "you're too young to recognise a daisy job when you get one." He levered himself out of the easy chair, too narrow for his Atlas thighs, and tried the comfort of the sofa. "For myself, I like the feminine touch. The old girls managed fairly well, I think, I expect they hated having to go."

He was sorry for young Hauser all the same. A bit of a girl, perhaps, with his soft hands and the curl in his fair hair, but keen as a tiger. A lovable boy like that, the quiet, romantic sort, was straining to work his arms off for the Cause, to march and fight and suffer; and here, in the epoch of their resurrection, he was wandering about a tasselled room, glaring at the barrel-bosomed dames between the bookstacks, rubbing his backside along the window-sill. Sauerborn undid another button to give his belly breathing-space.

"Cheerful old cow!" he said, pointing his foot at the sternest of the portraits, and went on: "You know, young Hauser, you'll get what you want in time. Work and plenty of it, man's work! It's the way things go. My dame, you know, she was mad with wanting a kid. Two years we were at it, tried like artillery corporals, and never a kid in sight.

Then they started, *thump, thump,* one on top of the next, like an orchard in October. Six in four years, six little blasted screamers, and every one as pretty as Papa, God strangle them! I go home of an evening and the dame shouts out from the kitchen, 'Georg! come here and let me tell you something.' 'All right!' I shout back, 'I don't want to know!' I know already, you see. Thirty-six weeks and then—*thud* again!"

"Children are all right," Hauser said absently. "It's prisoners I'm tired of. They stare at you all the time."

Sauerborn spat towards a rose-bowl.

"You get used to it, like all the nappies cluttering up the windows. Try growing a moustache!" he added, "—you wouldn't get so much on their imagination."

"I'd like to know what you mean by—"

"Achtung!"

At the first crack of heavy boots on the corridor parquet Sauerborn had gathered his limbs like a tortoise; in a moment Hauser was at attention beside him. The door shot open.

"Guard Hauser!"

"Sir!"

"When's your duty?"

"11.08, Sir!"

"This floor?"

"Yes, Sir."

"Good! Number 92 F in Room IV—you know the man, taken last night?"

"I brought him myself, Sir."

"I didn't ask you that. You're to read him this sheet, do you see, and get his signature. A separate signature to every clause is what I want. It's optional, of course. You must put it to him that things will be easier if he signs."

"I'll explain that, Sir."

"Exactly! It's a mark of a promising officer that he can make very clear explanations. You understand me?"

"I—yes, Sir."

Sauerborn waited till the steps had died away again before he flopped back on the sofa, leaving Hauser still at attention.

"You see!" he said, "a job of work already, with a slice of fun. Well, if you want a hand you've only got to let me know . . ."

The metal number plates had been ordered, but as yet the number was only chalked—'IV'—on the door of what had been the toilet parlour. The old notice was still pinned in one of the panels, *Members are politely requested to arrange for the services of the coiffeuse a day in advance,* and in the margin of this, for economy, the names of the present occupants were scrawled.

It was several weeks since a lady's hair had been trimmed in here, but the compound odour of shampoos and *frictions* lasted, vapid, as a kind of personality. The sun could reach these windows only in the early morning and it had to penetrate net curtains as well as tinted lozenges of glass. The linoleum had been rolled up and the cubicle curtains tied in a bunch, with a label *Not for present use;* the ointment cabinet was empty except for a sheet of prison rules pasted inside the glass. The room had the permanence of places that recur in dreams.

With the smile of polite surprise which belonged to the casting of his face, Max Dahlmeyer sat in one of the two basins, drawing aerial patterns with his pointed feet. Occasionally he felt in his waistcoat pocket for the watch that was no longer there, but he did not seem impatient; for him, the previous sixty years had really gone too fast.

"If only they had left the tools!" he said. "You know, Herr Doktor, I feel that time is never wasted when one is acquiring some new ability. The last time I was ill, and had to spend six months shut away in the country, I learned how to milk a cow. I've never milked one since, and yet I don't regret the patience I devoted to that study. When I get a bad notice in the papers—when some one writes that I don't get the full power out of my orchestra—I say to myself, 'Well, after all, I'm probably the only musician of my rank in Europe who can get the last drop of milk from the udders of a Holstein.' "

"I beg your pardon, but I just don't see!"

The dwarf Neuling, who was lying on his stomach in the corner, turned slowly over and let his watery gaze creep up to Herr Dahlmeyer's face. He seemed to have shrunk in breadth since Josef had met him in Ahlwarth's basement room, and the rodent energy of his movements had been flattened down.

"I don't see the good of knowing how to milk a cow," he said listlessly. "There aren't any cows to milk, you can't find a cow in a place like this."

Herr Dahlmeyer politely shook his head.

"You misunderstand me, I think! I was considering the advantage we would gain if the coiffeuse had left her tools —the long scissors and the clickety-clickety things. We could practise cutting each other's hair, and before we were all bald we might have become quite expert." He ran his narrow fingers through his own soft, grey hair and turned to Josef, who was leaning on the other basin. "Have you ever considered, Herr Doktor, the delights of the haircutter's art? The velvet hair of a young lady, a new one every hour, to let it run through your fingers, to bathe your hands in it! Occasionally you give a little pull, to see her turn and look up at you with big, reproachful eyes. You mournfully ask her pardon, and then with all your virtuosity you steer the clickety-click machine through the pasture of little hairs in the nape of her neck. Again, think of the excitement, the joyous expertise, in snipping a tiny curl to half-reveal the lobe of the fair one's ear!"

"I would rather prefer not to talk of women," Josef said; and Dahlmeyer understood.

"If they'd left a razor," Neuling added, "I'd know what to do with that."

"You'd have a go at some one's throat?"

"Yes—mine."

He was amiable, this Dahlmeyer; but what Josef wanted now was silence. The arid air of this small room, with its jeering glass, the feverish pattern on its walls, were a truckle bed where his thoughts would not lie still. If he could be alone in some dark place, wrapped up in quietness, he could gather all the misery which spread across his mind, suffer its flame so deeply that his power to feel would at last burn out. Then he would yield his spirit to a kind of euthanasia, sealing up the years behind, and shape himself to live as cattle do, taking each pattern of material things indifferently, seeking nothing beyond. He went across to the window, wriggling out the itch of his clothes, and stared through a broken pane at the brick wall a few feet away. He turned and walked to the other end, stepping over Neuling's legs; stood quite still and read through a notice about gratuities; turned and went back again. From his seat in the basin Dahlmeyer watched him.

By tricks of the wind the Rathaus clock was only sometimes audible. When they heard it strike, the three of them kept still to count, hoping they had missed it once and another two hours had gone. But it was only eleven.

At eight minutes past the key was turned and the three bolts drawn.

"Attention!"

Josef's hands came out of his pockets and his heels shot together, while Neuling hauled himself on to his feet. Gracefully, and like a bather trying the water, Herr Dahlmeyer let his toes down to the floor. Hauser slammed the door behind him and locked it.

"So we have the pleasure of another visit!" Dahlmeyer said.

"Silence!"

With his back against the door, Hauser fumbled for the paper, keeping his eyes on the opposite wall. (This Dahlmeyer, why couldn't they move him to another corridor!) He said:

"92 F, I have orders for you."

In the interval Neuling had been edging forward. His long, lipless mouth was working, and suddenly, like a knotted cord running over a pulley, the words began to fall.

"If you please, Herr Kerkermeister, it's only a small matter, it wouldn't be against the rules——"

"——I haven't time——"

"——it's only to send a message, a short message to Doctor Ahlwarth, Doctor Ahlwarth up at the hospital, I want him to see my wife, she's in a bad way, she——"

"Will you be quiet!" Hauser snapped.

"Yes, Herr Kerkermeister, yes, I'm not going to give any trouble. Only my wife, you see——it's the pain in her belly ——if you could just send two words to Doctor Ahlwarth——"

Hauser nodded.

"I'll send two words to Ahlwarth all right. We've got him down in the basement, with four more of your communist friends . . . You, 92 F, you're to read this paper and let me have it back when I'm round again. There's a place for your signature at the end of each clause."

Josef took the paper and glanced at the first paragraph.

"You mean——I've got to sign this?"

"It's not compulsory," Hauser said curtly. "I simply advise you to. It'll make things easier for you, that's all."

He turned and unlocked the door, hesitated a moment. Strictly, he should have read the document aloud——he would have to report that he had done so. But no, he wouldn't stop here now. He specially disliked this room. In some queer way this scum got on his nerves—he didn't know which upset him most, the bolshie or the yids. He said over his shoulder: "I don't want any row in here—you're being watched!" and marched away.

"Does that mean one has to talk in whispers?" Dahlmeyer asked.

He got no answer. Neuling was on the floor again, dribbling a kind of prayer that was full of oaths. Still at attention in the centre of the room, Josef read the document through twice, and then passed it over.

"This," he said, like a child faced with a paper on dynamics, "I don't understand it—what do you make of this?"

32

'EVIDENCE preferred in regard to Zeppichmann (J):

1. That by corruption he did, in the premises Handelstrasse 149 maliciously obtain and insultingly occupy the furnished apartment in the legal tenancy of a German.

   Admitted . . . .

2. That being of inferior race he occupied a salaried post in the Moltke Hospital, Hartzinnfeld, without proper competence for the duties of that post.

   Admitted . . . .

3. That on the 8th November in company with twenty-five other persons, to be later named, all members of a revolutionary (communist) society, he maliciously and with weapons and explosives did set upon and brutally injure five Germans in the street known as Zeugerstrasse.

   Admitted . . . .

4. That he did persistently behave with arrogance unsuited to a person of inferior race.

   Admitted . . . .

5. That at 7.15 P.M. on the 16th inst., in Adrianstrasse, he did obstinately refuse to give medical aid to a German woman, the victim of a street-accident.

   Admitted . . . .

6. That he did organise and develop complete plans for an act of revolutionary violence to be carried out on the occasion of an assembly of loyal Germans on the 26th February next.

   Admitted . . . .

"Yes," Dahlmeyer said dreamily, folding the sheet and handing it back, "I had a similar bill of delinquencies when I first arrived: written, upon textual evidence, by the same author. I rather think the little Hochhäusler must be the man—it's evidently somebody who once caught sight of a law primer . . . Is any single part of an item true, may I inquire?"

"No."

"I apologise. The answer to my absurd question is contained in the document itself . . . The problem that remains is the disposal of this work. I remember now what I did with mine: I twisted it rather skilfully into a windmill—really it was not a bad effort for a man who had never before made a windmill out of a bill of indictment. And then, finding our closet imperfectly equipped, I restored the paper to its original shape and put it to its proper use. Possibly some junior official is still trying to recover it. A very unpleasing duty."

Josef, still staring woodenly at the paper, said: "There'd be trouble over that!"

Dahlmeyer nodded. "There was! They were very, very much distressed about it."

He slid to the floor again, and with simplicity, as an elderly man might treat a shy girl at a party, he put his arm across Josef's shoulders, drawing him towards the window.

"It's so hard to give advice!" he said, scanning the wall outside as if it were a Tyrolean landscape. His gently pedantic voice had a coat of huskiness, like Speyer wine. "You see, one doesn't know how much another man cares about physical pain. Or about his outward dignity. The easiest thing is to sign the whole of it—the Hauser child was right about that. I won't deceive you: they treat one—very roughly, if one doesn't sign."

Josef said presently: "I may as well sign if that'll please

them. There's nothing to be gained by refusing, they'll 'prove' it one way or another."

"No," Dahlmeyer said thoughtfully, "no, that's not quite right. You can't prove something that isn't true."

He walked across to Neuling, who had fallen asleep in his corner, and examined the spectacle with delicate interest: the ugly mouth wide open, showing black stumps of teeth, the curious slenderness of the wrist lying across the forehead with its mighty, fibrous hand attached.

"For myself," he went on, as if addressing the sleeping man, "I like to think there's something they can't get hold of. That watch of mine they took away, it has a miniature of my wife in the back. I asked them to restore me that, as it had no monetary value, but they wouldn't do so. It's funny, the way people behave—they wouldn't even give me my wife's picture! So I said to myself, 'I've still got something inside me, and they won't get that!'"

For a moment Josef raised his eyes from his own finger-nails and stared at Dahlmeyer's face: beautiful, as even he could see, with the scholar's forehead and the grey, flamboyant eyebrows striding over brilliant eyes. He said:

"I don't understand."

Dahlmeyer was taking off his coat. He had folded it and slipped the bundle under Neuling's head before he spoke again; still quietly.

"What they really don't like about us is a certain quality in our minds. We recognise things for what they are, we refuse to believe that a fact can be wiped away by thinking, or turned into a different fact. That's what they really mean by our 'arrogance,' and because that quality of mind is one they can't get for themselves, their one idea is to destroy it in us. That—" he jerked his forefinger at the paper which Josef had let fall on the floor "—it means nothing in itself. As you say, they'll find some excuse to do what they want, it's only a device for saving them a little trouble. But when you sign that paper you're surrendering something. You're agreeing to their damnable doctrine that facts can be altered at will. And as soon as you agree to that you're coming down to the level of themselves. Of course I don't want to persuade you, you may see things differently, you have a right to consult your own interests." And suddenly his voice was salicin, with all the music gone. "But they tried it on me and it didn't work—it's never going to work with me. They've robbed me of all the rest—my friends, my art, my dignity. But I've something in my forehead, here, and here, inside my chest, that they shall never take away."

33

IT WAS a place of humid draughts, the Victoria Club, somehow the central heating had never worked very well. The smell of hot rust was there, from the entrance to the attic stores, a floating stuffiness pervaded all the rooms, no one was ever warm. The coldest part of the whole top-heavy neo-romanesque affair was the office of administration, formerly the club's debating room. But Commissioner Fietz didn't mind. A nip in the air made him feel younger, Paula had looked delicious this morning in her new pyjamas, his reservoir of boiling spirits was as deep as the sea.

He moved his chair back a little further, getting his stomach clear from the handle of a drawer.

"You see, Meisel, this fellow's giving us a bit of trouble. Lack of memory, perhaps—or shall we say, pig-headedness. I'm inclined myself to think it's pure stupidity, he's got a numbskull, ploughboy look about him—inbreeding, probably."

But Erich Meisel felt the cold, and his chair was very hard. He looked forlornly from the commissioner's face, of which the well-moulded parts had slipped a little out of position, to the board with *Mehr Licht* in poker-work above his head.

"But I don't quite see—"

"My idea," the commissioner said, "is simply that you should face the boy. I don't see how he can go on denying the facts when he sees you—he must realise that you know all about him. I wouldn't bother about it, myself, only some one's been fussing round my office in Gottwaldstrasse asking for some inquiry. An extraordinary person called Rupf. One has to be a little bit careful, Zeppichmann may possibly know some one influential in Berlin, and if there happened to be a song-and-dance I'd like to have everything taped beforehand. You'll do that for me, won't you! We've got him in the examination room now, Rutsatz here will show you the way."

"Very good, Herr Bevollmächtigte!"

He felt a certain resentment as he followed the guard, shivering slightly, along the corridor. He had understood that he belonged to an inner circle of the party, that the greatest service he could give was in the department of ideological organisation. Examining prisoners was a job for the rank and file; and as to this Zeppichmann, his single wish was never to see the stinking clod again.

At the foot of the staircase Rutsatz stopped. "I've something here," he said, "that you might find useful. We find it saves a good deal of time in these examinations."

It was a piece of rubber pipe some three feet long. Erich said, "Thank-you," and put it in his pocket.

So that was the method! For just an instant, as they turned into the lower passage, he felt curiously faint; and then, with a sudden spiritual enlightenment, his courage returned. He realised now that the time had come for his vengeance, avenging not the wrongs done to himself but the insult to his blood. The fellowship in which he had sealed his life, which had claimed the whole of his young and fierce devotion, was divinely charged with a mission to cleanse and purify his land. The task that lay before him was not the pricking of a single dirty clot; it was, in symbol, an assault upon the whole of the land's impurity: and in this sacred act he fought not as himself alone but as the archon of a nation, a Parsifal in which a people's holiness had been reborn. He touched the coil in his pocket and it seemed to have become the hilt of a sword. With a cold fire kindled in his loins and temples he forgot the smallness of his frame, the puny thighs and narrow chest, the way he must tilt his head to talk to other men. In this transfiguration the childish part of him had dropped away, he had come a warrior to his ancient heritage.

"Will you wait a few moments in here—I'll see if they're ready," Rutsatz said.

The examination, in the music room, had begun some twenty minutes before. On these occasions a certain relaxation of discipline was allowed: the officers engaged were mostly young, and the chance of a little comedy was considered good for their morale.

There was fog outside, and this room with its brocaded curtains was always a little short of light; so they had the electric chandelier switched on, and the standard lamp with its rose-silk shade, bringing the pleasantness of evening into the raw day. The heavy carpet was predominately rose, and the covers of the easy chairs were in the same warm tone. It was a pretty room, Hauser thought, as he lounged on the sofa: the furnishings old fashioned, but with the peculiar, mellow charm of all out-dated things. The other officers, half a dozen of them, sat and smoked in a row of easy chairs along the wall, leaving the central limelight to the prisoner.

It was left to Schulze-Behrend, the senior man present, to open the business. Tall and handsome, widely renowned for his wit, he sat on top of the Blüthner, drumming with his heels.

"So you maintain, my good Herr Doktor Zeppichmann, that you are a first-rate physician? You will not be offended, perhaps, if we conduct a brief examination of your attainments. To begin with, can you tell us where there is a muscle known as the Schlagbesen?"

"There is no such thing in the human anatomy," Josef said.

Schulze-Behrend frowned. "Oh, come, Herr Doktor Zeppich-hinterteil! When I ask you where a muscle is, it's hardly polite to say that it doesn't exist. Don't you agree with me, Tarnow?"

The man beside Hauser on the sofa, a swarthy youth whose growth had all been lateral, started to heave and squirm.

"I am bound to agree!" he bubbled. "Most discourteous!"

"I think," said Behrend gravely, "we shall have to give our friend a little demonstration."

That was Sauerborn's cue. With his slow, good-humoured smile he came up behind the prisoner's back, grasped the bottom of his jacket, and in one adroit movement jerked it off.

"I would ask you to be careful," Josef said. "I broke a bone in my shoulder—it's still rather weak."

"That must be a matter for a separate inquiry," Behrend remarked. "Yes, I've got it on the list: Cause of Damaged Shoulder. And possibly we could help with a little massage. Proceed, friend Sauerborn!"

Another mighty jerk and the shirt was off.

"And now, though we are slightly repelled by the colour of your skin, we shall endeavour to show you the exact location of the Schlagbesen." He slipped down from the piano. "Pohlse, I think you have a pair of dividers you could lend me? Thanks, comrade! Now, Herr Doktor Zeppich-Mutterring (hold him still, Sauerborn!), the Schlagbesen is to be found in the left side of the small of the back, *here!* One minute, I don't think I made myself quite clear. (Perhaps you would just turn the patient the other way up. Thank-you, Sauerborn!) Now, the exact position is—*here!*"

Through his giggles Tarnow managed to splutter: "I'm s-sure you're not quite right, Behrend! It's more over to the left."

"I bow to your superior knowledge!" Behrend answered modestly. "Here is the tutorial index, I beg you to demon-

strate your own view of the matter . . . Thank-you, Sir!
And once again, perhaps, to make our friend perfectly clear.
Thank-you! Has any other member of the committee any
alternative suggestions to put forward—or to drive in, as one
might say? . . . Very well then, we shall proceed to the
next item on the agenda, and ask the worthy doctor to give
us a little talk on Constipation: Twenty-Seven Different
Methods of Cure. One minute! The Doctor appears a little
sleepy. Perhaps you would lend me your cigarette a moment,
Grünwitz? . . . Yes, our friend seems definitely less sleepy
now. It would be a kindness, perhaps, if we allowed the
doctor to finish your cigarette while he is giving his lecture.
Wait! I understand that really learned doctors invariably
smoke by placing the cigarette in the left nostril. Perhaps
you would steady him again, Sauerborn, while I place it for
him . . ."

As the fun went on, Hauser, sitting quite still on the
sofa, hoped that it would not be carried to a higher pitch.
This kind of thing, he thought, was good for himself: it
should harden his nerves, prepare his spirits for the reckless
obedience which the Cause demanded. But he found it difficult to keep his eyes wide open, especially when they met
the prisoner's eyes. He wished the wretch would shout and
scream; there was something in his silence that made you
sweat about the neck and forehead.

". . . and now," said Behrend, "we might see if we
can do anything for the shoulder. These shoulders that get
damaged in attacks on Party Members are always so troublesome. (Have you got him tight, Sauerborn?) You, Grünwitz,
perhaps you'll help me with the massage. And you, Tarnow,
might work the arm a little, it's a great thing to get the
muscles loose . . ."

Hauser lit another cigarette. His digestion seemed to
be giving trouble. Only twenty minutes had gone, and he
supposed it would last for half an hour.

"Oughtn't we to c-cool his feet?" Tarnow was gurgling. "S-sit on his legs, will you, Pohlse, while I get his socks off!"

Soundlessly, the door from the next room opened a few inches, and in his furtive, rather ladylike way Rutsatz revolved himself in. He stood still for a few moments, with his head on one side, watching the progress of the inquiry with a critical eye.

"If the Doctor will forgive a moment's interruption," he said at last, "a friend of his has called to see him." He turned to Schulze-Behrend. "It's Group Development-Secretary Meisel—the Commissioner sent him down."

Behrend nodded. "Yes—bring him in, will you!" He signalled to the juniors to go back to their places. "You might stay where you are, will you, Sauerborn. The Doctor seems to want a little support."

"Perhaps you're right!" It was a pity, Sauerborn thought, that the play should be cut short; he didn't get much fun, these days, and really young Behrend was a master at this kind of drollery. But in point of fact, the prisoner had not much sport left in him; he was hardly on his feet at all—just hanging like a corpse on Sauerborn's hands . . . Yes, this Meisel who was coming in now was one of the stiff ones, so shy and formal that all the good spirits flew out of the room.

Erich saluted Behrend. He had one eye on the prisoner: on his body, not on his face at all.

"I understand that this man denies the charges brought against him?"

Behrend said: "That is so . . . We were rather hoping that he would save himself the ordeal of court-procedure, but—what can one do?"

"You might ask him," Erich said, "whether he still denies them, now that I'm here."

Behrend turned to the prisoner. (It was curious, he

thought, this shyness of Meisel's. Just at present the fellow appeared to be slightly drunk.)

"You—what have you got to say about it."

"I—still deny them."

"You mean," Erich said, his voice strangely low and hoarse, "you mean that I'm a liar?" His hand went into his pocket. Like the hilt of a sword, he thought, the blade of purity and vengeance, the glorious sword of Parsifal!

Josef faltered. Then,

"Yes—that's what I mean."

It was Behrend who actually whitened with rage.

"My God!—have you got him tight, Sauerborn?"

Erich waited for just a moment, savouring his ecstasy, before he stepped forward.

"All right then!"

34

THIS new country, the Weper valley, like a kind of music could be loved without being understood. He saw it first in the half light of a March morning, dull and distant shapes floating in a grey sea. When he noticed it again, leaning on his shovel and lifting his head for a moment, the boundaries were closer, loose curtains of green breaking the further reach. This Spring worked slowly, but the early days of June brought the sun to its fullest strength, and beneath that arc-light, which blistered your bare shoulders and shortened your breath, the pattern settled into solid permanence. A single farm down there, a russet roof studded with eyelids which stretched to shield a wooden gallery: below the pond a tail of brilliant grass, where the overflow slipped secretly to the lazy stream; and from the poplar fence a sandy track that having edged towards the brook strode over it by a wooden drawbridge and lost itself in the rising green beyond. That was a miniature, done in a crook of the stream with all a modeller's neatness; and the knoll which guarded it was wrought to scale, a thumb of goat-shaved turf with a sloping collar of furze. Farther and easterly the yellow land pushed up again, by easy curves, as you see a sleeper's form from the foot of the bed; and between the giant breasts of pasture land at its highest reach the sloping edge of forest showed like a Syrian beard. Leftward, the marshy pan of sheepland ribbed with wheat stayed low for twenty miles, the roofs of Weperbrücke shown like a steaming rag in the river's farth-est coil: only when the sky was cleaned with rain, and be-fore the fenland mist had gathered afresh, you saw that the level ground was measured off by the pine-capped bluffs of

Sigismund's gorge. In that extent the eye received no violence. Hamlets and scattered farms, the twelve-arched viaduct which bore the railway over Rudolf's Fen, were let into the gentle plain as easily as in a painter's wash; alone, the track of the new roadway crossed the foreground in a sloping scar.

This was a kind of safety, the field of his senses remaining always the same. In the three-mile climb to Cutting 28, where the string of trucks stood hungry beside a débris of blasted rock, he hardly noticed anything but the shoulders of the man in front. (You had to keep your step and distance if you didn't want a rifle-butt jabbed into your back.) There were cabins beside the track with elaborate carving over their doors, there were sometimes children staring at the gang, but he scarcely saw them. It was not until he had taken his position in the loading line, and the panorama was spread beneath him, that he seemed to come awake. Up here the charivari of birds was strong enough to pierce the clank of shovels, the hot air carried a whiff of wood smoke from the farm below, sometimes faintly the scent of dung. To the child of Richterhausen streets this weft of sensation was a second birth; and as its pattern grew familiar, the shape of all the years behind passed further into unreality.

That outside world, pasture and trees and the blue of distant hills, was held apart from him by the live electric wire which ran on both sides of the track; the old woman down there, leading the horses out to grass, might have been in another land; and yet he was more aware of it than of his own arena, the yawning truck, the gasps of the prisoner next along the line. His hands were calloused now, his skin would take the morning wind and midday sun and hardly pass the soreness on to his brain. Even the constant ache in spine and shoulder was losing force by its monotony. To be clad in a body which hurt, to feel your tongue like a rusty spoon, these were conditions normal to human life. He began to watch the flight of birds above the lamina of rock, to listen for the voice of the farmer's boy calling in the cows.

To Giessbach: when you're better I'll take you to Giessbach, I promise that my dear, we'll go there together, you and me. Like a line of poetry learnt at school, like the station cries on a familiar journey, that pattern of words was always echoing against the wall of his mind. In some way the distant hills started the tune again, and he once imagined that a place called Giessbach was hidden somewhere over there. But he would not let his thoughts slide back along that path.

By rule, no pause was allowed till twelve o'clock, when a whistle was blown for rations, half a pound of potato-bread with a mug of bohea, cold. If the stint of trucks had not gone down this 'hour of gratuity' was reduced from twenty minutes to ten.

But much depended on what the Disciplinary Works Director was doing. As long as he was about, the elderly Sergeant Busch would march up and down the duckboard path as rigidly as he had done for twenty years on the drill ground at Halberstadt, halting at intervals to urge them on. "You, cabbagehead, God rot you, put some kidney into it!" But from time to time the telephone would ring in the Director's little cabin, there had been some hitch in returning empty trucks, the Director breathing the fires of hell would emerge and march off down the hill. As his head disappeared Sergeant Busch unbuttoned his tunic, released a pumpkin of blue flannel and squashed it in again, expelling a load of boredom and dyspepsia in a mighty, creaking yawn. He would look all round, and clear his nostrils, and out of the top of his gaiters came the stump of a cigar. "Satan's teeth, my little cows, it's not so warm to-day!" He would sit on the edge of a truck and a smile would leak into his Saxon eyes. "It's better, I think—better for my old girl down there, the sun's been giving her diarrhoea." And then, with a kind of ferocity he would seize a prisoner's spade. "Here, Zeppichmann, give me that and I'll show you how it's done. Hell's navel, can you never learn! Go on, go and sit over there—you, lobster-bottom, Baruch, spawn of a cockchafer, you sit down as well, watch the way I do it!" There was muscle in the fat little man, he'd have a truck filled up in ten minutes, holding the handle of the shovel under his arm and doing all the work with his knees, *uuch! uuch!*, puffing at the inch of cigar all the time and chatting with the other half of his mouth. "A crew of ants—a crew of ants would make a quicker job of it than you knock-kneed yids. A lot of butterflies, I suppose that's what you are, a lot of butterflies out to enjoy the sun! I tell you, my small Thomas could load a truck quicker than any of you!" He stopped and spat. From one of the countless recesses in his shabby uniform came a crumpled snapshot of a dour, obese child, and in an offhand way, as one furtively tipping a waiter, he would pass it along the line. "Twenty kilos in his skin, and only three last month!" When the photograph came back he baptised it with a smacking kiss, tucked it away and set to work again. "Keep moving now, you bastards, I do two trucks myself while you do one!" And Josef, squatting on the end of a sleeper, feeling a little of the ache flow off, stared fixedly at the country beyond the wire.

It was best for him to be surrounded by such simplicity: the sergeant's gravelled voice, the piebald skull and scrawny neck that belonged to Herr Baruch, truck-rails narrowing down the hill. You did not have to worry here, you made no plans. When darkness came you took your place in the marching line and they led you back to the other half of your world. It came to feel like the rhythm of changing seasons, this tight monotony.

An effect like that of morphia came from pouring out his physical reserves, with the air and light washing all day against the bare skin of his torso. He was half asleep by the time they reached the barracks, he went through the routine of soup-queue and blanket-queue like a marionette. Sometimes, when the whistle was blown for bed, he could not concentrate enough to undo his boots, and would even fall asleep on the concrete. Then little Baruch, the darting sparrow of a man who had once owned the largest drapery in Stettin, would kneel and take the boots off for him, whispering "Tchtt, old lazybones, you must never buy boots again without your mother's advice!" and with the help of Dahlmeyer, who was still in protective custody and who slept nearest the floor, he would heave him on to his sleeping-shelf.

He slept, as a rule, like animals in safety: a lump of flesh and bone with only a shallow movement of the chest to show it is still alive. Now that the weather was warmer the blanket was enough protection; he had grown accustomed to the feel of the slatted shelf. He hardly woke when, at the first promise of daylight, the reveille whistle was blown. Only his body got itself down to the floor, his hands gathered the boots and presently he was marching up the hill.

But sometimes the cough which he had contracted in his earliest days of imprisonment woke him up with its violence. Then he lay awake for an hour or more, in a kind of stupor but with his eyes open, his senses shallow but acute. Below him Dahlmeyer gently snores; above, the restless body of Baruch is always wriggling, making the slats bulge and creak, while he carries on an endless conversation. 'Not in the same quality, not at 53½! I know, but what about the quality? Take it, my love, take it and write it off! Then we'll move Fräulein Lehmann into the millinery and everything will be all right. Get it down to RM 96 and we'll all go to supper at Ricasoli's . . .' The shelves go on for thirty yards, in the three layers there are forty-five men between here and the latrine, where the barbed wires cross and the next section begins; from this stack of bodies out-of-use come tides of sound, snoring and little groans, occasionally a boy's sobs or an eerie, shuttered laughter. Beyond the wooden wall the sentry's boots ring on the concrete; forty paces, the stamping turn, and forty paces again.

The wall came two feet short of the iron roof, the intervening space being webbed with wire. He woke one night when the moon, low on that side, revealed the whole barrack in milk-blue light criss-crossed with shadow; and seeing the dark line of bodies, and the sentry's bayonet passing along the gap, he thought he was still in the train. He wondered at its quietness, for in all the fourteen hours from Hartzinnfeld the train had rocked and hammered like a brewer's dray; and then, feeling that the journey had been so long, he believed it had passed beyond the steady world, and ran on silently through limbo, bearing its load of restless dead. Between the slats he looked at Dahlmeyer's face, the eyes open like the eyes of the newly dead and glossy from the moon's light. He tried to raise himself to see if Minna was there, but his muscle-will still slept and he realised thankfully that he too had died. 'The only thing is to write it down. Take the winter hose into stock and write the whole lot down to sixteen thousand. Sixteen thousand—surely that's low enough!' He wanted to tell Herr Baruch he did not understand, but his voice wouldn't reach so far; Dahlmeyer's face was receding into darkness, the train tipped over steeply, increasing its speed. The train ran through a market-square and the conductor came aboard, swinging by his hands along the corridor, a faceless man, he stood with his hand stretched out for Josef's ticket and the ticket was lost. They stood in a line with their hands held out, Herr Barthol and Frau Spühler wrapped in her quilt and Dr. Wildelau, they stood and moaned for him to find his ticket, and his arms were fastened down so he couldn't move. "Sixteen thousand," the conductor said; and that was more than Josef earned in two whole years, "sixteen thousand," the man repeated, "surely that's low enough!" The conductor began to grin, he grinned from his faceless head, the face took shape around his grin and became Herr Meisel's face. "I'll pay you in time," Josef said, "just give me a little time!" but he saw Herr Meisel's hand go into his pocket and the long black snake come out. He screamed, and a hand came up, a gentle hand, and held his wrist. "Hush, my friend!"—Dahlmeyer's voice—"hush, old lad, everything's quite all right!"

It was another night, but he thought it was the same, when he was woken by the light of an electric torch brushing across his eyes. Two of the guards were standing beside his shelf, the man they called the Münster Matador and the little chap with eyes like mushrooms in a bloodless face. It wasn't Josef they had come for; they gave Dahlmeyer a jerk in the ribs and he, as if he had been expecting it, got up and quietly went away with them. Josef remained awake, and in a little while they brought the old man back, carrying him by his arms and legs. They put him on his shelf again, and left him there; and until Josef fell asleep he heard him whimpering, as a child whimpers when ashamed of some private sorrow. Next morning, as they trudged up the hill, he noticed that Dahlmeyer was marching lame. That was the only difference Josef saw: in the ration pause the old man chatted to Sergeant Busch in his usual, courtly way.

Before the leaves had begun to turn, the prisoners were moved to Sondersumpf. The barracks here were not so good; the pinewood walls were rotten, letting in the wind, there was always an inch or two of water along the floor. Yet he found a kind of restfulness in the desolate country where they worked, lonely, staggering trees that rose from the early mist, the mournful green of rush and water-weed, majestic skies. There were birds he had never seen before which came across in steady companies like viking fleets, their long necks stretched like bowsprits, the sough of their feathers pricked with senile cries. As long as the sergeant's eyes were turned he would stand and watch that flight, wondering at their freedom. Only at dusk, when the labour brigade marched through the village, he sank to the lowest point of his dejection: for the sharpness of his sensibility was growing again; and smelling the cabbage soup from the cottages, and seeing the ragged boys who played about the street, he remembered that in a former life he had been as well-off as they.

This battle which had seemed to be won must still be fought again. Lying sick and faint on the floor of the cattle-truck, enduring in every bone the train's dogged advance, he had felt that Hartzinnfeld was being shaken away; and with the scene of old experience he thought its content would be gone, as if he had put all his possessions in a grain-sack and dropped it in the sea. The shreds and tags were coming to the surface now and the tides bore them in. Where the barrack path came out on the main road he noticed, day by day, the yellowing of the lindens, as he had seen them last year from the window of his room in Handelstrasse. He did his turn at cleaning out the warders' room, and the scrubbing soap they gave him was the kind Frau Spühler used. The days growing short, the cottage lamps were lit by the time they passed them in the evening, he would get a glimpse of an old man sitting to supper, of an iron bedstead in a shallow room. On a hundred tatters of experience his brain worked fretfully, as a dog will scrabble at old earths; and now, when the cold woke him early in the mornings, he could not escape from the dark invasion. Her face as she lay asleep; the whispered "Are you sure it'll make me well?"; the thin, bare arm lying against his cheek: their shape grew fainter but they would not stay away, those moments where the richness of the past was caught. They were like old menus mixed by chance with a traveller's gear, to catch his eye in lonely tracts, and set him hungering for half-forgotten tastes. The lines of her face were already dim, the very colour of her hair might fade, but the form she had left in him would not close up.

The picture he had tried to destroy, through the long nights in the Victoria Club, was coming into shape again: the picture of Minna waking up, that morning after he had last seen her, in the wretchedness and aching thirst which followed the peaks of fever; of her waiting for the crackle of the stairs under his feet. He had tried to believe that she was dead, that her shrunk reserves could not have held against the last assault. He had never convinced himself. And now he could not wish her dead; could not endure the bitterness that he should hear no word from her again, make no last gift of tenderness, never pour out his loneliness in the depth of her understanding. The time he had wasted at her side, hour upon hour, in conversation out of Plünnecke's book! Give him one more hour to talk with her, give him only a span of minutes, and he would so cover her with love and gratitude that all his pain would sleep.

That early period, between his waking and the whistle to get up, seemed infinitely long. It was giant relief to see his fellows come to life again, to hear their muttering as they jostled into line with boots tied across their shoulders; relief to be moving himself, for all his body's cramp and tiredness, shuffling along between the guards and damping his face at the range of taps; to smell new air, to listen for his number in the roll, to cover up the weariness of thoughts with a tissue of sensation. They had to keep close silence in the bread and coffee line, but there were ways of communication: a smile which could be changed to a facial-twitch if the guard looked round; a touch of the fingers to carry friendship to a boy who had been through punishment the night before. With only the privilege of animals, they kept their unity.

At this station the work was less healthy, but smaller in monotony. The foundation of the four-mile dam across the fen, to protect the workings lower down, was to consist of thousands of tons of rubble, which the prisoners transported in shallow floats. Propelling and unloading these, they had to wade through mud and icy water which sometimes came up to Baruch's armpits; as a rule the supervising engineers considered they could direct the operation best from the firmer ground, and the prisoners found themselves as much as a hundred yards from all authority.

"It is one of the evil jests of providence," Dahlmeyer said, "that she showers her gifts on us at inappropriate times. Only fifty-five years ago I used to long to wade about in a pond there was on my grandfather's estate. And my maritime ambition was always frustrated by diabolical nursemaids. Now, I am at liberty—indeed, encouraged—to practise the wader's craft all day long; and I find the odours of the bog disagreeable, and my limbs subject to rheumatism . . . If you, Herr Doktor, would be kind enough to shift the float on a little way . . ."

Baruch, taking a step backward to get out of the float's path, once more lost his footing and went down on his knees in the slime. Herr Liebenow the lawyer, working on the next float, turned round and tittered.

"Our friend Herr Baruch is a very religious man! He makes his devotions twelve times a day."

A shout from the engineer: "What's happening over there? If you stillborns think you can play the fool—!"

"What I complain about," Baruch said, scrambling up and shaking with the cold, "is the lack of economy. All this stuff we're throwing in here, it ought to be sorted out. There should be two qualities, the large pieces to go in the water, the dust and stuff on the mud. And there ought to be a bonus on the stints."

Dahlmeyer climbed painfully on to the float and took over Josef's shovel. "If only I had had our friend Herr Baruch in my orchestra! He would have tied a long wire between the ends of all the bows, and the time would have been perfect." He had got the shovel full but had to drop it before he could get the stuff over the side. "My legs!" he said, "if it isn't indelicate to mention such things, really they —give me—a lot of discomfort. No, all right, I can manage!" He had heaved a good shovel-full over this time, he was pleased, he hated to be beaten. "By the way, I don't like that cough of yours. Can't you think of anything to do about it? What's the good of being a doctor?"

"I used to be," Josef said dully. "I'd forgotten about that . . . Here, I'll shovel again. You, if you please, pretend to be spreading the stuff. It's all right, I'll stand in front of you."

"We should regard it as a favour," Baruch muttered, "if the Doctor could refrain from throwing gravel down our neck."

Dahlmeyer, done in for the present, knelt at the bottom of the float and made baling motions with his arms; he looked sidelong at the stuggy young doctor who, grunting and sucking his lips, was doggedly lifting a mountain of rubble over the side. There was some improvement, he thought: the boy had not made such a long speech since leaving Hartz-innfeld; his chest was pitiably shrunk, his skin, exposed to the whole of summer, had burnt to a dirty café-au-lait; but a little of the animal dullness had gone, his eyes seemed to find definite objects and hold them. It was like watching a baby's progress: the first genuine smile, the first turn-over from stomach to back. If they only left the boy out of the punishment roll another few weeks . . .

A shout from behind startled him so much that he nearly fell into the water. The engineer had managed to steal up to them unawares.

"One of you sods was talking! Which was it?"

" 'Twas I," Dahlmeyer said at once.

Baruch turned round sharply. "My turn!" he said to Dahlmeyer, almost angrily; and to the engineer: "I was talking to myself—it's a habit of mine. The professor didn't say a word.

Josef stood gaping.

"It was me talking," he said suddenly.

"Or rather, coughing," Dahlmeyer interrupted. "I suppose you couldn't possibly get hold of a linctus of some kind for my friend here? As—as a favour."

"What exactly d'you think I am?" the engineer inquired. "The Ghetto's Own Private Medicine-Man?"

Dahlmeyer removed an imaginary lock of hair from his right ear. It was one of the graceful tricks which had added to his popularity with the Munich audiences, and he could not remember that the hair had been cut off.

"No," he said, smiling. "I only suppose you to be a creature made by God in His own image."

The engineer wound up the argument:

"That's enough bloody lip from you," he said.

There was pleasure, large in a world sparing of pleasures, in seeing the daylight begin to weaken, the figures of men on the farther floats gradually blurred against the scrub. The day's work had to finish then; for in the darkness, it was thought, a man might jump the wires and run at top speed across the marsh to freedom. The first half mile towards home might be painful, men hobbling and falling on the stony track with the guards cursing them; but when they reached the road a little blood had got to their legs, and the spreading warmth seemed worth the biting pain in knees and feet. Where they stood for the evening ration a concrete wall kept off the wind; the dim electric bulbs upheld the illusion of being warm, and a cup of tepid broth was something to smack your lips on after six hours' fast. Even the guards were somnolent now: they could overlook a man who leant his shoulder against the wall, so long as he didn't drop down asleep. For a moment, as you passed the hatch, you caught the cheerful sight of burning coke, sometimes a whiff from the orderly officer's cigarette. You might be lucky to-night, and get a blanket without any holes in it. At least (if you were not on late fatigue) there was nothing more to endure between this and bed.

The storm-lanterns swinging at each end of the sleeping-racks brought the captives closer together: a small, friendlier world, with the lines of wire and concrete posts rubbed soft. Enjoying the heat from each other's breath and bodies they bandied little, nervous smiles. They had come a whole day nearer death.

It was Baruch who crept along to Josef's shelf that night, an hour after the whistle had gone; found Josef's hand and pressed a tablet into his palm. "Something for your cough!" he whispered. "I saw the Matador had them—stole one out of his coat."

And Josef sucked it gratefully, but the cough was worse that night, angry enough to keep even his exhausted body away from sleep. In the morning, putting on his boots, he noticed for the first time a freckle of blood on the slats where his head had been.

35

BY MARCH, Baruch had 'gone flat': that was the phrase in current use to indicate a special kind of symptoms. It was curious and disquieting to Dahlmeyer that Baruch had gone that way, for his small, shopkeeper's body had withstood the hardships better than many more robust ones, and the whimsical quickness of his mind should have saved him. It happened, however, and it appeared to be final. Overnight, as it seemed, Baruch's eyes took on the childish look which so many of the others had already. He ceased to be friendly, winced if you turned towards him. He laughed a great deal, without any reason, and the laughter always ended in tears. He made a little doll, wrapping a piece of rag round a cork he picked up in the road, and carried it with him everywhere, kissing and petting it. He cried when the guards took it away.

Dahlmeyer was grieved at losing his companionship. It was a serious depletion of his personal wealth, for he could not live without people to love and talk to. It was rumoured among the guards that Dahlmeyer had gone flat himself, but that was a clumsy diagnosis. He talked to himself because he had to use his voice, and because the punishment for that offence was comparatively light.

When the weakness of his legs became a nuisance to every one—twice in a week he had to be carried home by two of the stronger prisoners—they took him off the dam construction and gave him barrack duties. At these he was very slow, but thorough: they saw to that. One of the guards, a youngster, was put to superintend him as he scrubbed the floor of the guards' mess; and to this boy, who leant against the wall with his hands in his pockets, he was always talking.

"Do tell me, what were you doing before you started this job? What sort of home had you? A nice one, I think—I can usually tell."

"That's no business of yours. You're not supposed to talk. That bit you've just done isn't properly clean. Do it again."

Dahlmeyer worked himself back, moving the bucket and brush.

"It only interests me," he said, "because I always wonder why certain people have to drink such a lot. As a rule I think it's the result of boredom——"

"Do you want your bottom kicked?"

"No, I should be sorry if you did that. Up till now you've never kicked me when you were sober. I like to think of you as two different people—sometimes a drunken youth who can't help himself, but normally a nice fellow, intelligent and human, like my own Lazar: one that I could be fond of—indeed, one that I am growing fond of already."

"Are you comparing me with a young yid?"

"Let me ask you something: compare me with your own father——"

"I can't. He was killed in the War. I hardly remember him . . . you're missing out the corner, I've told you about that before!"

"I'm sorry—I shall reorientate my operations . . . You hardly remember your father—yes, that explains so much. But if you don't remember his face, you carry instead something else he has given you—the thought of his bravery and devotion. In that way you remember him. And I, who can't see my son any more, I try to use his share of my affection on some one else. To me, every boy is my Lazar. I want them all to have his courage and sweetness. I can't bear to see a fellow of Lazar's age letting other people make dirty marks all over his mind. I want——"

"There are dirty marks all over the floor," the guard said sharply, "that's what you've got to worry about." He went and looked out of the window, lit another cigarette. Why couldn't they put some one else on this job! It made you feel like a child, a mother-cuddling child, listening to this old fool. "I don't want any more talking!" he said.

"But listen, old friend—"

"*Silence!*"

There was still young Zeppichmann, and Dahlmeyer had certain hopes of him. That cough was very bad, but the toughness of the man's physique could withstand it as it seemed to withstand so many rigours. There were brains in the square, granite head: one saw them in his neat handling of the rubble-float, in the almost instinctive alteration of his manner for answering different guards. One saw in his eyes, too, that behind their dullness he was thinking, thinking all the time. Occasionally he smiled now; the smile came and went as if some one let up a blind in a lighted room and clicked it down again at once. His apathy was not all genuine, Dahlmeyer thought: a certain stolidity, combined with strict obedience, was the best demeanour for keeping out of trouble.

It was more than sentiment: in Dahlmeyer's mind the issue was of huge importance. His own course was virtually finished, he hoped to save his sanity and that was all. But if from this holocaust of human spirits a single one was saved, that man might bear the genius of his race to a new and more splendid fruition. Living within a herd of broken men, machines that only worked and breathed, faces unlit by any understanding, he still believed that one would emerge in whom the poison had left no live infection: a giant in ghostly power, to break in pieces the gates of brass, to make the crooked places straight and the rough places plain.

He hardly slept at all now. Sometimes he sank just below the surface of consciousness, as the aged do in their chairs, and saw old scraps of experience in the brilliant clearness which belongs to surface dreams; the crowded artists' room of the Meistersaal, his Rahel in her silver cloak coming to meet him along the lakeside terrace of Bellaggio. But throughout the night he was always aware of the slats grooving his side. When he knew that Josef was awake, on the shelf above, he talked to him constantly, using a technique he had brought to perfection. His voice, quiet but very clear, was so pitched that it reached exactly to Josef's ear; as the guard's footsteps came along the gangway it blurred into a whisper, changed to a snore; and presently he picked up his theme again as if there had been no interruption.

". . . A relief, in some ways, that here one can commit no solecisms. When I think of all the dreadful mistakes I used to make! I was at a drawing-room concert once, I saw an old man who looked very shy and lonely, all by himself in a corner, I went up to him and said, 'It's nice to find some one who hates all this flapdoodle as much as myself.' And all he said was, 'Then find my equerry, God damn it, and make your complaint to him!' So stupid of me—he was my host, and an Archduke into the bargain. And then there was that time in Milan, when the audience were all giggling—yes, I actually heard them giggling, all through Brahms's Symphony in F. At the end of that I gave them a lecture, I said in my dreadful Italian, 'You Milanese, you call yourselves the greatest amateurs of music in the world. I regret that I find you a gang of hooligans!' Then the First Violin touched my arm and told me there was a big yellow label with 'Dr. Dahlmeyer—let out waist' pinned to the back of my coat . . . Now here it's so different. One could be covered with tailors' instructions from head to foot and nobody would notice. One never has to be ashamed of anything. It makes life rather dull, perhaps, but what a relief! . . ."

The cough was starting again, and for a minute or more Dahlmeyer's berth shook with it, as if a quick-firing gun was in action on the barrack roof. Then, surprisingly, a faint voice came down from the darkness.

"It isn't what you do here—that doesn't matter. I'm ashamed of what I used to do, that's all it is."

"Were you unkind to people?" Dahlmeyer asked, as if he were inquiring about the local customs in a country he hadn't visited.

"Unkind? I don't know. Yes, I was, yes, that's it! I didn't care if I killed her or not. Or only—well, I wanted the experiment to go all right."

Dahlmeyer pressed no further: the slightest pressure on a man with a sick mind, the smallest show of common curiosity, and you ceased to be of any use to him . . . The guard was approaching again.

"There's a lot of coughing going on," the guard said. "It's a nuisance. Who is it this time?"

"I was only clearing my throat," Dahlmeyer said "—or possibly you heard my stomach rumbling. One's stomach is so capricious and so devoid of tact. I very much regret any disturbance I may have caused you." He waited till the guard had unlocked and re-locked himself through to the next section.

"Don't you think," he went on, "the only important thing is your knowing that you were unkind to her and hating yourself for it? I mean, if you were really a rotten creature you wouldn't realise you'd done anything wrong." He sat up and stretched to take hold of Josef's arm. (This was called Mutinous Correspondence, and incurred heavy penalties.) His voice grew warmer, vibrating with excitement. "It's important, this, it's very important indeed. You've got to realise that you're not a rotten creature, you're a very good creature, I can tell you that, I know it. These people here, they try to take away your belief in yourself. You mustn't let them. You know, I've done the most terrible things myself. I once got rid of an artist—a very good artist too—simply because he fell in love with my Rahel. I just couldn't bear to have a man about the place who was making sheep's eyes at my wife, I simply sacked the fellow. But I don't keep on punishing myself for that, I think of some of the decent things I've done. You have to, in a place like this. I've given my name to help some really dreadful performances, I've said that certain young musicians were men of genius when I knew that they were incurably second-rate— just because they were hard-up and hopeless. It costs much more than money, to hand over your name like that. And then I always think of one faultless performance of the Passione symphony, it was in St. Petersburg before the War, just one performance in which the whole swift power of Haydn's mind took possession of us, I was literally sweating with excitement and I knew, I knew that we had reached the pinnacle of interpretation, I was certain it would never be done so perfectly again. I remember the notices next day were very sad and spiteful, but what did I care? I had enjoyed the greatest moment of my life—I can feel it now, I can see the exact shape of the walls which were in my eyes while that mystery was passing through my mind and hands. It becomes a part of yourself, like your arms and legs, an experience such as that. Don't you think that those are the only real values! Not what we possess, but the difference our possessions make in ourselves. Not the things people do to us, but the result of their actions in our own being. You, it's possible that you may see the end of this. You may live for many years, till this period of your life looks like a narrow strip of darkness across the road far behind. The highest moment in your life, the moment when all the inward richness that a man carries about is completely realised—that may be still to come."

His voice was dropping again, but not for the guard this time. The pain that hung on his shoulders and round his legs was being drawn together into one place: a kind of rendezvous for all his pains, a spot not far below the left nipple to which he could have pointed exactly with his finger. It was happening more frequently nowadays, this mobilisation of pain, and it always tightened up his breathing. He had to make a struggle before he could go on again, an effort like that of tearing the body out of nightmare.

"Listen!" (faintly) "Listen, Zeppichmann! I want to tell you something I believe. I believe that evil can't crush out the virtue which we have in common, it can only stamp it into a smaller compass—like a kernel, you see, a tiny kernel of virtue, hard as steel and desperately powerful. You've got to hang on to that—I haven't any chance—you've got something valuable to look after and take out of this place. I mean, you've got to keep your own integrity, you've got to keep your mind very clear." Another effort, and he was fierce now. "Don't let them get their fingers on to that, don't let them persuade you that their own silly routine of hating and hurting is the proper business of human beings! You know it isn't, you know that yourself, you know that the spirit of man is worth infinitely more than that . . ."

When daylight came he looked sidelong at Josef's face and wondered if his moralising had been a waste of breath. 'I have become an old man,' he reflected, 'and perhaps a little absurd.' This was nothing but a young peasant, as his grandfather might have been: cadaverous cheeks and Polish forehead, mouth tough as a mare's, with shallow, powerful teeth; the labourer's eyes fixed stubbornly on his swollen fingers, as he stooped to the painful job of getting on his boots. 'I have read him from my imagination,' Dahlmeyer thought. 'He may yet take something out of this place, but I sow my platonism on frostbound soil.'

Yet it seemed that he had won some friendship. When his legs became so bad that he could not get as far as the guards' quarters, and was utterly useless, they let him stay on his berth all day. And at night, when the rest came to bed, young Zeppichmann always gave him some attention. In the darkness he would feel a bony arm creeping under his shoulders and a blouse, carefully rolled, would slide beneath his head. His face would be wiped refreshingly with a damp rag, his legs shifted to a better position, very slowly and with curiously gentle hands. All that was done in silence, and when he murmured, "Thank you, thanks old friend!" and took and kissed the creeping hand, he only heard a laconic whisper: "It doesn't matter."

So he was troubled, in one of the endless, lonely days, by catching the name from two guards passing on the other side of the wall. '. . . This bastard Zeppichmann.' 'Zeppichmann? he's out with the gangs I suppose . . .' One Lübelt, a little hunchback creature with a baby's mind, brought him a cup of cabbage in water if he happened to think of it during the day; and he asked this man, "Have you heard anything about Zeppichmann—you know, the one who sleeps on this shelf here?" Lübelt didn't seem to understand; he tittered in his schoolgirl fashion, and put the cup down on the floor and went away. But within an hour he was back again, trembling with mirth.

"Zeppichmann, you said? Zeppichmann who sleeps on this shelf up here? There's news for him, they're telling me, there's a bucket of trouble for him!"

The punishment list was generally announced just before lights-out, so that the men concerned could sleep on the anticipation. Dahlmeyer listened with trembling attention that night.

'2803 Baruch . . . 0201 Lorenz, 4615 Lubnau, 1158 Maass, . . . 0079 Rosenstein, 3304 Torge, 2806 Winkelmann. Schluss!'

Schluss! Dahlmeyer closed his eyes and let his head fall back. So Zeppichmann was not on after all, his ears had deceived him that morning and Lübelt had been talking nonsense as usual. The relief, the blessed, overpowering relief!

And then, opening his eyes again and leaning over the edge of the shelf, he saw that Zeppichmann wasn't there.

He called softly, "Does any one know what's happened to Zeppichmann?" and got no definite answer: some one had seen him in the supper-queue and that was all. The flood of anxiety poured in again. He tried to tell himself that nothing serious could have happened: whenever they had something up their sleeves for you they either put you on the list or else took you out in the middle of the night; most of the guards would be at their evening meal now, the rest too busy to bother about delinquents; probably Zeppichmann had merely been shifted to the barrack on the other side of the yard . . . It was useless, he couldn't appease himself, he felt powerfully that something was wrong.

In a minute or two the guard would be coming back to turn down the lights. Dahlmeyer put his legs over the side of the shelf, lowered them carefully and tried them on the floor. The right leg wouldn't take any weight at all, but the left had still a little endurance. With his arms on the middle shelf he worked himself slowly towards the door, while the others watched him in silence; they thought the old man had gone flat at last, those who were able to think at all. He had got right to the door when the guard reached it from the other side.

It was Eichner on duty to-night, a ploughman from Mecklenburg, six-foot-four in his boots. He said, as he kicked the door open, "You, what in hell are you doing there?" Dahlmeyer let go the shelf and stuck himself right in the doorway, leaning against the jamb. He said:

"I want to know what's happened to Doctor Zeppichmann."

"Zeppichmann? What in hell is that to do with you?"

"I want to know."

Eichner bent down and took hold of Dahlmeyer's ear:

a trick of his, rubbing some one's ear between forefinger and thumb.

"So you want to know about Zeppichmann, do you?"

"Yes. And I may perhaps mention, in passing, that a man in my condition becomes remarkably unresponsive to the kind of braggadocio in which you specialise."

"If you want to know about Zeppichmann," Eichner said, working the ear gently to and fro, "I'll tell you. Herr Spülicht Zeppichmann is in the Lieutenant's office. And if you want to know just what sort of a picnic he's having in there—"

Dahlmeyer said: "I do want to know. I want to see the Lieutenant myself. In fact I'm going to see him—now." He jerked his head free—he had too much pain round him to notice an extra stab of it—and set off along the gangway; lurching from side to side, grabbing at the stanchions of the sleeping-shelves. He had covered ten yards before he toppled over, and then he had to go on hands and knees: another four yards, and Eichner was up to him.

Eichner stooped and picked him up, as a girl would pick out a weed with shallow roots. He got the ear again, one ear and a fold of flesh from the other arm.

"So you want to see the Lieutenant?"

"Yes, I'm afraid I must insist on your taking me. At once, if you please!"

Eichner raised him a little way from the ground and let him drop.

"You needn't trouble, Herr Lumpenferl! The Lieutenant will come to you!"

In the office Josef was still waiting, and he had stood there for thirty-five minutes before the Lieutenant arrived: Karl Tsechner, Doctor of Ethics from Hamburg, always found that he could do his best constructive thinking while he smoked an after-dinner cigar in his bedroom. "You can clear out!" he said to the guard as he came in. "Don't go far,

I'll shout if I want you." He sat in the swivel chair and flicked through a pile of papers with a cashier's dexterity until he found the one he wanted. Then he looked up at the prisoner.

"A piece of news for you!" he said.

It was the human side of penology which really interested him. Organisation, discipline—he left all that to the underlings, only dropping a thunderbolt here and there if he detected signs of inefficiency. The variation in social and racial types, the development of the individual mentality in confinement, those were the subjects which occupied his insatiable curiosity. Since taking over his present post he had already filled four loose-leaf binders with classified observations.

"You know already," he said slowly, scrutinising the slumped body with the nervous hands, the haggard face with its rather curious, wandering eyes, "you realise the reason why it was originally found necessary to put you out of harm's way. When you were examined at Hartzinnfeld you appeared to show no understanding at all of the serious charges brought against you, and people who cannot understand the nature of crime are dangerous to the general public. You follow that?"

"I—I don't know."

Dr. Tsechner adjusted his pince-nez, caressed his very small, smooth chin. Another man would have flared up at such an answer, but Tsechner had infinite patience. A bout of coughing had started, and he waited till it was over. He knew that kind of cough well enough: it was frequently associated with a criminal psychology and was due, he supposed, to some kind of nervous disorder. He wrote on a slip of paper: 'Send inquiry to Dr. Marquardt about association of nervous cough with delinquent types.'

"You must try and control that!" he said without harshness. "Well, I now have information of a more serious charge against you. It appears that eighteen months ago you undertook the treatment of a German woman patient for pulmonary tuberculosis, without informing the authority under which you were then employed, and without any competence in the appropriate branch of medicine. What have you got to say about that?"

It was hardly necessary to ask. Tsechner would not have believed that the fellow could go whiter than he was already, but that was what happened.

"You mean," Josef asked, "you mean—she's dead?"

"Fortunately for you," Tsechner said slowly, "or perhaps unfortunately for you, she is not dead. In fact it is this woman—Minna Wersen—who has brought the evidence herself."

The knock of a giant's fist sounded on the ply-wood door, the guard Eichner came in and saluted. He said:

"Have to report, sir, prisoner died in Barrack IV."

"Was it really necessary to interrupt me in the middle of an important interview?" Tsechner asked mildly.

"Special circumstances, sir. Prisoner was attempting escape."

Tsechner got up. "Ah! Then perhaps I'd better come along. Call Ulbrich and tell him to keep an eye on this man. Who is it that's died, did you say?"

"2916 Dahlmeyer."

"Dahlmeyer? Let me see—yes, yes I know the man. You mean Dahlmeyer the musician?"

"I don't know about that, sir."

"Ah, you are not an amateur of music! You miss a great deal, Eichner." He turned to Josef. "Yes—you want to say something?"

"I . . ."

"Yes yes, what is it?"

"I admit it, I admit everything. I'll sign a statement, I did what she said, I might have killed her."

Tsechner, although not many things surprised him, was faintly surprised. He would not have associated this man with the 'confession' type; nor would he have expected, in so coarse a subject, this sudden breakdown of all control, this utterly childish sobbing and clutching of hands.

"That is admirable," he said. "I'll see you again later . . . In Barrack IV, you say?"

Josef started to follow him along the passage, shouting, "I tell you I did, I swear that's true, I tried to kill her! I tell you——" until the guard Ulbrich put the bull-jaw hold on his left arm and got him down.

36

ON THE scheduled 'F' route the air liners pass right over Sondersumpf. The village is too small to be noticed, only the fen shows as a dirty puddle shaped like a flattened heart. In a little over ninety minutes, flying in the northerly direction with a following wind, they will be over Hartzinnfeld. The Moltke Hospital, on its private hill, is a landmark: pilots trim their course when the red roofs disappear beneath the starboard wing: the long, white building which stands apart from the others is the Tuberculosis Block. When the clouds are low the liners sometimes come down to five hundred metres, and then a passenger may notice the row of crimson blobs along the gravel square. As soon as the wind gets into the northern segment the blobs vanish away; it happens so regularly that the sign could be used as a rough weathercock. There is, in fact, a weather-vane over towards the main block, on top of the power-house, but Dr. Vollmuth knows almost by instinct when the wind has changed. He touches No. 5 in his row of bells; Stefan the boy automatically puts down the shocker he's reading and goes out to the terrace to help the nurses wheel in the beds. Five minutes, and the whole forty are tucked away like apples in a packing case. From above, the gravel now shows clear, there is just the white box on the blue rectangle. Stefan returns to his book.

"I haven't done Chalet 14," Nurse Pichel said, and Nurse Kremerhaus said, "14 can wait a bit, she's not one of the grousey ones."

When you are ill for a long time you see the world with a child's eyes. People's faces are far above you as they stand by your bed, they talk among themselves of activities which are right outside your reach. For every physical need you are dependent on these huge omnipotents, and are content to be so: your thoughts live chiefly in a country of their own. In that condition Minna had spent the summer. When the wind was away from north they wheeled her outside; as soon as it grew cold they pushed her in again. So she could fall asleep with her face to the pine-wrapped hills beyond Mühlholz, and wake to see only a wooden wall. It did not make much difference. "Such a quiet little thing!" they said, "gives hardly any trouble. Perhaps just a bit—you know," and Nurse Pichel, nodding, said, "Of course they get like that!" They had put her things all together in the cabinet beside her bed, the things she had brought from Handelstrasse: a poetry book or two, a quite expensive nightgown that some one must have given her, a couple of grubby exercise books such as children cram into their satchels. They had pinned above her bed the two pictures that she seemed to treasure, a photograph of a spectacled girl and a cheap litho of Antonello's Crucifixion. The regular notice stood between them, '*Patients are earnestly reminded that rowdiness is not allowed. K. Vollmuth.*' Besides a reading lamp and a patent receptacle for sputum there was not much else in this small room.

"Of course she's not the class you expect to get in a Block like this. They say the gentleman's paying, the gentleman that brought her."

"Well, my dear, it's a relief, that's all I can say, to have some one who can go half an hour without putting her fist on the bell, class or no class. And they say that classes have all gone out now. And I've heard her use quite long words, you know."

"Very interesting case, Sister says it is. Doctor Vollmuth sent the X-ray for Doctor Dittmer to see, and that's a thing he hasn't done as long as anybody can remember . . . That my bell? That's the old Graefe bitch wants the frying pan again."

"But you told me you'd left her on it, half an hour ago."

"My dear, now I come to think of it . . ."

The voices were thin and constant in pitch, as if the same record were played again and again on a cheap gramophone; but when they spoke to Minna herself they were held right down to a practised kindness. The voice of Frau Graefe was the trumpet of a wounded bison, it broke like a foghorn's cry into the murmurous racket of moving shingle, 'Will no one in this house of pestilence attend to me!' From the next chalet the sound of Fräulein Jansen's voice would bore through the wall for half an hour at a time, peevish and puffed, "The doctor said I wasn't to be left alone. It makes me go all scared, being left alone. The doctor says . . ." At ten o'clock each day a rumble started at the end of the block, a muffled baying like the echo of vast upheavals underground; Dr. Vollmuth was starting his morning tour. All day long the coughing answered back and forth, now sharp and agonised, now weary and prolonged, the foundation on which all other sounds were laid.

But at night it sometimes ceased entirely, and if you were awake then you felt a tide of silence flooding in, as when the tick of a bedside clock suddenly stops.

In such a quietness she woke—it was only a few days since Herr Rupf had brought her here—and listened for familiar sounds, the creak of boards in the passage, Herr Barthol's porcine snore. She could not understand the altered shape of the room, the pattern of windows faintly lit by starlight, she called, "Herr Doktor! Doctor Josef!" but no one came.

She felt for the glass of water which Josef had always left within her reach, and as her fingers found the reading-lamp she remembered the look of the room she had come to;

but not the way she had come. It was a kind of prison, she thought. And now from the sleepy clouds a shiny face came back, the face of the man they called 'Herr Direktor,' and a butterfly-collar kind of voice. "I'm afraid you've made a mistake, young lady—that Zeppichmann was an ignoramus, he had not the smallest right to interfere with your case." And then, from just outside the door, "Well, Vollmuth, have it X-rayed by all means, if you think it's interesting. But the plates must be sent to me, I wish to deal with the matter myself . . ." In a mind almost empty of sensation the echo of those sentences was clear and strong: and they seemed to tell her why she was imprisoned here.

It was simple enough to wriggle out of bed and feel her way to the door. Surprisingly, they'd forgotten to lock it. With one hand against the wall she started to walk along the covered terrace, thinking, 'I must get away now, the chance won't come again.' Her legs were like birch rods feebly lashed with string, but she was not surprised to find them awkward after such long disuse. In a mile or so, she thought, she would learn to manage them again. It was cold out here; but to feel the weight of the blankets gone and breathe the night's damp vigour was like getting out at a country station after many hours in the train. While others slept the naked world belonged to her, and freedom seemed to give such power that her body's feebleness was only a petty hindrance. Her legs already had the tiredness of a Monday evening, but she would not pander to their obstinacy. A lighted window showed far over to the left, somebody there might give her help she thought, she left the wall and started to walk boldly in that direction.

Just two steps and her legs folded up like the sides of a camera. She found the boy Stefan looking down at her, saying, "Fräulein! Oh, Fräulein! Aren't you feeling well!" and afterwards she felt herself being carried back to bed.

So: I must wait, she thought, I must wait till my legs are right.

She wrote in her book: 'In the mornings all the hags are fussing round, and then the hags' father with his baby face and his voice booming like a tiny gun, a great old sheepdog of a man and Nurse Pichel's a bitch to snigger about him, all of them are scraping and twiddling and putting things in your mouth so as you get no peace at all. But in the afternoons they let you alone and then I twist the pillow round my ears so I can't even hear the Jansen moaning and spluttering, and then I shut my eyes but I don't go to sleep. Then I am all by myself with nothing but the Crucified and my beloved, that is my peaceful time when I can get myself better. There's nothing wrong with me now, my beloved burnt all the T.B. thing away, it's only my legs being weak. I can't draw the strength into my legs with the hags all fiddling about and changing the bedclothes and bothering about the motions, I can only get myself well when they go away. My body's always so tired with the bedclothes rubbing and the crumbs that get in after every meal underneath the damawful-looking nightdress they give you here, my body can't get any rest as long as it has me inside. So when I am all alone I let myself float out, and then my body can be very still, without any twitching and wriggling, and it doesn't cough at all. Then I am all wrapped up in quiet like being wrapped in a warm cloak, like the time my beloved found me shivering and wrapped me round with his winter coat, then I am very light with the tired body left behind, I am like the great white cloud which I saw lolling in the high sky with the sunshine pouring over its belly, I send the sunlight down into my legs and my body floats and swells with the creases smoothing out like when I put Herr Spühler's shirt in the washtub. When the Kremerhaus comes to wake me up I go back into my body, the Kremerhaus is old and sometimes lovely with hands like a kitten's paws, when the

Kremerhaus comes I glide down to my body again, the body's fresh and smooth with not so much ache in the back, and every day some more of the firmness has got back into the legs.

'To-night I shall try the legs again. I shall go on using the legs a little every night till I get them strong again.

'. . . Yesterday a man called Dr. Dittmer came and seemed to be nice, but he asked me questions about what Beloved did to me so I knew he was the Herr Direktor's spy. I said I didn't know anything about what Dr. Zeppichmann did. To-night I shall put Beloved's book under my pillow or else they'll try to steal it away . . .'

But Dittmer came again, and sat on the side of her bed in the way that Josef himself used to, smiling at her with his whimsical mouth and friendly eyes.

"You mustn't tell Doctor Vollmuth I came to see you— you won't, will you! Of course he's a good man, Doctor Vollmuth, a splendid man, a most admirable person—but somehow he doesn't care to have people like me messing about in his department . . . Now look here, I'm going to show you something. A picture of the inside of your chest, would you like to see that?"

"I don't mind."

"Ah, you mean you don't care about it! Very well—"

"No, I should like to see it, I want to!"

"Well then, here it is! Now look! On this side it's practically all right now. That messy part that you see there on the left side, it used to be like that on both sides, the whole way across. A few months ago, that was—at least, I think so. You see, I look at these pictures through a special glass, it shows me far more than you can see with your bare eyes. Well, that's why you're feeling so much better, it's because the right lung is practically healed up and the left one is well on the way to being healed. No, that's not quite right. The healing on your left lung seems to have stopped, and we don't know how to get the job finished off. At least, I don't, and I'm pretty certain that Doctor Vollmuth doesn't. If only I knew what it was that Doctor Zeppichmann used to put into you—"

"He didn't put anything in!"

"Ah, I think you've forgotten, Fräulein. Those little marks on your arm—"

"Will you leave that alone, please!"

"Of course I will! . . . Now when Doctor Zeppichmann made up that stuff to put into your arm he did it from a piece of paper he had. (You see, I know all about that kind of thing, he and I used to work together.) It was a paper with something like a cooking recipe on it—you know, so much flour, so many potatoes—only it would be in signs mostly, the sort of signs that doctors and chemists understand. Do you think you ever saw a paper like that?"

"No."

"You see, if I could find that paper, I could make up some of the same stuff, and then Doctor Vollmuth would put some more into you, and that would make you perfectly all right again. At least, I'm pretty sure it would. And I know Doctor Zeppichmann would like me to do that. Don't you think he would?"

"You'd better ask him."

"But, my dear Fräulein, I don't know where he is. These wretched policemen, I can't get them to tell me." He got off the bed and stood where she could see his face in the full light. He moved his eyes away from her and let her examine him, his untidy hair and dirty overall, the whole of his simplicity. Then he said: "It would be so terribly nice if you could trust me! It's not only you I'm thinking about, it's Josef Zeppichmann. He—he's a good man, you know, a clever man, and he got treated very badly in this hippodrome. I'd like to do something for him, just for old friendship's sake. And I can't think of anything better than going on with his job. You're his patient, you see—that's how I think of you—and you ought to be treated the way he planned out."

She said: "There's no one could do it like him."

Dittmer nodded. "That's true. But we could work on the same lines—the right lines—if we could get hold of his basis; I mean, the notes he made, something of that sort. Apparently they couldn't find anything in his room—nothing of the sort I want—and I thought you'd probably know something about it. Didn't he have a book or something where he wrote things down?"

His pleasant eyes were turned on her again. He waited patiently for her answer.

She asked abruptly: "Do you mean I'm going to get just as bad as I was? If I—if you can't find out what Josef did?"

He answered her seriously, as a doctor talks to a private patient: "No, I don't mean that. Of course, it's a possibility. If we don't get this trouble of yours cleared up altogether there's always a chance that it'll get the upper hand again. Then all Josef's work would be undone. But I think it's more likely you'll stay much the same as you are now."

"And not get any better at all?"

"I wouldn't say that. You're getting proper treatment here—I mean, you're getting the right kind of food, and clean air and that sort of thing. It all helps. You ought to feel steadily better. But you won't ever be *cured*—at least, I don't believe you will—unless we get you back on to Josef's treatment."

"But I'll get a bit better?" she insisted. "Well enough to walk about and do things?"

He was still patient, still serious.

"You ought to ask Doctor Vollmuth about that. But— yes, I should think you've got a good chance of becoming what I call a half-powered person. Some one who isn't ill

enough to be in bed, but who isn't ever really well. Of course
it'll take you a good long time to get as far as that even."

He put his thumb nails together and stared at them as
if some one had done an amusing picture there. It was a
symptom he had always shown when he had something difficult to say—proposing marriage or dismissing a lab-boy. He
made his last effort:

"You're sure you can't tell me anything? I'd like you
to—I'd so like to do something for poor old Zeppichmann."

Everything he had was in those words: his boyishness,
the sweetness which he so seldom revealed to any one but his
wife. And again she evaded him.

"This picture," she asked innocently, "can I keep it?"

"If you want to—I've got other copies. Only don't let
Doctor Vollmuth know, I do beseech you!"

She nodded, putting the radiogram under her pillow.

"And if you want to know about Josef's treatment," she
said gravely, "you must get him to tell you. Yes, the police
must find him for you."

"But—"

"And if the police won't tell you where he is you must
find out from that camel-faced man, the one they call 'Herr
Direktor.' It was him that had Josef put away, I know that.
The Director didn't want people to know that Josef could
cure people better than his dam-awful hospital, so he first of
all sacked him—"

"Now listen!" Dittmer said. "Really, you know, you
mustn't—"

But she was blazing now.

"I tell you I wouldn't give it you, not if I had a whole
bucketful of Josef's stuff. It belongs to Josef, Josef half-
killed himself finding how to make it, and now they've
smashed his job and had him locked up they want to steal
the rest of what belongs to him. It's no good your talking
all sugar-lips, I'm not a baby, I know what you're all trying

to get out of me. And you won't get it, not if you send all
the stinking doctors in the place to talk baby-talk at me, you
won't make me say anything I know. It belongs to Josef, do
you hear, it belongs to him!"

It was hard, Dittmer thought as he walked slowly back
to his own quarters, that the muck which all the fools kicked
up should fall into his lap. He was raging inside, but not
against the girl. That inspissated numbskull of a Wildelau,
what had he said to her? . . . Back in the laboratory he
once more put a set of the Wersen plates in his own apparatus and set his eyes drilling into the shadows. Did Wildelau really understand anything at all about the nature of
T.B.? What did he mean by 'healing as the result of natural
processes'—what processes, what nature, when the girl had
spent the winter in a filthy little attic? And by what infernal
right did Wildelau use the word 'unimportant'? Unimportant! Was he, Dittmer, raving mad, or was he the one sane
man in a gymnasium of imbeciles . . . ?

Minna's outburst had its natural consequence. Nurse
Pichel found her flushed and comatose, the temperature was
high that evening. She had a fit of coughing, which was rare
now; it was followed by her special kind of pain, the feeling
that hot, stale air was being blown through her stomach and
head. But she was happy: rejoicing in victory, and in the
prize she had won, the picture of her own chest which was
now tucked away in Josef's book, a companion for the earlier
pictures.

The effects lasted. For more than a week she lived in
fluid dreams, believing sometimes that she was still in Handelstrasse, sometimes that she was back at school. Voices were
distant in those days, and faces oddly large; shapes that appeared and vanished like those at a ticket-office window, the
portly, solicitous face of Dr. Vollmuth, Nurse Pichel's darting eyes and bevelled chin. But this will pass, she thought

in the times when she was lucid, the sickness will pass, and the smoky pain, and I shall continue on my journey.

It is all right, Josef, it's quite all right! Men can plant a separate life in you, but you've given me a new life of my own, that was your gift, beloved, and I shall keep it safe. You were stupid and stiff, little Josef, you hadn't any kindness in your mouth like Dr. Dittmer's, you never gave me any sweetness in your words like the people here, but you always came to me when I wanted, Josef my dear, beloved Josef. We've lost our little room, beloved, the room you cleaned up when it was me who had to clean the rooms, our room, Josef, where you always sat and smiled at me and frowned at the little bottles. We've lost the dam-awful old bed, the bed I was on all that time, where you went off to sleep that night with the broken shoulder. It's all gone away, the smell of your old coat and the noise you made coming up the stairs, the way you scratched your mouth when you were tired so I shouldn't see you yawn. They wouldn't let you be, a man so good as you, they wouldn't let a serving slut have a man like that. They stole you at night, beloved, they waited till I was asleep, they've hid you away so deep I can't find you any more. But I'm going to find you, Josef—listen, listen, my dear—I'm going to find you and bring you back. Look after him, Jesus, keep him, Sweet Crucified, keep my beloved, keep him until you've got me ready, don't let him die. Patience, my dear one, you must be patient, Josef beloved, you must be patient a little while more. When I'm strong, Josef, I'll come to find you, I'll come, I'll come, I'll come as soon as I'm strong, I'll come and take you away, beloved, I'll take you to Giessbach, we've promised we'll go together there.

Listen, Josef, listen! They've got me shut up here so I can't help you, I tried to get away but I can't walk very much. It's just my rotten legs, it's being in bed so long, your legs go all rotten and they won't take you. But I practise them at night, when the night-sister's gone to the other end of the block I practise them on the floor, I can get across the room and back quite easy now and never holding at all. They hurt a different way now from what they did and they're fatter at the top part, I keep on rubbing them and I feel the bones coming back. Sometimes I'm tired and I only want to sleep and try and dream about you, then my body's lazy and it won't get out of bed. But that doesn't last for long, I make it obey me, I put the pillows away and make my body sit up by itself for an hour every day. You see, this body's what belongs to you and me, my Josef, you did all you could to make it right and I've got to do the rest myself. I don't mind about it hurting, but it must do what I want, it's got to learn to obey me. It's like an old ship that I'm trying to get to the other side of the world, I've got to keep on going into harbours to patch it up, and all of that wastes time, but it wouldn't be any good if the ship fell all to bits before I find my beloved.

The nurse says it's going to take at least six months, the old nurse, Nurse Kremerhaus, with the squeaky shoes and the smell of radishes, Nurse Kremerhaus says they may let me go in about six months, and then I must go to another place where I can be in bed most of the time. But I'll try not to let you wait as long as that, I'll try to be quicker than that.

I've got your book, beloved, and the big envelope with all the papers and the photos. I'm keeping it safe, dear one, I won't let any one get hold of that.

I'm tired now, the hags have been in and out all day and trying to make me talk, Fräulein Jansen's been moaning and squeaking ever since this morning, her voice is like the old fiddle the blind man used to play up and down the Handelstrasse, it's a voice with a stale smell in it, it rubs its way into you like the breadcrumbs up and down the bed. Oh, Josef, I get so tired, lying and lying here, and the door keeps opening but it's never my beloved coming in. The hags put in the thermometer like putting a fork in a sausage, they don't hold my arm up quietly like you always did, they look at me as if I was a lump of food on a plate, they're never shy, the hags aren't, they never look away suddenly and start mumbling, they never smile all of a sudden like you did, beloved, all their smiles are ready-made and hard and useful like their hard white cuffs and their hard white useful hands. They won't let me have the door shut because Dr. Vollmuth says I've got to have the fresh air even when it's coming at me in a bloody hurricane, they won't give me anything to read but kids' books, they won't let me sit the way I want or have my bed so I can see along the terrace, they ask me over and over again how I feel now, as if I felt any different and as if I'd tell them, they keep washing me all over all day long with an awful hygienic kind of sponge. I'm tired, Josef dear, I'm tired, I only want to shut my eyes and feel your great rough hand come on to my forehead, I don't want to hear any more of the hags clattering about and Fräulein Jansen's voice. But to-night I'll feel stronger again, and when I've been quite quiet for a time I'll be able to do my leg practice and to-night I shall practise lifting things, which I ought to be able to do, and to-morrow I'm going to be very obedient and patient when the Kremerhaus is washing me, so I can ask her to get RM 1.50 out of my savings bank and get me a book on cooking and things so I'll know how to look after you.

Dr. Vollmuth says that next week I can walk a bit on the terrace when the sun's out, and the week after that perhaps I can walk all the way to the lavatory with the Kremerhaus holding my arm. I shall walk so they don't see I've been practising it over at night, that's to begin with, and then I'll walk a lot better so they think I'm getting well very fast, then perhaps in about a month Dr. Vollmuth will say I'm all right now and I may as well go.

It's getting nearer, beloved, the time when I'm going
to find you is getting nearer, I'm going to make it hurry,
I'm not going to have any more bad turns, I'm not going to
let my silly body do anything it wants and be lazy and hold
me down all the time. I can breathe better now, I don't go
like an old broken pump whenever I try to do anything,
I'm getting so I can keep my head steady and awake even
when my body's hurting me and trying to make me stupid.
I'm not going to give you an ill person to look after any
more, you've done enough of that, my darling, all that sitting up with me and going downstairs to get fresh water and
coming to me in the night when I had the smoky pain. You
won't have a very strong girl, beloved, like they advertise
for in the servant columns, but she'll be strong enough to
do things for you. I'm getting it ready for you, Josef, I'm
going to have my body so it can run about for you and get
the things you want, and isn't too awful for you to look at
all the same.

Oh, Josef, Josef my dear, my beloved, where are you
now? Can you see the sunshine from the prison where you
are? Oh God do at least let him see the sun.

The summer's all here, and they put us out along the
terrace. The buildings over there are shivery in the hot
light, you smell the dust and the hot grass. In the morning
it's all clear like water fresh out of the tap, you can see right
over to Mühlholz. The sun comes leaning over blowing a
hot sleepiness on to the blankets, the great grown plants in
Dr. Vollmuth's flowerbeds are all tired out. When it's dark
again the voices sound from right down on the roadway, as
clear as in the frosty weather, sometimes it's children singing, and they seem so close to me and there's so much peace.
But you're so far away, beloved. The summer's going that
we should have had together, soon they'll be putting the
beds inside before the afternoon sleep. The summer will all
be gone, Josef, and we haven't shared it at all.

But when it comes again we shall be at Giessbach. At Giessbach, beloved! In the long hot days I shall have my head on your chest, while we lie on the brackeny hills.

I'm too tired to write any diary now.

Oh God oh God I can't help being obstinate, I don't want any of the things I ought to want, I only want you to look after Josef and give me back a good enough body to look after him myself. You gave me Fräulein Rother, and I did say thank you for that, didn't I, and I didn't make an awful lot of fuss when you took her away. But you won't take Josef right away because I love him so much? I'm trying all the time to be thankful for what I've got already, the books that Fräulein Rother gave me and the flowers and mountains growing in them, the sun coming on my face and not having any washing-up to do, the hags all trying to make me feel better and always smiling even when they're tired and their legs ache. Oh God I know I'm stupid and selfish, when Fräulein Jansen's T.B. hurts more than mine, I never try to be kind to the poor Graefe woman who lost both her sons in the war when her bed's put next to my bed, I know I laugh at the poor floppy Kremerhaus when she isn't looking and her hair gets loose out of the tablecloth. But oh God won't you forget about all that, won't you put it off for a year or two, and let me find Josef first before I start doing something unselfish for all the miserable people. Or won't you let it all come on my body, I don't mind how much my body hurts, I'm used to that, you can make it worse if you think you ought to, only don't let it get any weaker, please oh God let my legs get stronger and my head get so that it won't go dizzy and lazy when I try to do things. I know I ought to be humble but could I put off being humble for a year or two because to find my beloved again I've got to be fierce and strong? If I could just have a few days with him, or perhaps just one day, at Giessbach, lying beside him on the hill, with the sun on our faces and the sweet tasting wind brushing through leaves, with Josef smiling a bit while I get the bread and cheese ready, then after that I'd be humble. And surely it isn't a bad thing to look after a man who's got a way to cure people's T.B. I wanted to do a lot of things, I wanted to paint pictures and be important and have people talking about me, but I've given up all that, I promise I've given it all up, I only want to be useful to Josef now.

It's quiet now, the night nurse has gone back to her own room. The blankets feel very warm, because autumn's coming, they still leave the door open and my face gets cold. I can't do any leg-practice to-night, the smoky pain's got me just for to-night, I can only keep quiet and still. I'm quite alone, Lord, I can't even hear Fräulein Jansen snoring, I'm trying for a little time to keep Josef out of my heart so that you can have it all to yourself. Oh Lord I don't want to put you against God, because you can't ever be, but I want you to forget you're God and just be kind and loving to me like you always said. I'm humble enough now, I won't get less humble whatever you do for me. Oh Lord I can't get the strength back quick enough, I keep trying to do it all by myself, using my mind as hard as I can, but it all comes so slowly and I don't know what's happening to Josef all this time. Oh Lord there's no need to love me any more, I want it all to go to Josef, I want the whole of your dear love to go to him. Only I want it to be through me, I want just to be used for helping Josef. Couldn't you make use of me like that? Couldn't you lend me for a little time the hands with the terrible holes, couldn't I have a very small part of the heart you had in the Garden and the way you didn't shout out when the nails went in? I'm puzzled and frightened now, I don't know how I'm going to find him, I feel like a baby all alone in here with the darkness round me like a cave. But you can come into the darkness, the soldiers couldn't even stop you, and Dr. Vollmuth can't

stop you, you can go through the cold night into the darkness where Josef is. Dear Crucified, there weren't enough
people on the hill to take the things you had to give them.
If all you had to give is still running out you can let some
of it go to Josef, you must, dear Christ, you must make your
love drive on as far as that, and the fighting strength you
had go into me . . .

She wrote in her diary, towards the end of November:
'I went all the way to the end of the hospital drive and back
again without holding on to the nurse. The trees are all bare
now, and the smell of smoke is like when he first used to
come and see me. I've got to be in bed for the rest of to-day,
my legs are aching, they creak like the trees in the wind,
and I've been coughing rather a lot, but I didn't let Nurse
Pichel hear. I am perfectly well now, except my chest hurting now and then, I have got very strong indeed.'

37

AT HANDELSTRASSE 149, in the room where Josef had lived, Erich Meisel woke up suddenly before it was light. The melancholy which held his mind like a tautened strap seemed to have come from a dream, but he could not remember what the dream was. By degrees he recalled what had happened the day before: the letter from Karl von Schüttenwalde which had killed his hopes of escape from Hartzinnfeld.

He groped for the bedside switch that Josef had fitted and turned on the light. The letter was in the pocket of his coat, which hung on a chair beside the bed. He read it again.

'I am afraid the position you applied for in the Frankfurt Headquarters has gone to another Party Member who, though not having your social standing, has rather more experience in the kind of work which the post involves. I am so sorry.

'I have made some inquiries about the Jew, Zeppichmann, that you mentioned in your letter. I understand— from a report which reached me in rather a roundabout way —that this person did not adapt himself properly to the new state construction work allotted to him and is believed to be dead now.

'Believe me, my dear Meisel, yours in true comradeship . . .'

What was the good of that! He wanted to be certain.

It was just after four o'clock. Handelstrasse slept. Only the wind, stronger towards dawn, chivvied the leaves about the roadway, fumbled at curtains through the open window.

He left the light on to protect him against dreams and

lay still, waiting for the warm tiredness of his body to over-wrap his lurching thoughts. His eyes closed and he saw the corridor stretched out, a voice that came to him without any sound said, "Take this, Herr Meisel, you may find it use-ful." He tried to plant his feet hard on the floor but found himself sliding, sliding, towards the door he knew so well: the panel with two cracks, the baroque finger-plate. He shouted, "No! I won't go in there!" and his eyes opened again.

A door banged. He listened intently, and thought he heard footsteps, somebody coming down the attic stairs: a halting step, the feet brought together on each stair: and now it was coming along the passage toward this room.

The handle of the door was in the corner of his vision, it seemed to be moving. He tried to turn his head that way but the muscles of his neck were locked, the whole of his body was stiff. He did not see the door opening, he only knew that some one had got inside.

The visitor moved quietly. There was only a rustle from the papers lying on the desk, a faint click from the handle of a drawer. Then the smell came nearer, a kind of soap and the smell of chemicals.

Erich whispered: "Listen, Zeppichmann, you'd better not come any nearer! Listen, there's something I want to explain, I want—"

A shadow leant across the side of the bed, a cool breath touched his forehead. His voice broke out through the narrow channel in his throat, a tearing pencil of sound: *"Hilfe!"*

As he lay spent and paralysed a door opened in the further passage, he heard the approach of bedroom slippers. Frau Rupf came in.

"Was it you screaming just now, Herr Meisel? What's the matter?"

Her sharp, everyday voice severed the cords which held him, he managed to turn his head. He said:

"The doctor—over there—behind the curtain. Don't let him—*keep him off!*"

He was out of the bed and cowering behind it. Frau Rupf, in her practical way, went and poked the curtain with her fist. She said:

"What do you mean? There's nobody there."

38

COMMISSIONER FIETZ was driving into the town office by the upper road which went past the hospital; that route was three kilometres longer, but he always thought it worth while to avoid the traffic. He took the bend by the Moravian chapel rather faster than usual. As he came round he saw a woman wandering near the middle of the road, he put all his weight on the footbrake, swerved, and stopped, tyres yelling, with his near front wheel on the footpath and his rear wing actually touching the woman's skirt. He got out, and for something like four seconds regarded the woman in silence. She was quite a young girl, pale, small-featured, with rather fine dark hair. The blue coat and skirt gave her the appearance of a child dressed up in its mother's clothes. She was holding a clumsy parcel. The small, new hat was of a deafening green. Fietz said:

"You, young woman, are extraordinarily lucky to be alive."

The girl said: "How do you know? Being alive isn't so bloody amusing. Why couldn't you blow your horn?"

She then, suddenly, sat down.

"Here, what's the matter?" Fietz said. "The car didn't touch you, did it?"

She said, "I can sit down if I like, can't I?"

"You'd better get in the car," Fietz said. And as she made no movement he picked her up and put her there, parcel and all. "Where were you going to?" he asked.

"Into the town. Wait! Where's my hat?"

The hat had fallen off as she collapsed and was lying in the road.

"Please get it!" she said.

Commissioner Fietz got out again and recovered the hat.

"Do you want it on?"

"Well, it wants brushing, doesn't it?"

Fietz brushed it with his clean washleather gloves.

"Is that all right?"

"That'll do."

Fietz placed the hat on her head, considered it critically and altered the angle. Really the little slut was rather enchanting in a vulgar way. He backed off the footpath and drove on down the hill.

"Now then, what part of the town were you going to?"

She said: "You can put me down by the Bülow fountain. Or anywhere round there, you needn't go so far as the fountain if you're not going that way."

"That's very kind of you. You're sure there's nothing else you want me to do?"

"No, that's all. Wait! Yes. I want to know the name of a good lawyer."

"Ah, now that's more difficult! Lawyers are never good, they're a pack of scoundrels, the whole lot of them. What sort of lawyer? I mean, is it to get you out of some trouble?"

"Yes."

"Then take my advice and go to Doctor Kunig. Doctor Kunig in the Ruhrstrasse. Mind you, I wouldn't have anything to do with him myself. He's a rascal like all the rest of them, quarter Jew, I shouldn't wonder, only we can't prove it. But when you get on the shady side of the law it's the shady people that know how to help you. That's worth remembering—only don't tell any one I told you." He chuckled. "I'd have that man under lock and key if I knew how!"

He stopped the car at the corner of Gimpelstrasse.

"Will this be all right for you?"

"Yes, this'll do."

She didn't look at him as she got out of the car, her eyes were loaded with her own thoughts. And Fietz was disappointed, for any one who was young and feminine inspired his tenderness.

"Are you sure you feel all right now?"

"All right? Oh yes! Oh, and thank you!"

"Wait a moment!" Fietz fumbled for his purse and took out a note at random. "You'll want something to pay Doctor Kunig."

She accepted the gift, tucked it away and suddenly smiled. "Oh, that's kind. That's fabulously kind! God bless you!"

He stayed to watch her drifting along the pavement, unsteady and apparently aimless, swinging her parcel by the string, colliding with people and taking no notice, till she was out of his sight.

It was only nine o'clock, the Romanisches Café was empty. She sat down at the Oberkellner's No. 3 table, the one he usually kept for the staff of *Hartzinnfelder Zeitung*. Probst, the waiter on early duty, brought the coffee she ordered and the *D.A.Z.*, then he stood a little way back and went over her appearance in the mirror, as his habit was at slack times. This was something a little apart even from his experience, the dead-white face and the monstrous clothes combined with such assurance, the masculine way in which she was frowning up and down the columns. He saw her shudder, and wondered for a moment, had she any underclothes? She crossed her knees, and he was relieved to see that at least there was a petticoat, an inch of striped flannel showing from what might have been a nightdress. But it was crazy, in March, to be abroad without an overcoat. He slipped through to the service lobby and brought back his own coat, which happened to be a new one; short enough for her, though rather full in the front.

"You will please excuse me, gnädiges Fräulein, but I thought perhaps you had forgotten your coat this morning. I wondered if you would care to put mine round your shoulders—just to get you home?"

She looked at the coat critically.

"Can I try it on?"

"But certainly!"

She buttoned it and went to the glass. She laughed then.

"But it's nice and warm!" she said. "Yes, I'll take it, please. But I think I'd better buy it, I may not be coming here again." She produced the note that Fietz had given her; the waiter was surprised to see that it was fifty Marks. "How much would that be, please—the coat and the coffee?"

He was thrown off his balance, he didn't know what to say.

"The coffee, 30 pf—but—but I should be happy for you to keep the coat as long as it's useful. I mean—I didn't really mean to sell it. But if you like to have it—"

She nodded. "You're very kind, Herr Ober. I think I'll give you an I.O.U. for it—you see, I haven't much money to spare at present. What is your name, please?" She borrowed his pencil and wrote in a margin of the *D.A.Z.* 'Minna Wersen owes Herr Probst at the Romanisches Café one man's-overcoat.' "And I'll pay for the coffee now."

When he brought the change she was standing up, with one hand on the table; a little unsteady, he thought.

"Excuse me—you are feeling quite well, gnädiges Fräulein?"

"Like a trace-horse!" she said soberly. "Oh—and which way is it to Ruhrstrasse?"

Ruhrstrasse, narrow and smelling of glue, fumbled towards the Deichselberger market between old harness

shops and a knacker's yard. Next to the Konditorei Cöpenick
a rusty plate said 'Dr. Kunig. European and New World
Trustee-Agent,' and a narrow staircase went steeply from
the pavement to a distempered passage smelling like a swim-
ming-bath. Nearest the door with frosted glass in it an old
man sat with his hat between his knees, as if he were waiting
to catch his loosely-fitted eyes directly the tethers broke.
Further along the deal bench was a trio of women, not old,
but appearing to have been warehoused for some time, and a
youth with herpes. They wore in common a steady patience,
as those who are used to waiting. From time to time a pink-
ish girl with the top of her stays poking out her art-silk
blouse, with one stocking crouching in many dewlaps about
her ankle, would march across to the frosted door, open it,
slam it again, and say triumphantly:

"Doctor Kunig is still engaged. He is on the telephone."

When she noticed Minna, she put on her smile: it was
like the best kind of artificial pearls, Fräulein Meissner's
smile, hardly distinguishable from a real one.

"It'll be a long time before he gets as far as you. Is it
something important?"

"Yes. Very important."

Fräulein Meissner came nearer and bent towards her
ear.

"Are you going to have a baby or something?"

Minna considered the question.

"Yes," she said, "I'm going to have a baby. Or something."

Fräulein Meissner went to the frosted door again, and
called inside:

"Another illegitimacy just come!"

An adenoidal voice said: "Hell burn and blast these
strumpets! Go away!"

"He oughtn't to talk about an expectant like that!" one of the women said.

Presently the old man was called inside, and was there for half an hour. His thick voice sounded through the door like an old lorry climbing a hill, "I told her I wasn't going to pay for the wire as well as the posts . . . I don't see why her brother-in-law can't pay, two of the steers belonged to him . . . Well, what I told her was it wasn't right my having to pay for the wire as well as the posts . . ." The woman with the face leaning over to one side went in next, and had ten minutes. At twelve o'clock Dr. Kunig himself came out, twisting his small body into a shabby overcoat. He said as he passed, "Next client at 2.30," and went off down the stairs.

Minna had the advantage of being nearest to the stairway door. She caught it before it shut behind him. Dr. Kunig, without the appearance of physical exertion, moved quickly. He went down the stairs like a sailor, he was thirty yards along the street by the time Minna got to the pavement. She saw him reach the corner and turn left towards the Technical Institute.

She went after him at a run, holding the green hat on with one hand, the other clutching the parcel and the slack of Herr Probst's overcoat. She hadn't practised running, her legs seemed to go in all directions like the wheels of a dumbwaiter. But her quarry was still in sight when she turned the corner, he was walking rapidly along the other side, she called faintly, "Dr. Kunig!" and ran without looking across the road. People were stopping to stare now, every one in the street seemed to be interested in Minna except the man she was after. Dr. Kunig moved like a pilot's cutter in a busy harbour, deft and rapid, and reaching a crack between two shops he disappeared there.

She thought she had lost him. But the little alley, after two right-angled turns, came to a dead-end in a café-bar.

A waiter who was throwing scraps for the pigeons put his hand on her arm as she came to the door, "Excuse me, this isn't a place that ladies usually come to!" but she gasped, "Important!—Doctor Kunig," and went inside. The place was full. Dr. Kunig was already seated at a table near the service-door, sowing the ash of his cigarette on to the *Lokal-Anzeiger*. She took a chair across from the next table and sat down facing him.

Dr. Kunig did not look up. Without moving his head he could see the untidy parcel she had laid on the table, the stunted epicene hands; and he never wasted any movements. "A double Bismarck," he said to the waiter, "and the small 12.30." His cigarette had hardly wobbled; the fly which had overhauled his rusty hair started to zigzag down his face, but he did not bother to brush it off. It was the face of a croupier in a second-class resort, the taut skin grey and lambent like a frozen pond, lips crimped like perished rubber; and his fingers, deeply nicotined, gave off the odour of violet ink. He reversed the paper and his eyes ripped down the first column on the stockmarket page. He said, as he jotted figures on the back of an envelope:

"I do not see clients except at my office during business hours."

Minna was silent. Her chest still seemed to be using wind a little faster than her stomach could pump it up, her throat was full of dusty phlegm. But when the waiter returned with Kunig's order she said, "I'll have the same, please—the 12.30 with a double Bismarck," and her voice was unexpectedly steady. She leaned across the table and looked straight into Kunig's face.

"Tell me please, what's it going to cost me, what I've ordered?"

He said promptly, still writing, "1.65. Another 25 if you have coffee as well."

She nodded. "Very well. That means I can offer you—

let me see—fifteen Marks for your fee. No, I'll make it 15.50—only I'm not going to wait about in that dirty passage all day, I want you to give me advice straight away. 15.50—you can take it or leave it."

"I can leave it," he said.

"And I'll pay for your dinner as well. With coffee."

"I can still leave it," he said. "I don't want your sort of case at all, it takes up all my time, I'm sick and tired of it."

"What do you mean?"

"You're the one that's going to have a baby, aren't you? My secretary told me——"

"Your secretary? Oh, oh yes. A baby, yes."

"Well, all I can say——"

"Very soon," she added. "I mean—almost at once. I think it must have brought it on, having to run after you. I feel——"

"Good God!" For the first time Kunig looked up from the paper. "Here, you don't think I'm a medical doctor, do you?"

She shook her head. "No, that isn't what I want. I've got plenty of those, the place I come from is crawling with them. It's about Josef. I want your advice about him."

Kunig's eyes wouldn't leave her now. God in Heaven, the girl was pale! Was it possible—? With that fantastic overcoat one couldn't——

"If you really feel bad," he said sharply, "I'll get the waiter to put you in a cab. You'd better——"

"No, no I don't want a cab. I can wait a bit—half an hour I think. It's about Josef——"

"You send Josef to me," Kunig said, squeezing the words past the end of his cigarette. "You send that fellow to me, and I'll——"

"I can't he's in prison."

"In prison—where?"

"That's what I don't know. That's what I've got to find out."

"What's he in prison for?"

"I don't know that either. It's what they call 'Political Safeguarding'—something like that—"

"Then I'm not interested!" Kunig said baldly. "I regard the police as fully competent to manage their own business, I'm in wholehearted sympathy with the government's determination to protect the community from undesirables."

He picked up the top sheet of the paper and held it as a screen across the table; but the sheet was torn at the fold, he could feel her staring through the aperture. And presently he heard her say:

"I only thought that as Josef's a Jew, and you being partly a Jew yourself—"

"*Be quiet!*"

He looked round sharply. At the next table a young business man was imitating Jannings and his two companions were heaving with laughter. Old Gütschow, on the other side, seemed to be deep in his paper. There was a stranger at the table next to that, but he was eight feet away and at present giving his order. Kunig beckoned the junior waiter.

"This lady doesn't feel very well, I'm going to take her home. Ring up, please, and get a cab for me." He waited till the man had gone and then leant over the table. He said quickly, almost inaudibly, "The food's no good here, I'll take you to the Reichsadler, get you something you'll like. Go along and wait for me at the end of the alley. I'll settle up here and be with you in five minutes."

She did as she was told. When a taxi drew up she said, "For Doctor Kunig?" and sat down inside. In less than the time he had given Kunig joined her.

"Where to?" the driver asked.

"My office in Schmolldamm." He wound up the window. "And now," he said quietly, "I want to tell you something. I've got papers in my office proving that my eight great-grandparents were Aryan. You can see those papers if it interests you. And then—listen!—if you say to me or any one else that I have Jewish blood I shall bring a slander action against you. Do you understand?"

"Oh yes, I understand. And now, about Josef—"

"Who was it who said I was a Jew?" he demanded.

"He didn't, he only said you were partly one."

"Yes, but who?"

"My chauffeur."

"Your—?"

"I mean, the man who drove me in this morning. I don't know who he was. Some kind of policeman, I think."

"Why do you think that?"

"Well, he said he was going to put you in prison as soon as he got a chance."

A corner of Kunig's mouth folded in; it was his equivalent to smiling. But the smile stopped as the fearful moment in the café returned, the girl's intense eyes spearing the *Lokal-Anzeiger*, the prickle round his neck and ears. She was lying back now like a woman of fashion in her own landau, while he bumped and swayed on the occasional seat, and he did not find her amusing any more. The one thing he hated was not to understand the accidents of life, and this was something he did not understand at all: a contraption of boisterous hat and flopping overcoat, bedraggled parcel, stubborn and lucid eyes clutched in cadaverous cheeks and forehead, he could make nothing of it, and before he got to the Schmolldamm it would have cost him nearly seven Marks.

"So this policeman friend of yours sent you to inquire about me?" he demanded suddenly.

She asked: "Why are you so frightened if there's really nothing wrong with you?"

"Answer my question!" he said.

The car had stopped, held up at the Zeinstrasse crossing. She got up and opened the door.

"It's not my business to answer your questions—"

He grabbed her back, just as the driver let in the clutch.

"Sit down, you little fool!—"

"What are you doing with me? You said you'd give me a nice dinner at a hotel. Now you're—"

"Did I? Yes, I did. Well, first I want to know what else your policeman friend said to you."

"I'll tell you," she said "—when you've given me advice about Josef."

Kunig lit a fresh cigarette.

"Right then! Josef: he's the father, I suppose?"

"The father?"

"The father of this child you're going to have."

She smiled. (It was odd, and not unpleasing, Kunig thought: the way a smile would suddenly flood this deathly face.)

"The baby, you mean? Oh no, Josef isn't its father. I wish he was. No, no one is. I mean, it's all just myself."

"Oh my God!" Kunig said.

"I mean—I made that up. That awful blonde you keep—"

"Then tell me," Kunig said furiously, "who is this Josef, what is he, what's he got to do with you, and what in hell's name are you wasting my time for?"

"I'm not wasting your time, you're wasting mine. I told you I'd pay for the consultation—"

"Well, get on with it!"

She said patiently, "Josef was my doctor—I used to have T.B., you see—he was my doctor and he had a special sort of stuff he put into me to make it better, he made it lots better, he would have made it quite all right only the dam-awful Nazional-sozialisten got the government and of course the first thing they did was to put Josef in prison. And now

I don't know where he is, I got Herr Rupf to ask the Commissioner but the Commissioner won't tell him." Her eyes had shut, and her voice grown weaker: she was palpably unused to so much conversation. But her deckled voice, after a moment's pause, came again with a ferocity that astonished him. "Only I'm going to find him and get him back. You understand that? Even if I get no help from you or any other lickpenny scrivener. He belongs to me, I'm going to have him back!"

The cab turned into Schmolldamm and stopped at 46. Kunig paid the driver and marched into the entrance hall. He said over his shoulder, "You'd better come up to the office!" and she followed him into the lift. His office here was on the first floor, he used it largely for trustee business. The old carpet bought recently at a sale in Hanover, the middle-aged sofa which had never been sat on, all the ingredients were meant to suggest a pleasant living-room; all the anxieties of a hundred lives were tied up with yellow tape in the long walnut cabinet; and the place had no more life than an art museum. Minna stood just inside the door. Dr. Kunig, standing by the table with his black homburg pushed back from his forehead, lighting a new cigarette and signing a letter with the other hand, said:

"You'd better tell me who you are and where you live."

"I'm Minna Wersen," she said. "I don't live anywhere at present, I've got to find a job. I'm a skivvy by profession, when I find a job I'll live there till Josef marries me."

"Where did you spend last night?"

"At the Moltke Hospital. I'm supposed to be still there but I escaped this morning."

"Escaped?"

"They said I was still ill, they said I wasn't strong enough yet to do anything, only I knew I was—"

Kunig stretched for the telephone. "I can check up on that . . . Get me the Moltke Hospital . . ."

She ran across the room and seized his arm.

"If you tell them where I am—"

"Shut up! Go and sit down!" He tried to shake her off, but her grip was tighter than he expected, and he suddenly felt her teeth pressed against his arm. ". . . Is that the Moltke Hospital? This is Heinricke the Florists. We have been asked to deliver some daffodils to a Fräulein Wersen at 'Hartzinnfeld Hospital.' Can you tell me please if you have a patient of that name? . . ." The grip on his arm relaxed. ". . . I beg your pardon? She left this morning? You have no address? But no doubt the forwarding address will reach you presently, and then perhaps you will be kind enough to let us have a telephone call? Inner 209 . . . Infinitely obliged!"

He went across and opened the door of his secretary's room. "Thora! Get through to Fräulein Meissner, will you, and tell her I won't be over before three-fifteen. Oh, and then go down to the Kurchen Kaiser and get a lunch tray— for two—a lot of food, something expensive." He wandered over to the window, hissing a little tune through his nose, shut the window carefully, went back to the passage door and locked it. He was like a householder sleepily doing the bed-time round, he didn't look at Minna, his thoughts seemed to be in another country. He said at last, standing in the middle of the room, fiddling with a ring of keys, tracing the motif of the carpet with his toe,

"Why don't you sit down! There's no need to stand up there like a weatherbeaten signpost . . . This Josef, did he ever overcharge you?"

"No, he never charged me at all."

"A pity!" he said, "that's a great pity. One might prosecute him for an overcharge. He didn't ever borrow money, by any chance?"

She said: "I don't understand. I don't want to prosecute him—"

He turned to face her then.

"Listen! You've got to start by realising this. You can't deal with these bastards in any ordinary way, these excremental hooligans who put human beings in cages for their own hellstunk amusement. You're not negotiating with civilized people, you're dealing with apes. And you can't deal with apes and not get muck on your hands. Now see here! It's no use asking the Commissioner or any one else what they've done with your Josef, they won't tell you. I've never traced one man that way—and I'll tell you for your private information I spend a great part of my days and nearly all my nights trying to trace one victim or another. There's only one way to start the ball rolling, positively only one. If you want to find a man who's disappeared you've got to bring up something against him. Then if he's still alive they'll produce him—six times out of ten. They like that—you get me? They like to have a definite charge, something they can make a song-and-dance about. If you handle it properly you can get something like a proper trial and a definite sentence, with at least a chance of the man getting out at the end of it. I say a chance, mind! It doesn't always work. And in any case you've got to take the hell of a risk. Well, there you are: you've got to make up your mind whether the risk's worth taking."

Minna said slowly: "You mean, I've got to accuse him of something?"

"Exactly! Something that sounds serious and can be proved not so serious. For example, you might allege that this—what did you say his name was?—you might allege that this Doctor Zeppichmann gave you careless or inefficient treatment. We might get a row of doctors arguing over that till all's blue, since no two doctors have ever been known to agree about anything. What do you think about that?"

"I don't know . . . You're sure there isn't any other way. Any way I wouldn't be hurting him at all?"

He looked at her obliquely. The colour of that face—madness, madness, to have come on a trip like this! And yet she was still sitting bolt upright on the hard chair, intent, aggressive, with the parcel like a fat woman half-undressed perched on her knee. The curse of it! He was wasting half his time with these political cases, missing lucrative business every day: only yesterday he had faithfully promised Erica that he wouldn't risk handling any more . . . But this was one he couldn't resist. There was something here to test his wits, something with the smell of battle in it. And this outlandish object, this faggot of skin and bone swaddled in tweed, she suddenly seemed to him worth fighting for.

"No," he was saying, "no, I'm sorry, but there isn't another way."

39

IT DID not seem quite right to Herr Oelschläger that there should be a bowl of flowers on his desk. His taste was good; and flowers, in a Police Divisional Legal Office, seemed to him as well placed as caryatides on a factory by Corbussier. Was Fräulein Bruder responsible? He would have said, as she sat there hunched-up over her short-hand book, that she had as much imagination as a pile-driver. He finished dictating:

" 'In all the circumstances comma therefore comma I feel that the proper course is for Zeppichmann to be brought back to Hartzinnfeld for further examination semi-colon and if you agree with this view I shall be glad if you will arrange for the necessary instructions to be given full stop.' That's the last of that batch."

Fräulein Bruder, with earnest obedience all over her flat, stupid face, got up and went to the door. With an effort, Oelschläger overcame his shyness.

"One moment! Am I to suppose that it was you who put these flowers here?"

Fräulein Bruder gaped. "Well—yes. Yes, it was."

Oelschläger removed the prismatic spectacles from his big, studentisch face, leaving it curiously naked and young.

"To honour my engagement?" he asked.

"Well—yes, Herr Reichsanwalt!"

"Well, that was—that was very kind. Most thoughtful! Well, that will be all, thank-you."

"Thank-you, Herr Reichsanwalt!"

In a scurry of embarrassment, Fräulein Bruder fled to the B Section Typists' Room. "Luise!" she called, with her head round the door, "Luise, I'm just going up to Cashiers' to check my stamp account. Answer the Big Man's bell, will you!" She went on to the end of the corridor and swiftly down two flights of stairs, out on to the pavement; looked round quickly and slipped across to the hairdresser's on the other side of the street. "Can I have an appointment to-morrow, my usual time? Just a trim. Thank-you! Oh, might I use the phone one minute? Thank-you so much!" She shut the door of the telephone closet carefully. "Inner 185 . . . Gertrud here. I've just seen a letter on the Important One's desk, about J.Z. J.Z. has made a confession, apparently. He says he wanted to kill the girl . . . No, that's all I could get, I only saw the bottom half. The Important One has asked for Z to be brought here . . . Yes, I'll let you know when there's anything more. Auf wiedersehen!"

Dr. Kunig put his elbow on the cut-out and immediately raised it again. "Get me North 100." He leant back against the wall, picking his nose with thoughtful artistry. Why, he thought, why why why must the fellow throw his hand in just when his plans had been worked out so neatly! Of all the dirty strokes which had come his way in the last twelve months, this was surely the most exasperating. "Is that the Moltke Hospital? Have the kindness to connect me with Doctor Vollmuth!"

Instinctively, he corrected the set of his lapels, pulled out the flaps of his pockets.

"Doctor Vollmuth? Herr Dönel speaking. You will remember that you were kind enough to grant me a short interview on the 9th of this month? Yes, and you were good enough to show me a portion of your Department, most interesting, an unforgettable experience, I was deeply grateful . . . No, I'm afraid my inquiries as to Fräulein Wersen's present whereabouts have yielded no results so far. I needn't tell you that I'm doing everything I can . . . You will forgive me, perhaps, for troubling you again—there is one small point on which my memory is not altogether clear. I think you told me that a radiograph of Fräulein Wersen's chest was made shortly after her reception. Now I am not quite clear as to the deductions you made from that. Perhaps you would just tell me, in general terms——"

The ambassadorial cough which came along the wire brought back to Kunig a complete picture of Dr. Vollmuth's face. Smiling faintly, he took the receiver a little further from his ear. Dr. Vollmuth was well launched:

". . . myself am always inclined to treat radiographic evidence with a large measure of caution. You will realise that a radiogram almost invariably shows fortuitous or quasi-fortuitous shadowing which to all but the most experienced observers might be taken as indications which in reality are contradicted by clinical observ—I beg your pardon?"

"Oh—excuse me!—I was just asking you, am I right in supposing that your radiologists give you a note on their own scrutiny when they deliver the plates? I mean, I take it that men who are solely concerned with work of that kind may sometimes have some helpful contribution——"

"Frankly, Herr Dönel, I feel that my own deductions, imperfect as they may be, are at least fortified in the case of tuberculous subjects by a diagnostic experience extending——"

"No no, you misunderstand me—if I may say so, Herr Doktor! I was only suggesting that a specialist like yourself, and in your position, must sometimes find it that it's not humanly possible to cope with all the details in the work of a great Department; and I thought that possibly, on some occasions, a report on certain radiograms from some intelligent junior man——"

Vollmuth said with a certain emphasis: "It is a doctor's business, Herr Dönel, to cope with the humanly impossible. I have, in fact, shown the radiograms in question to Doctor Dittmer, the head of our bacteriological laboratory, but that was purely—I beg your pardon?"

"I think," said Kunig, in the thin falsetto he kept for these occasions, "I think there must be something wrong with the line . . ." He rang off, rubbed his nose, and reconnected. "Northern 100 again, please! . . . Be so good as to put me through to Doctor Dittmer in the Bacteriological Department."

Still holding the receiver he yawned, fumbled for a pencil-end and began drawing on the wall: a profile of Vollmuth, done with billowing pothooks. He scribbled underneath: 'W definitely anti, V probably anti. D to cancel W + V? Girl to remain neutral, otherwise patently unreliable. Sell O idea of demonstrating impartiality?' Then the wire came alive again, he licked his palm and rubbed the scribble out. He heard:

"No, you fathead, over there! I said— Put the—blasted —stuff over there! Hullo hullo hullo! You, who are you, are you there, what d'you want?"

"Doctor Dittmer?"

"Who d'you think?"

"Ah, this is Herr Dönel, party-attached Solicitor. Doctor Vollmuth, whose opinion I value very highly, has recommended me to apply to you for——"

"Balls, my dear man! Doctor Vollmuth never recommended any one on earth to apply to me! Vollmuth thinks that I'm a crazy mountebank, and I think that Vollmuth's a fuddle-pated old wet-nurse——"

"Exactly! Yes! My own feeling is that Doctor Vollmuth, while undoubtedly pre-eminent in his own field, is inclined to be too empirical in his view of——"

"What?"

"I say, I have been talking to Doctor Vollmuth about a patient of his called Fräulein Wersen, and——"

"She isn't! She got away. And I can tell you there aren't many of Vollmuth's patients so lucky as——"

"Indeed? Well, it appears that radiograms were made

on the reception of the case, and from these Doctor Vollmuth deduces——"

"Never you mind what Vollmuth deduces! You could
X-ray the boiler of a steam-engine, and Vollmuth would
say it was an elderly female patient with pneumoconiosis.
I tell you, if I knew as little about medicine as Doctor Vollmuth——"

"Just so! You mean that from your own examination
of the Wersen radiograms you conclude that the treatment
she received before admittance to the hospital was unques-
tionably sound?"

"What? Say that again! My dear sir, I never said anything of the sort! You don't expect a man of science to go
making wild statements of that kind? Shouldn't dream of
saying such a thing! All I'm prepared to say is that Vollmuth is wrong, whatever he says. And as for that man
Wildelau, he's a good deal wronger still. I tell you I knew
the boy—Zeppichmann, I mean—he used to crash about in
my poor little department here. And when Wildelau says
that Zeppichmann's a knave and a fool I say that Wildelau's
just talking plain hogwash. Look here, you're not writing
all this down? Who did you say you were—a lawyer? Now
look here—hell, what's going on? What d'you say? Something wrong with the line? I should say there dam well is
something wrong with the infernal line . . ."

Kunig, releasing the cut-out, started his next call.

"All the same, I'm not happy about it," Oelschläger
was saying. "As a legal man I dislike a case of this kind."

Little Herr Siegert, perched on the edge of Oelschläger's desk, shrugged his shoulders. He said:

"I don't see why. If you've got a confession the whole
thing is simplified, that's all."

Oelschläger took another turn across the carpet, stroking the silky hair above his ears.

"Yes, but why did he confess? And for that matter, why did he want to kill the girl? Of course it might have been out of pity—"

"That isn't the point. The ethical purpose of the law, as I see it, is to preserve the integrity of the State, to defend the State against the actions of people who are hostile to it. That seems to me the supreme conception, raising Law from a mere code of inter-individual adjustment to a manifestation of the State's highest virtue. And if—"

"Yes, I know, I agree! But surely the Law becomes less able to fulfil its highest functions whenever it's seen to work clumsily. I mean—"

The telephone purred. Oelschläger took the receiver and placed it carefully in the recommended position.

"Reichsanwalt Oelschläger . . . Oh, is that you, Kunig! . . . In re Zeppichmann, yes. Yes, I was going to write to you. Certain information I've received makes me doubtful whether the case is one demanding public examination . . . Of course, yes, I have the interests of your Client in mind, but I must point out that it's exceedingly unlikely that any funds will be found to meet her just claims. It's very unfortunate. I understand there was only a trifling savings-bank account, and that sum was naturally requisitioned to meet the public expenses connected with the man's arrest. I should like to say, I am very much obliged by the help you've given me. Your attestation was of great value. I beg your pardon?"

Kunig was drawing little figures in the air. He said:

"Well, perhaps it's hardly worth mentioning in the circumstances. I was only going to tell you that you might get an adminicle of some interest from Doctor Dittmer at the Moltke Hospital. You probably know that he's the most noted diagnostician they have there, and I understand that he took particular interest in my Client's condition when she was admitted. My feeling was that the evidence of a man of that kind might give a little extra rigidity to the construction of the case—I mean, from the standpoint of public reaction."

"Dittmer—I'll make a note of the name," Oelschläger said. "I am most obliged." He rang off and turned to Siegert. "Have you ever heard of a man called Dittmer, up at the hospital? Kunig seems to think he might be useful over this Zeppichmann business."

Siegert said: "You want to keep clear of doctors, if you ask me. They go prosing and prosing in their abstruse jargon till the Judge goes off to sleep."

Oelschläger took off his spectacles and cleaned them with a piece of cloth he kept in the middle drawer, marked "Cloth for cleaning Spectacles."

"Still, I'd like to have all the corroborative evidence I can get. To me there's something very unsatisfactory about confessions—I mean, from the legal point of view."

Siegert gave his shoulder a friendly shake. "You're a man who doesn't know when he's lucky," he said, wandering towards the door. "When you're dealing with anti-racial poison of the most virulent kind, which is what you seem to have in this Zeppichmann of yours, the quicker you get the job wiped off the better. That's how I look at it." Humming *Röslein auf der Heide* he tripped across to the automatic lift and buttoned the third floor. In his own office he picked up the house telephone.

"Herr Fenrich there? . . . Ah, Martin, comfort my spirits, I've just had twenty minutes with friend Oelschläger! . . . Yes, he takes life very hard—it's that Zeppichmann business on his mind now. You know, I'm just a little worried. It's another of these cases which that Kunig man has jogged us on to, and so many of the good Kunig's little prosecutions seem to wobble rather. I can't help feeling that Oelschläger is a bit over-conscientious in the academic sense. He fumbles, if you know what I mean. Of course nothing's more important than upholding the rules of legal procedure, but—don't you think if some one dropped a hint to Meiricke he'd impress on our friend the need for a certain dynamism in his performances?"

There was a moment's pause before Fenrich's voice, neat and certain like the strokes of a sciabolist, came back:

"I think, perhaps, yes. Only Meiricke's gone to Frankfurt. Leave it to me. I'll send a line."

It was four days later that Oelschläger found a letter from Herr Meiriche on his desk:

'. . . appears from the memorandum sent to me that Zeppichmann is a specimen of particular insolence. Realising not only the State-importance of such cases as these, but also the probationary nature of your own present position, you will I am sure make special efforts to ensure that justice is done to Zeppichmann speedily, determinedly, and exemplarily. There must be no failure through academic narrowness."

Large and powerful in body, given to forty-kilometre walks and solitary climbs, Oelschläger was not often affected physically by his worries. But to-day his head ached all morning, he actually snapped at poor Fräulein Bruder when she murmured something about a summary for the Zeppichmann file. He left the office early, and sat down after coffee to write at length to his fiancée, who was at Dresden with the German Girlhood Forward-Communion.

'. . . mind a good deal strained by the Zeppichmann business of which I wrote to you in a former love-letter. My little precious, it's a shame to burden your sweet mind with these professional troubles of mine! But you must forgive your old Heinrich, who only wants to share the whole of himself with you and who strives so constantly to be worthy of you. The problem here is to satisfy my own standards of practice both as a man of first-class legal training and qualifications and as a loyal servant of my Country. It is of the utmost importance that I obtain the required verdict, but it is also important to me that I should obtain it in a way of which my professors would approve. The criminal is in Hartzinnfeld now, and yesterday I saw him. He is in a sullen, obstinate state, partly due, I think, to poor physique, and I could really get nothing out of him. If he were brought into any public Court his evidence would be quite unsatisfactory to a properly trained legal mind. So I feel it is essential to have other evidence which is patently reliable, and this is most difficult to obtain. The Director of the Moltke Hospital is ready to testify to the man's bad character, but he speaks of the young woman Wersen with a noticeable lack of sympathy, owing to her having left the hospital without his permission, and his professional deposition was made in terms which seem to me dangerously imprecise. Dr. Vollmuth, who was actually in charge of the case, also appears disinclined to express himself in a manner which would be conclusive as to Zeppichmann's guilt. Herr Fenrich has talked of bringing pressure to bear on these gentlemen and also on some of the hospital nurses. I myself, however, have found that expert witnesses often speak with an observable lack of assurance when their testimony has been prepared under too-close guidance, and I consider that such a lack of assurance might react unfavourably upon pressmen and others who do not wholly understand the objective of our Justice. Dr. Kunig, on whose helpfulness I rely so much, (he is not of our own social standing, but a diligent and honest spadework lawyer), has recommended me to examine another doctor, whom he believes to be sounder in his views. I am seeing this man to-morrow, and I shall also re-examine the young woman Wersen, who is a foolish and feeble creature (though of course deserving of compassion) but may chance to give me further assistance.

'My little gem, dearest of loving hearts, think of your Heinrich who sometimes finds life's road so steep and rough when you are not close at hand to comfort him . . .'

40

DR. DITTMER came in his blue serge and his soberest mood. Oelschläger's peremptory letter had alarmed him, he realised now that he had talked foolishly to the man who had telephoned, he was half-afraid of a slander action. "It's on the second floor," the porter said, "you can take the lift." But the lift was of a new type, he didn't understand its mechanics and he didn't trust it. He went slowly up the stone stairs, thinking, These lawyers, they have a devilish trick of making you say what you don't mean to.

Abominably clean, the place was: not a scratch on the lincrusta dado, not one spent match on the landing; and everywhere the warning, *The fines for spitting are: 5 RM, first offence, 20 RM, subsequent offences.* Reaching the second floor, he was suddenly inspired, he leant over the banisters and spat down the well. Ah, a fine plop it made! He felt better then. These legal gasbags, these portentous ignorami who wouldn't know the difference between staphylococci and leucocytes, one could only treat them as children. And after half an hour in the waiting-room he was moderately angry.

At eleven o'clock Oelschläger rang for Fräulein Bruder. "I am ready for Doctor Dittmer now." He took a handful of papers from the top drawer and arranged them on his desk in such a way as to indicate pressure of business combined with orderly methods. At Dittmer's entrance he half-rose and bowed. "Doctor Dittmer? I regret having kept you waiting, several of my colleagues are indisposed and I find myself particularly busy."

"I must tell you," Dittmer said, "that I've been spitting down the well of your stairs. Tell me, please, who do I pay the fine to?"

Oelschläger hesitated. "Well, I—I think perhaps the porter should be informed in the first instance . . . Do please sit down! I've sent for you to ask your professional opinion on a matter—"

"You mean the spots on your neck? Well my advice is to avoid all these doctors, they're quacks, the whole—"

"No no. It was about a certain Minna Wersen. I understand that you were responsible for her treatment at—"

"I'm sorry, no, I wasn't."

"I mean, I believe that you were called in to give a diagnosis when this patient was first admitted?"

"No, I'm sorry, I wasn't. You say that I should tell the porter about my spitting down the well?"

"What? Yes, the porter . . . Do you mean that you know nothing about the case?"

"Well, I've seen the girl once or twice."

"Ah, then presumably you made some observation as to her condition?"

"I saw the radiograms, if that's what you mean."

"The radiograms, ah, yes! And did those tell you anything?"

"They suggested something."

"Yes?"

"Do you mean that I actually pay my fine to the porter?"

"Yes yes, no doubt he'll accept it. I'm asking you— what did the radiograms suggest to you?"

"To me, personally, they suggested that the girl had been treated with injections."

"Injections, ah yes! Injections of what?"

"That's what I don't know."

"But you can say, I take it, whether the—the material used was good or bad?"

"No, I can't tell you that till I know what material—as you call it—was used."

Oelschläger touched the bell and waited in silence for Fräulein Bruder. "Fräulein Bruder, go and present my compliments to Herr Fenrich, will you please, and ask if he can spare me a few moments." He turned his chair a little and crossed his legs, as if he were taking Position 2 for a fashionable photographer. A good-looking fellow, Dittmer thought: but must he go through such convulsive antics with his jaws and throat every time he spoke?

"I think you will have to try and take me a little more seriously," Oelschläger said with hardworn patience. "I am really inviting you to put your professional knowledge at the service—not only of an individual—but of the State. You, as a doctor, are concerned with the State's physical welfare. I am concerned with the State's moral welfare. And just as your task is to make war on poisons in the physical body, so mine is to extirpate poisonous elements from the social body. Now, there's no need for me to go into details. Suffice it to say that a certain Zeppichmann made a pretence of giving treatment to Fräulein Wersen; we have ample evidence that the so-called treatment was ignorant, if not actually malicious; and what we require now is an adequate description of that 'treatment' in medical terms. Naturally there's no need to give precise details—actual formulae and things of that kind are usually of small legal value. I simply require you to say—ah, there you are, Fenrich! May I present Doctor Dittmer . . . I was just explaining to Doctor Dittmer the importance—the social importance—of our having a clear statement about Fräulein Wersen's condition when she was admitted to the Moltke Hospital."

Dittmer said: "Yes, but I'm still not perfectly clear. You say that it doesn't matter about the precise formula which Zeppichmann used?"

"Exactly—"

"All you require me to say is that he used *a* formula?"

For a moment Oelschläger hesitated. "Well, to be more precise, we require you to say that the treatment he adopted was harmful."

"You mean, I'm to say that he should not have used tuberculin?"

Oelschläger glanced at Fenrich.

"That should be good enough," Fenrich said.

"Or," said Dittmer, "putting it more broadly, that tuberculin treatment is a bad treatment."

Oelschläger nodded.

"Or rather," Fenrich said, "that it was a bad treatment in this particular case."

"You mean, having regard to the circumstances of the case at the time when the treatment was begun?"

"Precisely!"

"And I take it you would like me to substantiate my statement by giving a description of the condition as it was at that time?"

Oelschläger said: "That would be helpful, yes."

"In spite of the fact that I never set eyes on the girl till some six months afterwards?"

With a voice like broken glass Fenrich began: "I don't know if you think you're amusing, Herr Doktor——"

Oelschläger coughed.

"I've already told Doctor Dittmer that he would be well-advised to treat this business seriously, if he——"

"It seems to me," Dittmer said, "that if any one's not being treated seriously, it's me. You bring me here. You keep me waiting about half the morning. You say you want my professional opinion, by which I suppose you mean my opinion as a scientist. And you then tell me what that opinion is to be. You expect me to make exact deductions from certain very complicated data, and the fact that ninety per cent of those data are unknown seems to you to make no differ-

THE FIRE AND THE WOOD 333

ence. Well, if that's your interpretation of the word 'serious'—"

"Be quiet!" Fenrich snapped. "Listen to me! If you
think you can talk in that strain to people in our position
you're in for trouble, d'you understand? Listen! We know
already that Zeppichmann did his best to poison the girl—"

"Then why bother me?"

"Doctor Dittmer, I warn you—"

"One moment!" Oelschläger said, ringing his bell.
"There may be a way of convincing Doctor Dittmer that our
conclusions are not so groundless as he seems to suppose
. . . Oh, Fräulein Bruder, is Fräulein Wersen here? Then
bring her in, will you?"

The three men waited in frozen quietness, like amateur
actors when an entrance cue has been missed. When Minna
came in she went straight to the chair she had sat in for a
former interview. She smiled briefly at Dittmer, and sat
with her eyes fixed on Oelschläger's face, as the devout gaze
at a preacher, while Oelschläger studied his blotting-pad:
his chivalry forbade him to look directly at a young woman's
face, and his eyes couldn't stomach the hat. Fenrich, standing by the window with his hands in his pockets, ran over
her like an audit clerk: an interesting face, he thought, the
brilliant eyes oddly at variance with the sulky mouth and
stud-nail chin; but faces were secondary, and if you took off
her clothes—such clothes!—there would be nothing worth
attention. It was Dittmer who spoke first.

"You're a naughty girl, you know, running away from
Doctor Vollmuth like that. You're not fit to be away from
the hospital, you know you're not! If I told Doctor Wildelau—"

Fenrich tapped the floor with his toe.

"I don't think you were asked to say anything!"

"All right, please!" Oelschläger wished now that he
had left Fenrich out. "Listen please, Fräulein Wersen. You

know that we're all very anxious to help you, we want to punish the man who did so much harm to your health. But lawyers have to be very careful in the way they work to make sure of being perfectly fair, even with people they know to be blackguards. That means that we've got to find out as much as we possibly can about what this Zeppichmann did to you. Now will you tell me again exactly what you remember?"

Minna shut her eyes. She said feebly: "He—he put some stuff into my arm."

"We know that already!" Dittmer said.

"Perhaps you would like to question Fräulein Wersen?" Oelschläger suggested.

"Yes," Dittmer said, "yes, I would," and at once regretted it. There was something here he didn't understand. These people were talking as if the girl had a down on Zeppichmann, and he'd always imagined it was just the other way. He said with hesitation: "You remember, Minna, I was asking you about Doctor Zeppichmann's papers, whether you ever saw any papers he had when he was treating you, notes and things? I expect he kept a notebook—I should think he may have had it in your room sometimes to write down things he wanted to remember."

Her eyes were still shut.

"Yes," she said, "he did."

"Do you know what happened to that notebook?"

"No, I don't."

Fenrich said: "There was no such book among the personal belongings collected by the police. I checked the list over last week."

Dittmer ignored him. His mind was moving now.

"Listen, Minna! I think we've got to be fair to Doctor Zeppichmann, as Herr Oelschläger says. Herr Oelschläger wants me to tell him exactly what Doctor Zeppichmann did to you, so that he can see just how wrong it was.

I could do it perfectly well if only I could see that notebook. You say you remember his having a book like that, and it must be somewhere about, since he couldn't have taken it to prison with him. Now can't you remember anything that would help me to find it? Do try and think! It's important, this, it's very important—it may make all the difference."

If only she would open her eyes! One glance, and he could have told her everything he didn't want to say aloud.

Minna said, "Yes, I—" and stopped.

"Yes—?" He had guessed long ago, and he was certain now that she knew exactly where the notebook was. "Yes—?" he repeated.

"We can't wait all night!" Fenrich said.

But they had to wait nearly a quarter of a minute before she spoke again.

"Yes, I—I remember now. He told me—I think, yes—yes, he told me he kept the notebook hidden in his room. In some very secret place."

"Why?" Fenrich asked.

"I don't know. I think he—I think he must have thought it might get him into trouble, his giving me that stuff."

"Well, he was right about that!"

"What part of the room?" Oelschläger asked. "Did he ever tell you that? Did he ever give you any idea?"

"No. No, he didn't."

"The simplest thing," Fenrich said didactically, "is to get it out of the bastard himself. If need be, take him to the room he lived in and make him find it. That would probably save trouble."

Minna said quickly: "That's no good!"

Fenrich, who had already forgotten the girl, turned his head; and was surprised to see that she had come to life again.

"What do you mean, no good?"

She said slowly: "I mean—he wouldn't tell you, he wouldn't show you where it is."

Fenrich smiled. "We can be wonderfully persuasive."

"Yes, but he's—he's very obstinate. He wouldn't want any one to see that book, he wouldn't find it if any one was there. The only thing—"

"I think perhaps I'll take him along myself," Fenrich said. "If I—"

Oelschläger stopped him. "Wait a minute, Fenrich!" He turned to Minna. "What were you going to say? 'The only thing—'?"

She seemed to be confused again. "I only thought—I thought he might get it if no one was there."

"I don't quite understand," Oelschläger said. "What do you mean, 'if no one was there'?"

"I mean I thought—if you took him to the house and said, 'You're free now, we don't want you any more,' I thought he'd probably go straight and get his book."

"Yes," said Fenrich, "get it and destroy it!"

Minna shook her head. "No, he wouldn't do that. It was full of things he wanted—medical things. He told me. No, he wouldn't destroy it, he'd take it somewhere else."

"You seem to be very sure about Zeppichmann's ideas!"

"I don't know anything about his ideas. I only know people don't throw away things they've taken all that trouble over."

"Trouble? You mean—"

Dittmer said shortly: "She's right about that. A scientist never destroys his notes."

Fenrich yawned and went to the door. "If you'll excuse me, I've got rather a lot to do . . . I personally see no reason for any monkey tricks, I think it's just a waste of time. If you want that precious book of his, make him cough it up."

Oelschläger waited till the door had swung-to, then, "This house you're talking about, where is it?" he asked.

"Handelstrasse 149."

He made a note. "Very well! I think that's all I want to ask you this morning. Thank you!"

"Thank you, Herr Reichsanwalt!"

She walked steadily enough to the door, but the handle seemed to elude her. Dittmer saw her groping with her hand several inches above it, he went across to her swiftly and took her arm. "Wait!" he said, "I'll come along with you . . . If you'll excuse me, Herr Oelschläger——"

"One moment!"

Oelschläger was doubtful, he didn't like the idea of two witnesses leaving his office together, he lived in a horror of collusion. Dittmer hesitated. And in a moment Minna had pulled away from him and opened the door.

"I think, possibly——" Oelschläger said.

"——Do you realise the girl's ill?" Dittmer demanded. "D'you realise she'll probably collapse in the street!"

"Ill? In that case, perhaps——"

But Dittmer was gone already. Oelschläger, still staring at the door, opened the third-drawer-left and felt for his aspirins. The interview had been far from satisfactory: this Dittmer, he seemed to be a curiously childish person. But at least the girl had shown some intelligence in making that suggestion . . .

By the time Dittmer reached the top of the stairs Minna was half-way down. He called, "Wait a moment!" but she only went faster, the handrail gripped in her armpit, her feet falling on odd stairs like a cat's paws on a keyboard. At the first-floor landing she stumbled and came down on her knees, but she was up in a moment and starting the next descent. "Minna, stop!" he shouted again, "there's something I want to say!" A clerk coming up with a load of letter-books swerved out of her way, a goggle of typists stopped and gazed with penguin eyes: in the Police Divisional Legal Office it was abnormal to see a white-faced girl staggering across the entrance hall with a scientist in clamorous pursuit. He caught her as she reached the pavement.

"Minna, listen a moment!"

She turned like a vixen. "If you think I'm going back to be shut up in that lazar-house——"

"No, Minna, I shouldn't dream of it. I only want——"

The car in which Kunig had sent her was still waiting. She got in and closed the door, nodded to the driver to go on. Dittmer put his face against the window.

"That book," he called desperately, "get it and give it to me. I'll look after it!"

"It belongs to Josef!" she called back.

The car moved away.

41

LYING right across the seat of the car, she seemed to be very sleepy; it was the heat in the Herr Reichsanwalt's office, she thought, and having to think so hard. But before the car reached the Schmolldamm she managed to rouse herself and knock on the partition.

"I want you to take me to Handelstrasse. Handelstrasse 149."

She lay back again, feasting on the comfort of the sprung seat, and was surprised to find herself there so quickly; going by tram it took you twenty-five minutes altogether.

"Are you feeling all right?" the driver asked as she got out.

"Yes, perfectly all right."

The front door latch was down. She felt for the key on the ledge inside the porch and let herself in. There were sounds from the kitchen, and suddenly Herr Spühler's voice called, "Is that you, Herr Barthol?" As quietly as possible she slipped up the stairs and along to the Professor's room.

"May I come in?"

"Yes, come in!"

Frau Rupf was alone. She was sitting on a hard chair by the stove, there was something curious about her, something wrong with her eyes. Minna, standing just inside the door, said:

"I'm sorry—I wanted to see the Herr Professor. I forgot—he'd be at the school now."

"No," Frau Rupf said, "he's not at the school, he

doesn't go there any more. He's out looking for another post."

"He doesn't go to the school any more?"

"No. And if you want to know why, you can ask Herr Meisel. *Herr Meisel, you remember him?* Herr Meisel overheard something my husband said about the new education. Well, that was all that was necessary."

Minna nodded. "Herr Meisel, yes! . . . Well, perhaps I can see the Herr Professor another time."

Frau Rupf had lost the outer skin of her lethargy. She said, like an old woman at the end of a long day, "You must—you must come and sit down, you can't stand there, you don't look at all well. Why did they let you out of the hospital? Arnold will be cross, they shouldn't have let you go before you were quite well. Wait a minute, I'll make you some coffee. You know where I keep the coffee-things—no, sit down, I'll get them myself." She was wandering about the room, stopping to straighten a picture or an ornament in a quick, irritated way. "We shall not be here very long," she said. "We've got to find somewhere cheaper now. But of course that's of no interest to you. You look cold—put your chair nearer the stove. It was a great pity Frau Spühler didn't send you to the hospital earlier on . . ."

Here, in a room she had so often scrubbed, Minna sat on the edge of the easy chair, woodenly, with knees together and feet apart, hands in her lap. Her eyes followed Frau Rupf about the room. She said abruptly, as children make random answers to a teacher:

"It wasn't Doctor Zeppichmann's fault. He'd have made me all right if they hadn't taken him away."

Frau Rupf looked at her sharply. "That was Herr Meisel too!" she said. "He wanted that room."

"He's still there?"

"Yes."

"Oh! . . . I was hoping—I was hoping he'd gone."

"Why?"

"I don't know . . . Only Josef may be coming back sometime. Not for long, I don't mean. I just thought—he wouldn't want to see Herr Meisel again."

Holding the little tray with the cups and coffee jug, Frau Rupf stood staring down at Minna, as Pharaoh's daughter stared. The cups began to jingle foolishly in the saucer and she put the tray down. She went and looked out into the passage and then locked the door.

"I don't know what you mean!" she said. "Doctor Zeppichmann—I thought he was dead."

"No, he isn't dead."

"How do you know?"

"The Herr Reichsanwalt told me."

"Tell me about that!" Frau Rupf said. "I want to know. Tell me everything about it—it's all right, there's only Herr Barthol next door, he's as deaf as a judge."

All her apathy had gone now. To Minna's surprise, she felt for a cigarette out of the Professor's box; struck a match with quick, masculine impatience, lit it, and sat on the arm of the easy chair. Rather clumsily, like a boy in his first flirtation, she put her anaemic hand on Minna's shoulder. "You mustn't be frightened, I won't let anything out!" And as she listened to the stumbling recital she was snatching mouthfuls of smoke with petulant energy, murmuring, "Yes . . . Yes, go on! . . . So!"

"Then you've no idea when they're likely to bring him?" she asked at length. "I mean—what time of day? . . . Well, it would be night, surely. They always do things late at night, those swine—they don't want people to know what they're up to. Yes, it's sure to be night. And I suppose they'll hide some one in the room, that's the sort of thing they do."

"I didn't think of that," Minna said. "I hoped—"

"Never mind! You must leave all this to me, do you

understand! Only I may want you to write a letter to the Herr Reichsanwalt—I haven't thought it out yet. I must—"

Minna said, "But wait—please!" With the heat of the stove and Frau Rupf's quick voice the feeling of hopeless weakness had returned. She had thought of Frau Rupf as a mere mosquito, a nuisance that didn't matter; she was frightened by the intensity in these little, hat-pin eyes only a few inches from her own. "Please—I was only going to say—I thought there might be some way of getting Herr Meisel away from the room before he came. I thought we could have just a few minutes alone, Josef and me."

Frau Rupf shut her eyes. "No," she said, "no, there's a better way than that. You shall tell the Herr Reichsanwalt that Herr Meisel's away, but really he'll be there all the time. Yes, I want him to be there—you must let me have my way about that, and then I'll do all the rest for you, I'll pay for a car and everything, I can manage that." She got up and started fumbling in her workbasket. "My measure-tape—what in God's name has happened to it! I want to measure down from the balcony—it can't be more than two metres . . . You must leave it all to me, I don't mind if they send me to prison for it so long as I get it done the way I want. But Herr Meisel's got to be in his room, you understand! That's my part of the profits . . . Are you feeling bad? Wait, I'll get you some water . . . Now listen, I'll tell you what I think we've got to do . . ."

42

JOSEF said over and over again, to the man who sat beside him, "I don't want to go back to Sondersumpf. Please, I don't want to go to Sondersumpf!" The man next the driver, turning round, said, "Oh, for God's sake—!" "You, Jude, just keep your trap shut!" the other said, and Josef felt the blow of a heavy boot against his shin.

He thought it strange that the train should swing round a corner, passing so near the houses. And now he knew it was not a train but a motor-car. The windows were dull with condensation, the lights came past like fireships on a frantic tide. The car fell slack on its tow and was jerked forward again, the engine guttural, as they started to climb in middle gear. A tram slid by, and an unseen hand wrote *Konditorei Braun* through a patch of darkness. He put his hand to his wrist, where he used to keep his tram ticket under the watch-strap, and was surprised to feel the iron ring.

The car stopped and they put him out on the footpath, took the handcuff off his wrist. "Right—you can get along now!" Fenrich said.

"Get along?"

"You know the way, don't you! You're free, you can go home now."

He knew nothing, except that he was in a dark street. He started to walk the way they had left him facing, feeling with his hand along the wall from one lamp-post to the next. A fit of coughing stopped him, he leant against the wall doubled-up and tossed like an epileptic. When it was over he had forgotten how he came to be here, but catching the sound of heavy feet he went on quickly, expecting to feel the butt of Ulbrich's rifle in his back. All the houses were asleep; until, suddenly, a red curtain showed like a postage stamp suspended in the darkness, and from over there the notes of *Stille Nacht,* played with a stumbling caution, fell pertly into the frozen air. That drunkard's dance had been in his ears before, shaking the numbers out of focus as he worked on a calculation. He knew where he was now.

He reached the house, and felt along the ledge for the key. It must be late, he thought, but the door wasn't bolted. The passage light was off, but he knew his way all right: the edge of the coatstand, the newel post, the turn in the stairs: only his body was heavy to-night, heavy and very cold, and the work of pulling it upstairs took away his wind. He halted when he reached the landing.

He was tired, it must have been a busy day, though he could not remember; but I ought to see Minna, he thought, I ought to have a look at Minna before I go to bed. He listened for a cry from her, or the murmur she often made in sleep, but only heard, from the farthest room, the snores of Herr Barthol like gumboots dragged out of liquid mud. The house had fallen into its deadness, the kitchen smells were cold. He could not think how Minna had been when he left her at dinner-time.

It came back to him as he started to labour up the attic stairs: he hadn't seen her since last night, and that had been within the crisis-radius of the last injection. She had been sleepy then, the temperature a point or two above the normal; and he remembered promising to be with her soon. It was wrong he thought, it was foolish to have left her so long alone.

Then his desire to see her grew hot and huge, he wanted to touch her skin and smell her hair. He wanted to see her thin arm come out from under the blanket, he wanted to hear the hoarse voice say, 'Oh, Josef, you look so tired!' It was the feverish thirst of a long march through an August day, the violence of a tired swimmer's arms when his feet can all but touch the sand. He called, "Minna! I'm coming!" thrusting his voice through the weight of wind on his chest, he stumbled up the last four steps as if they were catching alight behind him, jerked the door ajar with his shoulder and turned the switch.

The rusty bedstead was still there, with the hessian pad lolling over the side. There was a shirt of Minna's on the floor, with half a comb and a sheet or two of *Hartzinnfelder Zeitung* furred with damp. His own tools, the top of a thermometer case, inspection torch, fragments of flasks, were all over the place, lashed with cobweb. The top window was broken, the smell and the ghost of the room had leaked away.

He picked up the shirt.

He turned out the light and went down the stairs again, slowly, holding the shirt against his mouth. The muscles in his face were cramped, as if a hot plaster were solidifying inside his cheeks, and yet his forehead was sensibly cold. Gratefully, a fluid warm and thick like coffee was oozing down the sides of his nose.

I will have a sleep, he thought, and in the morning I will ask them to take me back to Sondersumpf.

He felt his way along the passage towards his own room, opened the door and turned the switch. But the light would not go on. Then he became aware that some one was calling him.

It was hardly more than a whisper, "Herr Doktor! Herr Doktor, I want to speak to you!" A woman's voice that he knew, but he could not put a name to it. A fillet of grey light showed where the passage turned, he shut the door again and went that way. He was tired and cold, he didn't mind where he went to. "The light," he said, "there's something wrong with the light in my room."

Frau Rupf took hold of his arm, whispering, "It's all right, it's quite all right, just come into my room, I'll see to your light later on."

43

SOME loud noise must have woken him, Erich Meisel thought, for he had taken his usual sleeping-pill before going to bed and now he had been jerked from heavy sleep to full wakefulness. He fancied that the street door had slammed, but he could not be sure. He reached for the bed-head switch to see what time it was, but the light would not go on.

Curiously, he had dreamed about the light. Young Hauser in the Police Department had been asking officiously, 'Why isn't there a light in here?' and some one had said in the mean voice of Frau Rupf, 'I tell you, there's something wrong with the electricity. Herr Spühler's going to attend to it to-morrow.' Those words were shuttered and remote, like a nurse's voice following a patient into anaesthesia; in the first few moments of his wakefulness they were covered by the tide of new sensation. He only wondered, now, who had slammed the door.

What was that! Some one was coming up the stairs, he thought, and instantly he felt the creeping coldness in his stomach. He remembered, then, something which Richter the neuropathist had told him: 'Whenever you think you hear strange noises, stretch all your limbs as far as they'll go, and then try to think how you'd express those noises with letters if you had to write them down.' He stretched, and for a few seconds that alone was effective, the noise abruptly stopped. He turned over to go to sleep, and the noise started again, the footsteps came along the passage, haltingly, and passed his door, and went on up the attic stairs. Once more he stretched, with all the coolness he could find he tried to analyse the sounds his nerves had made. And through the field of his mental struggle a voice like the shadow of Zeppichmann's came sharp as a blow, *Minna! I'm coming,* and hard on that the crack of a latch and the wheeze of the attic door.

The light, he must have the light, he must get to the other switch: in thought he was over there in a moment, but his body was dead as a ship aground, even his arms would no longer move. A stretch of silence quickened his powers, it was his body which seemed to act of itself now while his will would have held it back. His feet were on the floor, his hand on the chair where his clothes lay, when his straining ears caught the footsteps once again; and now they were coming down.

The current which has moved him is cut, he is prisoner again in the cold body fastened against the chair; his breathing seems to have stopped, only his heart still lives, a new and separate life, gathering violence like a falling rock. All his sensations are dulled, leaving his ears the field, and his ears are tied to the flat uncertain steps which come towards his door. The flat, uncertain steps: he counts them, eight . . . nine . . . ten and then they stop. He hears a little cry, and he knows that cry, then the handle turns and the door is opening, he sees a man's shape standing there, dark against darkness, and the door is closed again.

The evil thing had gone, he thought, and once again he was free. The pace of his driving heart began to flag, slowly the grip on his muscles was released, and he made another step towards the door. A new noise came. Only the murmur of a man's yawn, but within the room. He turned, the curtain moved an inch, the side of a man's head showed on the paleness of the window. The thing had got inside.

It was not altogether instinct, it was partly an act of courage that made his hand go slowly back to the chair. His coat was there, spread over the back of it, and his automatic was in the outside pocket. In a few long seconds he had got the pistol over to his right hand, in a single motion he aimed at the curtain and fired.

Fenrich, waiting impatiently in the porch, heard the shot and the animal scream which followed it. He shouted, *"Pohlse, here!"* and the man on guard at the side of the house came running towards him. There were three more shots. Before the third, he had reached the top of the stairs, with Pohlse at his heels. The lights all over the house were coming on like a theatre sunrise, there were people gathering in the passage, a frightened old woman said, "In there! In there!" He kicked open Erich's door and tried the switch, he called, "Pohlse—Sauerborn—some one get a bulb for this light!" They got him the ancient bulb from the end of the passage, he felt his way over to the socket and the room came into sickly, yellow light. "Hauser!" he said, "what's ha—"

Hauser had fallen against the curtain in such a way that his knees held it down, and his head had come right through the wash-worn fabric. So, to the middle of the room, only his head showed, as in a drawing-room conjuror's illusion, his chin held up where the tear of the fabric had stopped. His open eyes seemed intent on the further corner of the ceiling; his mouth had a wry, deprecatory expression, which was made more whimsical by the ribbon of blood passing from his lip round his chin in an inverted question mark. The man sitting in his pyjamas on the edge of the bed, whom Fenrich recognised as Herr Meisel of the Secretariat, was grinning at this spectacle with frozen merriment: the automatic lay in tidy alignment with his bedroom slippers on the floor. Sauerborn went up and shook him by the shoulder but there was no reaction. It might have been a wax mannequin that he was shaking.

Indeed, he looked rather like a mannequin, Frau Rupf thought, as she stood at the door and peered over Herr Spühler's shoulders. She would have liked a brighter light on the scene, but it was good enough. She padded back to her own room and raised the corner of the blind. Two pinheads of light, showing through the leaves of Lerche's orchard, began to move as she watched them. She heard the hiccough of a gear-change and the rising, feebling drone of the car's middle-speed. The corner of her mouth tightened, she let the blind fall and got back into bed.

44

IT IS Josef sitting beside me, dumb, with his head lolling on the back of the seat. It is Josef's hand, this cold hand that I'm holding, though it's thin and knotted like an old woman's hand. It is Josef's hand, though it seems to flinch away when I try to stroke his fingers. I can only see his face when the street lamps brush across it, his eyes are open but he doesn't seem to look at anything.

It's stuffy in here, I want to go to sleep and I want to be sick. I can't breathe fast enough to keep my head up, it tires me to breathe so fast. I don't want to do anything any more, I want to lie back here with my cheek against Josef's arm, to let my breathing stop and my body grow small and light. I mustn't go to sleep, I mustn't go to sleep, my head has got to be clear and sharp to look after Josef.

"Josef! Josef!"

But he didn't answer.

The car tilted as it turned to run along behind the barracks, avoiding the brightness of the Schmolldamm. Headlamps swinging from the park showed the face of Herr Rupf old and white as he sat stiffly in the other corner, gripping the bamboo crook of his old umbrella, drumming on his knee. The knife of frosty air through the crack of the dividing window smelt for an instant of wooded hills, the lights of the Nissen Sport-Café poured yellow on the misted glass, the car screwed left and grumbled up the cobbled carriageway of Wulfgasse. In Bruddestrasse it stopped.

Strength, oh God, strength now!

They stood forlornly on the narrow footpath like country passengers waiting for a train, the car jerked off backwards to turn in the brewery entrance and the friendly smell of it floated away. The opening to the river-steps was only a few yards on, the river wind poured round the corner like a lynch-mob. From the lamp at the brewery gate the light was spun as far as the road's turn, showing the roadway empty, torn posters beating like pigeons' wings along the brewery wall. A voice said, "Wersen? Fräulein Wersen?" A shadow moved and became a dingy overcoat with a chubby face clutched in its collar. "From Doctor Kunig! Follow me, if you please!"

He took the fibre attché case which Minna carried—she wouldn't give him the parcel—he went ahead of them down the steps, a schoolboy hustling his parents through the fairground, squashed hat planted between his spreading ears, fat small feet churning like a camshaft. The light from the road gave out, the steps dived into nothingness. "Come, Josef, come!" but he lingered on the topmost step, insensible to the wind soaking his cotton boiler-suit, hands held together as if they were tied. She took his arm and urged him on, half dragging, half supporting him, green hat and sprawling parcel clutched together in her other hand, Herr Probst's overcoat thrashing and cuddling about her legs. "We must hurry, please!" the guide called back, and Herr Rupf, holding Josef's other arm, head down against the wind and feet pawing for the steps, repeated, "Come, Herr Doktor, we must hurry!" He let them have their way with him, he pitched and stumbled down the steps like a man asleep. The steps drew clear of workshop walls, the river showed as a grey sleeve stained at the golden buttons, wharfhouse roofs a cardboard pattern cut sharp on frosty sky. They bundled all together round the second angle of the zigzag and lunged along the half-way terrace, clawed and crumpled by the wind.

They had reached the final flight when Josef started coughing. The first convulsion tore him out of their grasp, he knelt on the steps curved over like a bridge and shook as if a wild creature was struggling to get out of him. When Minna stooped to put her hand in his armpit, a trick she had learnt from him, he shrank away and rolled on his back, bringing up his knees to ward her off. The guide, who had reached the foot of the steps, came stumping up again. "Really—ladies and gentlemen—I beg you—I beseech you to hurry—they won't wait for you after the hour!" "We must carry him!" Rupf said. "The only thing is to carry him."

But when they tried to get hold of him again he wriggled away, breathless and whimpering, he began to crawl down the steps on his knees, and over-balanced, and rolled the whole way to the bottom. They saw him there a dark heap like the contents of an overturned market stall, motionless; Minna ran crying down the steps, and Rupf plunged after her, clutching the parcel she'd dropped and both their hats and a spoke of his own umbrella. But Josef was up again before they reached him and staggering towards the river's edge, letting out a chesty noise that sounded like laughter. It was the guide who caught him just in time, and the others closed round him, he was passive again now, he hobbled along between them murmuring, "I want you—finish me off—God's Own sake—finish me." Drunks, the ferryman's wife thought, as they came through the light beneath her window: the broad one in the middle swaying and retching, the shameless girl clinging to his arm and lurching as he lurched, a windswept old somnambulist dragging them both along and a podgy dwarf hustling them like a sheepdog. "A shame on you!" she suddenly squeaked, "go on home, the lot of you!" and slammed the window down.

Minna's eyes had shut. It was like that early night at the hospital when she had walked out from a dream to try her legs; she felt the same disconnection between her inward power and the muscles that should have served it. But Josef

was here, though this arm felt narrow as a girl's it belonged
to him; precious Josef was here, and presently he would
start to look after her. She had only, for a little while, to
hold away the brown fog lapping at the edges of her brain,
to stiffen for a little longer the bones which propped the
growing weight of her head. Another effort, a little longer.

The sounds which linger in a town at night had fallen
behind, the concrete underfoot had given place to gravel. A
husky, melancholy voice said, "You're very late, I thought
you weren't coming!" She opened her eyes and saw close to
hers a shrunk face, bristle-piled, with a drooping cigarette
burnt all along the side. "Your clocks are fast," the guide
said shortly, "you ought to keep your clocks right!" He was
pressing something into Minna's hand. "The papers," he
said, "those are the papers Doctor Kunig's got out for you,
you'll have to look after those." "Right, come on then, if
you're coming!" the hairy man said.

"Where's the parcel?" Minna asked. "I must have the
parcel!" Rupf gave her the parcel, and held her hand for
a moment, murmuring without a trace of hopefulness, "God
with you, Minna—it's all right now, I know it's going to be
all right!" The black shape of the boat seemed to be quite
close, she stepped there as you would walk from one room
to another, missed it, soaked a stocking up to the knee, landed
in the bows of the boat on hands and knees. But the parcel
was all right, she had it grasped against her stomach with
her hat and Dr. Kunig's papers, it hadn't got wet at all. They
were helping Josef into the boat, he lay down in the bottom
and started coughing again, the boatman took his place to
scull from the stern. "You'll understand I'm taking no responsibility!" the boatman repeated. "I'll do what I'm paid
to do, but you'll understand that I'm taking no responsibility."

The fat little guide stooped down to shove out the bows.
He said: "You'll remember—be careful about those papers.

Doctor Kunig was very strong on that, it's taken him a lot of
work."

The breeze had got into Herr Rupf's umbrella and
prised it open, he held it at arm's length as if he had just
come down by parachute, shaking with cold he was raising
his hat and pouring hard-worn, useless smiles into the darkness. He called across the water: "When I next have the
pleasure of escorting you I trust to be in more elegant trim!"

"You understand, I'm not taking any responsibility!"
the boatman said.

The figures on the bank were absorbed into shadow, the
fabulous shape of a dredger moved to stand against the place
where they had been. With them a continent had gone, the
insistent reek of river weed washed over the smell of gas
works and the farther sounds hung loose and brittle like
an echo. Oddly, there was no wind here: the cold enclosed
them tranquilly, like wet clothes. "I've got the book," she
said, "you know—the book with all your figures, and the
photos of my chest," but he wasn't through the coughing-
fit, he didn't hear. When she touched him he rolled to the
side of the boat and knelt there staring over into the water;
knowing what he thought of, she held tight to the side of his
suit. The sound of a child whimpering came as if from below
the water, a wooden wall slid up and the side of the boat
bumped hard against it, a triangle of light broke from the
darkness above their heads.

"You got them?" A woman's voice.

"I got them. But I'm not taking any responsibility, I
told the gentleman that . . . Will you get aboard, Miss!"

She stood up in the bow, weak and hazy, felt for the
side of the barge with numbed hands. The distance now
seemed huge, an ocean of water in between, and she doubted
her strength to get across; but a pair of hands came down to
catch her by the arms, with careless power the woman pulled
her up and over. They couldn't make Josef move. He knelt

there in the lethargy which terrified animals show, he didn't
stir when the rocking of the boat brought his forehead hard
against the barge's side. Only his lips were moving all the
time, ". . . finish me off—she can't do anything worse to
me—why can't she finish me off . . ." Until the woman
leaned far over and linked her fingers behind his back, the
boatman put a casual shoulder under his buttocks and they
tumbled him on to the deck.

In the cabin's warmth, by so much light as the lamp on
the table gave, Minna sat beside him and studied his face:
the ragged, lifeless skin, the festering scar between his eyes.
She hardly realised that Frau Krückel with a mug of coffee
in each hand was silently watching them. He was coughing
again, but not tumultuously: the little, explosive cough
which goes on and on between your chest and stomach: and
she knew it so well, that cough, that although it never
plagued her now she could feel its echo in her own thin
chest. His eyes were open, he was staring at her as if he
didn't know how far away she was, less fearfully now than
with an aching curiosity. She could have eased herself by
weeping; that should have been her body's response to the
sight of this familiar face, so unfamiliar and so pitiful. But
she would not take the comfort of that feebleness while he
was needing her protection. She felt for his hand again, and
was grateful that he didn't pull it away. She put her forehead
against his cheek, waiting for his love to break through and
answer her.

45

SOMETIMES she felt a moment of hunger for the attic room in Handelstrasse, damp patches on sloped ceiling, odour of old blankets and medicine: that place had belonged to them, and she would have guarded, womanly, the frame of realised things she had made her own. With a room you have known for a long time you leave a little of yourself, you are that much altered: a person you have known only in that place cannot be the same elsewhere, and you are not the same to him.

But Frau Krückel was kind; and in her shallow cabin, with its knobbly chairs and photographs of the Imperial family in fretwork frames, with its china vases and tasselled fringes all along the shelves, the smell of celery and paraffin enrobed you quickly with a new familiarity. She had not very much to say, Frau Krückel, as she stood by the Börsig stove, sometimes stretching out to re-fasten the safety-pin in Willi's trousers or to wipe his small nose with her apron, always stirring her nameless stew. When she caught sight of a friend on a passing barge she would put her head out of the window and suddenly split the air with her broken voice, "He! Trudi! How goes! . . . Not too bad!" and return to her cooking; for the rest, she scolded the child laconically, smiled shyly at her visitors, murmuring, "Better to-day— out there. We are getting some spring at last," and at once put her huge hand to her mouth, stroking down the black moustache as if she would hide the source of her indiscretion. At intervals Oskar came in from the deck and asked if she was all right. "Not too bad!" she always told him, and he kissed her sturdily on the goitre and stumped away again.

She was kind, Frau Krückel, she did not seem to mind their invasion of her small home; and since Minna's papers showed that they were Georg and Else Freyberg she had made up a bed for them at one side of the tackle-house.

In the dark hours Josef was not easy for Minna to look after. For a long time the cough would keep him awake; and then, asleep, he would twist and flounder, groaning so loudly that she feared the sound would carry aft and wake the Krückels' child. For an hour on end he would hold a senseless conversation with some one he called Herr Dahlmeyer, sometimes he called her own name, as the dying call out the name of God, and begged for her forgiveness. Often, when she had just fallen asleep, she was roused again by his shouting in her face, "It's a lie, I tell you, it's a bloody lie!" and would find his hand fiercely gripping her arm or throat. To soothe him, then, she would light the candle, and prop him up against her arm, and stroke his hand, talking sleepily until the terror of his eyes changed into recognition. Then he nodded drowsily, and in the gaunt, cadaverous face, shown weirdly by unsteady light, a smile would start. "I'll make it right, Minna!" he said, "I'll make it right with you!"

Her own sleep was always shallow, as in the hospital, and the first light brought her to its surface. But she had to fight, each morning, to uproot her body from the growth of weariness that held it down. Shivering in the early cold she went to the cabin, where Frau Krückel was already giving Willi his breakfast, and came back with Josef's coffee in one of the cracked mugs. At this hour his sleep was quiet, his face in that serenity was the face she knew; and this was happiness, merely to squat beside him and to watch his face, thinking of the days when she had had to conjure it, until the eyes would open (like flowers, she thought, like summer flowers) and he would faintly smile. When he had drunk his coffee she soaped his face and shaved him, borrowing a razor

from the engine-hand who lived in the bows. She delighted
to prolong this fussery, and he suffered it without impatience, never minding her clumsiness. Sometimes he reached
for her hand and felt it over as if it were a curiosity, sometimes he said quickly, hoarsely, "It won't be long, Minna, I
won't be such a nuisance for long. Those people—those
people at Sondersumpf—they took it out of me. It won't be
long . . ." She dressed him, still lying on the bed, in old
clothes borrowed from Oskar Krückel; and when the sun was
warm she called for Oskar's help to get him outside. His legs
were uncertain: walking with confidence along the narrow
deck he would suddenly stumble and clutch her arm, almost
pulling her overboard. She was only at ease when she'd settled him on the tarpaulins piled amidships, tucked round
with the overcoat Herr Probst had lent her. That was where
he spent most of the day; a discarded, sprawling figure,
sometimes in a child's contentment and sometimes distrait,
forehead crumpled and scarred hands in fretful antic: while
the engine just behind him poppled ostentatiously, the
high banks dawdled past, the barge crept steadily towards
Bad Fels.

"There'll be trouble," Oskar said, "when you get to
Bad Fels." With the tiller lodged in his concave stomach he
stretched and put his giant paw on Minna's shoulder, staring
at her forehead as if a magic word were written there. In the
leather, Rodin face the eyes were kind and anxious, blue like
the sky a little after sunset: he was frightened of nothing in
heaven or earth except the smell of offices and the sight of a
printed form. "It's no concern of mine," he said, "only Bad
Fels is full of nosey parkers. There's nothing those people
won't look into. The way you came aboard, well, it's no concern of mine, but it didn't look like an honest job to me."
The child Willi had crawled to the very edge of the deck,
he stretched back absently and caught him by the scruff of
the trousers. "Nothing but nosey parkers!" he said.

Minna nodded and went on with her work; she was pegging Willi's clothes on a long marline from the engine-house to a pole in the steering-well. Presently she put down the basket and went forward to where Josef lay.

"Josef, are you awake? Josef, you do understand, don't you, that we're Georg and Else Freyberg? Just for the present—you do understand that? There'll be a lot of people in uniform—at Bad Fels—a lot of men in uniform will come and ask us questions. You've only got to say you're Georg Freyberg, like it says on these papers."

But she saw that he was frightened.

"You mean—the Police?" he said. "The Police are coming on to this ship?"

"But you've only got to tell them you're Georg Freyberg!" she repeated.

He was quiet for a time, thinking it over. "You must tell them," he said hesitantly, "you must tell them you're nothing to do with me. They all know who I am. You must tell them you're nothing to do with me."

She wasn't listening then, her thoughts were caught in another current. She said, "You know that we're not going to Giessbach? Doctor Kunig—he's the man who looked after me—Doctor Kunig said it wasn't safe to go there. We've got to go out of the country to start with, we'll have to stay out until the politics have settled down. Next year, perhaps—next year I think we'll get to Giessbach."

He said soberly, with his eyes closed, "Yes, I thought of that. That's what I'd like. I promised I'd take you to Giessbach."

"But we've got to be out of the country for a time," she repeated. "That's what Doctor Kunig said, he knows about that sort of thing. Listen, Josef, I've thought it all out. When we get out of the country we'll find a doctor and tell him about your stuff. I've got Doctor Dittmer's photos, you see, they're in your book with the other ones, everything's in the parcel all together, all we've got to do is to give it to some good doctor, then he'll tell all the other doctors, then we shall get some money, and when the politics have settled down we'll be able to go to Giessbach."

He didn't answer for a minute or so, and she thought he didn't understand. He was ill, poor darling Josef, the cough had been bad last night, and she found it hard to explain to him the plans which were all neat and clear in her own head. "You see that, don't you?" she said. "The first thing is to tell some doctor about your stuff."

"That's done with!" he said at last; abruptly, without emphasis, as a man who discards an old suit. "I've forgotten about that, they made me forget about it, those people at Sondersumpf."

She said nothing.

"Minna!" he called, and opened his eyes. "Oh—oh, it's all right. I thought you'd gone away. I don't want you to go away, I want you to stay with me till—what's the matter, Minna?" Then, "My dear!" he said, "my dear—"

"I've got to go—a few minutes," she said. "I promised I'd help Frau Krückel—not very long—" She took his right hand, where the inside of the thumb and forefinger was bitten away with sores, and kissed it, and put it back under the overcoat. "Not very long!" she repeated.

She wouldn't talk about the book and the experiments again, it was a worry to Beloved. She had meant to show him the book, and how she had done it up in grease-proof paper, and the photographs which Doctor Dittmer had given her to show how well her chest had got. But she wouldn't do that now, not just yet. She understood why those things troubled him, she had seen it in his eyes: he could only think how the pricks had hurt her, and how he had meant her to die if the experiment didn't work all right. She understood that, she understood it clearly: and the pain she had seen in him was repeated in herself as his coughing was always repeated, and the twisting cut of it was sharper than any pain of her own.

There were shirts and things of Oskar's still to go on the line, she would have to shift all Willi's things to get room for them. It made her giddy, this stretching up, it made her feel as if an iron hoop were gradually tightening beneath her breasts. But the five minutes' rest had put back a little of her strength, she thought she could just get it done.

The great trees which had sauntered past all morning were far behind them now, leaving the foreground bare: a steady wave of reddish earth, green-combed, a quilted petticoat of sad and flippant greens draped out from the nine-papped hills. The river turned, feeling its path to westward, the naked sun coming round against her eyes washed all the colour into feebleness and a squad of silos stood like hellish sentry-huts with a fog of light behind. That alteration brought into her face a wind still prickly from April frosts but smelling faintly now of wakened earth, strange but already known, the smell of coming out of school one late afternoon in Easter term. She had been sturdy then, she had beaten Else Strauss in a race to the pump. And now the weakness tethering her seemed separate from her body, a passing inconvenience, while she herself was changeless, sharing at once the tireless power of the barge, vigour of tranquil earth, unearthliness of shaggy hillsides carried on wind and light. Remembering the laggard march of hours in Handelstrasse, the stifling load of feebleness she had carried there, she seemed already to have won her resurrection. Her reason, whispering, said the journey had just begun: this time of quietude was leaking out with every hiccough of the *Weimar's* engine, Josef was not yet free, he was only moved into a larger cage; and though he belonged to her to-day, as a child belongs, this Josef was not the man she hungered for, he was only the child who would grow into him. So: it was enough, she thought, to have him as her

child; enough for to-day's contentment. The ruined city lay
in siege, the enemy had first to be driven off and then by
stone on stone the houses would have to be rebuilt. It will
take a little time, she thought, it may take all summer and
the winter following, it is a good thing that I have grown so
strong.

For a moment the iron hoop about her body bit more
fiercely; her breathing had grown quick and shallow, and
when she glanced at her hands she saw they were entirely
white. With the vague smile which showed all her mouth
like a ruined churchyard Frau Krückel came to her side,
bearing another basket. "These too, my sweet, if you will be
so kind . . . To-morrow, Oskar says, to-morrow night we
ought to reach Bad Fels. Bad Fels, you know—wonderful
shops there. I'll buy a honey-stick for Willi . . ." But
Minna couldn't stretch to hang up anything more just now.
She begged a cigarette from Oskar and went into the cabin
to smoke it, the cigarette went out, she lay back on Frau
Krückel's berth and shut her eyes, feeling pleasantly the current of tingling warmth which she supposed to come from
the stove. It was stuffy here, with the odour of laundry over-
laying the habitual smells. She would have liked to go forward and lie where Josef was, but her legs would not do that
just yet. Willi pulled himself up by her skirts and knelt
across her stomach, dribbling apathetically on to her neck.
"He is fond of you, the little one!" Frau Krückel said.

When she overcame the feeling of sickness and went
back to Josef the river had bent again; with a ten-mile wall
of basalt cliff blocking its westward course it had turned
north-easterly, and the sun, still bare and lower now, put all
the land ahead into unnatural definition, limpid, as if Corot
had coloured over a Dürer engraving. The breeze falling
into the barge's wake left an illusion of stillness, the rustle
of the bow wave as it felt along the nearer bank was quiet
and constant like a silence. From a day's full light the sliding

fields seemed to breathe more warmly, smelling of summer, all the horizons had drawn closer now, the small and homely hills sat arm in arm at shepherd's-call from the approaching bend. This shrinking and that vividness confused the eyes' mensuration. A cottage seen so clearly and so small must have its roof at shoulder height; the farmstead creeping out from behind the tackle-house would be a model for a child, made very realistically with a tiny haywain and with little cows to match. And as the farm drew near, and the gabled dairy passed so close to the *Weimar's* gunwale that it seemed within arm's reach, it kept its unreality. They were like the image in a telescope: the wooden bridge that joined the steading to an avenue of limes, the railway track sidling through young corn, a church's steeple guarded by its daughter-spires: they belonged to a country close but separate, as if she stood apart from it in time as well as space.

The road which had broken through the hills came gingerly towards the river, skirting the barley fields, hiding behind a larch coppice, from which it suddenly emerged to become one with the embankment. It followed faithfully at the river's turn, squeezing beside the top-heavy post-house, and now there were children riding home from school, an old man on a rusty tricycle, and the squat thatched houses closed their ranks until they hid the meadows behind. The houses grew towards an urban dignity, narrow and high-bonnetted, each patterned storey a brow to the one beneath; the wooden balustrade along the embankment changed to a wrought-iron fence, and a tradesman's van, brilliant in yellow paint, came bouncing over the cobblestones. They passed below the bridge, where a sandstone pier was spread like a waiter's hand to hold a wooden toll-house; the sudden whiff of motor-cars brought the engine-hand from his lair in the bows, Frau Krückel threw out a line and the *Weimar* came to rest with her fenders nudging the landing-steps. "A crate of hens for Walter Heimbach—a crate of hens from his

uncle!" "All right, I'll try and find him!" The porter standing on the steps saluted, he bowed to Frau Krückel and the
child holding his hand waved her handkerchief. The people
taking their evening stroll along the quay stopped to gaze
at the panting barge, a soldier with a girl on his arm, an old
woman encircled by tiny dogs, they smiled and blew kisses
to Willi, they called to Frau Krückel that he was a sonsy
boy. The shadow of the toll-house lay along the barge, the
street beside them was in yellow sunshine; you had said the
sunshine must be permanent in this quiet town, where every
one was very old or very young, that the fall of shadow was
as constant as the finialled gables. Where the river wall
bulged out to make a landing stage the Kaffee Schaale had
set three tables, the Burgermeister and his wife were sitting
there in their motoring clothes with the little manager of the
Mannheim Bank and his two enormous sisters, the sun lit
brilliantly their grave, contented smiles. They nodded pleasantly to the engine-hand, they raised their glasses towards
the toll-house window, where an aged military man sat
smoking in his crimson skull-cap with a solemn pigtailed
child on either side.

"That man over there, is that a policeman?"

"No, beloved, that's just an ordinary man."

His hands were cold, she pushed them back beneath the
overcoat and drew it up about his ears. She said, "It's quite
all right, beloved!" and she thought it was quite all right.
The sun held all the quay in a peculiar stillness, the street
smelt homely of new bread and harness, nothing could hurt
them in this quiet town.

"Herr Heimbach, here he comes!" and the little crowd
drew back. Herr Heimbach with his wife and two small sons
came proudly down the steps, Frau Krückel carrying one
end of the crate made a little curtsey to Frau Heimbach,
Oskar saluted in the military style and the men shook hands.
"A good voyage, Herr Krückel?" "So far—an excellent

voyage!" "And we left your uncle very well," Frau Krückel said. "The little brown bird is called Susanne," Oskar explained, "she is delicate, your uncle says. I told him I could accept no responsibility." Frau Heimbach had a stick of barley-sugar for Willi, a woollen scarf for Frau Krückel and an old penknife for the engine-hand, between them they all bundled the hen-crate up to the quay and the ladies sat on it there. Herr Heimbach paid for glasses of Pilsner to be sent across from the Kaffee Schaale.

"Frau Freyberg, aren't you coming?" Frau Krückel shouted. "Aren't you going to join us in a drink?"

But Minna would not leave Josef alone.

"Her husband is sick," Frau Krückel said, "he coughs a great deal at night." So young Franz Heimbach was sent to get a bottle of Giebel's Mixture from the chemist, and the lookers-on, overhearing that a poor woman with a sick husband was aboard, moved innocently along the quay to get a better view. There was not much to see: the top of a young man's head, the rest of him covered with an overcoat, and a pale girl in a shoddy dress who stared at them with sullen defiance. But a grey, lopsided woman suddenly took off her victorine, leant over and threw it down to the barge. "For you, my dear—that dress isn't warm enough." There were sounds of coins clinking, and presently Herr Ratzel the watchmaker came shyly to the waterside. "A few of my fellow-townsmen would like to make you a little gift—a little memento of Neubeck-am-Dieler—something towards your husband's medical requirements . . ."

It was growing dark when they got under way, the street-lamps began to cast their own pale dawns along the roadway. A window here and there was lit in the narrow houses crowding the Old Quay, to show a row of heads bent over a yellow tablecloth while papa said Grace, a woman undressing her child for bed. A boy sitting astride the last bollard waved his handkerchief, the lights behind were drawn together, the last fretful bleat of a motor horn was smothered by the *Weimar's* engine. Clear of the town the breeze came sharper, they had left the young summer behind. "Supper!" Frau Krückel called. That gentle place had only been a twist of the passing unreality, the *Weimar's* sides were the borders of Minna's world again. Josef had fallen asleep, she was quite alone.

Josef was warm under the overcoat, with the victorine round his ears. She wouldn't wake him and take him in just yet, she wasn't ready for the close light of the cabin and Frau Krückel's villous horizontal voice.

It is Josef sleeping here. It is too dark to see his face now, but it's Josef's shoulder pressing and hurting my arm and the warm breath coming into my face has Josef's smell. The cough has been hurting him all afternoon, the jagged, inside cough, making him cross and tired with me, poor Josef. It's good that he is sleeping now.

But she wanted him to wake again, she was always impatient when he slept. When Josef slept he went away from her, not to the country of her own feverish sleep but to some cold place she did not know, where sometimes he would shrink away from her touch and at times cry out at her with blasphemous abuse. Then it was hard to wait for his return, enduring the fear that he was finally lost. The cord that held him to her was of several pieces tied together with clumsy knots; at some time when he wandered far away one of the knots might give.

And now the passing of that small town had left her lonely. There she had seen a place she might have belonged to, faces she might have come to know. She had heard along the quay the carol of laughter, which sounded seldom in Handelstrasse and seldom in the Moltke Hospital, she had heard a man's soft voice say, 'Liebling!' and a young girl's voice, 'Du bist mir immer so grossmütig!' Those were of her own sort, the people gathering the evening sun a yard or two from where she had stood, their rustling voices sounded of low warm rooms in modest streets. So easy, to have stepped across to the landing stairs and been among them for a while. The woman who'd given her the fur would have offered some work perhaps; she was kind, that old woman, she would have let Minna rest when she was giddy and feeble in the legs. Perhaps she lived in one of the old houses facing the quay, where you could watch the barges passing from your window, perhaps her husband was grave and gentle like Herr Rupf and they had gentle, humorous children. And Josef? They would have found some place for him, they must surely have left him in peace till he was well again.

That was evasion: for the thoughts which huddle and gossip in the mind's shadowed border were murmuring that Josef would not get well. The picture her mind had kept of Josef standing beside her bed had already grown feeble, overlaid by the limp, numb creature who would lie and follow her movements like a baby following a candle flame. And as he had ceased to care about the work which had once possessed him, so he seemed to have lost all interest in his own existence. The summer they would spend in Giessbach had come no nearer, it was more remote. The vessel she carried off was badly broken, before she brought it to safety the fluid might have leaked away.

And yet to rescue him was her necessity: not out of pity for something broken and thrown aside, nor yet for the memory of his tenderness. Her mind when it was sleepy and fluid could paint a whole new life for her, a quiet room in a house with newly painted shutters, bedroom slippers lined with fur, some one to help with the washing-up and the whole of Sunday free. The vision soared romantically, gathering friendships and vast achievement, her photograph in the magazines. But always Josef was there, Josef waiting for her on her free afternoon, Josef coming first to praise her success. And now the colours of the panorama had grown too feeble, she saw its grandeur as touring scenery stacked in daylight against a theatre wall, and only Josef was left. So little of him. But a movement of his lips in the way he had used to smile, the unconscious carefulness with which he pulled the overcoat to cover her shoulder as they lay together, these like the glow of light in tiny valves betrayed the goodness he had kept for her. For her, because she knew that she had first awaked it. That part of him, unique and powerful, belonged to her like the pulse of her own heart; and the glory of it was that it belonged to him.

"We're tying up at Zappeln," the engine-hand said as he went forward. The light of his lamp fell on Josef's face, ugly in sleep, with the broken lips apart and a stream of phlegm all down his cheek. She whispered, "Josef, it's time for supper!" but he didn't stir. In the tightening darkness the trees went past like chariots and horsemen. It was cold now.

She felt like fever in the blood a boiling spring of gratitude: to the people of Neubeck for their kindness, to Frau Rupf and Dr. Kunig and the nurses at the Hospital, to Fräulein Rother and God. In all these months she had lain useless and still, people had tended her, people had helped her plans. She had taken something from them all, and the kindness she would have given back lay stored and waiting for release. The face of a hunchback woman cleaning out the Moltke chalets, the whimper of a tired child in the Siemenstrasse, these returning like the notes of an old tune became a cloud of hungry eyes and pleading voices, these were an empty sea which the river of her charity could never fill. But the gates were shut against that outlet and the sluices locked. Here men had broken what she loved, here they would steal and crush the little they had left of him; and till she was free of those, the power and stench of them, her stream was fastened by a thin, steel wall of anger. So, it must go to Josef himself, the whole of her gratefulness, the power for loving she had gathered in so many lonely days, her pity and her hunger. And surely there is room, she thought, surely now that he has lost so much there's room for him to take it all.

Be patient, God, and let him stay with me, don't let yourself be jealous of Josef, don't let him be hurt still more because I love him so much. Josef has taken so much pain, his hands are all torn, he's frightened and his back's so sore, the cough hardly ever lets him sleep. You don't care what his cough is like, it's like a squirrel twisting in your chest and biting with jagged teeth. Josef was giving all himself to take the cough away from other people, that's what he was doing when they came to hurt him, he'd go on doing that if he got strong again. Surely you can see the goodness he has, surely you know how much more use a man is than a girl. You've given me so much, the sun coming on my bed in the morning, the laughing I had out of Dr. Vollmuth's face and the little fat child that waved to me at Neubeck, I don't want anything more, I only want you to take it away and give it to Josef. Oh God it hurts me to have such a load of happiness and strength, it's like a fountain that has caught alight, I can't hold it back any more and I can't find the way to let it out. Josef is part of me, Josef's the only part that's any use, take all my strength away oh God oh Christ take all my love and mix it with your own and pour it into him.

46

NOISE came into her sleep like thunder, she turned and saw through a hole in the door a great beast thundering towards her with flaming eyes. It passed overhead, the red glow from its belly lit a spider's web of girders. When the smoke cleared there was only a small, red light in the tangle of steel, the clatter of wheels left a vacuum in which the husky voice of Oskar Krückel said, "Well, how was I to know?"

She went outside and along the narrow deck to where Oskar stood with his lamp. It was raining. The man beside Oskar was like a figure in a tailor's window, a little officer like a girl in breeches was standing stiffly behind him. "Well then, let me see their papers!" the big officer said.

The train had left the air full of its smell. Like a huge loaf not quite risen Frau Krückel hovered at the light's edge. "If the Herr Kapitän will come inside, I can have some coffee ready in half a minute—"

"This is her," Oskar said, "this is the woman I told you of, the one that brought him aboard."

The officer turned to look into Minna's face. His head was high over hers, she saw above the glow of his cigar a close moustache, eyes like water seen far down in a well. "You've got Zeppichmann?" he said, "Josef Zeppichmann?"

"I got him? No."

"But he's aboard?"

"You mean the Jew man? He got off at Zappeln."

Oskar caught her by the arm. "You didn't tell me! Why didn't you tell me?"

"It was nothing to do with me."

"But you brought him on board. You said—"

"I didn't. The Jew was hiding up in the front, where you've got all those barrels—"

"Langer!" the officer said. "Go and phone through to Zappeln. Make it lively!"

"Very good, sir!"

"You won't find him," Minna said. "He was quick, that man." She felt for a cigarette of Oskar's that she had in her stocking. "A match, if you please!" Absently the officer gave her one. "Thank-you!" She turned and went back to the tackle-house.

Josef was awake.

"Minna! Is that Minna? Where is it? Where have I got to?"

"I don't know, I think it must be Bad Fels."

"Bad Fels?"

"Yes. Go to sleep, beloved, go to sleep, I don't want you to talk now."

"Why can't I talk?"

"I'll tell you later on. Go to sleep now!"

"Minna! I heard some one talking. Some one out there. Who was that?"

"I don't know. Oh, it was only some men. You must go to sleep now."

She would sleep herself, she was heavy and aching with sleep. But here the night was busy with noise, the draught through the broken door felt thick and stale. Here their bedroom was part of the sleepless town, the boards above her seemed to throb as a long train plodded over the bridge, the voices trickled on in the following silence. ". . . a Jew like Oskar said, but I said I thought he wasn't a Jew, seeing what it said on their papers. Oskar and I of course we always want to do what's right . . ." "I'll have a look for myself!" the officer said.

She met him outside the door. She said, "I wish you'd

find somewhere else to go if you've got to keep on talking. I'm trying to get some sleep."

He said: "You've got a man in there."

She nodded. "My husband's in there. He's ill, he's not to be disturbed."

"Ill? What's the matter with him?"

"I think it's smallpox."

"I think you're a liar."

He pushed her aside and opened the door. He called back, "Here, you, bargemaster, I want that lamp!"

"All right!" she said. "Only don't blame me if you get a bug in your belly!"

He hesitated then. Some one was coming across the quay, and he shouted, "Is that you, Langer? Buck up! You've put that call through? Good! Here, give me a hand!" He climbed over to the quay, and she caught the words ". . . sending a doctor down . . . till you hear what he says." She called, "You may as well send a proper doctor while you're about it, I don't want any boosy vet!" and went inside again.

Josef was sitting up. She found his hand and felt him shaking like the floor of a factory. She said, "It's all right, Josef, it's all right, he's gone away now, the big man's gone away!" He didn't answer. The trembling gradually subsided, she thought he was falling asleep again; but when she tried to settle him with his head on her shoulder he pulled away. "What is it, beloved, what's the matter?"

"My shoes, I want my shoes!"

"Your shoes? Not now, it's not time to get up yet."

"I want my shoes!" he repeated.

The sound of his breathing, a stiffness in the leg that was pressed against her side, made him as clear to her as if she could see his face. He had shown this mood sometimes when he knelt by her bed writing up his notes, fiercely preoccupied. And now he had found one of his shoes and was trying to put it on, catching his breath with the pain it gave him to bend over.

"Josef! Beloved!"

He said, as a stranger would, "I'm going now. I'll find that man, he may as well have me."

"Josef!"

"You're to stay here!" he said. "You understand?—you're to stay here. You must say you're nothing to do with me, you didn't know who I was."

But finding his other shoe she had pushed it behind the oil drums which made a wall to their bed; and he was still hunting when a storm of coughing came, to leave him breathless and exhausted. She was master of him then, he lay across her thighs as limply as a dead bird. She whispered:

"Josef! Josef, beloved, it's all right. We'll talk about that to-morrow, you mustn't worry yourself."

The after-quake died off; he was still awake, she thought, but the cords between mind and body were slack. Afraid of his escaping, she pulled a piece of wool from his jersey and tied it into her hair. She must sleep herself now, she must gather a fresh bodyful of strength before the doctor came. But her shoulders were cramped in that position and she couldn't move without disturbing Josef. Over on the quay a single lamp above the Herrenklosett showed dully the shape of the little officer, rigid and watchful.

A new idea was shaped in her drowsiness. The stuff that Josef had used to make her better, surely it could take away Josef's cough as well. It was all in Josef's book, she supposed, how to make it and how to put it in; she had only got to show the doctor Josef's book . . . "Josef, are you awake? Josef, when the doctor comes I thought I could show him your book. Your book, you know, about the stuff you put in my arm, the book with all your notes. Josef! Josef, are you awake?" The shape of the little officer rose and fell in the subfusc light, rose and fell, the water must have got under the quay, the quay rising and falling on gentle waves. The sky was thundering again, stirring the brown hot waters in her throat, they had got a piece of wood screwed on to her back and were trying to break her spine. When the light drove at her face she knew the doctor had come, but she thought it was Doctor Vollmuth. She tried to get up and felt a violent tug at her hair.

"One minute, Herr Doktor, excuse me please, it's my hair, I've tied it to Josef's jersey."

"Tied it to his jersey?"

"I didn't want him to fall off the barge. You're to shut the door, please, it's cold outside, Josef mustn't be cold."

He obeyed the sharp command, put his bag down on the floor and looked for kneeling space. He was tall and mighty-bellied, there was hardly space for the three of them in this small room.

"A man with smallpox, is that right?"

"Yes, Herr Doktor, smallpox, he got it from a bad drain in Hartzinnfeld. It's mostly on his legs." She was planning to jog the arm in which he held his torch, but realised now she was coming awake that a doctor couldn't be tricked for long. "Or it might be T.B.—that's what I used to have."

A lone engine ambled over the bridge and stood fussing like an angry nursemaid above the wharfmaster's office, the oily breath of it drifting into the tackle-house thickened the smell of cigarettes and sleep. With his shoulder jammed against the wall, a floor-bolt sticking into his knee, the doctor tried to turn Josef over. "Here, let's have a look at you!" He was tired and he had a headache, babies two nights running, hospital Board to-morrow at nine. "You, Fräulein, please hold the torch a minute." But he knew almost before he had looked: with this breadth of shoulder a fellow should weigh not less than eighty kilograms, and there was hardly fifty here. Then he saw the caved eyes and cyanosed lips. "What do you mean?" he shouted to Minna through the hushing of the engine, "what were you talking about—smallpox!" The young man had got hold of his arm and was trying to say something. "What's that?" the doctor bawled, "I can't hear you!" The girl was shouting in his ear, "—Must you keep kneeling on my arm!"

With a final stertorous violence the engine pulled away, and then Josef was coughing: the monotonous, grumbling cough that might go on for twenty minutes. The doctor, losing patience, said, "I'll have to get this man up to the hospital, he must have a proper examination." Minna said no, he was not to go to the hospital. She was fumbling with a parcel she had pulled out from under the palliasse. "Listen, Herr Doktor, I want you to give him treatment here, I've got twenty-five Marks, I can give you that in cash." She pushed a soiled exercise book in front of his face. "It's all in this book, the stuff you ought to put in for T.B., it's what Josef found out himself. It's some stuff you have to put in his arm." Josef stopped coughing. "Give me that!" he snapped. "Give it me, Minna! No one in Germany's going to see that book!"

Minna returned the book to its brown paper and started to tie it up again. Josef was right, nobody here was fit to know about his stuff. And now she was glad, for it meant he had not given up. Suddenly her objective was magnified: Josef and his book, she would get them both out of the country as she planned long ago, then Josef would start to work again . . . "Well then, we shan't need you any more!" she said to the doctor. "Thank you very much!"

That accorded with the doctor's own thoughts. His practice had been varied, but he was unused to working on his hands and knees in a dark rabbit-hutch, surrounded by rods and ropes, infectious sputum and unbalanced bohemians. He said laconically: "Yes, I think I can make my report now . . . Oh, your name, by the way?"

Minna said: "Our name is Freyberg, F-R—"

"Zeppichmann!" Josef said distinctly. "My name is Josef Zeppichmann, I'm the person they're looking for, this girl is nothing to do with me."

The night had fallen into stillness. The little officer was still at attention, perhaps twenty paces away.

The doctor smiled faintly: in the reflected light of the torch Minna saw his smile. "It was not very hard to guess that!" he said. "It's a pity, isn't it, a great pity!"

And indeed, he was so much moved that a spring of phlegm, comfortingly warm, had started in his throat and nose. The young Jew was plainly of a coarse type, and too much wasted in physique to be of the slightest use to any one; but the girl, she was ill too, and there was something rather emotion-stirring in the way she tried to protect him. The doctor was fond of young children, and in her helpless eagerness there was something to remind him of his beloved grandchild Käthe. But he was a patriot also; and this little triumph would show these new officials that a man nearing sixty-eight could still do service to his country. "I am really very sorry!" he said, and tried to open the door. But the door seemed to be stuck.

Minna said rapidly: "Listen, please, Herr Doktor, listen please! It's very important for Josef to get out of Germany, it's very important, do you understand! He's a doctor himself, you see, he understands about T.B., he made me quite all right when I had T.B. You can understand, you being a doctor—"

"I understand my duty to the state!" he said. "Will you please let go this door!"

She moved her hand, but only to catch hold of his thumb. Her nails were long.

"You don't even want to know why they put him in prison?" she said. "His being a doctor like you doesn't make any difference?"

Josef said hoarsely: "Leave him alone, Minna! Let him go!"

"No, I don't want to know!" the doctor said.

Minna let go his thumb. She whispered:

"All right, go on! Go on, you grinning toad, get out of here, go and tell them what you like! Tell them what a bold man you are to catch a dangerous chap like him, tell them how clever you were to know it wasn't smallpox. No, tell them you've cured him, tell them what a fine doctor you are as well as a bloody spy! Go on, go and snivel to them!"

He went back along the narrow deck as if it were a tightrope, holding firmly to the little rail. It seemed, as Minna watched him, to take a long time. From the Krückels' room came the noise of Willi tirelessly wailing, it covered the doctor's steps so that he seemed to tread soundlessly, a solid shadow large and faintly ludicrous with a shallow hat squashed on to the big head, the feet fumbling across the gang-plank, body doubled with the weight of the tiny bag. Minna called suddenly, "Wait! I'll carry your case for you!" and went after him along the deck. But her body was in its lazy mood, it wouldn't go fast. He didn't even look round, he went straight on to the little officer.

She got as far as the gang-plank and had to sit down there; sit still and watch the two shadows against the Herrenklosett. It was cold, sitting there. Willi's wailing came to a pause as he gathered breath for a new attack, she listened intently and caught the doctor's voice.

". . . perhaps infectious, yes, but nothing so very serious. I'll look at him again in the morning. You understand, of course, that I'm not taking any responsibility . . . Good heavens, no!—he's as good a German as I am. Comes from Hamburg, a family I happen to know. No, I haven't any doubt, not the smallest doubt—though of course I can't take any responsibility . . ."

47

"MINNA! Minna, are you awake? The book, the book with all my notes, what have you done with my book?"

"I don't remember. I'm sleepy, beloved, I don't remember. Yes, it's in the parcel, the brown parcel."

"This parcel?"

"I expect so."

"Minna, listen! Listen, dear one! You'll be sure to look after it, you'll look after my book? You'll do that, won't you?—give it to the foreign doctors. That's all that matters, you see—all that work I did. It's right, you see, they ought to go on with that. Minna, are you awake? Listen! You needn't tell them it was me, don't tell them it was me who did all that. They'd say it wasn't any use, they'd say a Jew couldn't think of anything to do people any good."

"All right, Josef. I'll do all that. Only I'm sleepy now."

"It doesn't matter about me, you see. You won't be able to get me out, they won't let you. You mustn't mind about that. Dear one, you mustn't mind about me."

"Where's your hand? Give me your hand, beloved, let me kiss it, let me kiss the sore place!"

"Dear one, you understand? It's what Herr Dahlmeyer says."

"I don't know who that is. I'm sleepy, beloved."

"Herr Dahlmeyer, you must remember him! I saw him—no, I forget, I don't know what's happened to him. Herr Dahlmeyer says we mustn't let them get it. They'll smash it up, Herr Dahlmeyer says."

"I won't let them spoil it, beloved, I won't let them spoil your book."

"It's what's in the book, that's what he meant. All the figures and things, they'd be angry with the figures being right, they'd make people think it was all wrong. Herr Dahlmeyer, he told me about that. It doesn't matter about me, only you mustn't let them steal the book."

"Darling Josef, I'm so sleepy now!"

"Poor Minna! Wait, I'll put something under your head. Isn't that how you like it?"

"Darling Josef!"

"You, you're so good! So good!"

It was all right if Josef thought she was good. And she sank again into the warm still waters, where her body was light and charged with force, her understanding clear and strong. Here she could care for Josef as he should be cared for, here she had dignity to guard him. "No, I am sorry, the Gräfin must come another time; my husband can't see any patients to-day, he is busy with important research . . . Yes, Josef, I understand, I won't let the children disturb you, I'll take them all out for a walk. We'll go for a walk up into the hills, the high hills over Giessbach, we'll take our dinner up there and sit and look down over the lake." The things about her now were all familiar, a soldier's sleeve and his fingers in her hair, Fräulein Rother's voice and an old quilt smelling of cheese, the taste of peppermint and a door's long whine and snow on a broken window-sill. Here the sun was always at early evening, and the wind like a man's cool hand on your forehead, the wind scented with bracken and turf, the wind's voice through the furze like the breathing of a child in sleep. Here anxiety was only a stream across the road, cold at the feet's first touch; they were all at her command here, the spreading officers and the pale lawyers in their pince-nez, the crackling coifs of nurses, doctors with delving melancholy eyes. Something was still to do: ahead the hoar-toothed mountains stood blue and sheer from the valley's edge, the next day's march would bring her against that wall. But her lungs were stored with the resinous wind and her legs like vaulting pistons, however lustily Josef climbed and fought she would not be lagging behind. The air was still, a little cooler now, and the birds' chatter fell to quietness. The mist gathering from the hills was close and sweet like chloroform, like many satin curtains sweeping down it wrapped her into shade.

The darkness grew so tight that she was suddenly alarmed. She cried out, "Josef!" and he caught her by the hand. Yes, he was always there.

Awake, she felt her feebleness return, the sickness in her throat that would not be satisfied. She could carry her power to the very surface of sleep, but there it slipped behind; the current was at hand to bring her body into trenchant life, she had only lost the switch to turn it on.

Perhaps she had gone back a little way: to-day her eyes were not so clear, the distant view was hazed, objects close at hand unnaturally magnified. But it was better not to grow well too soon, for then she might forget how Josef felt. She watched him now as he sat on the oil drums, his swelled, retracted eyes intent and serious, the scarred hands fumbling for a pocket that wasn't there; and felt new gratitude that he was ill like her. In Handelstrasse the boundary had always stood between them, that he had power to come and go while she lay invalid. There she had loved the touch of his hands and his forehead rumpling over things that puzzled him, while his very self stayed far beyond her tallest reach; and now, with his body shrunk and his breathing always caught by a little pain, the barrier was down. Her pride in him stayed fast, but he had come within her own humility.

"Josef, beloved, wait! Wait a little, I'll get you your coffee soon!"

But he pointed and the two cups were already there, on the floor beside her.

In the narrow circle which she saw distinctly there were always faces, a new face each time she opened her eyes: the face of Willi and of Oskar, and now some doctor's face, a spread of loose, tired flesh with features too small to fill it, not Dr. Vollmuth but some doctor who had come into her dreams. "I should advise you to go to Doctor Reuther—when you get to Zurbergen—Doctor Reuther, he's the man who'd understand this person's case." He spoke almost in a whisper, the muscles of his eyes twitched in the difficult light, his lips were damp with nervousness. "I say that quite unofficially, you're not to mention me—Doctor Reuther, he's a friend of mine, but you're not to mention my name." She looked again and he had vanished, and now it was the pinched and stolid face of the engine-hand, the root of a cigarette on his drooping lips, the wandering oil-rimmed eyes detached and friendly. "You won't get him past the Revenue, not sick like that, they won't let anything past that's sick." He turned and spat across the deck, he grinned in his stupid way. "I'm sorry, but that's the way of it, they'll stop you at Zurbergen." She heard him whistling along the deck, and now the shape of the railway bridge had melted away, and the engine was grumbling again.

"I'll think of an idea," she said. "I'm tired now, I'll think of something later on."

The drizzle starting at Bad Fels had grown to a steady rain, it followed at the *Weimar's* side with the noise of escaping steam. Behind that slanted curtain the trees were sprawling shapes, petroleum tanks and cable standards passed like smears on a frosted glass. "At Zurbergen you'll have to see the Revenue, they come aboard at Zurbergen." The face of Oskar stayed for a long time, eyes inquisitive and anxious. Darkness came like a grey dye into the screen of rain.

"I've got an idea now. Listen, Josef, I've got an idea!"

But his breathing was thick and steady in the darkness, he seemed to be asleep. Frau Krückel came with bowls of soup and asked if she was ill. "No no, I used to be ill but I'm all right now, it's only a sort of giddiness in my throat. Please, Frau Krückel, I want some plaster, some plaster like you put on Willi's sore place, and something I can tear into bandages." Frau Krückel stretched her maternal eyes and scratched her moustache and grinned. "You must have your supper straight away, you mustn't let it get cold."

Daylight brought her a burst of strength, she was able to kneel up and do the bandaging. "You see, Josef, you've had an accident—that's what I'll tell the Revenue. You're not ill at all, not infectious I mean, you've only had an accident. It was in Bad Fels, you went for a walk round the town and a motor knocked you over."

He said vaguely: "I don't remember that, I don't remember any motor. I fell down some steps, I think it was at Sondersumpf, I remember I fell down some steps."

"Yes, you fell down some steps, and afterwards you were knocked over by a motor-car. Keep still, Josef, keep quite still, I'm going to put this right across your face."

"But I don't remember being knocked down."

"It doesn't matter. You've only got to say the same as me. You were knocked over by a motor-car."

He laughed then. And she could not remember his ever laughing before. He said, "You're so funny, Minna!" and repeated, "I was knocked over by a motor-car."

Then she was happy, remembering that Josef had laughed with her, forgetting that this time must soon be finished. It had become their own, this small place where you couldn't stand upright, their odds and ends were strewn all over it, some odour of their attic room had crept into the smell of paraffin. The engine's stammer was a settled part of their life now, like the noise of dragged shingle to those who live against the sea; lumps in the palliasse, nails that caught their clothes, were only the awkward turns you have in a long-loved house. And now, listening to Josef's incessant cough, she knew that any place was complete when he was there. His silences, head clamped and eyes staring at nothing; the patience of his ruined fingers fumbling at a shoe-lace, the sudden despair with which he gave the shoe to her; these with his gauche, spasmodic tenderness made up a country that was large enough for her to live in, she understood its weather and the curving of its lanes, these low colours were sufficient for the narrow prospect with her own sun warming them.

"There's still some of the stuff they got us at Neubeck. Would you like some more of that?"

"No, it's no good. These medicines, they only make them for money."

"Is it hurting now, that cough?"

"A bit."

"Is it like a piece of blue serge being pulled over where you breathe?"

"Yes, it's just like that."

"I know, it felt like that till you put in your stuff. Till the third or fourth time—it was different after that, after that it was only like a little hammer with a cushion underneath . . . I'll get a doctor at Zurbergen—at Zurbergen when we get to the Dutch side. I could show him your book."

"No, Minna, no, you mustn't show it anybody! Not till we're further away. They'd get it somehow, these people. It doesn't matter about me, it's only the book."

"It's all right, I won't show it anybody unless you say."

The rain's warp was closer again, smothering the lee bank, its noise on the roof hid every distant sound. In that eclipse the barge's motion seemed to have petered out, the day itself kept still. She thought, drowsy with the pain which had kicked behind her eyes all morning, There's no more fighting to be done, the people here are kind and we shall stay with them, nothing will alter now. There was sewing to do, a new hole in Josef's pocket and a scarlet ribbon of Frau Krückel's to go on the green hat, but she would leave it all till her eyes were steady. She would sit still now, with her back against Josef's thighs, and think how it would be when they got to Giessbach. To Giessbach: surely they could go there soon, surely no one could interfere if they promised to live quietly there! That was in the country they belonged to, Josef and she could do no harm in a little town like that.

She realised first that the engine's pulse had slacked, afterwards that the light was dull. A smell of brewery had grown about them.

"It's the Officer to see you, the Officer wants to ask about your papers": Oskar's voice.

The new face showing in the doorway was pleasant and well-kept and a little bored, the face of a celebrity admiring a new housing-scheme.

"You are Frau Freyberg?"

"Yes, and I've got a very bad headache. Perhaps you could come another time. You'll find us here any time, my husband and I."

"The Officer is very busy," Oskar said. "He's got hundreds of boats to inspect."

"And that is your husband?" the Officer asked. "I'd like to see his face without those bandages."

"I'm sorry, but the doctor said they weren't to be touched."

"The doctor?"

"The police doctor at Bad Fels. That's right, isn't it, Herr Krückel?"

Oskar said: "I don't know, I don't know about the bandages. There was a doctor at Bad Fels, yes, the Police Commissioner sent a doctor, he came twice."

"This photograph of your husband, how long ago was that taken?" the Officer asked.

"I don't remember. Oh yes, it was that day I left the gas on under a saucepan and it burnt the bottom off."

"And that would be, speaking more precisely—?"

"Oh, a month ago, I should think. It was that very old photographer in the Siemenstrasse."

"Yes yes, quite so—I see he was not a very good photographer."

"He's all right when he isn't drunk. When he's drunk he gets the distance wrong. I've got a photo of the inside of my chest, do you want to see that?"

"Well, no, not just now." He turned to Josef. "That is your signature, under the date-stamp?"

Minna said: "Yes, that's his signature."

But he wasn't listening to her. He said to Josef: "Will you sign your name, please, on this piece of paper!"

"He can't," Minna said, "he had an accident when he was under a motor-car, I had to bandage his hand."

"I thought you said the doctor bandaged him?"

"Yes, he said my bandage was all wrong, it let all the blood out."

"That's right," Josef said abruptly. "She's no good at bandaging."

With his eyes fixed on the papers, the Officer suddenly asked: "Where were you born?"

Josef said: "At Richterhausen."

"But it says here you were born in Hamburg."

"He doesn't remember!" Minna said. "He's ill, you see, after being underneath the motor. No one ever remembers being born."

The Officer put a finger on his chin. "You," he said to Oskar, "go and tell the corporal I want him!" He turned to Minna again, and said with a terrible gentleness, "I'm afraid we shall have to go into this a little further."

That smile of his, it reminded her of some one. Yes, it was Herr Meisel's smile. She shut her eyes and saw Herr Meisel's face, saw him standing at the door of Josef's room. And then Frau Rupf, Frau Rupf with her teeth deep in her lower lip as she sat at her little table writing to the police lawyer; her small, sandy voice: "There's only one way of dealing with these liars, you've got to think of a better lie . . ." If the pain in her head would only stop, if the man would only go away, just five minutes!

"It occurs to me," he was saying, "that these papers don't refer to you at all. I'm right, am I not?"

Josef said: "You'd better tell him, Minna."

"Yes," she said, "you're quite right, they're not the right papers at all."

The Officer nodded sagely. He was of nice breeding, he gave the impression that it was rather the regular course than otherwise to travel with false papers. He brought out a little book.

"And just why were you trying to get out of the country with passports that don't belong to you?"

She said haltingly: "Well, you see, we are in love, him and me."

"Indeed? But then, one can be in love in this country, can one not?"

"No," she said resolutely, "no, you can't."

"And—why not?"

"Well, you see, they'd have put him in prison."

"In prison? Why was that?"

"Well, you see, there was a man who wanted his room. He'd got a nice room—that was in Frau Spühler's house— he'd got a nice room and the other man wanted it, the other man was rich and he said he'd pay more and he ought to have it."

"But we don't put a man in prison because some one else wants his room."

"No, but you see, they had a fight, Konrad and the other man—that's why Konrad's all bandaged up. They had an awful fight and Konrad threw the other man over into the street and broke his legs. It wasn't Konrad's fault, of course, it was the other man having such silly legs."

"I see. And then you both ran away?"

"Oh no, not straight away, not until after the policeman had been. You see, the policeman came, and I told him Konrad hadn't meant to break the man's legs, but he said Konrad would have to go to prison all the same after he'd made his report, unless he wasn't there when they came to take him away, because there are people who think you oughtn't to throw people out into the street. And he told me a lawyer to go to, to get the papers and things. And the lawyer said we'd have to have some wrong names on the papers—"

"Wait a minute!" the Officer said. "I'm trying to get this down, I can't write more than forty thumping fibs a minute. You say the policeman told you to get your friend out of the way? That was rather particularly kind-hearted of the policeman, wasn't it!"

She nodded. "Yes, he was nice, that policeman. Some of them are bastards, but he was nice. And of course he hated the damawful rich man that Konrad broke the legs of."

"Oh, why did he hate him? It wasn't a Jew by any chance?"

"But of course, that's what I was telling you! That's why Konrad wasn't going to have him taking his room."

Josef said feebly: "Minna, that's wrong, you shouldn't have told him that."

"I'd got to," she said, "I'd got to tell him that. He'd have found out most of it, anyway."

The Officer, with the pencil between his teeth, was staring into the darkest corner as if some creature was hidden there and he meant to have it when it flushed. He worked a wedding-ring over his finger-joint and pushed it back again. "You, Konrad Whateveritis, why didn't you tell the Party Committee about this man trying to get your room?"

Minna said: "Well, you see——"

"Be quiet, you!"

Josef said confusedly: "I didn't know anybody—it wasn't anything to do with me, the Party Committee, I've never had anything to do with politics——"

"Exactly! You're one of the short-sighted, self-centred individuals who left it to real patriots to do all the work. You knew that life was utterly intolerable under the old system, and yet you didn't lift a finger to help those who were struggling and risking their lives to overthrow it. Instead of that you go and get into a vulgar scrap on your own account, you alienate a lot of squeamish people and make it impossible for us to help you."

Josef said wearily: "I don't mind, I don't care what happens. He can have my room——"

"That's not what I was saying!" the Officer snapped. He turned to Minna. "What did you mean to do when you got him out of the country?"

"I was going to get a doctor to him, have him made all right. Then I thought later on we could come back, when it's all forgotten about what he did."

"Are you sure of that? Would you swear to it, that you meant to come back?"

"Yes, I'll swear that."

"How much money have you got?"

"About sixty-three Marks. That's including what the Commissioner gave me."

"The Commissioner?"

"The Commissioner at Hartzinnfeld. He gave me fifty Marks. Commissioner Fietz it was, I didn't know it was him, but I saw him again in the Police Office and they told me it was Commissioner Fietz."

"Oh, and what did he give you fifty Marks for?"

"He said it was to pay the lawyer. Only the lawyer he told me to go to didn't charge anything."

"And do you think the Commissioner would remember that? Supposing I telephoned and asked him—?"

"Remember giving me the money? Of course he would! If you tell him I was wearing a green hat and he took me for a ride in his car."

The Officer turned and shouted: "Corporal! Go to the dock office and get a call through to Hartzinnfeld—no, wait a minute! . . . Why did he take you for a ride in his car?"

"I don't know. I suppose he liked having a girl in his car."

"I'll speak to him myself," the Officer said. "You're not to go off this barge till I come back, do you understand!"

"Yes, Herr Kommandant! Oh, and can I have our papers, please?"

"No, you can't!"

He was gone. Her eyes stayed limply on the place where he had been standing, she saw through the coarse stipple of rain a row of barges flank to flank like elephants at rest, a sorrel horse nosing the window of a café-bar.

"I don't understand!" Josef was saying. "Why were you telling him all that?—it wasn't right, all that, I never broke any one's legs."

"No, but most of it was right." She didn't want to talk any more, she had finished her reserves. "It won't make any difference, he's going to talk to the people at Hartzinn-feld, they'll tell him all about us."

It was chilly now. The roof of the tackle-house leaked a little, letting drops of rain fall with a dreary gong-note on the oilcans, this day seemed to have gone on for a long time. She wanted to let herself fall asleep, but that would be surrender; and she was coldly angry because they all made her tell stupid lies and even that wasn't any use. She said drowsily: "If they come to take you away I'll try and push them in the water. Then you must go and hide somewhere, you see, you must get away and hide while I do that."

"I've told you," he said, "they can have me if they want. I'm no use any more. It's only the book . . ."

Some one came along the deck, she smelt a cheap cigarette and thought it was Oskar.

"Please!" No, it was the corporal, the corporal that belonged to the Officer. "These passports," he said, "the Emigration Officer dropped them quite accidentally on the quay; and he said I was to tell you, it's entirely at your own risk if you go across the frontier. Entirely at your own risk, he said I was to be very plain on that."

It was a soldier's face, an old-timer's, fried to a crisp; not a twitch on it anywhere.

Minna opened her own passport, the Frau Freyberg one. She saw on the second visa page the words 'Examined and found technically in order' with a date stamp. The same endorsement was in Josef's book. She said: "I don't understand—" but the corporal was already half-way along the deck.

She stared at the endorsement as Moses may have gazed at the tables of stone. She said to Josef:

"I don't understand . . . He's written that our papers are all right. That means we can go over the frontier."

"It doesn't," he said, "it's just some trick." He took the passports himself and got them into the focus of his remote, damp eyes. "It's just some trick of theirs. They try to make you sign things and then they get you. There's all kinds of tricks."

But she wouldn't listen to that. She put her head out of the door and called for Oskar, and presently he came, flurried and impatient. She asked him:

"How far is the frontier?"

"The frontier?" He took off his cap and stared at the

torn lining as if the frontier was hidden there. "The old bridge," he said. "We always take it the frontier's at the old bridge."

"And how far is that?"

"Why it's over along there. You can see it. Only it doesn't look like a bridge now."

"Very well!" she said. "I want you to go on as far as that—I want you to get us the other side of the frontier. Now, at once! It's quite all right—look! the Officer says here our papers are quite all right."

He didn't seem to understand. "But I can't go on without the Revenue!" he said. "He's got to see everything, you can't go past the bridge till you've got his ticket."

"Well then, you must get him. You must get him at once!"

"He's doing the forward hold," Oskar said gloomily. "It's nothing to do with me, he won't do anything until he's done the forward hold."

It seemed to take a long time. She heard distantly through the wash of rain the voices of two men checking each other's counts, of Oskar stubbornly repeating, "Well, that's the lading slip they gave me, it's nothing to do with me!" and then the cry of Frau Krückel, "Tell the gentlemen, Oskar, I've got the coffee ready, the gentlemen will take a cup of coffee, surely!" The barges alongside slumbered, the horse oblivious of the dray behind him wandered across the quay in search of pickings, it was not a place where people hurried. But the Revenue, when he came, was alert and friendly, a little tidy man with lightning smiles.

"This lady and gentleman are your passengers, Master? Yes yes yes! And these are your papers, yes! 'Technically in order'—curious, curious! But he's fond of long words, my very good friend on this side—a beautifully educated man, I have always supposed—in the Netherlands we can't afford to give such advanced education to government officials. . . .

And these are the photographs, yes yes yes. It hardly does you justice, if I may say so, Gnädige Frau! And this one is of your husband, yes. Perhaps you would be kind enough to come towards the light a little! Yes yes yes! The likeness would be excellent except for the bandages. I think sometimes that the art of the passport photographer is too advanced for a government official to appreciate—all I can do is to see if the sex is right. You have had an accident, I'm sorry to see. Not serious, I trust?"

"He was knocked over by a motor-car," Minna said.

"T-to! Too bad. You will please accept my sympathies! No bones broken, I hope?"

"I was knocked over by a motor-car," Josef repeated.

"A motor-car, yes yes yes! Too bad! And you have not had any other kind of illness?"

But Josef could not answer that. A coughing-fit had been gathering, it broke on him now and he was lost in it.

"He had things when he was small," Minna said.

"I beg your pardon?"

She shouted: "Measles and things."

"A nasty cough!" the Revenue said. "It must be painful, a cough like that. I should like to send a doctor, if you will allow me—there's an excellent Dutch doctor here, he might be able to give your husband something—"

"Yes—thank you—yes, that's very kind—but will you let us get over the frontier first! It's important, you see. You see, Herr Krückel has to hurry, he can't wait very long —the stuff in the hold would go bad—"

The Revenue looked unhappy. "I'm so very sorry, but it's a rule we have—all my work has to be done by silly rules. You see, I'm not allowed to welcome any one into my country if there's the least chance of his being infectious. I'm not suggesting anything—it's simply that I have to obey the rules—"

"But if I promised to take him to a doctor directly—"

"I'm very sorry. I'll send the doctor as quickly as I can."

Doctors and officers, officers and doctors, still more faces! Oskar had waited behind. She asked him: "Has the corporal gone away?"

"Yes, he's gone, but he thought the Officer might be coming back. He said the Officer didn't seem to be sure about something."

The horse had been driven away at last, a single pigeon waded about the empty cobble-way which the rain from a broken gutter flogged incessantly. Somewhere high up a woman shouted, 'Fritzi! Come in this minute!' and a window slammed. The noise of trams was feeble below the susurrus of rain.

"Josef! Josef, do you feel all right? Do you think you could walk a little way? The Officer may come back, we ought to get somewhere so he can't find us."

He was trying to answer her, she thought, but the cough had ground away his voice, the effort left him weak and tearful. She could carry him for half a kilometre, perhaps: but when she stood up the pain in her forehead kicked again, clapping a brown shutter across her eyes. She heard her voice cry suddenly, "It's no use!" and then Josef was holding and kissing her hand. They waited silently, the rain plopping on the oildrums, while the trams clanked into earshot and fretted away. Down river a clock gave five lugubrious strokes, in the window of the café-bar the gas began to show.

At last voices came, men's voices emerging from Willi's whimper, heavy steps of men along the deck, smell of cigar: the Officer, she thought, the Officer was back. She knelt and pulled the door as tight as it would come, she got her thin fingers fastened like wires on the rusty nails. "They won't get in," she whispered, "I won't let them in!"

"I'm very sorry to have been so long!"

It was not the Officer's voice. She let the door open and the Revenue was smiling at her. "I have brought my good friend Doctor Poortvliet. This is Frau Freyberg, doctor—and Herr Freyberg who has the nasty cough." An overcoat with huge lapels filled half the doorway, the doctor bowed and she saw a widely naked face, absurdly trimmed with a shallow hat and tiny ears. "A little catarrh, yes yes?" "I've got some coffee ready for the Doctor," Frau Krückel said.

They went politely away, leaving the doctor to do his work alone. Minna called after them, "Will you please have the engine ready to go, Herr Krückel!" and shut the door. "Be quick, please!" she said to the doctor. "It's this leg, the bandage wants doing again, please be as quick as you can!"

"Leg? Bandage?" His eyes hadn't settled to the semi-darkness, he was like a rat in a mouse-trap, trying to find somewhere for his legs. Huddled up with his back against the oildrums, Josef spasmodically coughed. "You must excuse me, please," the doctor said gravely, "but how long has that cough been going on? When did it start?" It was Josef himself who answered:

"I don't know. It started at Sondersumpf."

"At Sondersumpf? So! I—I have heard of that place." He was feeling in his pockets, he suddenly struck a match and held it close to Josef's face. "Yes!"—that was all he said.

In the silence that followed Minna tried to speak but no sentence would arrange itself. She was finished now, she was dead with weariness. One side of the doctor's quiet, reasonable face was lighted from the hole in the door, his lips were tightly closed and he breathed through his nose, audibly, as a boy does while some one picks a thorn out of his thumb. The voices in the stern went on and on, she strained to hear if the Officer's was among them but could only pick out Herr Krückel's voice. At least they can take me as well, she thought, I shall make them somehow, I'll make them take me as well.

The doctor spoke at last, carefully, beginning a prepared speech:

"You know, of course, that no one may enter the Netherlands having an infectious disease? I'm sorry to say——"

Josef stopped coughing. "It's not infectious," he said distinctly, "not in the ordinary sense." Strangely, when Minna had no voice at all, his was almost steady as in the old days. "Only the sputum is infectious. If you——"

"I'm sorry," the doctor said, "but this disease is on the official list." He paused, and his voice changed. "Listen, I want you to understand. It is my business—a part of my business—to guard the health of my country against any kind of poison that may come in from outside——"

"You can only get it from the sputum!" Josef repeated. "I know that—I'm a doctor, you see, it's my special subject, pulmonary tuberculosis——"

Minna said: "That's true, I promise that's true, I had it and he made me all right. Look, look here—where's a match? I want a match, please, Herr Doktor, can I have your matches—look, look here, I want you to see my chest! Wait, wait a minute—Josef, strike another match—look, look here——"

"—Minna, you're not to show him, not till we're out——"

"I've got to show him—look, look, Herr Doktor, look at this photo, that's what my chest was like. Look, look at this one, that's the one they took at the hospital, look, you see what it had got like then—that was after Josef put the stuff in my arm. And they want to get him and make him die—they want him to die, do you understand!—they don't want him to make any one else better, they only want to make him die."

The doctor took the matches and struck another one. It was Minna's face he stared at now. He said suddenly and simply: "Bastard sons of hellbegotten whores!" And then he said, with his face turned away from them, "There are other kinds of poison besides bacilli, and I shall not have them in my country!"

He began to grope for his things, his hat and gloves and surgical case, and as he fumbled he went on talking, with his voice low and rapid. "The sputum, yes, that's what is most important. You have a mug here—yes—yes, that's all right—but you must constantly clean it out. You, doctor, I rely on you to give your wife explicit directions. And you, Frau Freyberg, I rely on you to take all precautions. Every possible precaution, you understand! And you are not to leave this boat—not even to leave this cabin. At Rotterdam you will stay where you are until some one comes: I shall telephone to a friend there, he will come and transfer you to a steamer for England. You understand that? You understand that I rely absolutely on your good faith?"

"Yes, Herr Doktor!"

She didn't understand at all. They were to stay on the boat, some one would come and move them to a steamer: yes, that was perfectly clear: but why were they going to be left so long, why didn't the Officer come and put them in prison now? Her eyes had shut, tightly, as if a spring held the lids; the doctor, she thought, had gone away. She said, "Josef, why don't they come—why don't they come and put us in prison quickly?" but the words came out like ghosts, empty of sound. Some one touched her hand and she forced her eyelids up against the spring. It was the Revenue leaning over her again.

"Your papers, Gnädige Frau!"

He held the passports open and struck a match for her

to see them. 'Permission to enter for transit: limit, three days.' "I venture to wish you God-speed!" the Revenue said, but she still didn't understand.

Laced with rain, the day had fallen easily to twilight; vivid now against the dulness of the quay the square of light from the café-bar was starting to slide away. In the slum of cask and deal, funnel and marline, a headless pier grew up like a toadstool, "The old bridge," Oskar said, as he stumped along the deck, "that's what we call the old bridge, you see!" With his head against her arm Josef was sleeping, but the cough pursued him into sleep, sharp-nailed and pitiless. There was still one enemy.

48

"YOU say it was a girl brought you the book? A German girl?"

"Well, she seemed to understand my German—more or less."

"And where did she come from?"

"Well, Germany I suppose."

"Doctor Inning, you're talking like a fool this morning!"

"I'm sorry, Mac. No, she didn't say who she was or where she came from. She merely said she'd come back later on to see if I thought the book was 'satisfactory.' A fortnight ago, that must have been. Well, what do you think of it, anyway?"

McDonell milked the lobe of his right ear.

"I wouldn't say it hasn't some interest. It's done by a methodical man. And the formula has some interesting features. But of course, there's nothing to go on. I'd say it was a dangerous thing to play with."

"But the radiograms, what do you think of them?"

"Well, they might be very remarkable. You can't tell. There's naught to say exactly what kind of conditions he had the patient under. I'm not pretending to be a scholar of German, but there's something about special ventilation—"

"Well, no, all he says in his notes—as I understand it —is that he made some sort of top window. I don't see how the room itself can possibly have provided anything like first-class sanatorium conditions. Here—where is it? yes, it seems to have been a sort of attic."

"It is very well established," McDonell said didactically, "by all the leading authorities, that tuberculin treatment is no use, no use whatever, except under sanatorium conditions. And if—"

"—Exactly, that's what I mean! Here's this fellow with the music-hall name—what is it, Zep-something?—here's this fellow carrying out his experiment under the most crazy conditions and apparently getting away with it! Unless the radiograms are faked, or the dates are faked or something. Wait—this one's got a hospital date-stamp in the corner, so that's all right. No, the other one hasn't. But it's the same subject all right—at least, Grover says so, and he's not likely to be wrong. Well then, we've got the whole thing, haven't we? The basis of the theory, summary of previous experiments, actual formula, scheme of dosage, details of all reactions—and, the portraits-before-and-after-using. On top of that, I've got an idea that the girl who brought the book was the patient herself. Questions may now be passed to the Chairman on folded slips of paper."

McDonell said: "I agree, the man has been very methodical. But when you come to my time of life you don't expect to see the science of medicine turned upside-down because of one experiment—"

"No no, quite, of course not! All I'm saying is that on the face of it there seem to be grounds for making some more experiments."

"Some further experiments, yes, there'd be no harm in that. On animal subjects, of course."

"I've done that already."

"You've—?"

"I've done a group of Powell's rats—with a control—"

"But how did you make up the tuberculin?"

"Keenness and initiative, my dear Mac! You see, in the main it's Schulze-Manz's formula, and Powell can slap you together a Schulze-Manz any time you ask him nicely—"

"I know, but where did you get the Tuberculol Merck? You don't find that—"

"Ah, that's where we were enterprising! We telephoned to the Bidault laboratory in Antwerp, and they had it. A great stand-by, Bidault! And Keddlehart's had most of the other stuff."

"And you say you tried it on the rats?"

Inning went over to the window.

"Yes," he said quietly. "And with rather remarkable results."

"Ah yes?" These young men, McDonell thought, they always expect life to be romantic, they believe that marvellous discoveries will be made to-morrow if not this afternoon, they walk about as if they were in a play. "Nearly all the great disappointments in a bacteriologist's career," he said, "are in consequence of an ungrounded optimism based upon the results of animal experimentation."

Inning stared at his shoes. "I suppose so, Mac, I suppose so! . . . But you know what you're always quoting at me, that gag of Hector Mackenzie's—'No animal once infected with a lethal dose of tubercle bacilli has ever been saved by tuberculin treatment'? I suppose that still ought to hold good?"

"It does!"

"Then in that case I can't see why Powell's rats aren't dead—all of them. That's what's puzzling me, it's puzzling me like hell."

"You mean—you began by dosing them with tubercle bacilli? You gave them a lethal dose? What dose? What! How long ago? . . . Then in that case they're dead, they're all as dead as mutton. I don't mind what you say, they've just got to be dead."

Inning smiled. "Half of them are dead," he said. "Of

those, half had no treatment and half had Schulze-Manz—the standard formula. The rest are in two sub-groups. 'A' have been treated with the full dosage of this German fellow's stuff and 'B' have been done at half strength. The 'B' lot are failing—they won't last the day. The 'A' lot are going to survive—I tell you, Mac, they *are* going to survive, they're positively perky—and what's more, they're going to recover their full and perfect rathood!"

McDonell looked gloomily at the acid stains on his white coat. He said: "And even suppose Mr. Powell's rats are not actually dead, what do you propose—"

"I want a human subject!" Inning said abruptly. "By hook or by crook, I want to get a T.B. subject in Marshall-Henry's Third Stage—"

"And put that stuff in him, which nine doctors out of ten will inform you is deadly poison—?"

"But what chance has the man got if he's in the Third Stage? And what about the woman the German fellow used?"

"I haven't seen the woman and I haven't seen the rats—"

"Well, at least you can see the rats. Come on, come and have a look at them! Wait! I say—come and look here!"

Biting his moustache, McDonell went over to the window. "Yes, what is it?" Within, he was boiling with impatience to see the rats: they wouldn't—they could not survive a dose of tubercle like that. "What are you staring at?"

"Look down there!"

McDonell looked, and saw the view he had known for twenty years: the northern wing of the hospital stretching on to Nelson's Ride, a procession of iron stairways tacked to the precipice of smoky brick; the black wilderness of St. Matthew's coaling yards, 'For all your Ills take Darnley's Pills' drawn huge across the roof of Eastwood's Empire. The whistles had gone for dinner-hour, a grey glacier of cyclists swept south along the muddy street, squeezed hard against the kerbs as the trams wedged it apart: he had seen all that a hundred times before. He glanced at Inning's face and down to the street again: a pair of scrubs along there, trying to cross the road, a lean girl with a man's coat flopping about her boots, a gaunt young Jew with his tawny blouse tucked into calico trousers, they made a sally and stopped and tumbled back to safety. The man was in no hurry, he stood on the kerb with his feet apart, swaying a little, he held a rag against his mouth and turned his head slowly from side to side like a calf in a gig: the girl was bolder; clutching her nauseous hat with one hand and the man's sleeve with the other she pitched herself into the stream again and was levered back like a gate on a spring. They gave it up at last, the girl lit the end of a cigarette and they sat on the kerb-stone, leaning against each other, oblivious of the wheels shaving their toes, waiting with disdainful patience for the road to clear.

"And there," said Inning, "you have the woman her-self. Simply a part of our Service."

49

THEY were steep, these stairs, but this was a place you could understand, here at last was a smell she knew. "Josef, it's like the Moltke, don't you think!" but he didn't answer, he was several steps in front and he went on doggedly in the porter's wake, shoulders crouched and hands behind his back. In this great emptiness, a polished avenue of silence reaching from every countermarch of the coach-broad stairs, the hubbub of the street was thinned to a murmur, their feet on the stone treads gave the clangour of an army's march. Here you could breathe and they didn't push you about, a doctor and his wife were somebody here.

At the top of the third flight she sat down, and Josef noticed and came back to her. "Is something wrong?" "It's only the stairs, they've squeezed all the air out of my stomach." He knelt and did up one of her laces while she took fresh air and arranged her hat, he didn't seem to be out of breath. He was stronger, her beloved, the sea must have done him good, but his mouth ought not to bleed so much. The porter, swinging his weight from foot to foot, sulkily watched them.

To keep her body in action, it was like dragging a loaded sledge; the sledge ran free and fast where the snow was flat, and suddenly it was wedged in a drift and pulled you up, you had to rest for a time and kick and tug to get it moving again. But now she was quite all right, her wind was back and she was at her best to-day, she said, "Advance, if you please!" and followed the porter down the corridor, erect and dignified, her hand on Josef's arm. The alien doors went past like Sundays at school, *Dr. McDonell . . . Lab-*

*oratory Clerk . . . Storeroom 5 . . . Laboratory F . . .
Laboratory G . . .*

"Listen, Josef! You mustn't let them cheat you. If they
want to use your stuff they must pay you at least two hundred Marks."

"I don't want money, not for that——"

"But we're nearly out of money——"

"You don't do it for money, that kind of thing."

. . . *Dr. Inning.* The porter gave a cuff to the door
and at once, to show that laboratory doctors were neither
here nor there, jerked it open. "Mr. and Mrs. Freeburg!"

A fire of the English kind, although it was summer, a
pleasant untidiness, the English doctor smiling through his
horn-rimmed spectacles: nothing was quite in focus, for the
climb upstairs had fogged her eyes a little, but you could
manage things in a small room like this, and she felt so well
to-day. "So glad!" the English doctor was saying in his
curious, halting way. "I thought you had forgotten to come
back. This is Doctor McDonell, his German is even worse
than mine. He is a Scot, you see—a Scotch man," and that
seemed to be a joke, for the young doctor laughed and the
other Englishman with the grey moustache screwed up his
mouth and sniffed, so Minna laughed as much as she could.
"And this is your husband?" the young doctor asked.

Josef, clicking, said: "Zeppichmann."

"Oh—then you are—you are the Doctor Josef Zeppichmann who conducted the experiments? I—I do not quite
understand. (Will you not take a chair, Frau Freyberg—and
you—please!)"

The chairs were anyhow in the middle of the room,
they sat in them where they were; a little apart, she with
her hands folded and staring at the young doctor's face,
Josef perched like a hook on a picture-rail, his eyes to the
window. She said:

"It was Doctor Kunig, you see, he said that our name

would be Freyberg, Zeppichmann is the name he used to have, the name in the book I mean, he was called that when he did the experiment, only the police wanted to have him in prison again, you see——"

"Just one minute!" The young doctor went to the door and called, "Miss Brewer! See if you can find Doctor Schneider, will you please—ask if he can spare me a few minutes."

"You see, I was Minna Wersen when he put the stuff in my arm, I belonged to Frau Spühler then, I was Frau Spühler's kitchen girl, you understand, and I'd got T.B. So you see——"

"Oh!" The young doctor seemed to have understood at last, he was very like Herr Oelschläger, stupid but nice. "Oh," the young doctor said, "I was right then, you are the—the subject of—of your husband's experiments? I mean—the case described in this book, it was yourself?"

"But the photos," she said, "I gave you the photos of my chest——"

"Yes yes, exactly—only I didn't know——"

"But I told you, I told you it was my chest." She began unbuttoning her blouse. "Look, I'll show you——"

"No no, some other time——"

"But of course I'm quite well now. I was very ill, you understand, I was very ill indeed, and then Josef put his stuff in my arm and I got all right. I would have died, that's what they told me at the Moltke Hospital, Doctor Dittmer, that was, he was a very good doctor, he knew nearly everything, much more than Doctor Vollmuth, he said that I ought to have died, it was the stuff Josef put in my arm that made me all right."

Dr. Schneider came, and the room seemed to be crammed with doctors. "Here is a countryman of yours," the young Englishman said, "he speaks your language quite well —don't you, Paul!" Dr. Schneider bowed. He was young and handsome and his hair was nicely done, his white coat was clean, he was altogether different from the Englishmen. "And you are the mysterious lady?" he said. "My friend Doctor Inning here talks of nothing but the book you brought him! And is this Doctor Zeppichmann?"

But Josef had turned his chair and he wouldn't look round.

"Josef! Josef, please! This doctor here wants to talk to you."

He said in English: "Not understand. Not German. Hollandish."

Dr. Schneider's smile went out, he stood rubbing his chin. "My friend," he said slowly, "I left Göttingen more than a year ago. I couldn't do my work there. You understand?" And as Josef didn't answer, he said, "They had a talk with me before I left—you know the people I mean!" He pulled up a cuff and put his wrist in front of Josef's face. "Look! You know how one gets that little trademark?"

Then Josef was weeping, and he talked at the same time. "They can have the book, you see, these doctors here, I want these doctors to keep the book, but they mustn't let them have it—those people over there. Those people would spoil it, they'd make my stuff all wrong and say it was because of me. They're not to say that, you understand, they're not to say I was trying to kill people—I was trying to make people better, whatever else I did. Please, Herr Doktor, please, I don't want you to tell them about my stuff, not those people over there. I'll pay you—Minna, we've got some money left—I'll pay you—please! . . ." The cough took him and he had to stand against the wall for a minute or so, bent double, while the inkpots on the table rattled in their stand. Then he was calmer, as if some weight had rolled away, he stood and faced the doctors with something like a smile, he said, "I'm sorry—it was at Sondersumpf, that's where I got like that."

The grey Englishman had come to Minna's side. He asked her quietly, "How long—that cough, your husband? Some blood, yes? He vomits sometimes? No? He—he sweats—he sweats in the night? No?"

Josef was on his chair again and the young Englishman was asking him questions which Dr. Schneider put into better words. Then the doctors were talking together in English, and then Dr. Schneider was asking some more questions, which Josef seemed to answer without any trouble, though Minna could not understand them at all. "But what made you depart entirely from Kolbe's principle in your schedule of dosage? . . . Doctor McDonell thinks it was dangerous, the initial doses being so concentrated and the intervals so short. Don't you think there was some danger?" "But I tell you, it's absolutely essential. My new elements, my Psi Plus and Psi Minus, they're no good unless they're allowed their full strength in the first attack—the later injections would have no more effect than some old-fashioned tuberculin like Béraneck. Yes, and all my experiments proved that, you can see from the summary . . . Yes, it's dangerous, I admit that—it might be made less dangerous, I don't know, I wanted to try another new line, but I had to go to prison you see. It's a question of getting your subject at the right time. With the disease in the early stage it would be better to try less drastic treatments—" "Exactly, yes!" "—but on the other hand you can't inject if there's hectic fever, that would be overloading, I—nowadays I wouldn't take a risk like that. With Minna, you see, I—I wasn't thinking enough, I didn't realise . . ."

They will tire him, she thought, he isn't used to it, he doesn't like to talk so much. But she felt a pride in seeing them, these foreign doctors with their serious faces, all looking and listening to Josef; she felt as a shy painter does when he hovers near the door of the gallery, watching a little group about his own picture. And Josef, he was at his best now, he was talking with his hands as well as his mouth, some force he had kept in hiding seemed to quicken his eyes and voice. "You see, I don't want to hurt any one again. Only you've got to take the risk. Otherwise it's all lost, the idea I had. It was a right idea, I mean, I proved it was right, it's the only way of stopping the bacillus when it's taken half your lungs. Please, you can't just throw it away, an idea like that!"

Dr. Schneider was translating. He had his hands in his pockets and he sat with half his backside on the edge of the table, he knew the way to behave in an English hospital. His voice was quick and smooth, miraculously turning Josef's words to English as they passed from ears to mouth; the voices came and went like shuttles, the small room was a loom of strangely coloured words. "And you yourself, you've been through a bad time?" "At Sondersumpf, yes, the food wasn't good, it wasn't enough for the work you have to do."

At last Josef turned to her.

"He wants to examine me—the English doctor—he thinks he could do something for my chest."

"Which of them, Josef, which of the doctors?"

"The small one, the one with spectacles."

"But I like the grey one better, he looks as if he knows more."

Dr. Schneider said: "It's a good idea, you know, it's a very good hospital, this one, they'll give your husband a proper examination."

"How much will that cost?"

"Oh, but we shan't charge anything."

She hesitated: she had meant to wait until they had some money and then get a private doctor. She wouldn't have minded a private doctor, one who came to see Josef in their own room. Still, there wasn't really any harm.

"Yes, I'll allow that," she said. "It must be done properly, of course, it mustn't be just a cheap examination."

They took her to another room to wait while Josef was examined. There was a nice chair by the fire here, and a girl who was rather pretty in an English way but could only talk English; the girl gave her some cake and a glass of milk and a magazine with pictures of people shooting at birds.

In the pleasant warmth she went to sleep, when she woke it was after three o'clock. She was suddenly afraid that Josef had left the hospital without her, Josef was often forgetful in his dreamy moods. She wanted to say something to the English girl, she knew how to say in English, 'I want to see the Manager, please!' but the English girl was at grips with her machine, trouncing all the notes together and fiercely cuffing its long arm whenever the bell rang. The place was full of bells, there were screeching bells and bells that growled like angry cats, in the next room a telephone rang incessantly. At last Dr. Schneider came.

Dr. Schneider, leading her through the endless passages, the countless doors, asked her where she was living. "Doctor McDonell told me to ask you, he's particularly anxious to know about that."

"Oh, at present we live in Marianne."

"Marianne? Is that a hotel?"

"I suppose so."

"But where is it, which street?"

"In Goldflackestrasse. It's just round the corner from the boats."

"You mean the street with the statue at the end?"

It wasn't that one. But she thought, suddenly, that it wasn't safe to tell him, it wasn't safe for any one from Germany to know where Josef lived.

"Yes," she said, "that's the one."

"You're comfortable there?"

"Oh yes, very."

He led her into a room with a big writing-desk, it was full of doctors but Josef wasn't there. He told her that a bald little doctor with tired eyes was Dr. Mayneshott, and they made her sit in a chair, the English always wanted to prowl about in their rooms but they wanted every one else to sit in a chair. The old man in the corner was Sir Georg something, he was like the bust of Friedrich Schelling but older and much more stupid, with his bottom lip stuck out and his kind eyes staring suspiciously at the carpet he hardly seemed to be alive at all. It was the bald doctor who started the talking, while Dr. Schneider explained what he said.

"Doctor Mayneshott doesn't want to alarm you unduly, but he has found that your husband's lungs are in a very bad condition——"

"I know that!" she said. "He's got T.B. I had it myself once."

For a time the doctors were all talking together, in the English way, hardly using their tongues at all but pursing their lips and making fierce little nods. Then,

"Doctor Mayneshott thinks you ought to realise that your husband's case is serious. When the disease has got to this stage it's—it's very seldom that anything can be done."

She said, "Oh, but he's better now, he's very much better. He was very ill on the barge, he couldn't walk at all sometimes, but the sea did him good. He's quite different now, he's getting quite strong again."

The old man in the corner suddenly came awake. He said, finding the words one by one:

"You must understand, a man can not go on living without any lungs. He must have his lungs—to breathe. When his lungs are all destroyed by disease, then he—he must die. I am very sorry. I am very, very sorry. It was necessary to tell you that."

The doctors were all looking at the carpet as if they wanted to take it to bits and remake it themselves. One or two of them were making little English coughs. It seemed curious to Minna that everything in the room was the same, stains on the grey doctor's coat and the clock ticking. So Josef is going to die, she thought. So Josef is going to die.

She said slowly: "I want my husband to have the very best treatment. You must understand, he is a doctor himself, he is not just anybody, it's right for him to have the best treatment. I shall pay for it by degrees, I am going to find household work, I have a great deal of household experience. It must be understood, please, that my husband is not to be put in the pauper wards—the treatment will not be too expensive for me if he's only to live for a short time."

Dr. Schneider said, when the doctors had all talked again, pursing their lips and making their little nods: "There's no question of expense, the doctors here regard themselves as colleagues of your husband, they are all very glad to give their services. It's only a question of the kind of treatment. Now you know, I think, what tuberculin treatment is?"

"You mean, putting stuff in your arm? Yes, that's the best, I'll have that for Josef, please. I'd like—"

"But wait! There are many different kinds of tuberculin. In a case like this, Doctor Mayneshott's normal practice would be—"

She said: "I want you to use Josef's own stuff, the stuff that he thought of. That is the best kind."

The doctor with spectacles seemed to understand that. He said something to the grey doctor, the grey doctor frowned and shrugged his shoulders. The bald man was talking again, and Dr. Schneider was patiently, swiftly turning it into German.

"If Doctor Mayneshott had to decide himself he would prefer to use his own formula. He thinks it's just possible

to save the case by the use of a tuberculin he has thoroughly
tested, given under proper sanatorium conditions . . . Doctor Mayneshott is much impressed by the possibilities of
your husband's formula but he is inclined to think it unwar-
rantably dangerous . . . Sir Georg would allow your husband's formula to be used if you as well as your husband
himself appreciate the danger . . ."

She said: "I can't understand all that——"

His voice changed. "Of course you can't, I was going
much too fast! It's like this: with the kind of medicine Doctor Mayneshott generally puts into people——into their arms,
I mean——he thinks he might keep your husband alive for
some time. For some months——a year or two perhaps. It's
possible. If he uses your husband's own medicine it might do
him much more good, it might stop the disease straight away
from getting stronger and it might gradually conquer it altogether. That's what we *think*, from what your husband has
put in his book and some experiments of our own. But to
begin with, this medicine would make a very great strain
on your husband's strength——"

"——I know that, I know that——"

"——and Doctor Mayneshott isn't at all sure that your
husband is strong enough——I mean, in his body generally——
strong enough to bear that strain."

It was clear now, it was very clear indeed. She asked:
"Have they got to do it straight away, whatever they do to
him?"

"They'd like to," he said, "it would be much best to
start straight away. You see, the disease is getting stronger
all the time, in a very short time he'll have less what we call
'resistance.' "

She nodded.

"I want to see Josef," she said, "I want to hear what
he says."

All the doctors nodded and pursed their lips, the old

man went to open the door and bowed her into the passage. With Dr. Schneider and the bald man on either side she started on another journey; in an English hospital you had to walk along all the passages before you went into another room. Then they knocked at a door and let her go in alone.

It was a bedroom, made by very high walls with nothing on them. Josef was not in bed but he was wearing a dressing-gown. He sat in an armchair by the fire. A nurse was in the room, she was fiddling over a glass table and rattling things as nurses do. Minna said, "I don't want that bitch in here, can't you tell her to go!"

Josef said that the nurse could only speak English. "And you can't make nurses go," he said.

She stood in front of him, looking at his face. He was tired, she thought, he didn't look so well now.

"Do you feel all right?" she asked.

"Yes, I feel all right."

"All those doctors say that you're ill. I mean, they say you're very ill. The old man specially. But I think he's a bit mad, he opened the door for me. How ill do you think you are?"

He was looking at the fire. He said, "Listen, Minna, listen! I think I can make them use my polyvalent tuberculin. On me, I mean. You know, the stuff I wrote all about in that book."

"Yes, I know."

"They've tried it with rats, you see, the Englishman with spectacles, he's tried it."

"Oh. Did he think it was all right?"

"Yes, he thinks so. And you see, I've got to the right stage now. I'm in what they call the Third Stage. When you get to the Fourth Stage it's too late. They're quite good here, they haven't any new things to use but they know about things. It's just exactly right, you see. If I was only at

the Second Stage it wouldn't really mean anything, my
stuff acting all right."

"Will it hurt a lot?"

"I don't mind that."

"I don't want you to be hurt any more."

"I got used to that."

"Is it bound to act all right?"

He hesitated. "I think so . . . And you see, if it does
it proves what I thought. Two cases are very much better
than one, they always think one case may be just an accident."

"And then if it acts all right they'll use it on a lot of
people? People won't have T.B. any more?"

"Well, a lot of them won't."

"And will they call it the Zeppichmann medicine?"

"They might do. But I don't mind about that. Not
now."

She wished that he still minded about that.

"You want them to do it?" she asked. "You want it
very much?"

He said: "I thought you'd better decide." And then he
said, stumbling, "We were in it together, you said that.
When I did the last injection. You said it belonged to us
both . . . So I thought you ought to decide."

So he remembered that! He remembered the night
when she had made him give her another prick. And she
thought, I've got him back now, I've got all of him back.

She wished that she were in the old room again, with
her in bed, her feeling the burning hot stuff as it crept up
the arm. You couldn't see things clearly with Josef in this
new dressing-gown and the nurse rattling things and the
high, naked walls.

"I suppose it would be a good thing," she said.

Josef smiled then. He looked happy and surprised, as
if she had given her a present, and she was glad that it made

him happy. He said: "Yes—yes, I think it'll be a good thing . . . Perhaps you ought to find the doctors and tell them."

The doctors were talking to each other, a little way down the passage. Dr. Schneider came to her, smiling, and she said:

"My husband and I have made up our minds. We wish you to begin the treatment at once, with the Zeppichmann medicine."

Dr. Schneider looked at her curiously. "You do under-stand—?"

"Yes yes, I understand all about it. My husband has made it quite clear to me."

"And you?" he asked, "what are you going to do?"

"Me? I'm going to stay here, stay and look after Josef."

"Oh, but that's not allowed, I'm afraid."

"But that bitch of a nurse, she's in there."

"But she belongs here, you see."

"I see."

He said: "Look here, would you like to come to my house? My wife would make you comfortable."

"Oh, that's kind, that's fabulously kind!" But it wasn't safe, she thought; he might write to the German police and tell them where she was. "But I'd rather go to my hotel," she said. "Thank you very much, but I'd rather go to my hotel."

"Are you feeling all right?"

For a moment she thought of telling him that she was ill: she could say how giddy she was sometimes, and how her legs sometimes refused to work: then they might let her stay in the hospital. But another plan was uppermost: she would go to some place where they taught you to be a nurse, then they would let her come back and look after Josef.

"I'm perfectly all right," she said. "I can come back to-morrow?"

He nodded. "About ten o'clock. Ask for me and I'll make things all right."

"Can I see Josef again before I go?"

"But of course."

The nurse was still there, but Minna was bolder now. She went to her and said "Go away, please! Please go away!" The nurse said something you couldn't understand, Minna said "Go! Go!" and the nurse went off to complain to Dr. Mayneshott. Minna said to Josef: "You're quite sure you want it done?" He answered, "Yes, quite sure."

"You won't let them hurt you an awful lot?"

"Oh no, I don't feel things much. Not after Sondersumpf."

She wanted to warn him about the way you felt when the stuff started to work; but she couldn't put that into words, she had lost the habit of putting things into words. "I expect it will be all right," she said, and he said, "Yes, I expect it will be all right," and then, indistinctly, "I'm glad it's me this time."

She put one of the cushions underneath his elbow. That way it kept his shoulder up and then he didn't get the ache in his shoulder. (The nurse wouldn't know that.) After that she kissed him on the eyes, letting her tongue touch his eyelids, she said "Jesus mit Dir, liebe . . . allerliebster." The trousers he was wearing had a tear at the knee, but the nurse would have to see to it. She heard him say, "You've done too much—too much!" Some one with creaky boots was coming into the room (it wasn't their own room, any one could come). She kissed one of his hands and went away down the passage, straightening her hat.

50

AT LEAST he is in a warm room, and Dr. Schneider is kind. He is by the fire, he has no more walking to do and the police won't find him there. The book was all crumpled and the pages were torn but the doctors could read what Josef put, the young doctor with the spectacles has seen how clever Josef's medicine is.

At least that is over. I talked to them all and I walked along their passages, none of them thought I was ill and it shows that Josef's stuff can work all right.

But her powers had been at stretch too long. As far as Canon's Plough her legs were docile and her head kept up, she halted there and leant against a sandbox, immediately her hold was broken. She waited patiently: it was nothing new, this slackening of all her joints, this dry, stale air in throat and forehead: only the pain beneath her breast was of a new kind, a curious squeezing as of fierce hands wringing out a cloth. And that would pass.

She felt a hand upon her arm, a woman spoke and she caught the word 'Olreit?' "Tank — you, olreit!" she said; and presently, when the squeezing stopped, she went on slowly down the Plough.

In England the rain leaves a mist behind; the mist hangs low and brown between the smoky houses, breathes damp upon the windows of the shops and changes back to rain. Pavements here are clothed with a film of mud, stumps and cartons silting against the tramway poles are a tangle of slime. Only the tramway lines stay clean, and now the lamps of cars are changing them to threads of light. You know that night has come because the yellow glow from

417

windows gets more intense on the moistened paths; the people walking past are by degrees reduced to extras, dark audience to the lustre of the shops.

The long façade of Woolworth's changed to the darkness of the city library, from the tank of light that passed her next stiff women glared with freezing eyes, women in stays and stockings lounging on canvas chairs, brown girls in pleated drawers who brandished tennis-bats in their long, rheumatic hands. A giant radio poured syrup sound against the noise of wheels in mud, vast pyramids of cigarettes gave place to romantic dining-rooms, the shiny wardrobes to a dazzling hoard of necklaces and clocks. The English did not buy these things, they gave an anxious glance and hurried on, eternally pursued by haste, they mumbled 'Sorry!' as they bumped her with their prams.

She picked her way across the Knightmoor road, remembering that here the motors rushed at you from the right-hand side. At the Dame of Windermere she turned, free of conflicting light the long street stood in evening, it brought her through the sphere of small hotels and auctioneers to where, beyond the cattle trucks, the trawler funnels still showed faintly through the haar. The smells were fresher here, fish-oil and railway-smoke, dimly the smell of sea.

She found her corner by the shop, pink sweets and tartan toilet-rolls, torn flysheets hung along the wall; and now the shapes were all well known, Hind's Cooperage, the long half-mile of stringent living-sheds, Mackenzie's Bar, the Bolingbroke, the Pleasant Sunday Afternoon. The quay swept round to bring the arms of travelling cranes above the roofs, the light that crossed belonged to a collier's mast. Like a finger post the smell of vinegar broke out upon the street, she turned and steered for the yellow blind across the triangle called Flemings' Change.

At least he is warm and in a proper bed, at least the doctors will be kind to him.

In Mary Ann's you went through the dining-room to get upstairs; she hoped the room would be full to-night, and then she could slip past before they noticed her. But the *Goole Brunette* had sailed on the evening tide, leaving only a trio of regulars, a trimmer from the *Baltic Star*, a Polish engineer, the yellow gantryman from Preston's yard. The gantryman was asleep with his chair against the staircase door, the trimmer shouted, 'Gus, make way for the skirt!', the old man woke and spat and went to sleep again.

Old Kate came in from the back with a glass of Parson's Cock. "There *is* the bloody tart!" she said. She wiped the glass with her hessian apron and put it on the bench, she was narrow and semi-bald and five feet high, she came to Minna slowly like a cat ready to pounce. "Police been after you—you and your fancy!" Her stiff mouth smiled, her ruddled eyes went slanting to the White Horse card as if she read dark secrets there. She raised her voice, "The cops, you hear, they know your little bloody game! . . . Cryke! Polzy, can't you come and make her understand!"

The engineer did up his belt, he came and slipped his hand through Minna's armpit, feeling for her breast. "You hark to me!" His grey-white face was damply kind, smelling of Worcester sauce, he spoke a fast and slangshot German with a Danzig twang. "Police been round, you see! They want to talk to you, you and your boy."

"But we haven't done anything, Josef and me."

"Haven't done anything—that's just it! You haven't gone to report."

"I give their names," Kate said, "I give their names according to the law, I can't do more—"

"You shut your trap!" the Pole said.

He felt in the spanner-pocket of his dungarees and found a cigarette. "What about your papers?" he asked. "You know what I mean—got any papers? Here, let me see!"

She had them in her stocking, he took the passports, licked his thumb and flipped his way through the visa leaves.

"You haven't got the landing-stamp. Didn't you see the landing-officer?"

She shook her head. "Josef had got T.B., you understand, I thought they wouldn't let us in. We went round the back of the sheds, the sailor told us how to go, we got between the railway trucks."

The Pole nodded slowly, rinsing his lips, he seemed to be faintly pleased. "That means the clink!" he said.

"Prison?"

"That's right!" He looked all round, savouring his audience, he said in English, "She's for the clink!"

"But why?"

"Why?" he said. "Because you dodged the landing bull! They want this goddam country for themselves, see, they don't want any bloody Deutschen nor no one else, not unless they're snug with boodle. There's not the jobs, see, they say the aliens pinch their bloody jobs."

"But Josef's ill, he couldn't do a job."

"It makes no matter, they don't want aliens here." He went to the table, held the bottles together and whipped away the *Gazette* which served as tablecloth. "I seen it here," he said, and held the paper under her chin, a spread of English words and gravy-stain. "Last week, it was, a German wench, you see, a Jew, she was. It's all down here. 'Landed without a permit'—there you are. 'Failed to report.' A month, she got, a month in the bottom sort of clink. 'You're nothing but a bloody parasite,' the judge says, Mr. Anzelvick, that's the judge in this place, 'you and all your kind, a lot of flaming parasites, it's a bloody scandal, see!' That's what Mr. Anzelvick said."

"And she's in prison now?"

"With chains, I shouldn't wonder."

"And what'll they do when they let her out?"

"They'll put her in the boat," he said, "back to where she come from. Now hark to me!——"

But she would not listen any more, she pulled herself away from his hungry fingers and went to the door. "Let me walk, please!" and the old man moved his chair. She turned again in the doorway. "Tell me, please—the police, are they coming back? To-night?" The Pole passed on the question. "Yes," he said, "Old Katia here, she says the bulls are coming back if you don't report."

She felt her way up the damp stairs to the room that she and Josef had, groped for matches and lit the gas. It had seemed to be good enough, this section fenced by matchboard from a larger room, the single chair, the enamel basin perched on the window-sill: it was lifeless now.

The fibre case lay open on the floor, as it had been since they came; their sponge was on the mantelpiece with half a slab of chocolate, most of their things about the bed. She wrapped the sponge in a piece of paper torn from the wall and pitched it into the case, the other things went in on top. The case was shut and she had snapped the only fastener that worked when she saw her diary lying beneath the bed. What use? But she dragged it out, slapped off the furry dust and stuck it in her coat; pressed her face in the pillow where Josef's head had been and went downstairs again with the case under her arm.

The gantryman was being sick in a corner, with the Pole holding his head. Old Kate stood by and cursed him, Old Kate would not have noticed her if the other man hadn't shouted out.

"Ey! You moving on?"

Old Kate swung round. "Not till she's paid, she won't!" and stood against the door. "It's nine-and-eight, d'you hear! Cryke, what's the Bosche for nine-and-eight? For God's sake, Polzy, leave that spuck alone, come here and tell the slut it's nine-and-eight—four double-sleeps since Sunday night, and twenty Players, tell her it's nine-and-eight."

"She says it's nine-and-eight."

"Neun schillinge?"

"And eight pence."

"What's the pence for?"

"She wants to know what the pence is for . . . She says you burnt a hole in the blanket."

"Tell her the bed was full of bugs."

"She says the bed was full of bugs."

"Ask her who brought them in!"

The room was in a dusk of Nelson's Plug and the latest smell began to override the rest; she couldn't fight in a place like this. They squared at nine-and-six; she gave her only pound and the change came back in three half-crowns, a shilling, twenty Craven A and four three-halfpenny stamps. She supposed that that was right. The engineer would have had a kiss for rake-off but she got away from him and slammed the door.

The fibre case, dangling from its broken handle, seemed heavier now. She went along the street in zigzags, keeping clear of the lights. The Bolingbroke, Mackenzie's Bar, And How They Satisfy.

It was autumn-cold, for in this country they had no summer. She turned to go her usual way, along by the tram-lines, gleaning shreds of familiarity to clothe her solitude. They had walked together here, the day when Josef was so much better: a curious porch he had stopped to stare at, the smell from a barber's shop, these helped you to remake a world in which you had had your place. The bigger shops had shut and the girls came down the street in twos and threes, she saw a woman with a smiling child on either side, a soldier with some one buried in his arms. But against that happiness she held a picture of her own brief contentment, his kindness in Frau Spühler's house, the tackle-shed, with the *Weimar's* gunwale nudging the quiet hills, 'You have done so much, so much!' The tramway boards had shapeless names, the electric signs threw words she could not even say: but in Hartzinnfeld these knowing people would be strangers; and she had walked this way with Josef Zeppichmann, and all the solemn English doctors were pleased with the medicine Dr. Zeppichmann had found.

He would want his brush, she thought, the brush she had got him in Rotterdam. It was in the case, and she'd take it to the hospital straight away.

But along the Plough her legs got sulky; and the ache, the new ache which had first attacked her by the sandbin, was stalking her again. She stopped at the door of a teashop, the place was full but there were no police or soldiers there; she found a seat in the far corner and ordered a Wiener-wurst and coffee, a weary girl brought her tea and a sausage roll. At the other side of the table an Englishman with grey, untidy hair was pushing scrambled egg under his thick moustache. She leant across and spoke to him.

"Tell me, please, to find a school. Yes? A school for nurse, for sick nurse. I would learn the nurse, you see? You have nurse-school here, in England, yes?"

The Englishman looked scared, for a moment she thought he would beckon the serving-girl and have her taken away. But he said at last, in something akin to her own language,

"I'm afraid—I don't quite understand. You are German —yes?"

"Yes yes! I want to be a nurse, you see. Josef is in the hospital, I want to go and be his nurse. That's my husband, you see—Doctor Zeppichmann. I thought if I could learn to be a nurse they'd let me look after him. In the hospital, I mean."

He still looked frightened, his eyes went right and

left as if she had got him in a trap, he wouldn't look at her face at all. He said:

"My wife might be able to help you. She knows more about these things than I do. And she speaks German properly——"

"Your wife, yes! But where is your wife?"

"We're staying at Perry's Hotel," he said. "My wife will be there about ten o'clock to-night. I—I'm sure she'd do anything she could to help you."

"In Perries Hotel?"

"Yes, in Chandler Street."

"You have policemen there, in that hotel?"

"Policemen? No—I don't think so."

She nodded. "Very well, I will interview your wife," she said, "at ten o'clock, yes. Oh, perhaps you will take my bag, it's rather heavy for me to carry about, I'll take it when I come to see your wife. You will, please?" She saw that he didn't want to take her bag, but he didn't say No. "Oh, wait, I must get out Josef's brush." It was right at the bottom with the sponge, she had to pour all the other things over the table and then cram them back again. The man, watching her, looked more and more wretched; he was a very English man, and perhaps a little wrong in the head. She snapped the fastener again. "You must be careful of the handle, it's a bit broken, you see. And perhaps you will take this book, too, it's just my diary, it's rather a trouble to carry about."

The Englishman put the case on his side of the table and stowed the book in the big pocket of his grubby raincoat. "And—is that all?" he asked.

"Yes, thank you . . . Oh, no, something else!"

She stood up and undid her coat. "This coat," she said, "—perhaps you will do me a great kindness. I really had it for Josef, he wore it when we were on the barge. It belongs to Herr Probst, you see, I told Herr Probst I would send him the money or else give him back the coat. But you see, I don't understand the postal office, I don't know what you do. I've got the stamps here—look, four stamps, they gave me those at Marianne, that ought to be enough. You will be so very kind as to send it for me?"

"But where are you going?" he asked. "You can't go about without a coat—it's raining—surely it could wait till to-morrow—"

She said decisively: "It may be raining over there too. Herr Probst is quite an old man, it isn't right for him to be without his coat." She folded it in a rough bundle and put it on top of the case. "The Romanisches Café, that's where Herr Probst is, the Romanisches Café in Hartzinnfeld. You'll send it there, please?"

He began to stammer, as if he'd got a fish-bone stuck in his mouth. "But listen—I—you—you don't look at all well. It's cold now, you oughtn't to go about without a coat—"

He seemed to be a very stupid man, he could not understand that the coat belonged to Herr Probst. "I shall buy another coat if I want it," she said. "Oh, here is some money, you will pay my bill, please?—I don't understand the English bills."

He pushed the money back. "We can settle later on. Only—"

"And I'll go to the Perries Hotel. In Schandler Street?"

"That's right—ask for Mr. Hutchinson. But listen, I wish you—"

"At ten o'clock!" The hospital might be closing for the night, she couldn't waste any more time. She smiled. "Auf wiedersehen!"

It was raining, as the Englishman had said; but Josef was under a good roof, it did not matter now. The scalding tea had left a sense of vigour, and the ache had withdrawn a little way. With the candid rain a freshness had come, breaking the weight of the town's close air, the rush of tyres on drenched macadam was the noise of wind in trees. People ran for the shelter of trams as the lighted boards broke round from Corporation Hill, a man coatless and bareheaded grinned skewly as he hurried by. So: they were not inflexible, they were not impervious to rain. And the rose light of the Empire Rex reached friendly across the gleaming road.

At the hospital the porter she knew had gone off duty. His substitute was young, cheeks flat and raw, eyes that always expected catastrophe. She was wrong, he said, there was no Dr. Zeppichmann here.

"But I leave him here! To-day I leave him!"

He turned and went on writing. "There's not a Doctor Zeppington, I've never heard of him."

"So, you will show me Doctor Schneider, please!"

"I won't—he's busy. If he's here at all."

"He is in bed, you understand."

"Doctor Schneider? More likely at the pic—"

"No no no—my man—Doctor Zeppichmann, he is in bed here. He suffers."

"Oh, he's a patient? Well, why didn't you—"

"He is patient, yes—I will see him, please?"

"Sundays and Wednesdays, four o'clock," the porter said. He got up slowly and showed her by the figures on the clock. "Sun-day . . . Wens-day," he repeated. "Comprenny?"

"But Doctor Schneider say I would go soon. To see my man. He is ill a lot, you understand. He—he can die. Yes?"

"Yes, I suppose he can . . . I'll tell you what, you come in the morning, then we'll see what we can do. And if anything happens before then, we always send—"

"In morning? Come in morning?"

"I don't mean all in black," he said impatiently.

"Not in back?"

"Cryke! Listen! You—can—come—in—the morning, get me?"

She said soberly: "I understand . . . You will give him this, please?"

He was writing again. "Right-o, leave it there! I'll send it up presently."

"You will give it?"

"*Yes!*"

"Viss—viss my lov? Yes?"

"Yes yes!"

With its traffic stilled the hospital was high and hollow, like Paradise in a child's dream: above, the mapless passages, men's voices very far away like voices on a trunk-line, the hollow tap of a woman's heels through the antiseptic silence. To struggle here was like digging holes in the sea.

She went slowly down the broad steps, and back towards the Plough. A man was standing by the petrol-pumps, she asked him, "Schandler Street?" and he answered with a jet of shapeless words, pointing towards the cable-bridge. She looked that way, there were two policemen talking below the traffic lights. "No good!" she said, and started up the hill again.

The noise of the city hushed with rain became a tinnitus, within its shelter her mind moved fluently. It had been no accident, the policeman standing by the light, it could only have been a trap they'd set for her. The Englishman who had talked about his wife: she remembered now how shifty he'd been, always avoiding her eyes. He had talked about the rain, trying to keep her in the café till a patrol had formed outside; most likely he had no wife at all, the hotel he talked of was an office of the secret police. So: she was not to be snared so easily, she who had tricked the officer at Zurbergen. They could have her when Josef was well again, when Josef was able to care for himself she would let them give her a spell of gaol, but not till then. To-night she would go on walking still she got outside the town; they wouldn't find her there; and in the early morning she'd return by another road, always eluding them.

She thought the town would end at the hill's crest, leaving her in open country; but the houses only rose and broadened there, the glinting tramlines strode into a valley riddled with light. Here, where a few scant trees grew up from cages on the kerb, the idle men who were cast like scoria about this town pursued her with their stagnant eyes. They were spies, she thought, and tried to hurry to the end of them. The Church of the Ascension passed, a steepled factory; a long wall trudged against her arm, the shrunken villas crowded up towards the road, in the dawdling lamps the rain hung down like fine-combed tops of wool.

51

A SWAN'S-HEAD reading lamp was the only light turned-on in the Reference Room. Inning took off his soaking coat and put it over a chair; carefully, so as not to disturb Mayneshott, who was lying on the couch.

But Mayneshott was not asleep. He said without moving:

"'s that Inning? Devil are you doing—this time of night—?"

"I'm sorry, I didn't mean to wake you. I'm just—interested, you know."

"The German boy?"

"Uh-huh. I thought there might possibly be an early reaction." He tried, in the thin light, to see something on Mayneshott's face. But Mayneshott's face never showed anything. "D'you mind my smoking?"

"No. Give me one, will you. Don't sleep these days. Can't imagine why. Bowels or something."

"You ought to let Croylewick vet you."

"Croylewick? What the hell does he know! Drug-peddling quack. Besides, I haven't the time. What time is it?"

"A bit after four."

"That all? . . . Well, if you want to know, there's been a hell of a reaction."

"Oh—"

"Father and mother of a temperature. Here, this thing's gone out, give me another match. Thanks. You know, Inning, I can't quite understand the Satrap allowing it. He's not the world's congenital gambler, most days. I thought it was damned risky myself, and so did McDonell——"

"McDonell thinks everything's risky——"

"It wanted twelve months' try-out in the labs. Not less. That would apply——"

"But the fellow had done all that. We've got it all in black and white. Anyway, he wanted it himself——"

"What the patient wants is neither here nor there. No, I'm not blaming you. You only gave your opinion, that's all any one can do . . . What makes me rather sick is that I saw a chance of getting away with it, using a modification of Telly's P.T. It was a Telly case, all right. My God, if I could have got him through, with a body all shaken to bits like that——!"

"But then we'd have learnt nothing."

The door was tapped and opened.

"What is it, nurse?"

"He's awake again."

"Restless?"

"No, only talking. He keeps talking about somebody called Darlmire. I think he wants something, I don't know what it is."

"I'll come," Mayneshott said. He worked his thick body off the couch and shook out his legs. "I say, Inning, you might go and get Schneider. He's in his room."

"What—at this time?"

"He thought he'd stop around—thought the lad might want him."

"Sporting of him!"

"He's like that, Schneider. I don't know why."

The bed in the Observation Room was huge, the gift of a benevolent ignoramus forty years ago. The young German looked quite small there. He lay very still. In the night-suit they had found for him, rather too big, he resembled his walking self as much as a cheap photograph. The eyes were brighter than they had been when he came; bright and far-pitched, steady in direction, like the eyes of some one looking up the street for his bus. That was the peculiar thing: that you could put yourself in the path of those eyes and they were not disturbed. It was, for the rest, a mammal's head, and of the human order: shrunken, and having lost its shape from being unreasonably used.

The nurse was sponging the forehead with pieces of cotton wool exactly squeezed-out. You had to do something. Mayneshott warmed his hand at the gas and slipped it under the clothes to feel the heart. There is too much white in hospitals, he thought: when a patient gets to this stage they should put something coloured on the pillow, then at least you'd have the relief of contrast. He asked uselessly: "The arm, is it painful? Schmerz hier?" The boy's lips opened, showing his teeth; the eyes did not alter, but Mayneshott knew from familiarity that that was a smile. The boy's hand was walking like a spider along the oversheet, it found the nurse's hand and held it. Mayneshott heard him whispering. ". . . es ist nun alles zu mir gekommen . . . Ich habe es von Dir abgenommen."

Schneider's footsteps hardly sounded on the linoleum, he could move with a peculiar quietness. He stood where the shadow was deepest, not venturing to approach another man's case. But Mayneshott knew he was there, Mayneshott knew everything, he knew without looking how long it was since a nurse had washed her hands. He went across, "We ought to get the wife," he said below his voice. "You took the address, I think?" "Yes, the Marianne Hotel, in Wellington Street." "Thanks so much. Nurse, get the porter on the house-phone, will you. Tell him to get the Marianne Hotel and then put the call through to my surgery. Oh, and you'd better——"

Schneider said abruptly: "Excuse please!"

Mayneshott was over to the bed almost in one stride.

"Steady, old chap, steady!" The figure had come to life, the boy was trying to sit up, fighting against the weight of the bedclothes. "It's all right, old fellow, take it easy!— Schneider, talk to him, tell him to lie still—"

Schneider was at the other side, he slipped his arm behind the boy's shoulders. "Quietly, old friend, quietly— nothing to worry about!"

Unexpectedly strong, the boy had got his trunk up straight, he was holding Mayneshott's arm as if it were his only safety. But with that he seemed to be satisfied, he sat quite still, his eyes began to move, left and right, left and right, like a clockwork figure's in a shop window. "The doctor," he said suddenly, the voice small but perfectly free, "I want to see the doctor."

"He's here," Schneider said. "No, the other side. Look, there he is, that's his arm."

Josef's eyes went that way. He said impatiently, "No, that's Doctor Röstel, he wouldn't understand. I want the young doctor."

Schneider said, "Wait, wait a moment, I'll see." He found Inning in the next room, he said, "I think it is you he wants, I'm not sure . . . No, I'm sure Doctor Mayneshott will not mind." They went back to the Observation Room together. "Look, I've brought Doctor Inning! He's the one, isn't he?"

"Inning? . . . Yes, Inning, yes, that's right! Where?"

"I'm here," Inning said.

The eyes came round, hunting.

"Nearer . . . Yes, the young doctor, yes. You had my book, you read it?"

"Yes, of course."

"Nearer . . . I was thinking, I was thinking all night, your thoughts go quickly down there. Nearer! . . . You hear all right? It's about the P.T. The Psi Plus—you know? —that's all right, I know it's all right. Where's the German doctor? . . . Tell him, please, tell him the Psi Plus is all right. It's the Minus, that won't do. Sepsis, you see. It all comes from the Minus. I know that now, it's all clear, it's perfectly clear. I'll write it—book, where's the book?"

"In the morning!" Schneider said, "it'll do in the morning!"

Josef shook his head. "Not time enough. It wants a lot of time, a lot more experiments. I'm so tired, I can't do experiments."

"I'll do them!" Inning said. "Tell him, Schneider, tell him I'll work on it, tell him I'll sweat my guts out—"

Schneider said: "Doctor Inning's going to do the experiments. You leave it to him, he's clever, he's the best research man we've got, he'll do it all right."

"Doctor Dittmer?"

"No, Doctor Inning."

"Inning? . . . Yes, that's all right. But not Minna, you're not to try with Minna again. I won't have that, you understand, I won't have anything done to her!"

"No no!"

"Can't you quiet him?" Mayneshott said.

Schneider said, "Listen, old friend—"

"They can give me another injection," Josef said. "—not yet, not just yet. Five days the first interval, not longer. Don't let them wait any longer—"

"—You leave it to me, old friend, I'll see to it—"

"It's got to go on, you understand! I promised Herr Dahlmeyer—"

"Yes, old friend, don't worry, don't worry any more, we'll see it goes on."

"Oh . . . Where's Minna? Tell Minna it's going on. I want Minna to know. Minna! . . . allerliebste . . ."

His eyelids had come down, he dropped asleep as babies do, the pulsing of a factory cut by a single switch. And as if it were a child, Mayneshott lifted him one-armed, patted a forme in the pillows and put him down.

Inning had moved away. He said at the door: "Do you think—"

"Quiet!" Mayneshott said. He was listening to the respirations, he put the back of his wrist against the cheek. "Nurse, thermometer. And that. Is that kettle on?"

The telephone was ringing in Mayneshott's surgery as Inning passed. He went in and took it. ". . . What, not in the book? You've asked the exchange? Well, you'll have to send some one—get a probationer or some one. The name is Zeppichmann . . . Well, why in blazes didn't you let Doctor Mayneshott know! You'd better get moving, that's all!"

He lifted the bottom of the blind and was surprised to see daylight. He let it fly and day possessed the shabby room like a blunt friend, the bottles on the shelf, the sight-chart. Schneider came in, blinking.

Inning said slowly: "You know, it's interesting. I've thought all along—I was talking to Grover and McDonell about it—I felt all along that what he called the Psi Minus is the thing that's not perfectly right. That's what I've got to work on . . . Do you think I've put Mayneshott's back up at all?"

"Back up? You mean, made him cross? I don't think so."

"Of course he thought it was a Telly case—"

"It's not that," Schneider said. "It's—well, you never like a man to suffer. Not when he has suffered so much before."

"But do you think he's in pain? I didn't think—"

Schneider rubbed the secretion out of his left eye. "They learn not to show it, some of them. You have to look at the corners of his mouth. And further up, beside the eyes."

"But you know, when you think of all the millions

who've got to go through this bloody thing until we've learnt how to stop it—well, you know, one feels in a way that the individual doesn't matter. Don't you feel that?"

Schneider stared at the Landolt balance on the table. "It depends which individual . . . That is one of the hardships in being a doctor and not being God."

Mayneshott came.

Inning said: "I say, I'm sorry if I—"

"Never mind, look here, will you—"

"—I say, the porter rang through, apparently the hotel's not on the phone—"

"That doesn't matter!" Mayneshott was taking off his coat. "Be a good lad—dispensary—here's my keys—go and draw me a ten-minim dose of Curvey's digitalis compound. 08CX. Not the Mulloch stuff, mind! Wait, you may have to make it up, give me a pencil . . . Wait, I'll want something else—can you read that? . . . Right, quick as you can!" He had swept everything off the desk, he shook out a roll of paper and fastened it to the corners. "Schneider, be a good chap and get that other kettle going—I've got an idea—I'm damned if I'll lose that boy. Just get me a drink of water, will you . . . Yes, nurse, what is it?"

She said "Will you come please—"

"Wait a minute—I'm getting something—"

She shook her head.

52

THIS street gets narrow, with a little shop abutting on the roadway. The red lamp of a level-crossing showed ahead. The shop was for old clothes and furniture, and the smell of it left soft by rain came down the street a little way. A dog was barking.

The moment when she recognised the street was very small, like the passing of a bird's shadow across a sunny window.

Here the cart had stood, creaking as the fat men put the long box on top of it. Mama was there, they said. The man had stood wiping the sweat from his red face and then the cart went off, the near wheel wobbling as it jerked across the railway-line. Somebody went to stop the dog barking, and a woman tall as a tree with great black beads was looking down at her. *So this is the child! I don't see what's to be done with it.* The railway gates shutting again and a smell of furniture in the damp wind; an impatient hand with prickly rings doing up her boots. Like a bird's shadow across a sunny window the moment was gone.

Its loneliness remained: the shadow of a grief for the child who had stood watching the cart. She turned back towards the main road, and the grief followed her, coloured with humiliation. As in the attic room, pain turned the eyes' far light inside, and now more brilliantly. That was a child not worth the pain of bearing: and this that crawls along the street,

Wie wenig, ach! hat sich entfaltet,
Dies Wenige, wie klein und karg!

436

There had been no stars. But somewhere the wet roofs were finding light to hold, slate roofs of little houses, the long iron roof of a builder's shed. The silence that had come was the sudden quieting of engines in the shunting yard; but it seemed the silence of expectancy, and the breeze teasing empty cartons along the path felt like an outpost of the new day. Safe now to go as far as the top of the hill; and when the day comes the porter will let me in.

Her legs were good again, able to keep their own slight pace and only jibbing at her weight; the body pain was quiet, like a child you carry carefully lest you wake it up. The rumble that had started far behind became an engine's voice and the first of the lorries passed her, climbing hot and tired towards the town.

The wall began, and Fräulein Rother's tired face showed palely in the long, pale shadow. *Minna, come here, why do you look so sad?* It was after her fight with Hanna Mundt and she was all alone in the detention-room, feeling the bruise along her side; the laurels dark against the narrow window, and no one had come to light the gas. 'Tell me, what's the matter?' and Fräulein Rother stood against the wall-map, the threadbare daylight on her thin hair. "I wanted to write a sonnet and it won't come out . . . I'm useless, Fräulein, I'm only a filthy waste." Fräulein Rother squeezed herself into the long desk and sat beside her, bringing a faint smell of primrose, held the paper in her thin, skilful hands. 'You haven't lost yourself in this, it won't come till you lose yourself . . . You can't be useless, Minna, you fit into the timeless purpose, no one who struggles can be a waste.' Another waggon laboured past, drawing the wall into its yellow light. The light went over the hill, letting the wall return to shadow, the voice sank back in the deep of memory. And Fräulein Rother was dead.

With darkness weakening, the small and busy noises had begun, the clack of fireirons in a house she passed, quick footsteps and a boy's whistle launched fearlessly against the drowsing town. Night's frightening sounds, small flutterings and clopping steps in empty streets, were overwashed in the rising tide: somewhere the machines had started, the first tram showed its lights at the crest and coasted down the hill. Across the clangour of its passage her ears caught Josef's voice, *Come quickly, Minna, quick!*

So still he needed her.

The pain grew rancorous as she tried to force her legs. But that was an old companion, which had first brought Josef to her side; she could hold it till she reached the top of the hill, and there perhaps it would let her go. The wall had given out and a monstrous church grew up, the street lamp showed a pale Christ struggling on its Calvary. Her steps got shorter but the paving stones still moved, the staring workmen fell behind, she passed the first of the solemn porticos. He had cried and she would get to him. He might have travelled deeply into pain, but that was a country which she knew.

And this was like release: to have her purpose narrowed again. No longer to search the horizon, but to go at a single mark; no longer to ask if she cared for his work as well as for himself, to match his need against a larger scope, to put the smallness of her strife beside the hugeness of the battlefield. Only to watch one face, only to beat away one enemy, to let her power of loving be lost in a single pity. Let that be enough ah Merciful, ah Crucified let that be enough.

The hill pitched sharper and the trees began. She would get there now. The coldness gathered from wet clothes was winding up inside, the fingers of the squeezing hand grew cold. On this steep length of road each pace took up a double breath, and with the drag of pain she could not make it fast enough. But the store would last, she thought, she would make it last to the top. Another tree had crept behind, leaves grey in the expanding light, the shape of red became a letter box and that was past. She called: "I'm coming, Josef—now!"

She felt no courage, only the fierceness that comes in war, brilliant like noise of trumpets, flame against fire. The kerb was broken and she fell, some strength unreckoned picked her up, she was running now and the stubborn pavement flowed like a swollen stream. Another tug of pain, an answering thrust, eyes shut, feet clutching at the path, legs driving them like broken canes: and the hill's resistance gave, her eyes opening saw mistily the street pitched down, and there, beyond the timber-yards, the ranks of windows in a smoky wall.

It was then her power gave out. One pause, a moment's rest: she sat down on the path, and pain, as if in timed assault, took hold and held her there.

The town was all within her reach, tied by the spreading wires: the firconed clocks, grey domes that nuzzled from the fall of roofs, a reckless tanglement of red and slate washed over by the crouching smoke to a curious unity. That way the quilt of cloud was fastened up, leaving the green sky bare and moist; and there, behind the pencil-work of crane and mast, the new sun's garnet stain crept out towards the pit-head wheels, the slagmounds of Plintire. It had the quality of dreams, this spread of solid shapes on liquid sky; and as a dream is private she thought, half lying here against an office wall, that this majesty which rain and dark had borne belonged to her: as though the crimson, spreading now to touch the skirt of cloud with fire, was squeezed from her own tightening pain. She whispered, "Josef, look there, I've brought you that!" But when she sought his eyes, letting the town slide into haze, she only saw a stranger's: a bunch of solemn faces peering down, the English voices murmuring 'Reit? Olreit?'

A sense of pitching motion, as at sea: and when she

looked again she caught a glimpse of steps she recognised, a long board shouting *Must raise £40,000*. But in the drumming noise the hospital had changed, the corridor was dim and wider now, reaching beyond her sight. The solemn doctors stood in line, their faces showing faintly through the darkness, the youthful Englishman and the Holländer the Revenue had found, they stood and bowed to her, the man they called Sir Georg was by the side of Dr. Dittmer, she thought that Dr. Dittmer smiled. Dr. Schneider whispered as she passed. 'Success, a great success!' and the word went down the line of doctors like a breeze through corn, 'Success, complete success!' So the medicine Josef had found was right, she thought; but she could not see him there. The train slowed down, an old man with a wooden leg came up to take her ticket, and across the shaded square the boys were racing on their bicycles. Beyond the old stone bridge the road began to climb, leaving the wide roofs far behind, and the scent of pines became so rich that she seemed to float upon its waves. She knew where she had got to now. She caught another scent, of a man's skin and tiredness. Then the sun came out and all the pain had gone, she called "Beloved!" and ran towards him up the hill.

BIRDLIP 1938
CRONDALL 1940.